BUYOUT

BUYOUT

Alexander C. Irvine

Ballantine Books DEL REY New York

A Del Rey Trade Paperback Original

Copyright © 2009 by Alexander Irvine

All rights reserved.

Published in the United States by Del Rey,
an imprint of The Random House Publishing Group,
a division of Random House, Inc., New York.

DEL REY is a registered trademark and the Del Rey colophon
is a trademark of Random House, Inc.

Library of Congress Cataloging-in-Publication Data

Irvine, Alexander (Alexander C.)
Buyout / Alex Irvine
p.   cm.
"A Del Rey trade paperback original"—T.p. verso.
ISBN 978-0-345-49433-7
1. Imprisonment—Social aspects—Fiction.
2. Los Angeles (Calif.)—Fiction. 1. Title.
PS3609.R85B89 2009
813'.6—dc22
2008055580

Printed in the United States of America

www.delreybooks.com

2 4 6 8 9 7 5 3 1

Book design by Liz Cosgrove

For L, of course,
and to the memory of Grandpa Bodary

ACKNOWLEDGMENTS

This book has gone through many incarnations since the first glimmer of the idea in early 2000, and along the way quite a few people have suffered through long conversations about it. Among the ones I haven't forgotten: Sam Hamm offered a wise critique of an early version, and Jeff Strickland clued me in to some interesting quirks of the insurance industry (I think while we were replacing the soffits on his house). The Los Angeles subway system envisioned in the book is derived from the proposal outlined by Get LA Moving. The legal expertise of Mike Kaplan was instrumental in convincing me to abandon an ill-conceived subplot about perjury. Scheming with T. Davidsohn provided continuous chuckles and occasional inspiration. Chris Schluep helped me see that what I had thought was the beginning of the book really wasn't, and was patient and encouraging when I needed both.

CRIMES CARRYING a life without parole sentence upon conviction include: kidnapping for ransom or extortion with violence, California Penal Code §209(a); murder with special circumstances, California Penal Code §190.2; perjury in capital case causing the execution of the defendant, California Penal Code §12; placing a bomb causing death, California Penal Code §12310(a); treason, California Penal Code §37; wrecking a bridge, California Penal Code §219; wrecking a train, California Penal Code §218; and using a weapon of mass destruction causing death, California Penal Code §11418(b)(2). The special circumstances are murders: (1) carried out for financial gain; (2) committed by a defendant who was convicted previously of murder in the first or second degree; (3) committed by a defendant who has been convicted of more than one offense of murder; (4) committed by means of a destructive device, bomb, or explosive planted or hidden; (5) committed for the purpose of avoiding or preventing a lawful arrest or attempting an escape from lawful custody; (6) committed by means of a destructive device, bomb, or explosive mailed or delivered; and murders in which: (7) the victim was a peace officer; (8) the victim was a federal law enforcement officer; (9) the victim was a firefighter; (10) the victim was a witness to a crime who was killed for the purpose of preventing his or her testimony; (11) the victim was a prosecutor or assistant prosecutor or a former prosecutor or assistant prosecutor; (12) the victim was a judge or former judge of any court of record; (13) the victim was an elected or appointed government official or former government official; (14) the murder was especially heinous, atrocious, or cruel, manifesting exceptional depravity; (15) the defendant killed by means of lying in wait; (16) the victim was killed because of his or her race, color, religion, nationality, or country of origin; (17) the defendant was engaged in, or was an accomplice in, the commission of, attempted commission of, or the immediate flight after committing the following felonies: (A) robbery; (B) kidnapping; (C) rape; (D) sodomy; (E) a lewd or lascivious act upon the person of a child under the age of 14 years; (F) oral copulation in violation of Section 288a; (G) burglary in the first or second degree; (H) arson; (I) train wrecking; (J) mayhem; (K) rape by instrument; (L) carjacking; (18) infliction of torture; (19) poison is used; (20) the victim was a juror in any court of record in the local, state, or federal system in this or any other state; (21) the defendant discharged a firearm from a motor vehicle, intentionally at another person or persons outside the vehicle with the intent to inflict death; and (22) the defendant was an active participant in a criminal street gang and the murder was carried out to further the activities of the criminal street gang.

BUYOUT

This is Walt Dangerfield. No it isn't. Or it is if you identify me by what I call myself instead of what my mother called me. With whom am I speaking? I choose homage over identity! That's Los Angeles. Here you change your name when you get off the bus. The rules are: fewer syllables, and don't sound Jewish. These rules have been in place for more than a hundred years, and are not to be trifled with. Marion Morrison, the world would have been a different place if you'd stuck to your guns. Ha! You're getting me, straight to you, and neither one of us knows who the other is. Media! Medi-a-ted! There is no straight! There is no face-to-face. All there is, is bandwidth. You see someone on the street, that's not a person. The person is in the profile, and the profile exists only with the wilderness of switched packets and quantum servers. We're all existing only in the moment between when a bit is one or a bit is zero. Uncertainty makes us, and the moment of certainty is when the tombstone is planted before you ever get a chance to think about your epitaph.

ONE

RUMORS HAD BEEN FLYING for days behind the energy-neutral windows of Antelope Valley Casualty. The company was being sold. A huge restructuring, with accompanying layoff massacre, was on the horizon. A big change in the regulations was about to be announced that would drive them out of business. Martin Kindred listened to them all on his way to the coffee machine, and listened to them all again on his way back. Then he kept working. Anything that happened up on the ninth floor might as well be the weather, was the way he looked at it. He had policies to revise and the first quarterly report of the year coming due in a week. AVC had had a tough go of 2039, and he was feeling a little pressure—make that a lot—to make Q1 of 2040 cheerful. The fourth-floor financial daemon was gloomy, and Martin pushed figures around his desktop, experimenting with different configurations to see which would go over the best on the ninth floor.

He was pinged, at ten fifty-seven, by Santos Queiroz, an AVC lifer who, by quiet obsequiousness and careful displacement of his mistakes onto subordinates, had gradually moved up to the ninth floor. Martin answered the ping with some reluctance, since Santos was more nervous about the Q1 report than he was, but answer it he did, doing his best to look professionally optimistic as Santos' face wiped out the unsatisfactory arrangement of figures on the desktop.

"Martin, hi, how are you," Santos said. "Listen, can you come upstairs?" By which Martin assumed Santos meant Santos' office, so he said, "Sure." When he got up to the ninth floor, he found Santos' office empty. Wandering in the direction of the conference room on that floor, he passed an open door and heard Santos call out to him. Backing up, Martin said, "I looked in your office."

"Yeah, I know, sorry about that," Santos said. There were four other people in the room with him. It was an unused office, with furniture left over from its previous occupant, whom Martin vaguely remembered as a manager of some kind who had left under a cloud having to do with reimbursement for adjuster's expenses. He didn't know any of the other four people, but Santos took care of that. "This is Kai Fonseca," he said, indicating a seated Hispanic woman who radiated the intense confidence of a college basketball coach. "She's a consultant working with us on liaising with Sacramento and Washington. Representing Washington is Victor Eads, who's with Senator Ron Dempsey's office." Martin thought Eads looked like an uglier, older version of his boss, the state's junior senator and self-proclaimed "law-and-order fundamentalist." The senator himself affected cowboy gear and cowboy pronouncements that would have embarrassed John Wayne, to whom he bore a cultivated resemblance. Next to Eads, bookending a leather couch out of the 1990s, were a matched pair of *Executiva californiensis*: tall, athletic, tanned, and wearing several thousand dollars' worth of tailored clothing. "And this is Scott and Jocelyn Krakauer," Santos finished up. "They're the ones who really wanted to talk to you."

Martin shook hands all around, in the order of Santos' introductions. Scott Krakauer gestured at an empty chair and started his pitch as if triggered by the contact of Martin's buttocks with its seat. "Until recently, Jocelyn and I were consultants to the private corrections industry, primarily in Texas," he began. "I don't mind telling you that's not a bad line of work to be in, but one of the things about Texas is that it gets you thinking big, right?" Eads chuckled, and belatedly Martin realized he should have, too, but by then the moment had passed. "We've been working on a project, the three of us, and Kai came in on it a little later. We thought we had it set up in Texas, and then Oklahoma, but one of the things about new ideas is that they're new, right? People need time to get used to them, and maybe some people need too much time. So then we thought of California. Out here, if you're not trying something new they send you to Nevada."

Which was the kind of macabre joke that told you something about

Scott Krakauer's personality. Since the Water Crisis, southern Nevada was largely depopulated, and you needed Code Orange clearance even to drive on I-15 to Las Vegas . . . although you could still fly there for nothing as long as you contracted to stay at one of the casino hotels and you subscribed to certain of the services they provided. Once, in college, Martin had driven out to Las Vegas and back, passing through Barstow at four in the morning both ways. The world seemed a little diminished by the fact that you couldn't do that anymore without being killed by desert bandits or careless checkpoint security on the outskirts of Sin City.

Scott was talking over Martin's woolgathering: "Plus, California is the other state that gets you thinking big. So here we are, and with Kai's and Victor's help, we're about to . . . well, this is where Jocelyn usually takes over." Scott leaned back and looked to his wife.

"Scott and I both used to be cops," she began. "Right here in LA, before we were seduced by the blandishments of the private sector. Now, nobody expects cops to be big thinkers. And most of us—them, I should say—aren't. But when you're a cop, you spend an awful lot of time waiting for something to happen, and idle hands are the devil's workshop." This last delivered with a smile both predatory and self-mocking. "Or so my grandmother told me. We've got an idea that's going to shake the bow ties off the insurance business. What's more, we're going to shake the pinstripes off the lawyers, and we're going to give the regular person a whole new way to look at life and death, prison and freedom. Plus, and I'm not afraid to tell you this, we're going to make an awful lot of money. We'd like you to be part of it, Martin."

Martin felt the force of her charisma. If she'd once been a cop, she could have gotten a confession from a corpse. "Part of what?" he asked.

"How much do you think it costs to feed, clothe, and house the average maximum-security prisoner?" Jocelyn asked in return. Martin had been raised to mistrust people who answered questions with questions, but he played along.

"Quite a bit," he said. He'd done some work with private prisons, insuring the facilities, and he remembered seeing six-figure-per-annum costs. "A hundred thousand?"

"Triple that," Jocelyn said. "And that's before the inmate gets old and you have to provide him with medical care. The actuaries tell us that the average murderer commits his crime at twenty-six years of age and will live to be eighty-plus. That's fifty-four years at more than three hundred thousand dollars a year. And that's in today's dollars, without anticipating uncertainties in future medical costs and legal expenses. We'll double that, given how squirrelly currency has been lately. So to incarcerate the actuarially average murderer from crime to death is going to cost us approximately thirty-six million dollars. For one human being to be in a six-by-nine cell. Excuse me: for one murderer to be in a six-by-nine cell. Thirty-six million dollars. Now, according to federal regulations, we're going to need to keep a certain amount of that money as cash on hand to ensure that we're going to be liquid for the foreseeable future. That's a reserve amount."

Martin was feeling the pressure to finish the quarterly report. "I know what a reserve is," he said.

Jocelyn grinned at him. "Not afraid to speak up. Excellent. That's the kind of independence we need." Behind him, Martin could feel Santos' gaze burning into the base of his skull, but he had work to do. His plan for the day didn't include a lecture on cost control in the corrections industry.

Still, the quicker he moved this along, the quicker he could get the report done. "Sorry," he said. "I'm just trying to let you skip to the good stuff."

"Which," Jocelyn said, "I will now do."

"If Martin will let you," Santos said.

"Jesus Christ, Santos." Eads threw up his hands, letting his pod fall into his lap. "I wanted you in this meeting, but now I'm starting to regret it."

Santos shut up, and Jocelyn glanced at the other four people in the room, checking them into silence before she went on. "There are studies showing that up to ninety percent of the prison inmates serving life sentences without parole—ninety percent—would rather have been executed." Studies, Martin thought, with maximal unspoken derision. But he didn't say anything. "So let's put together a hypothetical situation. You killed someone. You got caught. You got sentenced to life in prison without parole. You're serving your sentence, you've got nothing to look forward to but sixty years of bad food and gang rape and bars on your windows. Then someone comes to you and says . . ."

"I'll pitch it," Scott said. "Here's the deal. We're going to spend as much as thirty-six million dollars to keep you right here, just as you are, until you die. What if you could take some of that money and do some good? What if I said to you that I'd give you, say, five million, right now? Today. And you decide where the money goes. The company gets out from under a future obligation, and is therefore more liquid, and therefore more attractive to shareholders. The five million dollars can give how many people a new start? How many charities could that fund? How many kids can it put through college?"

The logic, Martin had to admit, was persuasive. He decided not to say anything.

"Apart from the money," Jocelyn said, "it's about control. It's about a prisoner taking control again, after his control has been taken away. It's about atonement, about the opportunity to put that money to work atoning for the act that put the prisoner where he is instead of pouring it into the maintenance of a life that's already been thrown away. Not that money can ever atone for the loss of a loved one, but the angle here is bringing some good out of a situation that seems to be nothing but negative and sorrowful."

Martin was starting to intuit where this was all going, but then Scott eliminated all doubt. "And the prisoner," he said, "agrees to finalization of the deal within twenty-four hours."

At the word *finalization*, Scott made a subtle gesture, two fingers of his right hand pointing at and pushing toward the crook of his left elbow. So this is where we get to the euphemisms, Martin thought.

Everyone was quiet, and the gap was Martin's to fill. "I hadn't heard about any of this," he said.

"Nobody has," Eads said. "We've kept the volume down while we got everything ready. Counting votes in Congress, lining up the right kinds of people in the corrections unions, DA's offices, that kind of thing. But it's ready to go now."

"And we hope you're ready to go, too," Jocelyn said. "As of Thursday morning, Antelope Valley Casualty is going to be Nautilus Casualty and Property, a subsidiary of ValCorp/KRK Holdings, which is a holding company we created to make strategic facility acquisitions in the corrections area. We launch with the first buyout announcements the next week, and then . . ."

"Then," Scott stepped in, "is when we really see whether the whole thing has legs. But we wouldn't be here if we thought it didn't. Our investors don't throw money away."

"They sure don't," said Victor Eads. "Not the ones I work for, anyway."

So the Krakauers had bought a bunch of prisons, and now were poised to add an insurance company to the portfolio so they could keep this buyout thing under one roof. They had at least one senator behind the project, and God knew what other kinds of clout. What did you do with an idea like this? Martin wasn't sure how they thought they'd be able to do it, who would be the clientele—or, most importantly, what they were asking him to do. There. A question he could ask. "What exactly did you want me to do here?"

"We're going to need someone to initiate client contact and generate deals," Scott said. "And we'd like you to be that guy."

"Sales?" Martin said. "What am I going to do, drive around to prisons and yell into the cell block if anyone wants to be executed?"

"It's a little more sophisticated than that," Jocelyn said.

"And we can do without the flip tone, Martin," Santos added. Just like him to play enforcer in a room full of people who could buy and sell him, Martin thought. But he played along.

"Okay," he said. "So how does it work? Who do I pitch? Is it lawyers? Do I contact people before their sentencing, just in case, or do I wait until they're serving their time? Hypothetically."

"Of course, hypothetically," Jocelyn said. "Some of those details are yet to be worked out. We're still doing the build on this thing, and if you're in, you'll have input about how those initial contacts are handled. You'll be our man in the field, and as the project grows and we bring more field agents in, your experience will be critical to making sure that they can hit the ground running."

"You're making about an even hundred thousand now, right?" Scott asked.

"About," Martin said, although the question meant that Scott already knew the answer.

"The way we have the numbers figured, that's about what you'd make for finalizing three buyouts," Jocelyn said. "Right now there are approximately three thousand buyout-eligible inmates in prisons under Nautilus control." Martin watched her watching him, and saw the change in the set of her facial muscles as she arrived at a decision. "Take a couple of days to think about it. Let us know by Friday, though, okay? We're going to need to move quickly." She stood, and everyone else in the room stood with her. "Thanks for coming up, Martin. I really hope this is going to work out for all of us."

At the door, Martin paused. "Hypothetically," he said.

Scott was walking him out. "Hypothetically what?"

"Hypothetically, what happens if someone takes a buyout and then we find out he was innocent?"

"This isn't philosophy, Martin," said Victor Eads. "Anybody who says that it's better to have a hundred guilty men go free than one innocent man die has never watched a guilty man walk free. We're not in a world that can afford to be high-minded."

HE WALKED BACK down the hall, waited for the elevator, and took it all the way down to the lobby. Martin was one of the few Los Angeles natives who enjoyed walking the city, as hostile to pedestrians as it was. And now he walked, keeping no track of where he went, the giant secret he carried deforming his sense of everything else around him. His pod informed him that it was 104 degrees and that he needed to put on his hat, but he'd left it up in the office. On every corner stood someone who might someday commit a murder, and if the Krakauers weren't just crackpots every murder might mean funding for a library, or ten years' worth of school lunches. Martin couldn't get his head around it; the ramifications stayed somewhere out at the horizon of his ability to comprehend. Was this really the kind of world where people did things like this, offered money to people to end their lives? And was he really considering it? He was. These were killers, rapists. Filth. The world was bet-

ter off without them. And the money . . . Martin couldn't sort out the ul-
timate ethics of the money. Was it a good thing or a bad thing if a Little
League field got a sprinkler system from a dead murderer imprisoned for
the crime of murdering a child who had played on that field two years
before?

Hypothetically.

In college, philosophy professors threw those kinds of questions out
to provoke discussion and set traps for the students they wanted to weed
out. In real life, Martin was thirty-nine years old, in a job that left no
mark on the world, and he was being presented with a chance to do
something important. Whether it was a good thing or a bad thing, that
was the question. Three thousand buyout-eligible inmates, Jocelyn had
said. Finishing deals on one-tenth of 1 percent of them every year would
equal his current income. Plus he would make a mark. This was a
chance. A chance to make a difference, and a chance to make some real
money. With that kind of money, thought Martin Kindred, I'd never
have to worry about making the mortgage again.

I look out over the cityscape. Did you ever do that, or did it make you feel like a tourist? Not me, ese. I look every chance I get and I think, people did that. People built those buildings and those roads and that harbor and turned the river into a concrete ditch. Then that wasn't enough, so they made movies, and everybody wanted to come here so they could have copies of themselves that were just a little bit better than the original. Immortality via celluloid! Immortality in thirty-five millimeter! Immortality in Super Eight! Except most of those you wouldn't want your mother to see. Then it wasn't enough to give live people immortality; we had to take dead people's immortality and eat a little bit of it, regurgitate it in hi-def digital. Immortality via pixels! Immortality via phosphors! Immortality via packet switching and broadband immortality! All so we can let ourselves off the hook for being turned off by what we see in the mirror. I look out over the cityscape, and that's what I see. I see an avatar of immortals who died not knowing they were immortal. I see the ghosts of stevedores and orange farmers. And I see a goddamn lot of drones and municipal cameras that ensure our safety by making sure everyone knows what everyone else is doing. Isn't that what it's always been about? We're all famous now.

TWO

"A CHANCE," Teresa said later, "to make your living from the deaths of other people. I can't believe you're even considering this."

Martin had taken the rest of the day off. They were over at his parents' house in Rancho Park. Casa Kindred was alive with kids. Martin and Teresa's girls, Allison and Kelly, churned around in the backyard pool with their younger cousins, Bart and Zack. There was much shrieking. Not for the first time, Martin wondered what gene it was that decreed that a child in a swimming pool must shout everything he said at the top of his lungs. On deck chairs between the pool and the house, arrayed so they could keep an eye on the boys, who were six and five, the adults staked out their positions about Martin's possible new job.

He hadn't wanted to tell anyone right away, but then he'd gone ahead and done it as soon as he'd gotten home. Teresa hadn't been able to believe that such a thing as life-term buyouts would be allowed; now that she was getting used to the possibility, she'd decided they were an ethical abomination. Although the last thing their marriage needed was more tension, Martin was relieved that someone had immediately taken an opposing position. She'd be able to argue against buyouts better than he would, which would help him see the whole thing more clearly.

Plus, he was used to having her disagree with him. It was the way of the last three or four years.

His brother Jason and sister-in-law Hannah were somewhere in the middle, as was Martin's mother. Felicia Kindred, cop wife and mother of a cop, had absorbed much of the cop's disdain for the niceties of questions about what rights convicted felons might or might not have. Underlying that disdain, though, remained the traces of a youthful idealism that even Los Angeles had never been able to erase.

"Funeral directors make a living from death, too," Vance said. "Shit, Teresa, you work for a defense contractor. Death's a big business." He was drunk enough to be contentious, a state with which all of them were familiar. "Jay, what do you think? How many times have you seen one get away who deserved the needle?"

Martin's brother shrugged. "Enough, I guess."

"See?" Vance said.

See what? Martin wanted to ask. His father and brother took everything the other said as if it were incorrigibly true by virtue of the fact that they, as cops, had said it. Martin had long since learned to recognize this, and recognize that he would always be on the outside of it. Jason was the favorite. This was the way of life.

"Assisted suicide's been legal for, what, thirty years?" Hannah said.

"It's not the same," Teresa said. "There's no profit motive in assisted suicide."

"There is in building missile guidance systems," Vance said.

Felicia turned on him. "Vance, that's enough. If all you're going to do is bait people, why don't you go play with the kids? You're sure acting like one of them."

The boys started yelling for Jason to come into the pool. "One second, guys," he called out. He drained his beer and then said, "I don't know, I don't see anything wrong with it. I mean, if that's what these guys want to do, they should do it. One more problem that everyone else doesn't have, you know what I mean?" He got up, jogged across the pool deck, and jumped into the deep end, landing with a booming splash as the kids screamed. They converged on him before he'd surfaced.

"Sure wish there'd been buyouts when I was on the job," Vance said. "Christ, the number of lowlifes I put away. I had to root for them to get shanked, and now they're going to go and pay these guys to take a needle. Cops should be on commission."

"That's the problem, isn't it?" Teresa said. "Think about how this market will develop. What kind of pressure will there be to keep a steady supply of willing inmates coming through the door?"

"Leave that up to Martin," Vance said. "Dotting i's and crossing t's is what he's good at."

"Vance Kindred, you are being an asshole," Felicia said. "You hear me?"

"I'm just saying Martin's good at that kind of work," Vance said. "Jesus Christ."

The old rifts, Martin thought. You got used to them or you let them drive you crazy.

"It's a good chance," Felicia said.

"Chance to do what?" Teresa asked. "Turn prisoners into profit? Increase shareholder value by putting a price tag on human life? I can't believe we're even talking about this."

"If I was in prison, I would sure as hell take a buyout," Martin said. "If it was that or a life sentence. Why not? What's to lose?"

"Life is what's to lose," Teresa said furiously.

"You've never been inside a prison, have you?" Vance said. "I wouldn't call it life. Still, this is a scam."

"A scam how?"

"I mean, who gets the money?"

Martin scooted his chair closer to his father's so they could lower their voices. He didn't want the girls knowing too many of the particulars about what he was about to be doing. Probably they would soon, but he didn't want to be the one to tell them. Oddly, he wanted them to come to him and ask, with half-formed ideas received from the culture at large, so he would have a chance to make his case. At least they wouldn't already have made up their minds when they came to talk to him.

Musing about authority wasn't going to help him with his own father, though. "The money goes wherever the client says it goes," he said.

"Bullshit," his father said. "Nautilus isn't writing these checks unless there's a benefit. What's the game?"

"They want to be liquid. They don't want a lot of cash tied up in future obligations. That's the whole thing, Dad."

"If you believe that, it's because you want to," Vance said. "There are a lot of ways to make money. What insurance company is going to start handing out millions of dollars every chance they get? What's the agenda?"

Jason and Martin used to joke that the old man thought he was Batman, since he always asked the World's Greatest Detective's signature question: *Who benefits?* And he was doing it again now. "Everyone comes out ahead. Nautilus gets flexibility, a bunch of recipients get money they can use to better themselves, and the client gets to make a gesture of atonement." His father snorted. "Go ahead, laugh," Martin said. "I believe that."

"Atonement isn't worth money," Vance said. "And if something comes with money, it's not really atonement. You want to buy and sell lives, son of mine, go ahead. I'm not going to get brokenhearted over more dirtbags taking the needle. But don't dress it up."

"It's what they deserve," Hannah said.

Vance snorted and dropped a hand into the cooler by his chair. "Shit, most of 'em deserve worse," he said, popping another can. "You said it's Scott and Jocelyn Krakauer you met with? I knew them right before I retired. Ass-kissers, both of 'em. But not terrible cops. Doesn't surprise me they'd come up with something like this."

"There was a guy from Ron Dempsey's office, too," Martin said.

"Of course there was," Hannah said. She might have been ambivalent about buyouts, but she hated Ron Dempsey because she hated all expressions of bravado. This made her a good match for Jason, who was as quietly professional as any cop Martin had ever met. Almost introverted, which he had in common with Martin. Neither one of them was particularly social. Jason had been a cop for nine years, and Martin still wasn't certain whether he liked the work or had done it because that's what Kindred men did—except Martin. Tricky place to be for a younger brother, Martin thought. To have your older brother bail out on the family tradition. It puts a lot of pressure on you to follow through even if you don't want to.

On the other hand, Martin thought, Jason's a grown man. I didn't sign him up for the academy.

"In a world where they're building houses out of bones in India," Vance said, "who am I to get precious about whether some trigger-happy banger can cash in on his own life?"

Teresa nearly spit out her drink. "They're building houses out of bones in India?"

"I saw it on the feeds somewhere. All the bodies that go floating down the Ganges, people pick the bones and use them. Why not? They use everything else."

"Think I'm going to take a dip myself," Martin said. He dove, low and flat, a race dive, hitting the water with a crack and skimming under the surface to the far wall. When he came up, the girls were coming after him. He caught them both in a bear hug, his daughters who had not yet outgrown the simple joy of wrestling in the pool, and dragged them over to Jason and the boys to start up a game of Marco Polo.

"I CAN'T BELIEVE you're actually going to do this," Teresa said on the way home.

Martin finished guiding the car into the smart lane on the Pasadena Freeway, and then he cut his eyes at the girls in the backseat. "How about later?" he said. Teresa sat silently fuming the rest of the way home to Pasadena. The girls, with their instinct for an approaching storm, vanished into their bedrooms without prompting, leaving Martin and Teresa alone in the kitchen.

"You're going to do this, aren't you?" she said.

Martin knew he was, but he also knew that when he said it, the decision would become one more wedge driven permanently into the marriage. If he started doing buyouts, it wouldn't matter if he stopped. The correction could never be as important to Teresa as the initial error. So he didn't say it just yet.

"T," he said, hedging, "I think it's the right thing to do."

"No you don't," she said. "But you'll keep trying to convince yourself that you do because you're thirty-nine years old and you've never gotten over the fact that your father doesn't respect what you do."

The conversation hardened into an argument, just like that, and Martin felt himself let go. "I'm not fighting about this, T. I understand that you don't agree, but this is a chance for me to do meaningful work. It's real, it has an effect on people, it can create some good out of something awful."

"You're kidding yourself," Teresa said. "About all kinds of things."

He didn't agree, but already they'd reached the point at which there were only a few things either of them could say that would calm the situation down, and neither one of them was willing to say any of those things. So Martin said nothing, and after a minute Teresa went into the spare room she used as an office. Work was her refuge from him. A snatch of an old song, one his father used to listen to, floated through his head: Well . . . how did I get here?

Martin sat at the kitchen table and cued up his work desktop. The house system wasn't as fast as the AVC daemon, but it would do to tinker with the report. If Teresa could run away into work, maybe he could, too. Instead of working, though, he found himself idly reading through the feeds about the Dodgers, the Galaxy, random bits of pop-cultural flotsam . . . he streamed the latest Walt Dangerfield, because there was nothing better when you were lonely late at night than listening to someone else who filled his own crazed loneliness with the sound of his own voice.

Then he got a ping from Charlie Rhodes. It was eleven o'clock, only twelve hours since he'd been called into the meeting. "Amigo," Charlie said. "Strange rumors are filtering out of your place of employ."

It was Charlie's business to know things. He was the kind of private investigator who avoided jobs involving people whenever he could. Charlie's field was investigating information: where it came from, how it got where it was going, who else was interested in it. He had friends who were deeply involved on the midnight side of the perpetual race between net security and gunslinging innovation. He was also Martin's closest friend, in fact one of the very few people Martin characterized as a friend.

"Probably all of them are true," Martin said. "But I only know about one. And what the hell are you doing spying on Antelope Valley anyway?"

For Charlie, spying on Antelope Valley was a simple matter of keeping tabs on things that mattered to his friends. It was hard to explain that to people when they knew your line of work required you to be obsessive about gathering information, but it was true. In fact, to Charlie it seemed that he was obsessive about information because that was one more way of making sure he knew about things that mattered to him and the people he cared about. There weren't too many of those, because like Martin, Charlie did not give friendship lightly and he was choosy about who he wanted to receive it from. He'd decided to get in touch with Martin this late because he was seeing chatter about an underground group organizing itself in response to a coming announcement that had something to do with Antelope Valley, and he was hoping that Martin would know what it was all about.

"Maybe they're going to start a guerrilla war against insurance premiums," Martin said, and Charlie knew Martin was avoiding something.

"Amigo," he said. "What's going on?"

"I swore I wouldn't tell," Martin said. "I have to talk to a couple of people at the office tomorrow, and then I'll probably be able to let you know." He was excited, Charlie could tell by the tone of his voice and the effort Martin was making to keep his face neutral. "It might be big, though, Charlie. It might be real big."

"What the fuck does that mean?" Charlie said.

"I'll tell you tomorrow," Martin said. "Right now I need to either finish this report or go to bed."

"Whatever," Charlie said. "Tell T I said konnichi-wa."

"Right," Martin said, and clicked off. Charlie sat in the room he called his office, watching nine different feeds come in on nine different screens, monitoring nodes and tinkering with a program that picked random messages out of random bitstreams like a grizzly bear swatting salmon onto a riverbank. He had a bad feeling. Whenever Martin avoided a topic, that meant that he was about to do something that he wasn't sure he should do. Sometimes he settled down and got more comfortable with his decisions later, but one of the things about Martin Kindred was that he was more willing to suffer the consequences of a bad decision than he was to suffer the second-guessing that followed a change of heart. Martin was looking forty in the face, his marriage was iffy, his job had turned him into a high-end cubicle drone . . . he was ripe to do something rash. Have an affair, spend too much money on a car, get some kind of odd cybernetic bodymod. Amigo, Charlie thought, I am going to be watching you. Because you haven't turned out to be very good at looking out for yourself.

Holy shit. Ho-lee shit. You know, I hate and despise vapid celebrity gossip as much as the rest of you, which is to say that I love it with an unrepentant passion that I am reluctant to share with people whose good opinion I value. But! Since I do not know you and therefore cannot reach any valid decision about the importance of your good opinion, I offer to you this juiciest of celebrity crime tidbit-tastic news. Carl Marks, loudmouth Marxist and film director of either genius or extreme imitative cleverness, has just been arrested for killing a woman who was either his girlfriend, or a high-class—by which is meant too expensive for you—call girl. Or both. The woman, a twenty-six-year-old native of Edmond, Oklahoma, who went by the name Andi Anton, was . . . well, she was an extraordinarily attractive woman. Yes. But she was also shot three times in a condo in Playa del Rey, after which she was not so pretty at all, or so I imagine, not having had the stomach to look at the crime-scene images. Can you believe this? Carl Marks killing someone? This is where communism gets you.

THREE

WEDNESDAY MORNING Martin walked through the AVC lobby, into the elevator, and out again on the ninth floor. He found Santos in his office and said, "Hey, Santos. Where can I find Scott and Jocelyn?"

"Where's my report?" Santos said in return.

"In the system," Martin said. "But you're going to have to find someone else to do it."

"I knew it," Santos said. He cast his eyes heavenward—ceilingward, anyway—and said, "Everybody wants to grab the brass ring. Everybody wants to do the new thing. You're going to be sorry."

"Could be," Martin said, "but at least I won't be working for you anymore."

Santos stood up, all high dudgeon and affronted pride. "You think I'm so bad to work for? You might wear a nicer tie when you're answering to the Krakauers, but I tell you what, what you have is a bad case of grass-is-greener-itis."

Which was something that only Santos Queiroz would ever have said. "Where can I find Jocelyn and Scott, Santos?" Martin repeated.

"They're already moving into the office where we met yesterday," Santos said. "I'm surprised you couldn't hear the scheming from downstairs."

Martin turned to leave and saw Jocelyn appearing in the doorway. "I thought I heard your voice," she said, reaching out to shake Martin's hand. "Come on and let's talk." When they got to the new office, Martin at first didn't recognize it. Overnight new furniture and carpet had been installed, and a daemon appeared at the door not to ask Martin if he wanted coffee but to confirm whether he wanted his coffee black, as usual.

"Please," Martin said, even though it had always seemed odd to say please to a subroutine. Scott looked up from where he was installing something behind a desk. "Martin, good to see you." He came over to the conference area, three couches facing one another in a U across a holo-enabled tabletop. A secretary appeared with hot coffee. Martin was a bit dazed with the speed of the transformation, and a bit seduced by the way it made him feel just to ride along on this wave, wherever it was going. Just think, he told himself. You could be downstairs slogging through the Q1 report. Don't fuck this up.

"Before my better half gets started," Scott said as they sat, "I thought maybe we could start going over a couple of things. First and foremost, a big part of this job early on is going to be press availabilities. If you're camera-shy, this would be a good time to get back to work on that report downstairs."

"I've never had a chance to be camera-shy," Martin said. "I don't think it'll be a problem."

"Just as important as getting our first few buyouts finalized is getting the word out about the good that the money will be doing," Scott said. "So part of your client interface is going to involve some direction as to where the money will be going." Jocelyn cleared her throat, and Scott broke off. "Okay. You're on board. We should get a couple of things signed and then plug you in."

Jocelyn spread several forms on the tabletop. "These are versions of your existing employment contract with Antelope Valley. The only things different are a slight tightening of your nondisclosure agreement and language changes throughout to reflect the creation of Nautilus. Oh, and we've made sure to note your new earning potential." She shot Martin a smile with this last sentence, and Martin couldn't help but smile back. He signed the forms where indicated, and the three of them relaxed back into their couches.

"When you start a new employee in sales," Scott said, "it's customary to provide the new hire with leads. We've done that with you. Already on your pod you'll find a set of files related to current inmates of prisons that KRK will own by close of business tomorrow. Each of them has expressed some interest, informally, in what we have to offer." Martin glanced at his pod, and sure enough, he had a new folder marked NAUTILUS. "You'll also find proprietary apps for secure communications with the office when you're on the road, and so forth," Scott said. "We don't use anything out of the box. When you're in this particular line of work, it doesn't pay."

"Be aware that there are going to be some protestors," Jocelyn said. "People will probably call you names. To the extent that you'll be a public figure, your family life will change. We're hoping it won't be a huge change, because that would mean the whole program is more controversial than we're hoping and anticipating it will be, but you should know that this kind of thing is a possibility. You should make sure your family is prepared."

Martin had a feeling, now that he'd slept on it, that part of Teresa's opposition stemmed from exactly this problem. Considering this, he decided he'd have to take the lead, make sure that she knew that he was concerned, too, that he was going to do everything he could to minimize the impact of the new job on the girls. Sometimes people needed to hear things, even things that they knew were true. "Okay," he said. "I'll do that as soon as I get home tonight."

"Good answer," Scott said. "Because we're announcing the program pronto, and because word of it has already leaked out, there's already a protest group forming itself. From what we understand, they're called Priceless Life. Right now they don't seem to be much more than a repurposed mailing list that was once devoted to anti-abortion rants. Once everything's public, though, they'll probably get more active."

"What are they waiting for?" Martin asked.

"My guess is they don't think we know they exist, so they're waiting for our announcement to jump on us, assuming we'll be surprised." Scott shrugged. "But if there's one thing us Krakauers like to do, it's anticipate all possible problems and have plans in place to address them. Avoid them if possible, but address them in any case."

"The situation is this," Jocelyn said. "I'll try to be as evenhanded as I can. We're about to start doing something that will make for great media, and will provoke strong reactions. You'll be at the center of it. If you're not ready for that, I can pull up those forms again and we'll go in another direction. Priceless Life will, I'm sure, make some noise in your direction. At the beginning this program is going to require a deft touch; if we can get through the first year without a large groundswell of public opposition, the scaredy-cats in Washington and Sacramento will start to come out in favor of it. So the question for you, Martin, is this: Are you ready for what will be a turbulent year, if it means the rest of your career will be something you never could have imagined?"

"I sure am," Martin said. The way he had it figured, he was in for a turbulent year anyway, what with the simmering discontent at home. Work issues wouldn't compare to that, and if he could be absorbed in his work, maybe it would offer him the same kind of refuge it apparently offered T.

Maybe he would even start to understand why she did what she did. Maybe a little work turbulence would be good for the home life. Who knew? If you could predict the future, it wouldn't be the future.

"Because let's be honest here," Jocelyn said. "We're going to completely reorient existing ideas of punishment, penitence . . . atonement . . . everything that we thought we knew about the legal and correctional systems is going to be thrown into question. Buyouts will be philosophical lightning rods from day one. You'll need to have done some clear thinking about the related issues before you get in front of a microphone, and we'll also be helping you with that. Still with us?"

"I'm not going to finish the report," Martin said.

Jocelyn and Scott both laughed. "Good answer," Scott said. "Take the rest of the day, look at those files, and let's meet here first thing in the morning. Sound good?"

Martin stood. "Yeah. Sounds like I've got some homework."

"You sure do," Scott said. "Oh, and Martin? I'm sure you've already mentioned this to your wife, but other than her, keep it to yourself, right?"

MARTIN WENT AND READ. He started at a coffee shop around the corner from AVC on a stretch of Wilshire that had been high-end office space since before he was born. The only difference was that now, with the clock just ticked over into 2040, there was a light-rail line bisecting the boulevard, and every storefront you passed spawned an avatar with access to every financial transaction you'd conducted in the last year. "Martin," one of them said smoothly, outside a lingerie shop, "hasn't it been a little too long since you came home with a surprise for Teresa?"

I cannot be the only guy, Martin thought, who would be greeted with pure incomprehension if he brought home fancy lingerie as a present for his wife. At the coffee shop he read and ignored the pings that came in. Several of them were from Santos, asking questions about the report that thirty seconds of effort would have resolved without the ping. I don't work for you anymore, Santos, Martin thought. I have signed my life away, taken a buyout to do buyouts. After two or three hours, and too much coffee, he got jumpy and took a walk. An hour or so later, he found himself at the La Cienega/Venice interchange with the Santa Monica Freeway. Cars and surface rail roared and screeched, planes roared in and out of LAX. Everyone was going somewhere.

Me, too, Martin thought. But where, that's the question. And who's coming with me and who will I be leaving behind. Or who will be leaving me behind. A week ago I was in a rut. A week from now everything will be different, and it'll be different in ways that I can't predict. It was enough to make you wish for maybe just a little bit of stability in the midst of change.

He pinged Charlie, who was on his most hated of jobs: a motel stakeout. Advances in surveillance technology had come with advances in the ability to invisibly alter videorecordings, as a result of which the private investigator still occasionally found himself stuck watching adulterous couples in motels or private love nests. Seeing the event personally meant the investigator could testify about it personally, and personal testimony still carried more weight with a jury than pixels. "Amigo," Charlie said. "Death would be preferable to this."

"I can't offer death," Martin said, "but if you want to know about what you were asking about yesterday, meet me at Temoc's."

Charlie of course agreed, because Temoc's burrito shack, on Sepulveda near La Tijera in the former home of a Starbucks, produced what were the the finest burritos in Los Angeles County by Charlie's reckoning. Also because Charlie was consumed with curiosity regarding the thing he knew Martin wasn't telling him. So he sat and he ate while

Martin violated his nondisclosure agreement, both of them keeping a sharp eye on Charlie's pod, which was loaded with anti-surveillance wares less than a week old, and so good they were illegal. In another two weeks they would be obsolete, but by then Charlie wouldn't have them anymore. In a city with nearly as many recording devices as citizens, it was a safe assumption that someone beyond your intended audience had access to everything you said. One solution to this was to hide out in a Wi-Free anytime you wanted privacy; the other was to hide in plain sight, deploy good wares, and count on the vast amount of noise to drown you out. This is what Martin and Charlie were doing. In the end, it would draw less attention, since surveillance instruments linked to the LA County Security Bureau recorded every entrance to a Wi-Free area. Charlie was a good deal older than Martin, with most of his sixth decade in the rearview mirror, and he could remember when people were actually able to do things nobody else knew about. Seemed like now, the distinction between public and private had become one of those ongoing little white lies that act as social lubricant. Those pants don't make your ass look big, and no, probably nobody in the government is peeking in while you roll a joint. Even a government with unlimited surveillance power is still a government with limited resources, so as a practical matter not much changed in everyday life—until someone came after you for something, in which case they came after you for everything you'd ever done.

But the background consciousness of being observed was maybe the more important consequence. In 2040 Los Angeles, nobody could be alone. Charlie kind of missed being alone. Which was why he kept his blinder wares up to speed, and why he and Martin sat in public and had conversations that if not illegal were certainly in violation of signed agreements. You just couldn't think about it all the time.

When Martin had spun out the whole scenario for him, Charlie said, "Jesus fuck. Amigo, are you sure you know what you're getting yourself into?"

"No," Martin said. "I readily admit that I do not know what I'm getting myself into. But I know what I'm getting myself out of."

"You're going to put needles in guys' arms so your employer can get more liquid."

Charlie had a gift, or so he'd been told, for phrasing uncomfortable truths in exactly the most uncomfortable way. He watched Martin grapple with what he'd said and reach some internal accommodation with it. "I'm not all the way behind the ethics of it," Martin said. "I don't think. But there's something to it, isn't there? The idea that a guy whose life would otherwise be wasted, and a drain on everyone, can be turned into something good?"

"Tell you what, amigo," Charlie said. "I hate slippery-slope arguments, but man. Where does this one end?"

"I don't know. It hasn't even started yet." Martin finished his lunch and flipped the burrito wrapper in the direction of Temoc's outdoor trash can, which had no explosives sensors on it and so was probably illegal unless Temoc had paid someone off to get grandfathered in. The wrapper missed, and Martin went to pick it up. "Listen," he said, "I need to get back to reading. It's going to be a hectic couple of weeks."

Get a problem, solve a problem, Charlie thought as he sat in his car with the air-conditioning cranked against the midday heat. He fiddled with the brim of his hat, which had gotten creased somehow, and now he didn't like the line of it. Plus the sweat stains were starting to discolor the fabric. Time to get a new hat, he thought. Also he had an idea about how to make Martin's change of fortune an opportunity for Charlie Rhodes as well. This was deep into rationalization territory, but Charlie thought that if Martin was going to get involved in this buyout thing, he was going to need someone watching his back. And maybe the best way for Charlie to do that was to offer his services to the Krakauers. Background work was Charlie's area. Now how did he feel about making money from buyouts, if it happened that way?

Not too good. Not too good at all. But if it was going to happen, it was going to happen, so it should happen in such a way that minimized the chances of Martin getting hung out to dry. And what the hell, if Charlie could make a few bucks along the way, where was the harm in that?

Casualties in the Niger Delta water war have reached half a million, with famine displacing millions more. That's the serious news for the day. Here at home, resettlement of Arizonans and Nevadans displaced by the failure of the Colorado River is said to be proceeding with minimal disruptions. But if you believe that, you haven't been seeing the same feeds I have. Phoenix, Tempe, and Tucson are all coded Orange. The D-Backs are on the road until further notice, playing their "home"—did you hear the scare quotes?—games in New Orleans, if you can believe that. No water to too much water. Back in Arizona, the new suicide hot spot is the remains of the Hoover Dam. Oh, and if you're not cleared Orange, stay away from the civic center until four o'clock today. Visiting honchos of somethingorother in town for talks about the water problems in Arizona and Nevada. Surprised they don't have the emirs of everywhere in the Horn of Africa here, too, the way they're killing each other for agua. But hey, if people over there didn't have something to shoot each other over, they'd all wake up and realize they live in a place where people shouldn't live, and then they'd all be here. Or in Canada. In any case, if your car doesn't pass Orange, don't drive downtown today. No word from Metro on whether there's a security pinch for the trains, too. Dodgers are up three-to-one in the fifth. Let's see, what else . . . did you hear about this buy-out thing? I tell you what, a whole lot of things have made me homicidal in my time, but man, that's incentive. You kill someone, we'll make your family rich! All over Cali, people are making lists of relatives they don't like and matching them up with people who need killing. Do I sound like I'm against it? Pero no! Anything that derails a lawyer's gravy train, I'm totally pro. A hundred and two degrees at LAX, a hundred seven in the Valley, ninety-six in Long Beach. UV index is thermonuclear. If you're outside without a hat, you would not be found competent to take a buyout, know what I'm saying?

FOUR

THURSDAY MORNING a press release went out announcing the restructuring of Antelope Valley and the creation of ValCorp/KRK. The buyout
program was teased, but without specifics, and Jocelyn did some press
while Scott and Martin huddled in the office over the files. "Usually I do
the press," Scott said. "Joss thinks they like me better than her. But
media strategy is my department for sure, so she's out there today while
we strategize. Every good marriage has a viable division of labor, right?"

"Right," Martin said.

"Okay." A holo gallery sprouted from the tabletop, twelve mug shots
of twelve lifers in three different Nautilus-owned prisons. "You've read
up on all these guys, right?" Scott said.

"I'm ready for the test," Martin said.

"Ha. Okay." Scott waved his pod at the top left image, spawning
records across the tabletop. "I think we ought to do him first because
he's white. Tell me what I'm thinking."

The potential client in question, Karl Felix Alexander, was serving
LWOP for the murder of a family named Uribe, in Reseda. The case
was pregnant with dog-whistle symbolism: Alexander was white, his victims Hispanic; there had been widespread outrage when the LA County
DA's office had abandoned its capital case despite evidence that the
Uribe children had been raped. "You're thinking that you never get a
second chance to make a first impression," Martin said. "If our first guy
is white, and kills Latinos, then you flip around the expectation about
who gets imprisoned and you disarm natural suspicions from minority
communities that this is some kind of sneaky eugenics conspiracy."

"Yeah, right, good," Scott said. "That's a big part of it. But there's another part, too. The only reason Alexander's still breathing is that the LAPD fucked up their processing of the crime scene, so even a public defender could convince a jury to ignore a lot of the evidence. Put rape and murder together, and add kids into the mix, and you've got a guaranteed capital murder case. But here's Alexander, who did all these things, and he's enjoying three meals a day." Scott winked at Martin. "Insert prison-food joke here. Anyway, the important thing is that Alexander's still alive because of a technicality. Justice failed because the people whose job it was to kill him didn't meet the standards of the law. So here's how we frame it, right? A buyout, for a guy like Karl Felix Alexander, is a chance to put things right—and a chance to put justice back in the hands of a human being instead of the criminal justice system, which nobody trusts. Particularly not the Latino majority of this fine city. We're going to go out with Karl Felix Alexander and turn him into a symbol of all that's wrong with how we do crime and punishment, and then we're going to turn him into a symbol of how the life-term buyout can fix that, can usher in a new era. Right?"

"Yeah," Martin said. "Right."

"Then we can roll out some minority clients to ease the fears of the Anglos, who still have all the money in town," Scott said. "This guy here, for example." The fifth picture in the grid expanded, and a new set of records appeared on the tabletop. "Alonzo Pickering. We go with a black guy second, and this black guy because he's locked up for killing both Anglos and Latinos. You read up on him, right? The thing with the plastic bags? You'd never believe someone would be so fucking dumb as to video something like that, but hey, these are the times we live in. And it worked for him, once the video got out onto the feeds he could argue that the publicity made it impossible for him to get a fair trial. So there he is, Alonzo Pickering, killer of six women, still breathing. Who's going to say we shouldn't do a buyout on him?"

"Somebody will," Martin said.

"Sure. We'll have that dialogue. But we'll shape it, we'll make sure that our initial choices frame it, and that it takes place using our terms. People are going to oppose buyouts, you bet. But we're going to get out front and make them play on our field."

Martin scanned the faces of these men who would soon occupy so much of his time. "You chose all of these guys because they present the same narrative, right?"

"That's right," Scott said.

"Have they all agreed that they want buyouts?"

"Not in so many words," Scott said. "We've been in touch with them and outlined some possibilities. You'll be the one who closes all of the deals."

"What if I go in and they all say no?"

Scott put a hand on Martin's shoulder and gave him a playful little shove. "Martin, come on, you've got to believe in yourself. If you make the case, they'll come around. Plus, we put these guys up first because they're already primed."

"Primed," Martin repeated.

"Nothing illegal. I mean, most of the law that will govern the situation isn't even written yet. But obviously coercion is off the table. That's in the charter as written. Although there's a funny story there. Ron Dempsey wanted the no-coercion provision cut, and only agreed to leave it in because a bunch of bleeding hearts said they wouldn't go for the charter unless it was explicitly spelled out. Me, I wanted to say that if someone's coerced, that would come out during the course of doing the deal, and then we'd call it off, but hey, compromise is good. Listen, as things go on we're going to be right on the straight and narrow about stuff like that, but for now—these guys, their cases are all about technicalities, they've got no room to bitch. We're not threatening anyone's kids or anything. We're just incentivizing the process in some informal ways."

Martin could see how Scott had gotten so successful in the consultancy racket. *Are these the kinds of people you want to be getting involved with,* is what his mother would have asked. The flip side of that question, though, was: Does it matter what the people are like, if some good comes out of what they do? Thomas Jefferson owned slaves. This was the moment when Martin could either back out or commit absolutely. Now he knew, from the depth and range of Scott's artful bullshit, that the buyout program was, for the Krakauers, solely a business proposition. That was all. And that meant that they would try to get away with whatever they could. But I'm going to be the one out in front of the world, Martin thought.

"I need a bit of reassurance here, Scott," Martin said. "I need to know that if I say a deal isn't good, you're going to go with me."

"I promise you, Martin. On a day-to-day, deal-to-deal level, it's going to be absolutely your call whether something goes through. Joss and I are counting on you to curb our enthusiasm, as a matter of fact. One of the reasons we picked you is that you have a reputation around here as a straight arrow. A guy who does everything exactly the way it's supposed to be done. We can't surround ourselves with gunslingers."

I am that guy, Martin thought. He was proud of that reputation, and careful with it. Even apart from his uncertainty about whether life-term buyouts were, on balance, good—although he was settling into a belief that they were—he was nervous about putting his reputation on the line.

"Are we still working together?" Scott asked.

Martin looked at the gallery of murderers hovering over the table-top. "Yeah," he said. "We are."

"Good. So these are the kinds of assholes who will be our initial clientele," Scott said, waving at the gallery. He had his pod in his hand, and accidentally caused a number of the pictures to expand as he swept the pod's eye across the holo field. "Whoa. Oops. Easy to make the case, right?"

"Sure seems like it," Martin said.

"And then we do availabilities at places where the money's going, right? Where it's having an obvious effect. First time one of the clients finances a new Little League field or an expansion of a day care, we're all over it. Make sure you let them know they have that option. I figure they're all going to want to give the money to their mothers or some-thing. Broaden their horizons for them, right?"

"Right," Martin said. Already he was getting sick of the way Scott used *right?* to prompt agreement. But he'd live with the shtick if it meant the job would go forward.

Scott was talking on his pod. "Hey," he said, and listened. "No shit.

He did?" More listening. "Yeah, that's what I would have done. Good news." He clicked off. "Funny thing just happened," he said, turning his attention back to Martin. "Your friend Charlie Rhodes just cornered Joss and talked her into giving him a job."

CHARLIE, BEING MANY things but not completely a fool when it came to his financial well-being, seized the opportunity to make himself indispensable when he had an epiphany about the potential havoc to be wrought on the process by unscrupulous, suicidal, or just plain crazy people who happened not to be guilty of a particular murder. He pressed his case to Jocelyn, who opened their meeting by saying, "Charlie, I'm willing to bet that over the past three years of planning this, we've thought of every scenario you can come up with. But let's hear what you have to say."

He decided to believe that this opening salvo was her way of laying the groundwork for financial negotiations after she discovered how insightful he was going to be. "Everybody's out for a quick buck, right?" he said. "The way I see it, you got potential problems coming from two directions. One, people who for whatever reason decide they want to cop to a murder so they can take a buyout. A guy with a terminal illness, for example. He confesses that he killed someone because the buyout payment is going to be worth more than his life insurance."

"We're not going to be doing buyouts on sixty-year-olds," Jocelyn said. "The numbers don't work."

"Right, but people get cancer in their twenties. And there's these new strains of AIDS, and whatever else. Anyway, the minute you get some do-gooder who can prove that someone gamed the system, there goes your political backing." Charlie piped some statistics about terminal illnesses in the eighteen-to-thirty-five age group to Jocelyn's desk. He saw her notice them, but she didn't say anything, so he went on. "Then you've got the people who will actually kill someone so they can get a buyout. A guy's suicidal, maybe, but doesn't want to leave his family out on the street. What does he do? He kills someone, takes the buyout, and he's got a delayed-action suicide together with a nest egg that will take care of his wife and kids. Even though they're probably the reason he wanted to do it anyway. You've got to have some way to prove that the crime wasn't motivated by a desire to get a buyout, and for that you need someone to do the investigation that the cops won't. They close the case, they're done. Ask any cop, they don't give a fuck why someone kills someone else, excuse my language, as long as they can prove he did. You were on the job, you know this."

"Excused," Jocelyn said. She had leaned back in her chair, and was giving the impression that she enjoyed Charlie's presentation. "We did have a vetting process in mind."

"I'm sure you did," Charlie said. "But you're going to need to go outside your regular kind of insurance adjusting. What if someone innocent is forced to go down for a murder he didn't commit? What if inmates in one of your prisons get together and pressure another guy to take a buyout? A guy who's spent his career trying to decide if someone's carriage house was in a floodplain isn't going to have the first idea about how to look for that stuff."

"But you will," Jocelyn prompted.

"I regret to say," Charlie said, "that I have spent much of my professional life interacting with people I wouldn't want to introduce to my mother. God rest her soul."

"How did you get access to my desk?" Jocelyn asked him. "Maybe I should be hiring you as a network security consultant."

"Nah. I don't work in-house. The hacks I get from guys who owe me favors because of other work I did for them. Your security isn't bad."

She gave him a long appraising look, a career-cop-turned-corrections-executive weighing the merits of a dime-a-dozen private investigator with no formal credentials. "Charlie," she said, "we had anticipated the situations you've outlined here, but you're right that we need to keep our noses absolutely clean on this. Every single buyout we do has to be provably free of any hint of graft, coercion, or manipulation of any kind. If I hire you to do this, you're going to have quite a bit of responsibility. Have you ever had that kind of responsibility before?"

"Not for long," Charlie said.

"It would be our strong preference to have someone on staff do this."

"No way," Charlie said reflexively, spurred by a warning signal that went off in his head at any instance of proposed professional commitment. "We can do a priority deal, though. I drop everything else when a buyout comes along."

After that it was all numbers. Jocelyn was so smooth glossing over their disagreement about the nature of his relationship to Nautilus that Charlie got the impression she'd wanted things that way all along. Close but not too close. That's how people like Jocelyn Krakauer got where they were. He had the strong feeling that he'd been had despite getting what he wanted, including an hourly rate close to twice what he charged for regular surveillance and data-chasing work. It was a good deal for him. Steady and reliable work meant that his two boys still in college could stop hounding him about money, and if the buyout thing took off, he could stop spending his nights watching strangers fuck through binoculars while his coffee got cold. No more hacking public security cameras and newsdrone feeds.

The stakes in each buyout case—not just the life and/or death of the client, although Nautilus paid lip service to that, but the reputation of the company and the continuation of the immensely lucrative buyout charter itself—meant that Charlie was going to have the entire company in his hands. It would be up to him to ensure that the Krakauers' golden goose would not be cooked.

He worried about being compromised, and he also had a long list of moral and philosophical qualms about buyouts, but he was going to do this anyway. For Martin, partly, because Charlie could tell even before a single buyout had ever been "finalized"—terrific job of euphemism, that—that if the Krakauers ever did decide to do something shifty, Martin was too much of a straight arrow to figure it out before it was much too late. Charlie, on the other hand, attuned as he was to the worst aspects of human behavior by his years of observing it, figured that he'd see a threat to Martin coming from a mile away. So if he was going to sell his soul to make money by implicating himself in the whole buyout process, at least he could tell himself that he was doing it partly out of friendship.

Jocelyn had been so easy to work with, and so willing to pay him what he asked, that he had the discomfiting sensation that she thought she was buying more than Charlie had in fact meant to sell.

But that was a problem for another time, and forewarned is fore-armed, et cetera.

MARTIN WAS HAPPY to have Charlie backing him up. "You couldn't be that against it if you're going to spend all of your time making sure I do it right," he said, to which Charlie heartily wished that Martin and his sanctimony would go straight to hell, and then he got them another beer. Yankee Doodle's was its typical Wednesday self, which was to say it was a place where Martin wouldn't have been caught dead if his brother hadn't been there. It was a post-adolescent playground that had also be-come a cop bar, primarily because there the cops could mingle with the post-adolescents. Jason bought a round, distributed beers to Martin and Charlie, and paused a moment to take it all in. "This place is some-thing," he said. "Sol's over there holding court."

Sol Briggs was an LAPD veteran, widely despised even by his col-leagues, who formed the obese and vulgar core of a group of cops who gathered at Yankee Doodle's to watch the talent. Jason had no use for him professionally, was a different kind of cop, but also knew that it did you good to appear at places like Yankee Doodle's since the tribe of blue had chosen this as a favored place. Martin followed the logic but didn't like it, and only went to Yankee Doodle's when he knew Jason would be there. Charlie appeared when he thought he might hear something in-teresting and possibly germane to a case he was working.

Ringing an acre of pool tables abused by people who couldn't play pool were several dozen VR booths and another several dozen video games so ancient they'd acquired a retro cool. Vance Kindred, during his days on the force, had been known to hoist a few at Yankee Doodle's because it reminded him of the old arcades he'd haunted in 1985. It was one of the rare places—which are rarer still in a place so single-mindedly devoted to fantasy and reinvention as LA—that seemed never to change. Charlie hated it despite his general liking for places that had history beyond the renewal of the last lease.

"I don't like this," he told Martin when they were topped off. "And I'm not going to like it. But if it's going to happen, I want to get my two cents in about the way it happens. You're laughing about this now, but you're going to wish you'd never known me when I'm breaking your balls because you want to do a buyout on a guy with brain cancer who was convicted because he agreed to take the fall for his nephew or something."

"My hero," Martin said drily. "Guess I better get some clients signed up so you can keep me on the straight and narrow."

"You'd be the only one," Charlie said. The more he learned about how the buyout charter had gone through, the less he liked it. Three months ago nobody had ever heard of the idea. Then out of nowhere, the Krakauers had bought into the former Antelope Valley Casualty, sold it to corrections conglomerate ValCorp Services, then arranged with ValCorp's directors to have their California operations spun back off, together with the insurance arm that had been Antelope Valley. Just like that, the Krakauers were managing directors of a vertically integrated corrections operation and insurance concern. But long before that, back when they were still consulting in Texas (or so Charlie had it from one of his hacker acquaintances, who had provided him the key to Jocelyn Krakauer's desk), the Krakauers had begun a campaign of seduction in Sacramento. The California legislature had for seventy years been notorious for its infantile need to be simultaneously innovative and tough on crime, and committees in both houses burned the midnight oil to frame a buyout program that would draw just the right amount of fire from human-rights types while throwing enough red meat to the law-and-order crowd. The governor was with the program, making nobly thunderous statements about prison reform and promising a new direction in corrections for a state whose prison population and incarcerations costs had tripled over the previous forty years. With the election of Ron Dempsey to the United States Senate, the final piece had fallen into place.

Martin didn't know all of this. He was just beginning intensive training along two primary lines to prepare him for his new vocation. First, a detailed study of California law pertaining to prisoner rights and the legal questions surrounding life-term buyouts, as well as a thorough grounding in the demographics of the state's prison population. Second, Martin was learning all there was to know about how Nautilus built, populated, and administered its growing network of medium- and high-security prisons: He was scheduled to visit every one of them and hob-nob briefly with their administrators. The Krakauers planned to get their administrative staff up to speed at a general briefing to be held next week at the new headquarters. There they planned to introduce Martin as the first of what would, they hoped, be a staff of agents as the program proved its worth and expanded. The newsnets were starting to get wind that something big was in the works, and Scott—the more telegenic of the Krakauers—put Martin on notice that he was going to be the public face of the program. "I'll handle the high-level political stuff," he said, "but you, Martin—you're going to be the face of the life-term buyout for Joe and Jane Public. And I hope you won't think I'm blowing too much smoke up your ass if I tell you that you're perfect. The camera likes you, you're a family man, and you come across as someone who can really explain why he believes what he believes. That's what we need."

It wasn't out of the ordinary to stage-manage something like this, especially in LA, but Scott's coyness was curious to Martin. He decided to let it go for the moment. "About the family-man thing," he began.

"I know," Scott said. "I know. Look, everyone's got troubles if they stay married long enough to get troubles. Do me a favor and don't get divorced just yet, okay?"

The official announcement of the program was every bit the media cluster bomb, at least in California, that Charlie had feared and the Krakauers had hoped. Priceless Life, a self-styled advocacy group cobbled together from the mismatched remains of turn-of-the-millennium pro-lifers and a smattering of anti-capital-punishment zealots, was screaming bloody murder to everyone who would listen. Various churches were starting to weigh in, and prisoner-rights groups were gearing up for their own crusade. Within the industry, early word was that the corrections union was going to be agnostic on the proposal as long as it didn't diminish inmate populations enough to affect staffing. Police unions were staying out of the fray, arguing that what happened to prisoners after conviction wasn't their problem. Politicians were grandstanding according to the dictates of their constituencies. A real controversy was at hand, and the newsnets couldn't wait for it to really get going. Charlie knew that Martin was in for more than he'd bargained for, and he also knew that he could explain to Martin exactly how this was going to happen without making the slightest bit of difference to Martin, who would plunge ahead because that's what he knew how to do. Martin was rolled out to do a couple of small availabilities, but at first the Krakauers kept him away from the live packs of reporters. He got comfortable doing videoconference interviews from his new office, and he noted an uptick in the number of attempted podjacks and intrusions into his car system, which was so old that it couldn't handle newer upgrades.

Despite their plans for Karl Alexander and Alonzo Pickering, it soon became clear that their best candidate for the inaugural life-term buyout would be one Jackson Ordonez, a former Santa Ana public-works supervisor. Jackson himself was on board, but he wanted Martin to go talk to his wife as well, since—as Jackson put it—"I'm not so good at explaining things to her."

Martin would have preferred Jackson just to thumbprint the form so they could get on with it, but he shook his head. "Fuck, man, I said I'll do it," he said. "But you go talk to my wife, see what she thinks."

While waiting for Leila Ordonez to answer the door—he knew she was home, since she didn't have a job and the family car had been impounded—Martin rehearsed his approach. His hardball pitch, to a new fish at Yucaipa or Nautilus-Valley, was going to be something like: Later you will want it. When you're sixty years old, and your children won't speak to you, and the prison surgeon has stitched your rectum back together three times and you wear a colostomy bag because you got shanked twenty years ago after giving the wrong guy a cigarette, and you've got another twenty-five years of the same to look forward to unless you're lucky enough to die of AIDS or a fast-moving cancer first—then you're going to want a buyout, and then I'm going to have a hard time making the numbers work. So now's your chance: to do what you can for your kids, and for your victim's kids, and for everyone else whose life was torn apart because you couldn't keep control. This, Mr. Lifelong Resident of Yucaipa Supermax, is the one and only chance you're ever going to have to be in control.

That was how he would pitch the guy who had to thumbprint the blinking field. But Martin knew that wouldn't work with the woman he's left on the outside, with her turmoil of mourning and guilt and anger and love and hate. Leila Ordonez opened the door, and he took off his hat even though it was ninety-six oppressive degrees here, on March 22. "Mrs. Ordonez? My name is Martin Kindred," he said and extended his hand.

She didn't shake. "Are you a Jehovah's Witness?" she asked.

"No," Martin said with a trace of a smile. "But I'm afraid I am selling you something."

"I'm not buying," Leila said. The sun beat on Martin's back. He tapped the bow of his sunglasses, and the lenses depolarized. A readout in one corner of the right lens reminded him that he had a parent–teacher conference at seven o'clock. This note scrolled out of view, replaced by a notification that someone on the block was probing his car's security. Martin sort of wished someone would steal the car so he'd have an excuse to get a new one.

"Mrs. Ordonez," Martin said. "I represent Nautilus Casualty and Property, which both owns and insures Yucaipa Prison."

Leila didn't finish shutting the door. Her husband had gone to Yucaipa about a month ago, just before the Nautilus takeover. He was serving a sentence of life without parole for the murder of a friend whom he'd caught in a compromising position with his mistress—of whose existence Leila Ordonez was not aware until informed by the police. Jackson might have escaped a life sentence were it not for the fact that he had left the house where his indiscretion occurred, and then returned to kill his mistress shortly before police arrived. The only reason he hadn't gone up on capital murder was his attorney's skillful manipulation of the male jurors' feelings about infidelity. When Martin read the transcripts, he determined that if he was ever up on a capital murder rap, he wanted Jackson Ordonez' lawyer.

"Nautilus is engaged in a charter program to create an alternative to life imprisonment," Martin said. "I've already spoken to your husband about it."

"If you've spoken to him," Leila Ordonez wanted to know, "why are you talking to me now?"

"Because it's customary to get the entire family involved in the decision-making process." The sun was killing Martin. He wished she would let him inside.

"Mr. Kindred," Leila said. "Say what you have to say."

"It costs something in the neighborhood of three hundred thousand dollars per year to feed, clothe, and house an inmate at Yucaipa," Martin began. "More if that inmate is particularly litigious, or lives a long time with chronic medical conditions. Your husband is twenty-nine years old, and according to the actuaries he will live to be eighty-six. Take fifty-seven years, multiply by three hundred thousand dollars, and you get seventeen point seven million. Add in the projections we have to make about medical care and legal expenses, and you can double that. So that's almost thirty-six million dollars we will spend on your husband while he spends the rest of his life in a six-by-nine cell. Now, according to federal regulations, Nautilus needs to keep a certain amount of cash on hand to ensure that we're going to be liquid in the foreseeable future. That amount is called a reserve, and it's typically twenty percent of the anticipated expense. In real terms, this means that Nautilus has to keep about seven million dollars sitting in the bank with your husband's name on it. And I am here to offer you and your family a significant portion of that seven million dollars."

"You're not going to just hand me this money," Leila said.

"I sure am," Martin said. "And it's tax-free."

"You know what I mean. What do I have to do for it?"

"You don't have to do a thing. Your husband has to sign on the dotted line, and once the buyout is finalized, I'll be right back here on your porch to transfer the money into your account."

"Mr. Kindred, you're starting to piss me off," Leila said. "What does finalized mean?"

"Well, Mrs. Ordonez, inmate interviews tell us that a good seventy-five percent of Nautilus inmates serving life without parole would rather be dead. Ninety percent of those are incarcerated for murder." Martin hesitated for a calibrated moment, weighing the risk of sounding preachy against the possible reward of closing the deal. He'd been holding himself back, being careful. Now maybe it was time to let go. "Most murderers, despite what they say, harbor enormous guilt," Martin went on. "A majority of them say at one time or another, particularly later in life, that they would willingly take the place of the victim, except in cases where killer and victim had an ongoing dispute. We've studied this fairly exhaustively, and one of the motivating beliefs of the life-term buyout program is that murderers should be given a chance to atone for their crime. Capital punishment by itself is capricious, unfairly applied, and does nothing to satisfy the loss and bereavement of the victim and loved ones. The life-term buyout, on the other hand, puts the inmate in control. He decides whether he's going to stay or go, and he decides how best to make amends, in the only way he can."

"You're saying that you want to kill Jackson," Leila said.

"I'm saying that Jackson doesn't want to spend the rest of his life in prison."

Only a fool would think that human life had not been scaled and valued since the first time a crowned head traded his best and strongest for shining stones or purple dye, black pepper or black gold. It wasn't about valuing human life; it was about asserting that human life has value. A buyout couldn't bring a dead person back to life, but it kept the lawyers and the courts out of the picture, and it wasn't driven by revenge. The wronged party couldn't ask for one, and no buyout agent could approach a potential client at the request of the victim's family. Only the guilty man could take the measure of his conscience, and only the guilty man could relieve the burden of the state and lay down his life to make amends for his transgression. It was about control.

Scott was a little more straightforward. For him, buyouts were a market-driven solution to a problem that no government had yet been able to untangle. Freed from the judicial morass, the life-term buyout cut to the heart of the problem with maximal efficiency and minimal empty gesturing toward sentiment. A ten million-dollar wrongful-death verdict against an unemployed pizza delivery driver was a meaningless waste of government resources and the time of twelve jurors.

But you couldn't say that to somebody's wife. "Jackson has an opportunity to atone," Martin said. "In another time, he would be on death row, at the mercy of the state. Now he can choose whether he wants to try to make amends."

"To who? Me?" Leila snapped, with a bitter laugh. "To his daughter?

You think that by making us rich, we're going to forget what he did? Get the hell off my porch."

"That's not what I think at all, Mrs. Ordonez," Martin said. "I think that Jackson has a right to make this determination, and a chance to consider the well-being of you, your daughter, and the loved ones of Warren Travers and Alana Kristiansen."

A risky move, bringing up the names of the dead. Especially since there was adultery involved. Consider it a test case. If it worked, then maybe try the strategy another time when it seemed right. If not, well, she hadn't kicked him off the porch yet.

"So you'd expect me to give them money?" Now Leila was just disbelieving. Her anger had faded away. Half of the sun's disk was behind the house across the street, but the remaining half blazed onto her porch with undiminished intensity. Martin played outside all day when he was a child; there were no children on the street here.

"In consultation with Jackson, you could decide which funds should go where," Martin said. "Ultimately it's his decision. If you don't want to go through the process without guidance, I'm happy to help, or I can provide you with some standard disbursement breakdowns that other clients have used."

Car salesmen have known for a hundred years that if you sell the woman on the car, you've sold the car. It was the same with buyouts. So to the woman Martin said: I am not here to tell you what to do. I am here to provide clarity. The situation is this; the stakes are these; the possible solutions are such. The newly single woman with a man inside—especially a man, like Jackson Ordonez, inside for killing his mistress—needed above all a sense of purpose, of agency and control. Martin couldn't provide that, but as the purveyor of the life-term buyout he could be the conduit through which Leila Ordonez discovered it.

"I believe," he said, "and I'd have to check to make sure, but I believe the disbursement amount we're talking about is just over five million dollars." The look on Leila's face told him all he needed to know. He excused himself after piping the necessary forms over to her, and then he walked back to his car.

Every day, Nautilus-owned prisons got three or four new inmates serving life without parole. Eleven, maybe twelve hundred per year, new chances to make his pitch. Martin only needed a strike rate of one in forty to add a zero to the amount of money he'd made last year.

It wasn't about wanting someone to die. It was about someone who already had died. And it was about atonement, and purpose, and belief that a human life was perhaps worth dying for.

Leila Ordonez had not said either yes or no. Martin thought of what Scott said about that situation: "If they don't turn you down right away, eventually they're going to say yes." And Jackson was behind it. So it would happen; after that conversation, Martin was pretty sure that at least she wouldn't try to talk him out of it.

People, Martin reflected as he started the car and pinged the office that the Ordonez deal was alive and well, know what life is worth.

We note with interest the scheduling of what we here at Dangerfield World Domination Studios believe to be the first life-term buyout performed on a human being. If you stream this later today, it will already have happened; then again, if you stream this later today, I might already be dead. Our foray into seeing whether insurance regulators will get themselves involved in assigning a dollar value to human life begins at oh nine hundred hours . . . unless, that is, you believe that it began the first time an insurance company denied someone a surgery based on a preexisting condition. Man, I remember when I was a kid we had this dog named Sesame. Don't ask me why. She got sick, and my dad took her to the vet, and Sesame didn't come home. Me and my brothers, we asked why. Well, kids, the old man said. Sesame was sick, and we couldn't afford to get her better. Couldn't afford it? Couldn't afford it!? Maybe we couldn't afford to make sure that Jackson Ordonez, for such is the moniker of the lucky first recipient of what our esteemed punditocracy is already calling the Golden Needle, maybe we couldn't afford to make sure that he would grow up and come to adulthood in such a way that he wouldn't off his girlfriend and her other boyfriend. How much would that have cost?

FIVE

THE BUYOUT of Jackson Ordonez' life sentence was finalized at nine o'clock in the morning on April 16, 2040. Outside, the mercury hovered around 110 degrees, and sweat evaporated from the foreheads of the forty-nine people who had just filed in from the waiting area to the viewing room, where the temperature was maintained at 68 degrees with 20 percent humidity. Of the forty-nine, three were preparing the sophisticated machinery of finalization. Federal and state law required the presence of a doctor and two technicians certified in the operation of the necessary equipment, with additional demonstrated emergency medical proficiency. Three other prison employees were present: a pair of bored guards and Yucaipa's chief executive officer, a career bureaucrat named Garret Lau who had been deputized into corrections about the same time Martin made his move into buyouts. A Catholic priest stood, gaunt and introspective, at the back of the room, behind fourteen relatives of Warren Travers and Alana Kristiansen. Just in front of them clustered twenty-two journalists, selected and personally credentialed by the Krakauers.

Martin was watching Leila, and incongruously it struck him that she was the embodiment of a line of poetry he'd read and improbably remembered, years before in college—solitudes crowded with loneliness. In black, veiled, she sat upright in the front row, not even turning her head when her husband entered the chamber flanked by another pair of guards and without ceremony laid himself down on the cushioned gurney, resting his arms by his sides with his palms turned up to expose the veins in his elbows. He moved as if he had rehearsed carefully, and understood the importance of the role he was to play.

The priest had already performed last rites and taken Jackson's confession. Now began the final equation of the buyout, through which one human being would be subtracted from the forty-nine present and five million dollars moved from Nautilus accounts to those of Jackson's designated recipients. The mechanics of buyout finalization were no different from those of the state-imposed terminations that preceded the buyout charter. The ritual aspect of life's end hung, hushed and self-important, over an event that Charlie Rhodes had once described as sacred purpose bastardized into efficiency. The men who buckled Jackson Ordonez onto the gurney went about their work with commendable focus topped only by the intensity of the attending physician, who would not have been more dedicated had he been performing heart surgery on a child. Into the midst of the scene strode Garret Lau, to remind everyone present that Jackson Ordonez had taken his final steps absent coercion and in full possession of his faculties. The onlookers thus reassured, Lau stepped back through the door of bulletproof glass into the viewing area, where he took up a position near—but not so near as to appear ghoulish—the stoic figure of Leila Ordonez.

Martin wondered what would happen if a client were to change his mind at the last minute. Legally Nautilus was on firm footing to pursue a finalization over the client's second-guessing; the client could no more take back his thumbprint on Martin's pod than he could unsign a marriage license. Still, the Priceless Lifers would have the proverbial field day with such an event. No one wanted to give them that kind of free notice and momentum.

"Sooner or later, a bad buyout's gonna happen," both Scott and Charlie had told Martin, and both of them—although, Martin imagined, for different reasons—tended to follow this proclamation with the same caveat: "Hope you're not the guy who does it."

I won't be, was always Martin's reply, and he believed it. Especially today, as it all began, as Jackson Ordonez felt the first cold spill of sodium thiopental into the basilic vein of his left arm. At this moment, even the most jaded or misanthropic spectator could not look away. The client's breathing slowed with the induction of temporary coma, and his body relaxed; the last motions were a slight curling and uncurling of the fingers of the left hand, as if Jackson Ordonez in his last moments of consciousness had beckoned to someone. After thirty seconds, at the quiet instruction of the attending physician, one of the technicians triggered an infusion of pancuronium bromide, which paralyzed every muscle in Jackson Ordonez' body, including his diaphragm. His breathing slowed, and as it stopped everyone watching realized that they too were not breathing, that through some bodily sympathy they had stopped their own signs of life as well. They inhaled slowly and self-consciously, and felt the air fill their lungs. Thirty seconds following the cessation of breath, a third bolus injection of potassium chloride swept away the last of what made Jackson Ordonez human. The attendant physician observed his monitors. One minute after the third injection, he went to the gurney and listened with a stethoscope. Replacing it in his pocket, he pronounced Jackson Ordonez dead as of nine sixteen in the morning.

"May God have mercy on his soul," Scott said, just loud enough for the journalists to hear.

Moving with a deliberate, almost anesthetized smoothness, Leila Ordonez got to her feet. She turned as if her body had grown unfamiliar to her during her transition from wife to widow. She walked up the aisle looking neither right nor left, and she did not notice Garret Lau as he fell into step next to her, his left arm crooked ever so slightly in the event she might reach for it. She did not, and shortly they were gone. "Without a hitch," said Scott. "Good eye, Martin."

OUTSIDE, MARTIN DID his first post-finalization media availability. Scott was right there in case things got out of hand, but Martin had trained for this, and he had the Krakauers' okay to refer difficult questions to them until he felt like he had his feet under him. At the podium, set up in a grassy corner of the Yucaipa grounds so a camera view would feature mostly hills and just a corner of the prison facility, Martin looked out over more assembled media than he'd expected. There were maybe fifty cameras, and eight or ten drones circling overhead. So it begins, he thought, and started to speak.

"With the finalization of Jackson Ordonez' life-term buyout," he began, "the innovative and socially invested charter program created by Nautilus Casualty and Property is officially operational. I have time to take a few questions before I have to leave and begin the disbursement of Mr. Ordonez' funds."

Immediately everyone there asked a question. At first Martin couldn't make sense of any of them, but he was surprised to find that his ears quickly learned to sort them out. The first one that sounded interesting to him came from near the front. "Are you concerned that you're taking the question of capital punishment out of the courts?"

"Ah, no," Martin said, reminding himself not to address only the reporter who had asked the question. "The existence of buyouts has nothing to do with the choices made by the district attorney's office or the judiciary. They have to do their work before I even know in any given case whether I'll be able to do mine."

"How will you know if your clients are being coerced?" This from a feedhead whose face Martin recognized but couldn't place. Not one of the big networks.

"The procedures in place to detect possible coercion are very strict," Martin said. "Part of the reason Jackson Ordonez was the first client of mine to finalize is that I rejected several other possibilities because I couldn't satisfy myself that the potential client was acting freely and independently to choose a life-term buyout."

On and on it went like that, with questions coming in that Martin and Scott had rehearsed, and Martin giving answers whose general wording he and Scott had sketched out weeks before. As Martin realized how well prepared he was, he got less nervous, and after twenty minutes—the amount of time Scott had suggested for the availability—he was a little bit sorry to end things. "That's all the time I have, sorry," he said. "The charter says I only have forty-eight hours to comply with Mr. Ordonez' wishes by finishing his disbursements. So you can understand that I have to get started."

Scott caught a ride with Martin back to the office. At the gate, they passed a small group of Priceless Life demonstrators. They were attracting some cameras, but the feeds were going to have a hard time making it look like a large or emphatic expression of dissent; Martin counted nine of them, and only one who was anything like telegenic. Their banners were homemade, and the podjack they sent out fell victim to Martin's car security before its avatar had fully coalesced on the windshield. "Amateurs," Scott said with a chuckle. "Probably they'll draw in some more malcontents and worried old women, but if this is all they've got today, Priceless Life is not going to be something we have to worry about."

After dropping Scott off at the office, Martin started right in on the Ordonez DBs. The charter required that he be personally present to transfer funds to each recipient, which was both a huge waste of time and a golden opportunity for publicity. The first two DBs today were both scheduled media availabilities. The first was an elder-care facility in Santa Ana, upon which Jackson Ordonez—with Martin's guidance—had bestowed three-quarters of a million dollars for facility upgrades and an outings fund. The feeds showed up to get video of Martin shaking hands with old people and discussing how the money would be spent, and he got lucky with one resident, a decrepit old Anglo who seized Martin's hand and said, "By God, that Mexican may have been a killer, but at least now he's trying to do something good. We sure can use it around here." Back at the office, Martin was sure, Scott Krakauer was high-fiving whomever he could find. Or he'd paid the guy off beforehand; with Scott you couldn't be sure.

The second stop was a park where Ordonez had played baseball and basketball as a child. Accompanied by Santa Ana Parks and Rec personnel who brought holo renderings, Martin outlined what would be done with Ordonez' bequest of a million dollars: complete reconstruction of three baseball fields, and a new soccer complex that comprised a full-size outdoor field and stands built on top of an indoor training facility. The media ate the renderings up, and the innovative design—commissioned by an architect who had built prisons for some of the Krakauers' consulting clients—drew praise for its economical use of scarce urban land.

"Killer start," Scott pinged when Martin was driving home that night. "The feeds got it all: the Priceless Lifers cut against the happy fucking old people and parks. Home run, Martin. And you did great. Catch you tomorrow."

They were off and running.

AT HOME, with the girls in bed, Martin had a glass of wine with Teresa. "I was wondering if you'd be happy or something," she said. "It's a big day for you."

"Not happy, exactly." Martin looked through his glass at a lamp, liking the rich diffusion of the color. He found himself minutely conscious of details—more alive in some way.

"Then what?" Teresa prompted him.

He thought about it. "Satisfied," he said. "In the way that you are when you're doing work that is satisfying, and you do it well."

It was her turn to think things over. "I feel like I should congratulate you even though I don't agree with what you're doing," Teresa said. "It's confusing."

"I feel like you should congratulate me, too," Martin said, joking a little. "I think this will be important."

"Could be," Teresa said. She drained her glass, toasted Martin with the empty, and stood up. "There are a couple of things I should finish."

And there went another chance, because she moved away and Martin wouldn't try to bring her back. "Okay," he said. "I'm beat. Guess I'll just hit the sack."

AND AFTER THAT a year passed without Martin even being conscious of its passage. He celebrated birthdays with the girls, and at some point became conscious that he'd marked off another year on earth, but buyouts consumed him. During each of the twelve months following the inaugural finalization of Jackson Ordonez, Martin clocked at least two completed deals. His total for the year was forty-one. At an average disbursement of close to five million dollars per buyout, a lot of money was pipelined into a demographic that usually only got big cash injections from lottery winnings or professional athletic contracts. Part of Martin's job turned out to be counseling clients about ways to direct

their money so it wouldn't be wasted. Facing a death that they had chosen, buyout clients approached their financial responsibilities with surprising diligence. Here Martin's financial-planning experience—he'd
started in that area at AVC before moving into policy—came in handy.
He made sure that part of each buyout was directed toward charities,
civic organizations, you name it. Those forty-one buyouts built soccer
fields and baseball diamonds, completed financing for renovations at
boys' and girls' club buildings, bought several thousand Meals on
Wheels, endowed scholarships for disadvantaged children . . . it was
work you could feel good about.

On a more personal level, Martin made more money in 2040 than
he had in the ten years previous. The girls' college funds got plump.
They were ahead of schedule on the mortgage. Everyone had new
clothes, new gadgets. For a while Martin was worried that the sudden re-
versal of the financial pecking order—Teresa had always made more
money than he had—would exacerbate the marital situation. Then, as
it happened, he realized that their problems had nothing to do with
money, and that things were going downhill at home partially because
of how well they were going at work.

His thoughts on these and other matters were forcibly clarified when
the Kindreds went out to dinner one night in February 2041. They
chose an old favorite, an Indian place called Hi Bombay!, in an old New
Urbanism–inspired part of La Canada Flintridge that had been redeveloped after the '29 earthquake. It was comfortable, not too far from the
house, and served decent food. Even Kelly, a frustratingly picky eater,
made an exception for Hi Bombay!

On this night, however, things started off poorly and then got worse.
The minute they sat down, an adjacent table called the hostess over. "Can
you please reseat us?" one of the women at the table asked loudly. "I won't
be able to digest my food if I have to sit next to him." She pointed at
Martin.

The confused hostess got the other table resettled and came back
over to the Kindreds to apologize. "I don't know what that was about,"
she said. "I'm terribly sorry."

"It's fine," Martin said. "No need to apologize." They ordered drinks
and an assortment of samosas. Both of the girls were looking in the di-

rection of the empty table next to them. Kelly looked confused in much the same way the hostess had; Allison's face was set in a very Teresa-like expression of suppressed anger.

"Celebrity," Teresa remarked, with a touch of acid in her voice.

There was no way for Martin to respond to that without making things worse, so he didn't. The samosas came, and so did the drinks. With some effort, a normal vein of small talk was established. Three times Martin's pod vibrated in his pocket, but he ignored it. This tenuous equilibrium lasted until midway through the main course, when Allison said, "Dad. There's a Priceless Life group starting at school."

This was the way children had of letting you know how much you didn't know about what they knew about you. Martin had been preparing himself for a conversation with the kids about buyouts, had in fact touched on the subject briefly a time or two and then let it go when they immediately shifted conversational gears. Never had he imagined that it would come up insistently in this particular way at this particular time. He fell back on the tried-and-true method of getting a kid to keep talking.

"There is, huh? Who's starting it?"

"It's weird," Allison said. "There's some of the real fundy girls in it, and then some of the hairy social-justice people. You'd never see them together, but now they're like best friends."

"How about we eat our dinner," Teresa said.

"Eat up, girls," Martin said. "But Allison, tell me more, kid. How many people are in it?"

She shrugged and wolfed down a bite of pakora. Allison had the manners of a starving dog, no matter what they did, so Martin and Teresa had decided a year or so before to just let it go. Eventually social pressure would accomplish what parental diligence could not. "It's kind of the hot thing all of a sudden," she said. "They've only had one meeting, but a lot of kids were at it."

"You think they'll stick with it?" Martin asked.

Teresa set down her fork. "How is she supposed to know, Martin?"

"She'll have a better guess than I will," Martin said. "What do you think, kiddo?"

Allison shrugged again. As quickly as the urge to talk had come over her, it was gone. Adolescence was encroaching on the oldest Kindred girl, Martin thought. From the looks of it, all of them were in for quite a ride.

The first thing that happened when they got in the car was a bandit avatar appearing on the windshield. "Public tension is often a sign of much deeper-seated issues at home," it began. "Flamini Therapeutic and Family Services can—" The car security purged it before it could get any farther, and automatically sent a complaint to the podjacking division of the local Better Business Bureau. Not that it would do any good.

"Well, for God's sake," Teresa said. She glared at Martin, and he could anticipate the chain of logic leading her to blame this intrusion on him. Never mind that the average citizen of the United States saw a dozen unwanted avatars a day; this one, at this time, was going to be Martin's fault.

One of the things about a surveillance society, in which anyone can know anything about anyone else, is that most people discover how unimportant and uninteresting they really are. Martin had always taken some pleasure in this. What did it matter who was looking, if there was always something more interesting than you for them to look at? The buyout program was beginning to change that. Now people did care about Martin, and his work was coming home in ways that made him uncomfortable and Teresa downright furious. Looking at her now, in the car, Martin could tell that she was biting down hard on a bunch of things that she wouldn't say in front of the girls.

He decided to stay in the open lanes of the Foothill on the way back to Pasadena. Actually having to drive the car would give him an excuse not to talk as much. But as soon as they'd gotten up to speed Teresa said, "Martin. Please use the smart lane," and he had no good reason not to, so he did. Then they sat listening to some new band that Kelly had downloaded until just after the Ventura Freeway interchange, when all of a sudden the proximity alarms went off and something banged hard into the back of the car. Martin seized the wheel, but the automated smart-lane systems had already corrected for the impact, and he let it go again, turning around to see what had happened.

An old pickup truck, one of the massive diesel models from just after the turn of the millennium, accelerated out of the smart lane and pulled up next to the car. Sitting in the bed, long hair streaming in the wind, a young man looked Martin in the eye. He held up his right hand, two fingers extended in an old-fashioned peace sign. Then he brought those two fingers to his face, one below each eye; and then he pointed them at Martin.

"Get a picture," Martin said. He was scrambling for his pod, too, but it had jumped out of its bracket when the truck rear-ended them. The man in the bed of the truck pounded on the wheel well, and the truck jumped ahead, accelerating away to the east before Teresa or Martin could freeze an image of it. Their car continued its controlled path down the smart lane as if nothing had ever happened.

Thirty seconds later a voice-only ping came in from the California Highway Patrol. "Sir, we've recorded an impact in the smart lane of the Foothill Freeway," said a blandly official female voice. "Were you involved?"

"Yeah," Martin said. "How is that possible?"

"Can you describe the other vehicle?"

"It was an old pickup truck," Martin said. "If you knew to call me, what about them?"

"Looks like we're having some trouble with the tracking system in that area. Could be that's why the proximity controls failed. Is your car . . . never mind, I see that you're still operating the vehicle. I'd like to remind you that filing an insurance claim is mandatory in this situation."

"Of course I'll file a claim," Martin said. "But I've got my wife and kids in the car. I'm a hell of a lot more concerned with how this happened in a smart lane."

"We're checking into that, sir," the voice said. "We'll be in contact if we locate the other vehicle so you can redirect your claim." The call ended.

After a silence that extended until they decelerated off the Foothill and onto Pasadena's surface streets, Kelly spoke up from the backseat. "Dad, how did a car hit us in the smart lane? I thought that couldn't happen."

"I don't know, Kel," Martin said. "There was a glitch somewhere." He was waiting for her to ask about the man in the bed of the truck, or for Allison to put two and two together and relate it to Priceless Life somehow, but neither of those things happened . . . or at least Allison didn't say anything about it. They got home without further incident, and Teresa disappeared to work without picking up the conversation. An hour later, he got a text-only ping from her: *I expect you to report this to the police. And I expect you to take measures to insulate the girls from the effects of your work. And I expect you to make sure that in the future our family time will be untainted by public reaction to buyouts. You owe us that much.*

Martin was simultaneously furious and guilt-stricken. She wasn't wrong, but it wasn't enough to be right. She was setting him apart from the rest of the family, as if the consequences of his work were different from the consequences of hers. She was never there. She was the one always asking him to be sure he got to soccer games and teacher conferences. And now she was dictating the response to work–family issues that came from his job, too? No, Martin thought. He didn't answer the ping because she'd trapped him again by being right in such a way that it left him no room to be right, too. What he wanted to say was *Look how great this is! Don't you see all the good coming from it? Haven't you been paying attention?* He wanted, almost, to turn into Scott Krakauer for a minute, and do the whole litany of school lunches and Little League fields and elder-care funding. *It's working!* he wanted to scream. *And all we have to do is see it through . . .*

My favorite Carl Marks movie? I'm glad you asked. It's Koba! That's the shit—a musical biopic of the Man of Steel himself, Josef Vissarionovich Dzugashvili, with Party officials in blackface to a beat of Isaac Hayes. As an aside, if that was my name, no fucking thing in the world would get me to change it. Robert Goulet's avatar as Koba himself is a masterstroke, and I'll fight anyone who says otherwise. Thing about Marks is that when he's on his game (and we will forgive him his trespasses, among which I would number British Library and Great Leap Forward), he makes you want to be a communist. Not because you give a shit about labor or because you even know what dialectical materialism is, but because it's cool, man. And there's one of his great contradictions. If fascism is partly the pure aestheticization of power, Carl Marks turns communism into an aesthetic proposition with his films, which is more or less a fascist act. He wants you to think, or so he says, and I don't think he's lying. But he wants the gosh-wow give-me-some-of-that reaction in the gonads, and that's where the real power of the movies comes from. Hot hot hot. Now that he's going to jail, if the wheels of justice grind to that conclusion, we have lost our greatest appropriator of the images of dead movie stars. I hope I sounded appropriately somber there.

SIX

MARTIN MADE A POINT of taking some individual time with both of the girls over the next couple of days, to sound them out, allay their fears, explain the situation as much as he thought was proper. The way he explained it to Charlie, it was a good opportunity to get the girls thinking about how sometimes people have to make difficult choices, and about how sometimes things that appear bad on the surface are actually good if you can take a different perspective. "You know that sounds like bullshit, right?" was Charlie's initial response.

"It might," said Martin. "But it also happens to be true. I don't think I quite believed in this at first, but now that I've been doing it . . . you've seen some of the stuff that the DBs are financing. How can you say that's a bad thing?"

"You put it that way, I can't." Charlie considered how best to approach the real problem here, which was that Martin needed to convince himself of something. Whether buyouts were good or bad was an open question, as far as Charlie was concerned. He was much more worried about the way that Martin was grasping at justifications. "But," he said, "that's probably not the only way to put it."

Martin looked around at the Yankee Doodle's crowd as if he was wondering how he'd ended up there. Sol Briggs had just cracked up a group of off-duty cops, including Jason. Briggs' partner, Meg Twohy, was nowhere to be found. She didn't need places like Yankee Doodle's. The older cops, the male cops, who had given up on being understood and fitting in with anyone but one another—they needed Yankee Doodle's. And Sol Briggs, from what Martin understood, also had a couple of off-the-books business ventures that involved Yankee Doodle's clientele.

"Jesus, Charlie," he said after a while. "Yeah, you can chop the argument some different ways. But how come every time someone does that, the point is to tell me I don't know what I'm talking about?"

"Okay, never mind," said Charlie. He got up, came back with beers, and changed the subject. "You want to know what the one time was I ever had a professional interaction with Sol Briggs?"

"Smooth," Martin said.

"Yes or no?"

"Okay, sure."

"He warned me off a case I was working on because the guy I was bird-dogging was one of his brokers. You know Sol moves stuff that disappears from evidence lockers, right?"

"No shit," Martin said. "I did not know that."

"Fact, amigo. That guy is not only lazy and a bad cop, he's dirty as hell. I don't know what keeps Meg Twohy partnered with him."

"People," Martin said. "Who knows why they do what they do? I don't even know why I do what I do sometimes."

Truer words, Charlie thought. "I called Sol on this," he said, "and you know what he told me? He said I wouldn't understand if I wasn't a cop."

"I heard that line from my dad, too," Martin said. "I keep waiting for Jason to say it, and that's when I'll know."

"Know what?"

"I don't know, man. Some things you never figure a particular person will say, and you figure that if they do, you'll know something about them. That's one of those things with Jason. I can't explain it. The only professional interaction I ever had with Sol Briggs," Martin went on, "was when I interviewed him about the Bragdon deal. He was the arresting officer."

"What did he say?"

"That Bragdon was a shitbag who deserved whatever he got. He's not a very verbal guy."

Bragdon, Charlie thought. That was the first inkling he'd really had of how powerful the idea of buyouts was, and how powerful Martin's shtick could be. It was six or seven months back, and Charlie had gotten to the courthouse late after the subway got hung up because of either a murder or suicide, no one was sure which. He ended up standing around in the back of the room until Martin tiptoed in just as the jury reported that they had a verdict. Track-mounted cameras whirred along the ceiling and walls to get three-dimensional holocaptures. Martin looked around, getting a sense of where everything stood. Often the atmosphere in the courtroom foreshadows the verdict, and this looked like one of those times. The assistant DA trying the case, whom both Martin and Charlie had met at a party once but whose name Charlie couldn't remember, was conferring quietly with someone on her team. The public defender looked defeated, elbows on his knees and shoulders rounded as he looked over some notes—probably on the next case he was due to take, since this one was going to be over in a few minutes. Christopher Bragdon himself was a big, sloppy mess of a man, maybe three hundred pounds on a frame built for two hundred. Jailhouse tattoos encircled his wrists and forearms where they stuck out from the sleeves of his orange coverall, and another tattoo of what looked like some kind of tentacle was partly visible emerging from his hairline on the left side of his forehead. Martin murmured into Charlie's ear. "Prototype hard case," he said. "Once I get the women on my side, he'll crack like an egg."

This was all part of Martin's method, Charlie learned as he watched Martin work. The thought of sitting and waiting for the messy, chaotic process of trial by jury to work itself out filled Martin with anxiety. So, as a buyout agent, he strolled in just before the curtain came down.

He picked out Bragdon's family members right away, in a cluster two rows behind the defense bench. The mother was there, maybe sixty-five years old, with something in her demeanor that led Martin to whisper, "Retired nurse." He pulled her name out of his pod: Charlene Bogosian. She sat between two younger women, neither of whom bore any family resemblance. Martin's sotto voce play-by-play continued: He guessed that Bragdon's sisters, if he had any, wouldn't have come to the hearing— especially since it clearly wasn't his first. Although, if the mood in the courtroom was any indication, it was likely to be his last. So that made them girlfriends, possibly mothers of some of Bragdon's children. Martin looked a little more closely at them. The first, on the mother's left, he pegged as a service drone: waitress, housecleaner, something like that. The other wore more expensive clothes and was the only one of the three in dressy shoes. Cubicle bot on the rise, Martin thought. The service drone would be the one to work on if there was resistance in the family; she would need the money more.

Charlie had noticed that no members of the jury had looked at the defendant since he'd come into the room. Too bad for you, Mr. Bragdon, Charlie thought. If they don't look at you, you're already gone. Martin slipped three business cards from his card wallet into his coat pocket.

The murmur in the courtroom subsided as the jury got themselves settled and the judge tapped his gavel.

Have you reached a verdict? Yes, we have.

What say you? Guilty of murder in the second degree.

Which together with the rape meant LWOP, unless something during the trial had persuaded the judge that Bragdon was a candidate for rehabilitation. Martin had his doubts about this; it was his business to know judges, and Jerome Hsieh was as tough as they came when sentencing time rolled around. As reaction swept through the courtroom—tears and angry shouts from Bragdon's girlfriends, grim nods and quieter tears from across the aisle, handshakes among the attorneys—Martin made his way down toward the front of the room, keeping an eye on the potential client. Bragdon didn't move for a long moment; then his head slowly fell forward until his chin was resting on his chest. Behind the exhalation of the crowd, the whirring of the holocameras on their tracks kept up a counterpoint.

Hsieh thanked the jury, and they sat in their box waiting for the room to clear so they could pick up their vouchers and go home. The last few feet of the aisle filled up with observers of various stripes—law students, court vultures, print reporters—and Martin's pace slowed as he eased through the oncoming tide. One of the first people to pass him was Bragdon's attorney, who had been up and out of his chair before the bailiff had even put the cuffs back on his erstwhile client; shortly after came the assistant DA, who nodded and said, "How are you, Martin?" on her way by. Martin nodded back, but his eyes were on the three women. "Mother first" had been his last words to Charlie, and now Charlie watched him perform.

He stopped in the aisle at the end of the second row. "Mrs. Bogosian?"

Charlene Bogosian looked up at him. The sadness in her eyes carried with it no shock. It was a longtime companion, familiar in all its dimensions. She was not one of those lucky people who never get to know sorrow except all at once.

"Mrs. Bogosian, my name is Martin Kindred. I won't take up much of your time, but I would like to make you aware of certain opportunities your son will have after sentencing." He handed her one of the cards, which at the touch of a hand other than Martin's began showing an animated Nautilus insignia: an abstract line drawing of a nautilus shell. Across this design, Martin's name and contact information unspooled.

The two younger women reached out, and he handed them cards as well.

"My sympathies for your situation," Martin said. "Please contact me if you think I might be of service."

"What is it exactly that you do?" Bogosian asked. "What kind of opportunity?"

"I work in the area of life-term buyouts," Martin said.

"Of . . ." It took her a moment to process what Martin had just said. Once she had, the weary sadness in her eyes flashed into an angry glare. She looked away from him, to her son disappearing through the door that led down to the van that would take him back to LA County Jail to await sentencing.

"If you'll excuse me," Martin said.

What happened next made Charlie think Martin was a natural: All three of them pinned Martin with looks of pure savage hate. But not one of them handed back her card.

SO MARTIN COULD be one persuasive son of a bitch, Charlie knew that for a fact. Even if it was a stained kind of brilliance. "What did the girls say, anyway?" he said, abruptly remembering where the whole conversation had started.

"I think Kelly has a better grip on it than Allison, actually," Martin said. He paused, as if making sure of his own opinion. "She went right along with everything I said. Her only problem was whether the prisoners really wanted to do it."

"Tough one," Charlie said.

"Not as tough as I would have thought. Hannah did me a favor there, by accident, I think. Back when I was first talking about this with the family, she compared the whole thing to assisted suicide, and I tried that out on Kelly. I think it worked okay."

"Huh," Charlie said.

Martin smiled. "Yeah, I didn't figure it would work on you. But there are parallels. Allison, she had a whole different take on it, but she's feeling more pressure at school than Kelly is. There's a Priceless Life club there."

"In the seventh grade?"

"In the seventh grade. So for Allison, there's a whole social component to her reaction." Martin shook his head. "It's tough for her. I try to make it easier, but she's hitting adolescence, so nothing can be easy."

Uh-huh, Charlie thought. You might be letting yourself off the hook there.

"The bigger problem is T," Martin said. "She won't listen to me, and . . . man, I'm starting to think that the buyout thing is going to be the straw that broke the camel's back."

Charlie wasn't sure what to say about this. Strange to think that a guy as persuasive as Martin was on the job could also fail to communicate the way Martin did at home. How many people are we? Charlie wondered. Immediately he scorned himself for having the thought, but he was remembering a feed he'd watched a couple of years ago, in which one of the heads had argued that the supersaturation of media and virtual realities had essentially created new personalities in the heads of everyone who lived in such an environment. Sometimes he wondered.

The next day he did something that, had someone else done it for him, he would have found nearly unforgivable. He talked to Teresa himself.

WHAT TERESA HAD never been able to figure out about the friendship between Martin and Charlie was how exactly it had begun. One day, as she remembered it, Martin had been sitting out on the porch complaining that he couldn't relate to any of his co-workers, and all his college friends had moved away. The next, Charlie had appeared, twenty years older than Martin and with a Chicago-style abrasiveness that set him apart from not just the entirety of Martin and Teresa's social circle but most of Southern California as well. Teresa didn't dislike him, really, but she didn't think that he fit, with his vulgar stories of stakeouts at by-the-hour motels and his physique that bordered on the slovenly and his comically bitter monologues about the string of ex-wives he'd left back in the vastness of the Central Time Zone. Teresa was happy that Martin was happy, but she was always a bit on edge when Charlie mingled with her engineering colleagues or the few co-workers Martin could stand to invite to a party without damning himself for insincerity. Charlie was a rock, a nigh-stereotypical midwestern blend of gruff candor and fearlessly devoted reliability. If you called Charlie when your car broke down in the desert, he would not only get there but drive past a burning building on the way. For him the world was divided into his friends and the other nine billion people who existed outside the firelight of Charlie Rhodes' friendship. One false note would have rendered the entire personality of Charlie Rhodes not only distasteful but downright nauseating—but there were no false notes. He was purely as advertised.

So suddenly Martin had a close friend, and as she looked back on it now, Teresa realized she'd been fighting a knee-jerk impulse to blame Charlie for the last ten years. She also recognized that this was a self-serving and ultimately nonsensical evasion, clumsily designed to absolve her of the share of blame she bore for the decline of her marriage. It wasn't even a good rationalization, since divorce culpability wasn't a zero-sum game. There was always enough to go around.

Further complicating her efforts to blame Charlie was the fact that she liked him, had in the years of his friendship with Martin developed her own friendship with him, and was now reluctantly facing the truth that even though neither she nor Martin would ever ask him to choose, all three of them knew that when everything was over, her friendship with Charlie would be a casualty of the divorce.

Now here he was on her desk screen telling her that he was worried about Martin. "And I might as well tell you that it's not because of you," he said. "You guys are going to do things however you're going to do them. But Martin's doing this other thing that I recognize because I did it. Your marriage comes apart and you start grabbing at straws, anything you can find to make you feel like you still know what you're doing in at least one part of your life. He's starting to do that at work, and since it's in the best interest of the girls that their father stay employed and reasonably sane—can we agree on that?"

"Don't be an asshole, Charlie," she said.

"Boy, if I had a nickel," he said. "Anyway, you get what I'm saying. Keep an eye on him. Let me know if anything seems out of whack to you."

"A whole lot seems out of whack right now."

"Yeah," Charlie said. "I guess it does. But listen, you guys still rely on each other for more than either one of you know or would admit. So if he's having a problem, you'll hear about it." He paused and cut his eyes away from the screen on his side. "It's gonna be a long time before the two of you stop needing each other. That's why this is so hard. Don't make it harder by pretending it's not happening."

"Asshole," she said. "Thank you. Now please go away."

"Nope. I got one more, and you have to listen to it because I'm gonna be sixty pretty soon." By which he meant he feared the slide into invisibility that was the inevitable lot of the old, and which happened much sooner in LA than anywhere else. Teresa and Charlie had talked about this before, and she knew he didn't discuss it with Martin. Now she resented his use of their previous confidence as leverage.

Still, it would be easier to let him say his peace than try to dissuade him—or let him know how she felt about the Charlie Rhodes School of Interpersonal Relationships. "Okay," she said. "One more."

"Before my first divorce, I got so hurt, I felt so misunderstood and rejected and taken for granted that I just stopped coming into the bedroom where my wife was. We had a sunporch on the back of the house, and I slept on it for months while we got our nerve up to do what she'd been wanting to do for a couple of years. And every night I slept out there—this is the important part—every time I slept out there, I hoped that would be the night she asked me to come back in. It wasn't about sex, or even winning. I just would have done anything if she'd asked me to come back in with her." Charlie picked at something invisible that had found its way into the corner of his eye. "But she never did."

"Okay, Charlie," Teresa said.

"Don't ever do that," he said. "Don't ever be the one who won't ask even though you want to."

And then her screen went blank, and Teresa wanted to call Martin as badly as she could ever remember wanting anything. She ran through her inbox, routed correspondence to where it needed to go, tinkered with the design of a solar array destined for the top of an airport terminal, looked at the time. She would need to work late again tonight.

LATER SHE WAS HOME. Martin slept on the couch, the TV showing a barely audible recap of the Dodgers game. She checked on the girls, knowing that Martin would have made sure they got where they needed to go. He was a good father. That was one of the things she was going to miss about him. Back in the living room, she stood watching him sleep and wishing that she'd had an affair so he would have an excuse to repudiate her. It would all be so much easier if he would tell her he couldn't stand to look at her, that she disgusted him, that she'd used their marriage vows as toilet paper and sullied the first blossom of love and belief that had brought them together. Strange, strange, to be wishing for something like that. Why couldn't she wish for everything to be repaired? Or better yet, restored?

Because, Teresa Kindred knew, she was exactly the kind of person who could not wish for something that she knew could not happen. Which meant, in the end, that she could not wish at all.

She watched her husband, and imagined what it would be like, this moment when she took another lover. Another man who would touch her with hands rough or tender—whom she would learn to know from his touch. Another man who would lower himself over her, rock his hips behind her, differently than Martin. His cock would feel different in her. He would shudder differently when he came, and the noises he made would sound different as he buried his face in the hollow of her throat. She watched Martin and she did not want any of this, but she knew it would happen. There would come a moment when she would walk in her front door and find another man on the couch. He would not know about her routines, her systems. She would have to teach him, and to learn his. How would he like his eggs? She did not want to be alone.

It was quiet, so quiet. At work it was never this quiet. Teresa could have been a ghost, with her sleeping husband on the couch and her sleeping daughters upstairs. How could she feel so distant from this when it had been her life for thirteen years? Charlie Rhodes saw right to the heart of it. He always did. In a realization both exhilarating and humbling, Teresa realized that this insight of his was why she had always been uneasy around him. She didn't like to be understood so completely. But Martin understood her, and she loved him for that. Charlie was also right that he'd been acting strangely, and she could only assume that he was right about why. Martin, she thought. What have you gotten yourself into?

What have you gotten *us* into?

Charlie was right, she thought. It never pays to be the one who will not ask. And I do need this. But I won't have it much longer.

Comes news that there's been a shootout in the middle of a flash mob down in Venice. Remember when you didn't have to be in a flash mob to shoot somebody in Venice? Oops. Marketing says I shouldn't date myself. Did you just outclick? You did not! You will not! Because this is Walt Dangerfield, and I remember when you could shoot somebody in Venice anydamntime you wanted to. I remember when it was possible to do something in LA and not have anyone know about it. I remember when the sky was full of 747s circling LAX and traffic choppers circling the Orange Crush, instead of drones circling the perfect vantage point to catch you planning to shoot somebody from the middle of your flash mob. I remember the first time I heard the phrase flash mob, and it was a bunch of fag-Mod English kids giggling till they wet their pants because they could send text messages over a cell phone and arrange to meet in a place all at once without anyone knowing. Incredible! Now, I got nothing against a good old-fashioned mob. You get wired up enough about something that you want to get out your pitchforks and torches, I say go forth and do it. That Frankenstein monster has to get burned, sometimes there's no two ways about it. Burn, baby, burn. Aaaahhhhhh, I'm a palimpsest! But flash mobs? How long before that particular fad is over? I'm hoping it's a generational thing. On in the 2000s, out by the 2010s; back in the 2030s, which would mean that any year now the whole thing will go out of fashion again and people in Venice will be able to fire at will. Man, I pray to God.

SEVEN

MORE OFTEN than Martin would have thought, people pinged him trying to get buyouts set up. Sometimes these were family members of a prisoner, sometimes prisoners themselves, sometimes lawyers. On most of these occasions, Martin did not pursue the deal; already, after just a year of doing this, he'd figured out that people who went looking for a buyout usually had ulterior motives that meant the deal wouldn't go through anyway. Still, he answered every ping that came in, because every once in a while he was solicited in such a way that he could proceed. He was on the way from Nautilus–LA County back to the office on a Wednesday in May, windows down to enjoy the unseasonably cool weather, when the windshield announced that he was getting a ping from Moon and Teller. A talent agency? Martin was enough of an Angeleno to know who Moon and Teller were, and also to have a brief tingle at the possibility that they were calling him because . . . what? Because they wanted to pitch him some kind of project? What would it be?

This was a running joke among Nautilus personnel: that pretty soon someone was going to make a movie about Martin. It was also a more darkly inflected topic of conversation between him and Teresa, who was afraid that Martin's minor celebrity would turn his head and lead him to do things he would later regret—not to mention things that might ruin whatever normalcy they still had.

And now maybe he—they—would find out.

Martin answered the ping, and the face of Daniel Moon appeared on the windshield. He was pushing seventy, with a careful beard, vanity eyeglasses, and an expensively restored head of salt-and-pepper hair. "Mr. Kindred," he said. "Dan Moon here."

"What can I do for you, Mr. Moon?"

"Well, I thought we might have a little chat between two professionals, seeing as both of us are in the business of making deals," Moon said. "Although it's rare that our clientele overlaps." He chuckled and then added, "Rare, but not impossible. The client in question is Carl Marks. I can assume you have some familiarity with his works, yes?"

Martin had a brief moment of speechless bafflement as he realized why Daniel Moon was calling him. If he hadn't been in the smart lane he would have totaled the car. Recovering, he said, "Ah, yes. I certainly know who he is." Actually Martin was much more familiar with the persona of Carl Marks than with Marks' films. He'd seen *Ernesto in Kinshasa*, but that was the only one. Well, and *Koba!*, even though he hated musicals. What he knew of Carl Marks was the goateed, beret-wearing face on the feeds, endlessly and vigorously pontificating about film, art, culture, capitalism, and anything else anyone asked him about. And more recently, the Carl Marks who was thrown out of his own trial because he wouldn't shut up, and was only present at his own sentencing because he wanted to make sure it was recorded for a posthumous documentary on his life and work. Martin had always written him off as a poseur who had successfully leveraged coverage of his persona to create a lucrative movie career.

"Well," said Moon. "I've represented Carl since *Anastasia's Bones*, and it looks like he'd like me to set him up one last time. If you know what I mean."

"Just so we both know we're talking about the same thing," Martin said, "are you telling me that Carl Marks wants to do a life-term buyout?"

"That's about the size of it. When can you come into the office?"

"The protocol in this situation is for me to consult directly with the client," Martin said.

"Oh, Carl's here," Moon said. He looked offscreen. "Carl, come here for a minute, will you?"

The director's familiar face crowded into the frame. "Martin Kindred, hi, it's Carl," he said.

"Mr. Marks," Martin said. "I have to ask before we go any farther. Are you undertaking this consultation of your own free will?"

Marks looked at his agent, who shrugged. "Just like you said, Dan," Marks said. Looking back at Martin, he said, "Insofar as anyone in a capitalist society has free will, yes. I am doing this."

Martin's calendar was empty for the rest of the day, or could be emptied for an initial consult. "Where's your office?" he asked.

"Directions are on your pod," Moon said. "Shall we say an hour?"

MOON AND TELLER, unlike the offices of larger agencies, went neither for flash nor for understatement so aggressive that you had to assume enormous expense. The office space, on Olympic not far from Twentieth Century Fox, wasn't all that different from what Jocelyn and Scott had done with the ninth floor of Nautilus. Daniel Moon came out into the lobby to meet Martin and conduct him into a conference room, where Carl Marks was scribbling with a pen on paper. Martin couldn't see whether he was actually writing, or just doodling. He didn't look up when Moon said, "Okay, Carl, everybody's here."

Martin sat in one of several empty chairs, about halfway down the table from the end where Marks sat. Floor-to-ceiling windows extended the length of one wall, looking out onto Olympic. The other three walls were covered with posters for Marks' movies. Martin began to feel a little unreal. "Mr. Marks," he said. "I'm a little unclear about how we can be talking about a buyout given your situation." On the way over, he'd caught up on the celebrity crime feeds. Marks was currently free pending an appeal of his conviction.

"I'm dropping the appeal tomorrow," Marks said, still without looking up.

"Against, I have to say, my advice," said Dan Moon.

"Then we should talk after that has happened," Martin said.

Marks looked up and put his pen down. "Martin. I'm going to do this. We can go through all of the hoops then, or we can get some of them out of the way now. I want to do this, I'm going to do this, and I want it to happen quickly. Ping whoever it is that does your backgrounding, put him to work on me." He produced a pod and tapped it a couple of times. "You've got access to everything now."

"Once Carl drops the appeal, sentencing will be a formality. We'll move it up as much as we can. Although I'm against this, and I have to tell you, Martin, I'm against buyouts on principle." Moon sighed and took his glasses off. "I'm trying to keep my personal feelings out of this. I have it on good authority that sentencing will be wrapped up by the end of the week, and everything else should be straightforward after that. Am I right?"

By the end of the week? Martin thought. He's going to drop the appeal on Thursday morning, and be sentenced by Friday afternoon? That's clout.

"Assuming it's all going to happen that way, I guess it won't hurt anything to get a couple of details out of the way early," Martin said.

It rubbed him the wrong way to say that, but clearly people like Daniel Moon and Carl Marks operated in a different sphere. If he was going to do business with them, he probably had to make allowances for that. He piped a quick message to Charlie with Marks' pod access information and a short text addendum: *Next client. Need to move fast.*

"So what do you need?" Marks asked.

"I don't feel comfortable actually signing anything before your sentencing," Martin said. "I'm more than happy to consult with you on how things might proceed, but the charter is very strict about when certain things can happen."

Marks nodded and started tapping his pen on the table. "So how does it work? I go behind bars, I ping you, you make sure I'm not being strong-armed, we sign some forms, and off I go. Something like that?"

"In broad strokes, yes," Martin said.

"So we can meet on Monday?"

"We can provisionally schedule a meeting for Monday, assuming your sentencing proceeds as you're planning."

Daniel Moon laughed. "In my business, all meetings are provisional, Martin," he said. "But yes, let's do it that way. Everything aboveboard."

"You're interesting," Marks said.

Martin wasn't sure what to make of this. "Excuse me?"

"You're not a cruel man, or a heartless man," Marks said. "But you make your living from the transformation of human life into capital. It's alchemy, amazing stuff. Adam Smith must be wishing he could be reincarnated."

"I'm not sure I follow you," Martin said. He avoided, or curtailed when he couldn't avoid, personal conversations with clients. Or potential clients. And he didn't feel like he needed to be lectured by a movie director.

"I'm not sure you do, either," Marks said. "You're the perfect instrument of the capitalist apotheosis. If I hadn't killed my wife, I'd make a movie about you. As things stand, that lapse in judgment means that I'm going to have to make part of a movie about me, and leave someone else to finish it."

Martin stood. His pod vibrated. Glancing at it, he saw a text from Charlie: *What the fuck?*

Good question, he thought.

"Mr. Moon, I'm afraid that from here on out, I'm going to have to deal with Mr. Marks directly," he said. "I appreciate the work you've done putting us together."

Moon spread his hands. "That's what I do. I put people together."

"You're an incredible bullshitter, Dan," Marks said. "You're one thing I'm going to miss about being alive."

CHARLIE PINGED HIM continuously until Martin finally answered him when he'd gotten back in the car. "Carl Marks?" Charlie said. "The director, commie guy?"

"That's the one. I guess he killed his girlfriend."

"Or a hooker, depending on who you ask. This is the first you're finding out about it?"

Martin headed back up Olympic, aiming for the office. "Hang on a sec," he said to Charlie, and sent a meeting request to Jocelyn and Scott. Back with Charlie, he said, "Yeah. I'm not a Marxist and I don't follow celebrity gossip. How was I supposed to know?"

"I'm amazed you could avoid it, amigo," Charlie said. "I mean, I try to hide from that shit, and I can't do it."

"Oh shit," Martin said.

"What?"

"Fuck, I just asked for a meeting with Jocelyn and Scott, and I wasn't supposed to be talking to Marks until he's sentenced. Now they're going to want to know what I wanted."

Charlie was quiet for a while. "Amigo," he said eventually, "be careful. That's not like you."

"I have to go, Charlie. Talk to you over the weekend." Martin ended the call and took a deep breath. Charlie's implication was clear, and he was right. Talking to Marks was against the rules. Martin knew better. More importantly, it wasn't something Martin would have done a year ago.

He fired off another message to the Krakauers, saying that plans had changed, and could they meet on Monday instead? Then he realized he'd just implied that he wasn't going to be around on Thursday and Friday. "Jesus Christ," he said to nobody. "What are you doing?"

It was four thirty, he was stuck in traffic on Olympic Boulevard, and all of a sudden Martin didn't have any clear idea of where he was going. Okay, he said. That was a mistake. And you compounded it, or almost. Probably Jocelyn and Scott won't care about whether we have a meeting tomorrow or Monday. But it was careless, and Martin couldn't afford to be careless. Especially not if he was going to be doing deals with people like Carl Marks.

He pinged his father, just to have something to do, and out of nowhere they decided to get out into the woods for the day on Saturday. Jason and Hannah would come. They'd have a picnic, hike around, maybe go somewhere that had water so the kids could swim. "You sound like you're losing your mind," Vance said.

"I do?" Martin said. "Where did that come from?"

"You're all over the place. You want to do this, you want to do that. Come on, Martin. I know you, and I know you don't call just to shoot the shit. What's on your mind?"

"Nothing," Martin said. "I'm turning over a new leaf. It involves calling just to shoot the shit. Where should we go on Saturday?"

They settled on Colby Canyon, in the San Gabriel foothills, and a good time was had by all, although Martin was more than a little distracted. He was sitting on the Marks thing, and true to their word, Marks and Moon had dropped the appeal and finagled an accelerated sentencing hearing. As of Monday morning, Carl Marks would report to Nautilus-Yucaipa to begin serving a life sentence without parole. It was becoming clearer and clearer to Martin that the ping from Daniel Moon had started one of those conversations after which nothing is ever the same. Buyouts were already controversial, but after a year the controversy was starting to die down; the Krakauers' campaign to focus attention on the good works done by disbursement money was working. Public opinion, though still divided, was starting to lean in favor of buyouts. Priceless Life had grown a little in the first few months, but— again, just as Scott had predicted—it wasn't a loud or influential voice.

Now the Carl Marks deal was going to put buyouts in a brand-new spotlight. A much brighter spotlight, with many more people watching. Briefly Martin considered turning the deal down, but he'd taken a look through Marks' files on Friday morning, and there was nothing there to indicate that finalizing the deal would be a problem. The only thing that set Carl Marks apart from Karl Alexander or Jackson Ordonez or Christopher Bragdon was celebrity. But celebrity was its own justification, as far as the feeds were concerned.

He tried not to think about it. There they were, splashing around in one of the many excellent swimming holes on the creek on a perfect late-spring day. Martin loved places like this, the hidden natural jewels of Southern California. The first few times he'd come here, graffiti and trash had taken the shine off the experience, but over the years either people had gotten less interested in tagging and littering, or the Angeles National Forest staff had gotten more interested in keeping it clean. He took a swim, let himself get pelted by the edges of the waterfall, then headed out for a hike with the girls. They worked their way along the creek until they got back to the road. Martin pointed out Strawberry Mountain and some of the other features. On the way back down, they passed the ropes from the top of the big falls down to the pool. The girls wanted to rappel down. "Since when do you know how to rappel?" Martin asked them, and they didn't, but they'd seen people do it and were sure they could, too. You had to love the confidence. Martin talked them out of it by pointing out that then they'd have to climb back up, and also that it was lunchtime. Both of them were starving and, having been reminded of their hunger, immediately got crabby. By the time they got back to the swimming hole, Martin was starving, too; they sat and ate, everyone together. The Kindred men bemoaned the fact that they'd forgotten their fishing rods; there was fine trout fishing in some of the pools that didn't have kids stomping around in them.

"God," Martin said. "I don't think I've been fishing in ten years."

Jason was nodding. "Me neither. We should go."

"Could get a charter, do some saltwater fishing," Vance said.

"Yeah, or throw a tent in the car and come up here for a couple of days," Martin said.

Vance shook his head. "Tent days are over for me."

"Not me," Jason said. "You think we can talk the girls into taking the kids for a couple of days?"

"Maybe you can. You're more persuasive than I am." Martin was bemused by the way Jason referred to Hannah and Teresa as "the girls." He wondered when was the last time someone had called Teresa a girl to her face. Also he wondered where his fishing rod was. Somewhere in the basement. The line was old enough that any halfway ambitious trout would snap it right off; he'd have to do a little restoration work before any fish were in danger of being caught.

Jason was shaking his head. "Man. Why did it take us so long to think of this?"

"Well, how often do the three of us get together?" Martin said. He lived in Pasadena, Jason was out in Silver Lake, Casa Kindred in between. They had lives, and it was easy to fool yourself into thinking that video conversation was just like being together.

"Okay," Jason said. "Let's go fishing. I'm off on Monday."

"I'm off every day," their father said.

Martin started to say that he'd take the day off Monday and go, but then he remembered the Marks deal. It had been nice to forget about it for a while. "Monday's tough for me," he said. "You off every Monday, Jay?"

"Right now, yeah," Jason said. "So maybe next week?"

"That I can do," Martin said. "Dad?"

"Days are all the same to me," Vance said. "I threw out all my calendars when I retired."

"Okay then," Martin said. "Next Monday."

HE SPENT SUNDAY morning working in the yard, and Sunday afternoon at soccer games. Kelly's team won 4–0, but Kelly was steamed because she hadn't scored. Allison's team held a 1–0 lead for most of the game before blowing it and losing 2–1, and although Allison had scored the goal, she was steamed at the loss. Martin said what he always said. "It's only sports, you know? You play hard, you try to win, but whatever happens, the sun's going to come up tomorrow."

"That's not the point, Dad," Allison said. She wouldn't say what the point was.

When they got home the girls disappeared to friends' houses, and Martin got to work on the house again. The house network had been acting hinky, and he needed to run some diagnostics and figure out if the problem was something he could fix. Lights weren't always coming on when someone entered a room, the clocks were out of sync with one another . . . he had a sneaking suspicion that the house daemon was just wearing out. The buyout windfall would come in handy if they had to do a house upgrade; much of the system had been on the verge of being outdated when they bought the house six years before, and now the whole thing was a dinosaur. "What do you think, T?" he said. "Upgrade the house?"

She was in the living room flipping back and forth between some kind of technical reference and a portable display. "Yeah, if we're going to sell the place, we're going to need to do something about that."

"Sell the place?"

She looked up at him, startled into being fully present. "You know," she said. "If we ever decide to."

"Oh," Martin said. "Right."

This June third, Allen Ginsberg would have been one hundred fifteen years old. In honor of him: City of baking asphalt, of madness blowing down from mountains named for martyrs, of thirteen million people strangling on the failure of their dreams, or the realization of their dreams, or the fatal realization that they were dreaming someone else's dreams all along, and now it's too late. City of fiber optic and chrome, where avatars of movie stars give you directions to hotels staffed by custom-coded daemons. City of the ghosts of orange groves, of vigilante flash mobs and outpatient skulljacks. Eighty percent Hispanic city, with fifty percent cops who can't speak Spanish. City of forgotten spaces. City of sawed-off shotguns under cash registers, dream factory at land's end, city of walking in celluloid footsteps. City of pitiless sunlight and exalted dawns. City of the long slog toward the permanent kinetic paradise of adoration and burgeoning traffic. God of thunder, you are absent here except below the surface of the earth, and we like you that way. We cherish, adore, and worship the fear that arrives with every temblor that isn't the Big One but might be when we first feel the ground jump and shimmy under our feet. Secretly we all want to crack off and fall into the sea.

EIGHT

WHEN MARTIN GOT UP Monday morning, he looked at the People and Happenings feed that the house service culled, feeling furtive and somehow ashamed. But there it was. Carl Marks was in jail. Before he'd even brewed coffee—the house system was having trouble timing that, too—he pinged Garret Lau out at Yucaipa and made an appointment to talk to Marks that morning. "He hasn't requested any visitors," Lau said.

"He contacted me last week, ah, after his sentencing," Martin said. "And asked me to come out today."

"Carl Marks wants a buyout?" Lau looked like this was the worst news he'd heard in years. Martin couldn't tell whether that was because he was a fan of Marks' movies, or because he knew what kind of feeding frenzy a Marks buyout would bring to his doorstep.

"I don't know," Martin said. "All I know is he wanted to talk to me. I wouldn't go putting out any press releases."

"Oh my God," Lau said. "You don't have to worry about that."

Somebody had told somebody, though, since by the time Martin arrived at Yucaipa, just before ten that morning, he had received more than a thousand messages and pings, and the car informed him that two drones had picked him up somewhere back around Ontario. "Goddammit," Martin said, and pinged Garret again. "Garret, what did I say about press releases?"

"I didn't tell anyone," Garret said.

"Well, neither did I, but the word sure is out," Martin said. He pulled up to the gate. On the left side of the access road, three vans were lined up, each with wireless arrays deployed and an expensively dressed feedhead lounging around at the back door. Until they saw him, when all three made a beeline for his open window. The gate started to open, and he drove away from their shouted questions onto the prison grounds. An avatar of one of the feedheads, Caitlin Frost, appeared on the windshield. "Hi, Martin," she said warmly. "I just know that you're going to have lots to talk about when you come out. Make sure you come to me first, okay?" She winked and disappeared.

Savvy, Miss Frost, thought Martin. Most feedheads didn't resort to podjacking, and many of those who might have didn't have access to the right kinds of wares to worm through the kind of security Martin had. He wondered if she had an ear to the ground inside Yucaipa.

That wouldn't account for the spread of the news, though. Hm. Martin abandoned that line of thought. He didn't even know what news had spread, exactly, or what shape it had taken as it spread. All he could do was talk to Carl Marks and see how things played out.

Martin hadn't kept close track of Marks' trial and didn't know his movies very well, but he'd lived his entire life in Los Angeles and understood that celebrities were like poisonous snakes. It was very important to handle them in a certain way. Maybe even more important with this particular snake at this particular time. He'd asked Charlie to run down various questions about the director's background and mental state. The short version: Carl Marks, 1994– (presumably) 2041, American-born director of digital films and pioneer in the use of digital avatars. Born Kenneth Weitzmann in Ann Arbor, Michigan. Graduated Huron High School, 2012, and University of Michigan, 2016, BFA in film and digital arts. The figure that emerged from the biographical information was a gifted artist whose art was ruined by his politics, in Martin's opinion. He himself wasn't particularly liberal or conservative. His politics were the politics of keeping the lights on and making sure the kids were safe and educated. Carl Marks was a throwback. He hadn't cast himself in his *Paris Commune* movie for nothing. He was looking for barricades so he could either storm them or take up positions to defend them. Didn't matter which.

And another thing that didn't matter was the lower-class commentariat's hunger for anything that would allow them to use the words *celebrity* and *scandal* in the same sentence. Martin wasn't sure how that was going to play out, but Charlie had warned him on his way out to Yucaipa this morning. "It's like the old soda fountain, you know?" he said. "You've been discovered, Martin. Now these fuckers, they're going to eat you alive."

GARRET MET HIM in the reception area and guided him through security. "Mr. Marks is already in the interview room," he said. Martin noted the honorific; he doubted Garret had ever called another prisoner Mister before, except during media availabilities. At the door, Garret added, "I'm really hoping that whatever happens, we can keep it under control." He looked around nervously, taking in all the security cams as if any one of them might be a covert feed.

"Me, too," Martin said. "I'll let you know how it goes."

He noted a transformation in Marks the minute he walked into the room. Gone was the distracted, disengaged nonentity Martin had met in Daniel Moon's offices. The Carl Marks sitting handcuffed in the Yucaipa interview room radiated the kind of self-assurance that came from a lucky combination of money, status, and ideological certitude. Martin took him in: the Bolshevik-style smartattoos, the tangle of beard and hair, the calm light in the eyes that you saw only in gurus or lunatics. There were more ironies here than Martin could untangle: the auteur who appropriated the valuable images of dead people, capitalizing on them to make propaganda films about the history and struggles of communism, and along the way make piles of money. Who could make sense of that? Whatever real human being had once occupied that body, he was long gone, replaced by a persona constructed for consumption. And so Martin got on with the final act through which he would be consumed.

"So you're here to sign off on the final intrusion of capital into the body of the laborer" was the first thing Marks said to him.

"Are you for real?" Martin sat down across the table. "I don't mean that to sound flippant; I'm serious."

"As real as any 'I' can be in a society of the spectacle such as this one."

Martin could already tell that this was going to be one of those conversations where he would need to run a little app known as Allusionist. It tracked, harvested, and sourced quotations and allusions in the course of a conversation. Terrific social lubricant if you were outside your normal areas of knowledge. He decided to skip it this time, though. Marks needed to feel superior, that much was already clear. So why not let him?

"I'm here, Mr. Marks—"

"Please. Carl."

"Okay, Carl," he said. "I'm here to jump through all of the regulatory hoops with you so we can proceed with your buyout."

Marks spread his hands expansively, all noblesse oblige. "At your service."

"You have pled guilty to the murder of Andrea Antonowicz, who went by the name of Andi Anton. Do you wish to contest that plea now?"

"No. Why would I? I did it."

"Do you have any appeals on file, or any plans to file an appeal based on the proceedings of your trial?"

"Nope."

"Have you been pressured in any way to consider taking a life-term buyout?"

"Nyet."

The rest of it was bookkeeping, making sure that Marks' disbursements were in order and that he fully understood finalization procedures. When they were through, Martin said, "Okay. I'm going to run all of this through the channels back at the office, and then we'll be ready to go. I'll have to come back here one more time to get you to sign off on the last set of documents and permissions."

"You know where to find me," Marks said.

HE LEFT NAUTILUS-YUCAIPA and walked into a storm. Drones whined overhead, flagrantly violating the prohibition on overflying the prison below one thousand feet. They were low enough to tell how long it had been since Martin had shaved. Outside the gates, San Bernardino County sheriff's deputies were keeping the road clear. Beginning about five hundred feet from the gate, Martin could see a double row of media vehicles stretching off to the first bend in the road. Inside the gate, Scott and Jocelyn Krakauer were waiting next to Martin's car. As he approached, both broke out their best smiles.

Leaning in close as Martin got within arm's reach, Scott said, "Let's chat in the car." He cut his eyes up at the drones. The car noticed Martin and unlocked its doors. He started it and turned on a music stream, which turned out to be a Calranian pop group singing in an impassioned Farsi-English-Spanish creole.

"One of Allison's favorites," Martin said, turning as far as he could so he could face the Krakauers, sitting in the backseat. They shared a grin that said, *Kids.*

"It's got a beat," Jocelyn said.

Scott reached out and punched Martin in the shoulder. "This is what you didn't want to meet about last week, isn't it?" he said. "Good call. You played it just right. You know this is going to be the one that takes us over the top."

"Which is why it needs to be perfect, and you need to be perfect," Jocelyn added. Their enthusiasm was rubbing off on Martin. He felt a little giddy. "This one's going to demand a lot of you, Martin. All the rest has been warm-ups. This is the big show."

"We just wanted to come out and give you a personal thumbs-up, right?" Scott said. Through his daze, Martin thought how odd it was, the way the Krakauers handed a single conversational role back and forth. "Now we're going to go run interference for you while you get this deal moving. Back to the office, ping Charlie if you haven't already, make this happen and pronto, right? Finish up whatever DBs you have to, but chop chop. Marks is the priority."

The rear doors slammed, and Martin watched the Krakauers walk out through the gate and in the direction of the assembled media. What did they think he'd done? Martin wondered. How had he played it exactly right? By talking to a potential client before sentencing and then keeping it to himself? Maybe. That was their world. I, Martin thought, have to be careful that it doesn't become mine. As instructed—although he would have done it anyway—he pinged Charlie. No answer. "Okay, it's on," Martin said. "Krakauers are doing somersaults, they're so happy, but they also want this to happen quick. Did you do anything on it this weekend? Sorry I didn't catch up with you. Was out with the family, and now the house system is squirrelly. Let's talk, unless I'm carried away by a swarm of feed drones."

He drove slowly past the police roadblock and between the rows of media. Off the right shoulder, just past the roadblock, Jocelyn and Scott were being available. Martin had a couple of DBs to finish up on his last finalized deal, one Jeromy Godbout. Routine stuff. He'd be back at Yucaipa tomorrow, if Charlie could race through the backgrounder. The fastest Martin had ever turned a deal around was four days. He had a feeling that he might be able to finalize Marks in two.

And then? Things would get complicated. If celebrity worked the way celebrity always worked, all of a sudden everybody and his brother would want a buyout. One of the miserable side effects of the charter program was that every so often, someone committed a murder intending to leverage it into a buyout. Martin wrestled with that, and in the end had to admit that it was simply a bad thing. Sure, people would kill one another for other reasons, but he'd heard of specific crimes committed for buyouts, and they gnawed at his conscience. Still, how many other lives were improved by the disbursement money? How many life-saving surgeries had been performed? How many kids had been vaccinated?

You take it on balance, Martin thought. He finished up the Godbout disbursements—except one at a clinic that was closed for some holiday so obscure, Martin didn't even know what religion it was for—sorted through the silt in his inbox, and pinged Charlie again.

"What?" Charlie said.

"What do you mean, what?" Martin said.

"I'm working on fucking Carl Marks, now leave me alone." Charlie glared at Martin from the windshield, and then added, "Amigo. We need to talk."

"Okay," Martin said, "let's talk. As long as it's not at Yankee Doodle's."

Sometimes I'm a little disappointed that more of you don't ask me who I really am. Not that I would tell you, but I want you to want to know more about Walt Dangerfield than that string of phonemes. And maybe you do, but don't ask because you figure I won't tell. Correct! The other thing is that I'm realer this way. You know how many eardrums vibrate to the sounds of my electronically reconstituted voice every day? Do you know? Lots. But you don't even know if that's true, because as far as you know you might be the only person in the world listening to me right now. What if you were? We'd be having a personal conversation right now. Intimate, even. Because even when I am talking to a million people, I'm talking only to you. And it hurts me that you don't want to know who I am, that you're so satisfied with the Walt Dangerfield who comes into your ears that you don't want to know about the Walt Dangerfield—not his real name—who eats cream of wheat and roots for the Lakers and walks every day to the deli around the corner because that's what he's done every day since way back in the fucking days when you used to go buy print newspapers. Outside. You prefer me not quite real, the way you pre-fer yourself mediated and wireless and not quite ever yourself. Do I con-tradict myself? Very well, I contrafuckingdict myself.

NINE

IT ENDED UP being at Flaco, a declining tapas restaurant adored by Charlie Rhodes because he felt himself declining and often wanted his surroundings to mirror that interior sense. New places made him feel old; old places grounded him; old places that were a little rough around the edges make him think the world might just be a bearable place after all. Thus empowered by his environment, he lit into Martin as soon as they'd ordered. "Amigo," he said, "you need to snap out of whatever fucking stupor you're in and notice a couple of things. One, buyouts aren't going to change the world. Two, even if they are, it's not necessarily for the good. Three, even if some buyouts are on the whole a good thing, which I'm not necessarily ready to admit, the Carl Marks deal stinks."

"It does?" Martin said. "What's wrong with it? He's guilty, he's got enough money that there's no way someone could be squeezing him, and there's nothing in the case that says he killed her just for the needle."

"Exactly my point," Charlie said. "Your average dirtbag doing life, he's got nothing. A buyout might appeal to him. But Marks, he could sit in prison and pontificate to his fans for the rest of his life. They'll probably even figure out some way to let him make movies. But no, he wants a buyout. Why? Because that's an even bigger platform for him. He's going to go out raving about capitalist running dogs or some antiquated shit like that, and then some film school asshole is going to make a movie about him, and he'll have what he wants, which is to be a hero of the revolution even though he's never done a goddamn thing except render images."

Their drinks arrived, and just as Charlie was about to wind himself up again so did the food. So instead of talking, he ate. "You know," Martin said, "sometimes I get the feeling that you see me not caring about something and mistake it for not noticing it."

Charlie kept eating. This was the part of the dance where Martin rationalized, and they might as well get it over with.

"You think I don't know that Carl Marks just wants to demagogue this?" Martin said. "Of course he does. But why should I care? The rules are the rules. He checks all the boxes that make it okay for him to take a buyout. That, and only that, is what I care about. Some of my clients hate their lives inside. Some of them want to help their families. Some of them really believe that they can atone for what they've done. It's not up to me to decide which of those reasons are better. Why does everything have to be better than everything else?"

"What the fuck does that mean?" Charlie said, even though his mouth was full.

"It means that some things just are. The buyout rules are the way they are. I work within them, exactly to the letter. Except I fucked up last week, as I'm sure you were about to point out. That was wrong. I won't do it again. But my reasons for not doing it are my reasons, and they don't matter as long as I do it, just like my clients' reasons for doing what they do don't matter as long as it's legal and ethical for them to do it. I'm not fucking stupid, Charlie. I'm well aware that the Krakauers use me to perform a function. You know what? That's called working for someone."

They ate in silence. Charlie was hungry, and also doing his level best to give Martin's perspective a fair shake. Try as he might, he couldn't figure out how Martin could stand his job. That's what it boiled down to. Part of it was Charlie's philosophical opposition to buyouts, and part of it was the particulars of how Martin was changing, invisibly to himself. Charlie had done some shady things in the past, pushed the boundaries of acceptable conduct, and he'd made his peace with those things. Probably he should let Martin do the same thing.

"Amigo," he said, "let's make peace. I get it."

"I see the downside, Charlie," Martin said. "I live with it. But you know what? I believe in what I'm doing. I also see the upside."

Charlie nodded, considering this. He wasn't ready to accept it entirely, but he could see where it was coming from. "Okay," he said. They had another drink, and then Charlie went home. On the train, he had a bad feeling that he couldn't shake. It had been there long enough that he'd nearly gotten used to it, this sense that an inscrutable doom hung over Martin, but something about the Carl Marks deal had made him more conscious of it again. Truth is, he told himself, you're a pessimist. It's not complicated.

Back in his home office castle on Kittyhawk Avenue—selected in large part for its proximity to Temoc's—Charlie ran through his back-grounder on Marks one more time. It was clean. There was no profes-sional way for him to return a report recommending against letting Marks take a buyout. He could have created one. Briefly he considered contacting an acquaintance who profiled as Klaatu, an insomniac gun-slinger hacker savant whose ex-wife Charlie had discovered ratting him out to a private security force hired by some of Klaatu's victims. Thanks to Charlie, Klaatu had avoided both a severe beating and the continua-tion of a treacherous marriage. Ever since, he'd been a valuable business associate, a forger and data wrangler without peer. If Charlie slipped him a few bucks, Klaatu could invent a reason to keep Carl Marks alive. Plus, Charlie seemed to recall that Klaatu had a geek-crush on Marks' movies.

It would be so easy, he thought. But it would be wrong.

"Amigo," Charlie said to his friend who was not there, "sometimes people have to make their own mistakes." He sent the final version of the Marks backgrounder, brushed his teeth, and went to bed.

WHEN MARTIN WENT back to get the last of the paperwork taken care of, he had to navigate a thicket of feedheads, print journalists, and even a few guerrilla avatars from the underground feeds whose operators were anonymous. One of them, an avatar of a 1970s-era Oprah Winfrey, blipped into existence in front of Martin as he was parking his car. "Given the demographics of prison populations," it said through his windshield, "isn't this just another kind of eugenics?"

This was one thread of the running (and one-sided, since Martin was rarely encouraged to answer questions) conversation surrounding the debut of the life-term buyout. Others involved the question of prisoner rights—were they really able to make a decision from behind bars without coercion? How would you know?—or more abstract questions of the value of human life and the intrusion of corporate power into the private sphere. To Martin's mind, buyouts were already starting to stand in for all kinds of larger questions that couldn't really be answered by your position on buyouts. So he stayed out of those conversations. For him, the life-term buyout was an expression of the value of human life, and a way for those who had transgressed civilization's most basic commandment to demonstrate their willingness to atone.

He'd said that once, to Caitlin Frost before he'd known who she was, and had been regretting it ever since. Her eyes had lit up, and her mouth curled into a hungry—but still very telegenic—smile. "Is that right?" she'd said. "We'll have to take that up another time. Perhaps a year or so into the program, when we all see how it's going." Then she'd moved on to another topic, with another interviewee, and Martin had made his way out of the studio to find irate messages from both Krakauers on his pod.

So he didn't say it much anymore, but Carl Marks had apparently seen the Frost interview. "Atonement, is it?" he asked when Martin entered the visitation area.

"Your motives don't interest me, Mr. Marks," Martin said.

"Oh, but they interest me a great deal. And it's Carl," Marks said, and waited. When Martin didn't take the cue, he went on. "Atonement. If I were to atone for a heinous act, how would I do it?"

"That's part of what I'm here for," Martin said. "Beyond that, I'm not qualified to comment."

"Oh, don't allow yourself to be compartmentalized. That's what they want," Marks said. "And yes, now that I've invoked the great nebulous They, you can dismiss me as a paranoid. Go ahead. While you're dismissing me, though, consider how many things you've been told you're not qualified to comment on. Why not? Because you're the one-dimensional man."

"Not even two dimensions?" Martin couldn't help himself. Marks was ridiculous, with his recycled 1960s rhetoric. The only reason he'd gotten as far as he had was that most people alive in 2041 didn't know how brazen he was in his intellectual theft.

"Mock all you want. But you find your second dimension. Then, if you can find it, that discovery might clue you in about what the missing third is. Or, if you don't like Marxism, let's go to French post-structuralism. You are the classic type of the man denied subjectivity by his culture. You are in every way an object, acted upon without ever acting, going through every day under the illusion of agency."

"Mind signing these?" Martin brought up the final disbursement forms on his pod and slid it across the table for Marks' approval. Marks thumbed the screen carelessly and slid it back.

"It's all part of the game," Marks said. "And you can't see it because you're one of the pieces. You're so far inside it that you see rules and think they're laws. You have insulated yourself with belief in a dogma that will destroy you in the end."

Martin, unsurprisingly, thought Marks had it exactly backward. In fact he had stripped himself of insulation. He was a live wire. Too much so, in Charlie's opinion.

"You'll see I'm right," Marks said. "But by then it will be too late."

EVERYTHING ABOUT THE Marks deal had to go perfectly. Martin knew this. Scott knew Martin knew this. Yet Scott still had to call Martin in, the day before finalization, and walk him through a series of intellectual propositions and boardroom fears that Martin already knew about.

"Sacramento, Washington, Washington, Sacramento," Scott was muttering as Martin came into his office at eight thirty. He looked up at Martin and said, "You don't know how hard this all is."

Martin didn't know what to say to this.

"You have a vision," Scott said. "You try to implement your vision. On all sides there are people telling you why it can't happen, for all these reasons that are valid if you happen to be one of those people. But I'm not one of those people. You're not, either, Martin. We know that something greater is out there. But I'm the one talking to committees and hassling lobbyists and making sure that congressmen feel like their asses are covered. Does this sound familiar to you?"

"No," Martin said.

"Right," Scott said. "That's because it isn't familiar to you, because you don't do it. I do. And then I come to you, and I ask you do to impossible things, and you go home to your wife and complain that I've asked you to do impossible things, but nobody ever stops to think about the impossible things that I do. Fuck!" he shouted, and then visibly took control of himself. "So. How's the Carl Marks deal?"

"Everything is like it should be," Martin said.

"Exactly what I wanted to hear. Jocelyn and I took early retirement five years ago, and we've spent maybe four years and eleven months since then working this. It can't fuck up, Martin. C-A-N-apostrophe-T." Scott ran a hand through his hair, a gesture that reinforced his youthfulness while conveying the impression that he was accustomed to dealing with weighty issues. "Sometimes I can't believe we've gotten this far."

O Captain my Captain, Martin thought with maximal sarcasm.

Scott turned to Martin and gripped him by the shoulders, as if he were sending Martin on a momentous quest with the fate of the world hanging in the balance. "You're our guy on this, Martin. I'm not saying you're perfect, but you're our guy. This whole thing is going to stand or fall with you. You've got the learning now, and you already had the temperament." Scott was massaging Martin's shoulders, and now he let go with one hand to make a conciliatory gesture. "Okay, maybe that's too personal. Sorry. The thing is, I saw it over and over again when I was on the job. You turn it into fuel, but you can't let it consume you. Belief. It's a controlled burn. Has to be."

He released Martin and said, "Take the rest of the day off. You've got to finish the Godbout thing, right? Do that tomorrow." Maybe the clinic that was receiving a big piece of the money would be open then, Martin thought. "Clock's ticking. Then a big morning on Thursday. Big morning. Feeds are going to be like schools of piranha." Scott shot Martin a newsnet-ready wink and sent him out the door with, "Oh, by the way. We transferred Marks to Nautilus-Valley. Better access. Hope you're ready."

HE WAS TELLING Teresa about these conversations later that night, in an effort to combat his acknowledged tendency to confuse independence with isolation. They'd been doing the counseling thing, with mixed success. She didn't like the way he kept work and family so separate, arguing that they needed to be pulling completely together, working by consensus. And she was right. He knew she was right. The problem was that from Martin's point of view she was sensitive to this issue precisely because she was prone to the same kind of compartmentalizing. From there, the conversation usually went downhill, and anyway it was a stand-in for much deeper issues that never quite came to light.

Tonight, though, Martin was making the effort. "Funny how we keep being convinced that celebrities are different even when we sit down and talk to them," Teresa mused. "And then we think we're different because we talked to them. It rubs off, or it's like an infection."

"I'd say infection," Martin said. "The feedheads are a plague, anyway." Lately he hadn't been able to leave home or office without some leering, plasticine newsreader trying to weasel confidences out of him. But the ego stroke was not to be taken lightly; he'd be lying if he said he didn't get a charge out of seeing himself on the feeds. It made him feel more real, oddly, this virtual multiplication of his visage, his voice. The newsnet machine was creating for him a persona, and he was participating.

Teresa, as usual, could read his mind. "So what's it like being famous?" she asked.

"I'm not famous," Martin said. "I'm momentarily prominent. Soon as Carl Marks is gone, they'll forget all about me."

"Not the Priceless Lifers."

But Martin didn't measure his worth by the attentions of zealots. Even zealots who could ghost into and out of smart lanes without leaving a trace, or spawn guerrilla daemons to hector him about the sanctity of human life when he went to the grocery store. Luckily the house system had held, so far, thanks to Charlie's dubious friends.

"Everyone needs something to bitch about," he said. "It's probably good for the program."

"The program," she repeated. "What about the family? The girls are getting interview requests. We need to step up the house security."

"I know. I was working on it Sunday, remember?" Cut to the chase, Martin thought. "You want me to quit and get another job? Is that what you want?"

"No, it's too late for that. I just want it out in the open—and I've said this before—that I don't think you thought through how this was going to affect us. And that goes back to some other things that we've been talking about."

And this was the moment where they were either going to go off the deep end into full-blown fighting, or they were going to both decide to back down. "I do think about that, T," Martin said. "I'll be more conscious of it going forward."

She looked at him for a long time, appraising him. Martin could see her deciding whether to pursue the issue further. "Okay," she said. "I have to go upstairs and finish some things for tomorrow."

There's your irony, Martin thought. She wants more family consciousness, and she's not wrong about that. But every night the last thing she does is work. We start a conversation about how we need to talk more about certain things, and then she stops talking. He'd had enough of ironies.

It seems wrong to ride the subway in Los Angeles. Just like it would seem wrong to wear a Red Sox hat in New York, or eat a ham sandwich in a synagogue. So I don't do it. I like to drive. I like to ride my bike. I even like to walk, which you're not supposed to do in LA, either. You remember the WALK-LA thing? How many million dollars did the city spend on sidewalks? How many trees did they plant? How many traffic patterns did they fuck up trying to sync stoplights so people actually had time to walk across eight lanes of traffic? And then, ten years later, the stoplights were all the same again, you still had to run across the street, the sidewalks were all busted up from the earthquake so you broke your ankle every time you walked a block, and the trees had all keeled over dead because of the holes in the ozone layer or some goddamn thing. We're good at dreaming out here, but we're not so good at planning. And speaking of the ozone layer, I'm going to say that one good thing about climate change is the return of the men's hat. Eighty years ago JFK killed the hat, and about twenty years ago it finally rose from its sartorial grave because we're men! We go bald! Except if we pay not to. But the hat is the one single salutary epiphenomenon of climate change. I don't give a fuck if you can grow pomegranates in Nova Scotia now; balance that against our climatological sequel Dust Bowl Two out there in Oklahoma or wherethefuckever. But the hat. There is nothing bad to say about the hat.

TEN

A TRUE SON of Los Angeles, Martin had loved cars since well before he was old enough to drive one. His first car was a gas-burning Toyota Corolla, only two years younger than he was and with 247,000 miles on it the first time he got behind the wheel. He nursed it to about three hundred thousand, learning a fair bit about cars along the way, before his father handed him off a '13 Mitsubishi Kivu, which at least was a hybrid; by then Martin had constructed elaborate rationalizations for driving a carbon fart, but he was glad not to hear about it anymore. He hadn't gotten his first fuel-cell wheels until five years before Jocelyn tapped him to be her buyout pioneer, and on the anniversary of that date, he'd bought himself a brand-new hydrogen Pontiac. The resurrected GTO was his first American car, his first car with full uplink and daemon interface. He got it in a rich, solid blue, and specifically demanded that it come with manual overrides on the road-proximity features. Martin was old enough to remember when you could actually drive a car, instead of sit in it while it ferried you somewhere. If he wanted to ride, he took the train; in a car, he wanted to drive.

The day he drove it off the lot, it had sixteen miles on it. As he got out of it after someone had T-boned him at a nondescript intersection not too far from the clinic where he'd finally done the last Godbout disbursement, it had a bit under five thousand. The number, 4947, was stuck in his head because it was the last thing he'd seen before three different airbags hit him like boxing gloves on the hands of a playful giant. John Wayne drawled a warning about possible injuries to any passengers, and informed Martin that he was calling in the cavalry. "Fuck,"

Martin said and got out of the car, ignoring the Duke's admonition that
a man never went outside without his hat.

Three men were getting out of the car that had hit him, an old diesel
pickup truck. The air was rank with the smell of backdoor biodiesel.
Martin swayed on his feet a little; the airbags saved your life, but they
sure didn't go easy on you doing it. "You okay there?" one of the men
said. "Never saw you there, ese. You musta run the stop sign."

"What's your hurry?" another chimed in. "Like you're fleeing the
scene or something."

Belatedly Martin realized that the three of them had formed a loose
half circle, penning him close to the open door of his car. "Let's, ah. Insurance," he said. "We'll get that out of the way." He shrugged. "Accidents."

"Accidents," the first guy agreed, nodding to his friends. "They sure
do happen." The three of them stood, arms folded. Martin's head was
clearing a little, and warning bells started to ring.

"We can just wait for the cops," he said. "The car called it in."

"Great," the first guy said. "You never know with signals around
here, though. Sometimes they don't go through."

"Never had any trouble before," Martin said, and only just then noticed that more people had joined the three who hemmed him in.
"Hey," he said. "You hit me."

"Wasn't me. I wasn't driving. Hey, Martin, everything go okay over
at the clinic, the Godbout thing? Real generous."

The punch-drunk fighter never sees the last one coming, and Martin didn't catch on to the meaning of what he'd heard until he'd replayed it three or four times. "Godbout," he repeated.

"Yeah, that was a nice thing he did, putting all that money into the
clinic. Those kids sure could use it." Coming closer, the spokesman for
what Martin was only just realizing was a flash mob spread his arms to
take in the people surrounding Martin and his car. Beyond them, cars
eased slowly by; behind them, horns honked. Nobody stopped. In the
windows of the nail salon across the street, two unoccupied stylists chatted with each other while they looked out on the scene.

"You've got maybe three minutes before the cops get here," Martin
said. It's the same truck, he thought. These are the same guys from the
Foothill Freeway.

"A lot can happen in three minutes." The mob started to close in. The leader held up his pod, and on its screen Martin saw himself leaving the clinic. "Just so you know, Martin. Priceless Life knows what you do, when you do it, who you do it with. If we wanted you, we'd have you."

Pocketing his pod, he took a step backward, and the mob quit contracting. Martin stood with his back to his car. He would not get in and shut the door. He would not be weak. "Who's watching you?" he asked. "Who's watching you watch me?"

"Those are good questions, ese. You keep them in mind." The leader's pod chirped and as quickly as it had appeared, the mob vanished. Martin leaned back and closed his eyes. From above he heard the lawn-mower sound of a drone, fishing for news, and he heard the pitch of its engine change as it circled back to take in the scene of two cars, the traffic easing around them, the bright glitter of broken glass in the hammering sunlight, the single man leaning against his crumpled car, eyes closed, not seeing all of the eyes on him. The drone circled, sending video out to its feedlist until the police came and one of the responding officers fired off an override that forced it away. He then introduced himself as Officer Cooper—these kinds of small courtesies being a recurrent fad among LAPD brass—and took Martin's license before strolling off to take in the scene.

At first neither Cooper nor his partner, one Kelvin Osorio, believed Martin about the flash mob, since he was unharmed and none of the cameras in the area had recorded anything unusual. "Do the cameras work?" Martin asked. Jesus, he was thinking. They disappear from smart lanes, they hack municipal cams. What's next?

"Above my pay grade," Cooper said. Osorio noted Martin's last name, inquired about a possible relationship with Jason Kindred, and upon hearing the answer started taking Martin quite a bit more seriously. Martin pointed out that they could have tracked the signal from his car daemon, and they considered this, Cooper a good deal more skeptically than his partner.

"Also," Martin added, "what about the three guys who were in the truck? Where did they go?"

"About that," Cooper said. "This truck has no plates, the VINs are removed, and it doesn't exist in any state motor-vehicle records after

2033. You couldn't drive this truck in Orange County for more than an hour without getting pulled over. No wonder they ran off."

"After calling in a couple dozen friends to stand around while they gave me a little warning?" Martin said. "Come on. This was planned." He knew they'd write him off as a complete paranoid if he told them about the last time he'd seen this truck. There was no record of it there, so for the police it wouldn't exist. When cameras were everywhere, nobody believed anything that wasn't on them. Without the image, there was no reality.

"They mentioned Priceless Life, you said," Osorio said. "That's the buyout group, right?"

"Anti-buyout group, yeah." Martin walked around to the passenger side of his car. The door and fender were caved in, and the shape of the engine block was visible on the fender, the truck's impact having acted as a stamping machine. The passenger window was all over the road, and the windshield was spiderwebbed. Air hissed slowly from the front tire on that side. It was going to be a while before he drove this car again. "I need to call my insurance company."

"Your daemon should have taken care of that when it pinged us," Osorio said.

"I know," Martin said, "but I want to make sure. I need this car for work. Also I need to get a tow."

Cooper was filling out the accident report, and Osorio was working on his own pod. "I don't want to sound demanding or anything," Martin said, "but I hope that's an incident report."

"I'll let you know when you're being demanding," Osorio said.

Martin reached into the car and got his hat. "So if you couldn't drive this truck without getting pinched," he said to Cooper, "how did they drive this truck without getting pinched?"

The cop shrugged. "Either they were from right around here and hadn't taken the truck out in a while, or something wasn't right with the transponder system in the area. We'll have to see if it's noticing expired plates on other cars."

"What if it is?"

"Then you can get paranoid, Mr. Kindred." Cooper went back to his report, and Martin started in on his own reporting. He called a tow truck and arranged for his car to be dropped off at the dealership in Pasadena. Then he called Teresa and let her know what had happened. After that, all he could do was wait while the arcane process of tow dispatching played itself out.

At least he had Osorio for company, now that the initial boilerplate of the incident report was done and the cop needed Martin to fill in some of the details. "I'm recording this, just so you know," Osorio said. "That okay?" Martin agreed that it was, and Osorio started asking him questions about where he'd been coming from and going. Getting the background set, was how he described it, before starting in on the accident itself. "So these three guys all got out of the truck and came over to you?"

"Yeah," Martin said. "I was a little dazed from the crash . . . well, more from the airbags, I think." He was now experiencing the beginnings of what promised to be a monstrous headache, and his nose felt swollen as well. It was coming clear to him that he had hit his head pretty hard, although when he ran his hands all over his face and scalp he couldn't feel any bruises or lumps. His memory of the minutes immediately after the accident had a dream-like, dissociative quality to it; part of the time he had a convincing recollection that one of the men from the truck had been wearing boxing gloves, and had punched him in the nose.

Osorio looked him over and asked—for what Martin thought was the third time—if Martin wanted medical care. "No," Martin said. "Good night's sleep and I'll be fine."

"Okay," Osorio said. "So these guys get out of the truck. What did they say to you?"

"Typical stuff at first; hey, I didn't see you, everything okay, that kind of thing. Then right away one of them stepped up and said something about Jerromy Godbout. A disbursement I just did on his case."

"That's your buyout client," Osorio said, in his cop-fleshing-out-the-record voice. "Did any of them say anything threatening?"

"Well, they . . . no. Not directly."

Osorio's tone changed just enough to let Martin know that he didn't want to bullshit around. "Okay. Indirectly?"

So Martin tried to explain the insinuations about the car daemon's ping being blocked, the vague menace of *A lot can happen in three minutes*, and what he saw as the implicit threat about Priceless Life watching.

"Especially since they already knew about what I was just doing. It was supposed to happen yesterday, this wasn't the schedule," Martin finished.

"Could be they just watched it on a feed," Osorio said. "You can piece a lot together from public records. Plus then there's you. You're the guy who's doing the buyout on that movie director, right? Tomorrow? People are paying attention."

"Then it just so happens that a completely untraceable truck T-bones my car while being driven by three guys with an interest in my professional activities? Come on, Officer. I get that cops are supposed to be skeptical, but something's going on here."

"I'm not saying it isn't. There's your tow," Osorio said. "Tell you what, ping me after you do your thing tomorrow. My information's already on your pod." A second tow truck, this one belonging to Santa Ana PD, grumbled up next to the private rig cranking Martin's car up onto its bed. Cooper and Osorio had the truck sent off to a city yard somewhere, and they each piped Martin a report after he thumbed his acceptance of their version of the facts.

Riding in the tow truck, Martin took a close look at the streets and the people on them. How many of them had been in the flash mob? he wondered. How many were watching him, keeping track of his daily round of appointments so they could plan when best to accost him? What would they do next time? The Krakauers had anticipated more Priceless Life activity because of Marks, and it sure was happening. Listening to his car bounce and groan on the towbar, he discovered that he was starting to bear a serious grudge against any and all Priceless Lifers. Buyouts were legal. They had been argued out in Sacramento, hashed through on all of the newsnet opinion programs, finessed in a variety of civil-liberties and religious forums. The consensus at this time was that they should happen, and Martin believed this, too. He was still ruminating when they got to the body shop, which was maybe three miles from his house. After half an hour of wrangling over insurance numbers and accident reports, the shop let him go home with a loaner slightly better than the old Mitsu that Martin had driven in college.

Teresa was waiting for him on the porch. "I sent the girls out," she said. "They're at the park until you go get them."

"Okay," Martin said.

"I want you to know that I'm really worried about you, Martin." Teresa wouldn't look at him, but he knew the timbre of her voice and could feel the emotion she was trying not to express. "It's one thing to believe in law and order, retribution, whatever. It's another to make decisions that put yourself in danger. You're not changing the world."

Maybe I am, he thought. He sat next to her and looked out on the street. Kids, stray balls, lawns. Flowering bushes, occasional piles of dogshit. Home. "What if this is going to change the world, T?" he said. "You didn't see the kids at that clinic today."

"No, but I saw our kids today," she said.

"Come on. That's not fair. What if I was a cop? That's a lot more dangerous."

"I don't know if that's true," she said. "And the world needs cops. Does it need buyouts?"

Martin let this sink in. "Guess I'll head over to the park," he said, and went to see his girls. Tomorrow was going to be a big day.

Today, Carl Marks meets his maker. Today, Carl Marks joins the choir invisible, and we will only have an endless succession of pontificating avatars in his stead. I'm not sure we're any worse off. I've been doing some reading about this buyout thing, as I'm sure you have, and here's one question: Where's the money going? Marks is old. Not as old as me, but he's well past the midpoint of his biblical threescore and ten. He's not worth as much in potential avoided expenses as your average twentysomething pizza delivery guy who gets in a fight with his dealer over an eighth of Kona and accidentally on purpose plugs him nine times with an old Glock he stole from his uncle. Now, he's made upward of a dozen movies. For most of them, he only had to license image rights and pay his code monkeys to render, and even if you, my onliest listener, never saw one of his films, there are two billion people in China. They did. And there are half a billion in Vietnam. They did. Carl Marks made some money. His family doesn't need the two million his buyout is going to bring in. So where does it go? I hope he sent it to me. In fact, I hope he put me in his will. Did I mention I loved Koba!? And hey, I take back all that stuff I said about The Long March. *I just didn't* understand . . .

ELEVEN

WHAT HE HADN'T counted on was the actors. Feedheads he was ready for, the slings and arrows, vilification and opprobrium—all of that he was already learning to handle. And a little dose of celebrity, Martin didn't mind that, either. But to have the whole thing turned into a performance, that rankled Martin to the core.

He walked out of his house at seven o'clock in the morning, already annoyed at having to drive a rental car, and found a guerrilla theater troupe doing the great execution scenes of Jacobean drama. Here was De Flores killing the innocent maid in *The Changeling*, Vindice poisoning the duke in *The Revenger's Tragedy*, Brachiano dying of Lodovico's poisoned hat and Flamineo killing Camillo in *The White Devil* and, at the center of it all, the strangulation of the duchess and her children from *The Duchess of Malfi*. The air overhead was thick with drones, and camera crews had trampled Martin's lawn into a mudflat. Two cops watched the performance with interest.

Martin walked up to them and said, "I don't want to be rude or anything, but what the fuck is this?"

The cops shrugged. "They have permits," one of them said.

"Martin Kindred!" the actors shouted, in unison. "*Morituri te salutant!*" And then they all fell over, pantomiming various gruesome deaths.

In a black fury Martin drove to Nautilus-Valley, where he found another group of costumed protestors performing a bloody masque on the street corner. Charlie met him and handed him a cup of coffee. "Welcome to fame, amigo," he said. Priceless Lifers chanted slogans and waved banners, the typical idiocy: LIFE IS BEYOND VALUE and KEEP YOUR

BOTTOM LINE OUT OF MY VEINS and on and on. Here the cops were a little more helpful. They cleared a path through the demonstrators and got Martin and Charlie inside.

The finalization chamber was built according to a standardized design. At the center of the room, a gurney gleamed in fluorescent light. Surrounding it, status lights blinked from various bits of machinery. There were two doors, one leading to the offices of the medical staff and the other to the cell blocks. One wall of the chamber was one-way glass, and a small room with theater-style seating for forty adjoined it. Martin entered this room and scanned the attendees. The family of Andi Anton, a crush of feedheads too important to stand outside in the baking sun, a handful of prison officials and politicians, and the Krakauers. Martin greeted everyone he felt it seemly to greet and stood near the wall closest to the Krakauers. Charlie leaned next to him, looking around like he expected to be thrown out at any moment.

The entry of Carl Marks instantly captivated everyone present. "Ladies and gentlemen," he boomed to his unseen audience. "What you see here is the revelation of this culture for what it has always been. A great unmasking, and the face of America is the face of the abyss looking back into the drooling collective visage of the proletariat. You are drugged, you are already dead. Capital has insinuated itself into your very bodies. It flows through your veins as this excellently lethal cocktail will soon flow through mine, making concrete and individual what has heretofore been abstract. But always present! These poisons flowed in the veins of the robber barons and the oil tycoons and the information aristocracy. They flow now in the veins of the bought-and-paid-for legislators in Sacramento and Washington, who legislate what they are told by their donors and cronies. I have killed, and perhaps I deserve to die. But my action was direct, and every day thousands die by the indifference and cynicism of boardrooms and committee meetings. I am you, and all of you will soon be me. Welcome to your brave new world."

"Render unto me a fucking break," Charlie muttered. Martin looked at the Krakauers, both of whom appeared to be thinking hard. Working out the consequences, Martin guessed. How much of Marks' speech would make for great feed, and how much would become grist for ridicule? No way to tell which way the commentariat would break. This was a wild card. The Krakauers hated wild cards. Martin would have bet his right hand that both of them were already writing new finalization guidelines that explicitly prohibited grandstanding at the scene.

Marks lay on the gurney, talking through the murmur of the staff, the tone of his voice not varying as they inserted IVs in both of his arms. "Martin Kindred is not the problem," he went on. "The Krakauers are not the problem. They are symptoms, they are agents of a system whose rules and extent they refuse to see because it has long since made them part of itself. This is my body, given for millions of dollars that I earn only because a market has been created in which my death is the commodity. Capital is the predator, a new link in the food chain in which humanity must acclimate to a lesser role. Welcome, and farewell."

He fell silent, and the attending physician gave the signal. Marks had a beatified look on his face, as if he were infused with the kind of immanent divinity that his politics would deny. It was not the face of a man who knew he was going to die. It was the face of a man annihilated by the role he had always been born to play, the face of a man who knew that this was his life's finest moment and that anything that followed would always pale in comparison.

When the doctor pronounced Carl Marks dead, a nervous rustle swept through the viewing room. People got up and left immediately, looking around them as if something had changed in the paint on the walls, or in the quality of the light. They were uncertain. Even if they were happy, and some of them were, they looked as if they expected something else.

The two exceptions to this were the Krakauers, who shook Martin's hand and led him and Charlie to the prison media room, where an availability was about to break out. "Let me preface things by saying that we're not going to comment on Mr. Marks' last words," Scott said. "It's our belief that the life-term buyout is an essential component of free expression that has for far too long been denied to many American citizens, and that extends as long as life extends. So."

A wave of questions broke over them, mostly directed at the Krakauers, but Martin could pick out a few aimed at him, and even at Charlie, whose presence there was of interest because he wasn't a Nautilus employee and most of the feedheads didn't know what he was doing there. Yes, they were very satisfied with how things had gone during the program's first year. No, this was not an attempt to increase the execution rate, nor was it an end run around existing capital punishment legislation. "The buyout is not a punishment," Scott said. "That should be obvious. It's an expression of social responsibility."

The pace of questions slowed to something approaching coherence, and Jocelyn stepped in. "This, by the way, is Charlie Rhodes. It's up to him to make sure that each buyout proceeds strictly according to regulations, and also to make sure that there is no hint of coercion or conflict of interest. He's done a great job for us so far, and he'll be a valuable asset moving forward."

Charlie, looking bilious, declined to answer any questions, and the assembled media returned their attention to Martin. There was Caitlin Frost, who had watched without saying anything until this point. Seizing on a brief lull, she called out, "Martin! Are you proud? Any regrets?"

"Martin will be making his own remarks at a later time," Scott said. "For now, let me just say that the finalization of the life-term buyout of Carl Marks is one more step in a brand-new relationship between the prisoner and his human rights. No longer are people going to be powerless permanently because they have entered the criminal justice system. No longer will they be forced to waste their lives in a six-by-nine steel cell, with no means of rejoining the community of human beings. Marks and I might disagree on the meaning of this," Scott added with a chuckle, "but he was correct in seeing this as the birth of a brave new world. I for one am very excited to be living in it."

Scott made a beckoning gesture toward the waiting police officers, and six of them closed around Martin and Charlie to lead them from the prison media room back into the glare and chaos of the street. Outside, the mass of demonstrators started throwing their signs and banners, plus an assortment of rocks and bottles and whatever else was at hand, the minute Martin and Charlie emerged. The Krakauers were smart enough to either stay inside or leave by one of the jail's direct exits to the parking garage. There's a lesson in there somewhere, Martin thought, as he crouched under a pair of riot shields held aloft by two cops who looked annoyed that they wouldn't be able to join into the mass asskicking that was about to commence.

And commence it did, with the efficient savagery that made the LAPD riot squad one of the most emulated in the United States. Martin saw little of it as he was hustled around the perimeter within which the beatings were being administered and into a police van. He sat inside, with Charlie and the six cops, for nearly an hour. Then the doors opened again, and Scott grinned at them from the sunlight. "Boy, I sure turned out to be right about the Priceless Lifers getting wound up. Pretty good day's work, gentlemen," he said. "Lunch tomorrow? It's on me."

Then he was off to work the feeds some more. Smooth, Charlie thought. If the Krakauers were anything, it was smooth. Selling-ice-to-Eskimos kind of smooth. You had to admire it, but Charlie saw Scott Krakauer for what he was: a con man, pure and simple. He was immaculately put together, handsome, glib; everything about him so polished and perfect that it couldn't be real. Even the veins on the backs of his hands were symmetrical. If the buyout program was anything other than a scam, it wasn't because of Scott, was the way he'd put it to Martin about a month ago, when they were leaving Yankee Doodle's. But Martin wouldn't be persuaded. "It's about results," he said. "If buyouts are a good thing, and I think they are, Scott doesn't matter. What matters is that we do them right. In ten years, nobody is going to care about Scott Krakauer's character. They're going to care that people who have committed murder have a meaningful way to atone for what they did."

Since then Charlie had known that a fight was brewing between him and Martin, but he didn't feel like having it right then, with everybody still buzzing from the Marks deal.

"Hey," Martin said, rescuing Charlie from his gloomy prognostication. "Let's grab some lunch."

"Nah," Charlie said. "I got work to do. Catch up with you later, amigo."

THE NEXT MORNING was Friday, and Martin got started bright and early on the Marks disbursements. Cracking the file, he saw that there were only eight. This was good news; the sooner he could knock them out, the sooner he could get on to making more deals. Marks' funeral was happening somewhere in West LA, siphoning off much of the media energy, but the disbursements were well attended. The first was a Marxist bookstore in Silver Lake, where the owner actually said *Viva la revolu-cion!* while the transfer of six hundred thousand dollars into his account was occurring. Nothing says *proletarian revolution* like a bag of money falling out of the sky, thought Martin. These people were ridiculous.

Two more were just like that. Absurd slogans, playing to the feeds, recipients of Carl Marks' largesse railing against capitalism while Martin made them temporarily rich. It was the strangest DB he'd ever done, that much was certain. Around one o'clock he got a ping from Charlie. Good timing, he thought. "Hey, Charlie," he said. "I'm in Santa Monica. Lunch? You would never believe this morning. I mean, have you been watching these people? It's amazing."

The look on Charlie's face brought Martin up short. Charlie always looked sour about something, but today he looked stricken. "What's up?" Martin said.

"Amigo," Charlie said. "I, you know, I troll the cop bands to keep up, and, ah . . . it's your brother. Fuck, Martin, I'm sorry, don't go anywhere, there's a car coming to get you."

And Martin heard sirens.

He didn't remember much about the ride. He was in the back of a police car, siren screaming, automated traffic-control daemons moving cars out of the way and turning traffic lights green in front of them. Martin called his father, and Teresa, but he couldn't remember what he'd said. What did you say? Jason is dead. Someone killed Jason. No, I don't know. I'm on my way over there, I'll call you as soon as I know something.

The police car jounced across shattered asphalt at the edge of an enormous rail yard. Martin didn't know where they were. Somewhere south of downtown. He heard train whistles and the curt interchange of voices. When he got out of the car, the first thing he saw was the ambulance, lights on and doors open. The EMTs stood talking to each other, not looking at the group of cops who stood in a ragged circle at the far end of an empty lot. Martin walked in that direction. A cop stopped him, planting a palm in his chest. "It's my brother," Martin said, and the cop stepped aside.

When he got to the circle, he saw Meg Twohy. She came up to him and said, "I'm so sorry, Martin." Beyond her, he saw crime-scene technicians picking through the weeds. Evidence flags stuck up from the ground. At the base of the fence, covered by a sheet, was the body of Martin's brother. His feet stuck out from the sheet. He was lying on his side, back to the fence, the ground dark and the sheet splotched with blood. Martin heard the snap of a camera, over and over.

"Who did this?" he asked.

Meg looked him in the eye. "We'll get him," she said. "You can believe that, Martin. We'll get him."

Charlie appeared next to him. "Amigo," he said. "Ah, Christ."

"We were supposed to go fishing on Monday," Martin said, and tears came down like a curtain.

It's not that I don't like cops. As the immortal Mickey Rourke once said in a movie based on the life of the immortal Bard of Los Angeles, Bukowski himself, I just seem to feel better when they're not around. Nothing wrong with that, right? I mean, when cops are around, it means that somebody did something wrong. Or that they think somebody did something wrong, which is often just as bad. So yeah, I feel better when they're not around. But that doesn't mean I want them not to be around, if you know what I mean. I have had occasion to need the cops, and whichever motherfucker out there iced Jason Kindred of the Los Angeles Police Department, I hope that when they catch him, no one is looking. Not too likely, I get that, but there wasn't anyone looking when he did what he did, and part of me just wants to say what the fuck about that? I didn't even know there was a place left in our City of Angels where you weren't in the field of at least one lens. Now it turns out that there are quite a few. I used to think that municipal surveillance was the last step on the way to Big Brotherville, but then it happened, and you know what? It didn't make any difference, because who the fuck cares what I do? Then I got used to it. Then I started to assume it was always there no matter where I went or what I did. And now that I know that's not true, it makes me a little nervous. My twenty-year old self is calling me a pussy right now. Godspeed, Jason Kindred. But I still feel better when cops aren't around.

TWELVE

NO ONE IN LOS ANGELES was a stranger to sudden violence. Even if you didn't experience it yourself, it saturated the newsnets and barroom conversations. Vigilante podjackers raised lynch mobs in response to raw police crime-scene vid and staged flash citizens' arrests that resulted in coroner's inquests more often than jail sentences. All of it was beamed out on the feeds and played live on subway station screens for the benefit of bored commuters. So every Angeleno was made intimate with the image of violence, and yet when Jason Kindred was murdered, the shock to his parents and brother was so thunderous and brutal that it sheared them apart from one another.

As the news spread, family and friends came to Casa Kindred, where Jason's parents Vance and Felicia sat stony and withdrawn, accepting condolences without remembering who gave them. Hannah veered from gently consoling her children to furious rages against any target that presented itself. She blamed Martin at first, and Martin could do nothing but accept it. Who knew whether Priceless Life had killed Jason? It was possible. The group's membership was currently on the receiving end of some hard questions from LA cops looking to take out their anger. But Hannah blamed them, too. Today she hated the police because her husband had been a cop. Grief has its own logic.

In the Kindred household blaming cops for anything was secular blasphemy, but Hannah could say what she wanted. Her rage gave Jason's friends from the job an excuse to unload their own discontents about the force, petty or philosophical depending on the character of whoever took up Hannah's jeremiad at a given moment. All of them knew somehow that their function as they stood in Vance and Felicia's living room, or milled around the backyard patio, was to ratify Hannah's rage. Through it all the retired detective patriarch of the Kindred clan sat silently, one hand on his wife's knee, until late in the evening he stood up and said, "That's about goddamn enough." Extracting a cigar from the humidor in the liquor cabinet, he took it to a chair in the far corner of the yard, across the expanse of xeriscape and swimming pool. There he lit it with rigid ceremony and sat, his distance and posture defying anyone to approach.

Lost his kid, the assembled cops and family friends said by way of excuse. They were looking for a way to impute weakness to Vance by judging his behavior inappropriate and therefore in need of excuse, but Vance Kindred needed no excuse. He'd joined the LAPD in 2000, left to spend two years with the sand flies and roadside bombs in Baquba, and then came back to the job until retiring in 2030 to teach courses at Pepperdine, where he passed most of his classroom time telling stories. If it wasn't gunfire in Gardena, it was the lazy, delayed pop of sniper rifles from the rooftops of Iraq, the sound like an afterthought slipped in between the bright spray of blood and the mechanical heartbeat of the medevac chopper. Vance had earned his moods, was the consensus among the impromptu gathering at Casa Kindred.

At intervals he would say, *Those fuckers*. To which those clustered at the other side of the pool to pretend they weren't watching and taking their cues from him would nod, and echo *Fuckers*. Only once did Vance display the kind of emotion everyone was expecting in the aftermath of the murder of his younger son. Sometime close to midnight, nearly twenty-four hours after they'd gotten the news and about an hour before people got drunk enough for fights to break out, some enterprising funeral service podjacked the pool-cleaning robot. It was on standby near the fence, and at first when it turned itself on those few people who noticed assumed that it was timed maintenance. Then it beamed a grainy holo of palm trees and sunsets out over the pool, and said, "In the hour of your grief, know that Ortiz Funeral Home will relieve you of every burden, so that you can see to what's important. An Ortiz representative can call on you whenever you wish, at the location of your choice. We take care of everything, so you can take care of your family. Simply say 'Ortiz' to schedule a private and respectful consultation."

Silence fell. The holo blipped out and restarted, but the poolbot never started speaking again because Vance threw his cigar aside and beat the bot into a tangle of wires and shattered plastic casing with his bare hands and feet. Then he stood there for a long moment, looking back and forth from his bloody knuckles to the ruins of the poolbot to the soggy end of his cigar, which floated in the pool surrounded by a slowly descending halo of ash. "Well, shit," he said after a while, and went to the shed for a net to dip the cigar out.

Through all of this, nobody seemed to notice Martin, who shuttled from his mother to Hannah and back to Teresa and the girls. He looked to his father but did not approach him, knowing that the old man was going to get through this the only way he knew how, which meant biting down on it and holding it until he'd grown used enough to the loss that he could pretend it hadn't happened. Martin wanted to go to his father, but when Vance walked away, it didn't do any good to follow. He would stay there dabbing the blood from his fingers, overhung by flowering vines and eucalyptus branches, until he was good and ready to come back. All his life Martin had waited for his father's attention. Now he would wait to ensure that his own attention rang true. Teresa, in her heart already gone, stayed by this man she no longer loved, finding a reservoir of tenderness toward Martin that she had long ago forgotten about and he had for even longer ignored. The girls turned to each other. No adult had anything to offer that could cushion or obscure the brute fact of Uncle Jason's death. Together with their cousin Bart, they clustered around Zack, who at six cried because everyone around him was sad and because he knew their sadness was because of something bad that had happened to his father. But the idea of death comes slowly and incompletely to six-year-olds, and Zack's tears came less from sadness than from confusion. His sister and cousins went to him the way they saw the adult women going to their men, sublimating their own partially articulated grief into caring for the male in their midst.

Many people said How are you, Martin, but few of them would have been ready if he had actually told them. Martin's feelings were a knot of bereavement, frustrated filial devotion, and lingering reflexive instinct to protect his distant wife from a grief that in truth she did not feel, but he believed in because it was his own. He could not say his grief, he could not console his father, and he could not open himself to the woman who in implacable slow motion was breaking his heart. Because his own heart was broken, he needed someone to come to him—but none of the gathered cops and family friends were the people who could reach him, or whom he wanted to reach him. Charlie had only just gotten there when Vance tore the poolbot apart, but right away he could tell that Martin needed one of three people to make him however briefly the center of their attention. His father was gone to the corner of the yard, his mother was now tearfully tracing the edges of Jason's academy graduation photograph, and Teresa was trying to wrangle all of the children into some kind of game that none of them wanted to play. "Hey, amigo," Charlie said when he got there. From the scene, he'd gone home to put out the word that the Jason Kindred murder was personal to him, and his people needed to get over their cop hatred and feed him what they knew.

"Hey," Martin said. He took the beer Charlie offered and added, "You hear anything?"

Not yet, Martin, Charlie wanted to say. Later you can try to fix it, to get redress or revenge, or even understanding. Right now all you should do is try to learn how to be in this new world where your kid brother isn't the golden child everyone loves, but the latest hero cop gunned down in the line of duty. But Martin couldn't do that. Because he'd never gotten understanding for his decision not to be a cop, the Kindred family profession since Vance's grandfather had come home from World War II and joined the force in Ypsilanti, Michigan, Martin needed to understand. He was the kind of man who took the things he'd always wanted to get from everyone around him, and transmuted his own impulses into the shape of those absences. Because he thought nobody understood him, he needed to understand everyone and everything. After college, when he'd gone to work for the insurance company that became Nautilus, Vance and Felicia had reacted with not just puzzlement, but outright anger. The only worse thing he could have done was become a defense lawyer. For Martin, the intricacies of risk, the crystal-ball projections about how and why things happened, gave him a feeling of control that he couldn't imagine finding in the endless treadmill of investigating and solving crimes that would just be committed over and over again. He'd long since given up trying to justify the choice in the face of Vance's cop evangelism, and over the years the conflict had died down because all of them had arrived at a tacit agreement not to address it.

Now Martin, without the solace he needed from people who needed solace as much as he did, leaned into Teresa as she came back from a provisionally successful child-diversion operation. "Hey, Charlie," Teresa said. They hadn't talked since his impromptu counseling session a while back. He figured that they'd still be cordial after Martin and Teresa got their shit together and finally got divorced.

"T," Charlie said. "How are the girls?"

"Coping, I guess," she said. Unconsciously she reached out to touch the back of Martin's shoulder, and Charlie saw her realize what she'd done and drop her hand away again. There is a quality to the way two people touch when they are falling out of love. A reaching after something that's already gone, and also a quiet reassurance—when you've spent fourteen years with someone, trying and failing to build a life, you want that person to know that both of you will survive. Perhaps even be happier. That's the thing that underlies all of the minor unforgivable slights of the divorce endgame. Charlie had seen Martin and Teresa do this before, in other public settings. They hadn't said out loud to anyone that they were splitting, although everyone in the room could see it, and so they enacted this strange, melancholy pantomime of togetherness and partnership.

Charlie had seen it before. Hell, he'd done it before, three times. The thought of all his marriages exhausted him. The end was always the same. Once you knew it was going to happen, you got to the point where Martin and Teresa were, when you looked at each other across the kitchen table, and both of you were thinking: Okay. How do we do this? There was the house, the question of which nights the girls would spend where. At least Martin didn't have to worry about going broke. They'd talked about money a little, during those mostly late-night occasions when the hovering specter of divorce became too substantial for either of them to ignore. Then they'd decided to put it all off for another day, as if the simple passage of time would do something to bring them back together without either of them taking action. And behind that decision to table the divorce conversation hung the question. How do we do this?

That was the question on Martin's mind this night, too, with his parents' house full of drunk and angry cops. There was his mother, surrounded by people pressing her hand, swearing to find whoever had done this. There was his father, alone, the force of his sorrow keeping consolation at a distance across the pool. His brother was dead. Martin, the unsatisfactory child who had chosen a most un-Kindred life, was now an only child. He sensed that this would be a burden. Jason was gone, and as they adjusted to his absence, there would be pressure to live up to all of the things he might have done. *How do we do this?*

CHARLIE HATED FUNERALS, but he would no more have missed Jason's than Martin's, or for that matter his own. He'd been friends with Martin for ten years, and known Jason almost as long. Younger than Martin by two years, Jason had gotten all of the standard-issue Kindred bravado and bonhomie. He was born to be a cop, and had joined the force the minute he'd completed a degree in criminal justice. At twenty-three, he was a rookie whose father was a department legend two years from retirement; when persons unknown fired a succession of bullets through his upper torso on the back lot of a machine shop on the edge of the rail yards between Bandini and Hobart, he was deemed a worthy successor to the Kindred legacy, with *future detective* written all over him. Now cops from all over the LA basin were showing up in full dress, and you could cut the sanctimony with a knife. Charlie hated cop funerals even more than regular funerals because at cop funerals it was expected that everyone would lie. People lied at all funerals, but at cop funerals the dead man was always the best cop any of them had ever known, or would have been if he hadn't been cut down in the prime of life with the potential of his career shining ahead of them all, a golden road of decorations and selfless guardianship that because of the violence they had all dedicated their lives to fighting would never be traveled. Or something like that.

It had been years since Charlie had gone to a cop funeral, but he didn't need a new suit because he'd gotten heavy as an adolescent and stayed the same since. He allowed himself secret and vaguely contemptuous chuckles at the other guys his age who still tried to fit into suits they'd bought ten or twenty years before. His years of being a PI had introduced him to a lot of cops, and taught him to steer clear of most of them, but Charlie didn't mind cops any more than he minded anyone else. He considered himself an equal-opportunity misanthrope. The pose was hard to keep up at the funeral for a good friend's brother, though. He met up with Martin and Teresa, who had not only their girls but Hannah's kids in tow. Glancing around, Charlie caught sight of Hannah, whose inchoate rage had burned out into numbness. No, Charlie revised his estimate. Catatonia. She was an animate doll, moved from place to place by the people who knew what she was supposed to do.

Martin and Charlie both knew that Hannah was a little too fond of certain pills, and they exchanged a knowing glance. "What the hell," Charlie said under his breath so the kids wouldn't hear. "I would, too, if I could. Who wouldn't?"

"Sure, but she's still got the kids." Sympathy wrestled with anger in Martin's tone. "You have kids, you don't get to fall apart."

Charlie shrugged. He didn't figure family permission figured into whether a person fell apart or not.

"Listen, amigo," he said. "Anything I can do."

"Yeah," Martin said. He gripped Charlie's shoulder. "I know."

Scott and Jocelyn Krakauer appeared as if summoned. They'd known Jason distantly when he was new to the force and they hadn't yet left the thin blue line for much greener pastures. "He was a terrific kid, Martin. And a terrific cop. We're so sorry," Scott said. Charlie bit his tongue because in this case, the boilerplate words expressed the truth. Teresa and Jocelyn were talking a short distance away, toward the open grave, with the kids orbiting around them. Most of the cops in attendance stood in a thick knot on the side of the grave opposite from where the pastor would stand, and behind the dozen chairs set up for immediate next of kin. Radiating from the knot was an air of impatient, frustrated violence. Going to cop funerals made cops want to nail somebody. Charlie wondered if any Priceless Lifers would be dumb enough to show up and lecture Martin about karma. That would be a quick way of removing yourself from the gene pool.

A few words said, a few tears shed, a show of support and a few spadefuls of dirt thumping down on the casket; that was about it for the funeral itself. The wake started at Casa Kindred and later moved to Yankee Doodle's. Nearly everyone drove even though the bar was close to a train station and thorough inebriation was mandatory. This was another thing Charlie hated—cop wakes and Yankee Doodle's both—but at least there was baseball on the vids. Theories circulated with the pitchers, and got more cynical as the number of pitchers in circulation mounted.

Teresa was there, as were Vance and Felicia. She watched her in-laws who wouldn't be her in-laws much longer, and she watched her husband who would soon be her ex. He was mourning his brother, and she tried to feel the impulse to nurture, to mourn with him, but all she had was a nonpharmaceutical version of Hannah's numbness. She had fond memories of Martin the way she had fond memories of her first boyfriend in high school; he had become past tense to her even though they were still married and the girls would keep either of them from ever being entirely past to the other. "You know what it is?" she said to Charlie. "We don't fight. We don't even disagree. We're roommates. That's all we've been for a long time, but as soon as we decide we don't want to be roommates anymore, then all of a sudden it's a divorce again. I think that's why we haven't done it yet."

Charlie considered this, and then said, "Am I supposed to relay this to Martin?"

"No. God, no. I mean, if you want to, you're his friend. I'm not going to ask you to keep secrets from him."

"If you want my advice, T?" Charlie said. "Get it over with. Right now you've got yourself fooled with the roommates thing, but roommates can bring people home. You can't. You got yourself in a perfect unhappy stasis, is what I think. Get it over with. I'll tell him the same thing."

"You haven't already?"

Charlie shook his head. "I sit and listen, I offer advice when asked. I don't make enough money to offer people advice about their marriages."

Both of them stood watching Martin for a while. He was part of a group of cops, one of whom was obviously telling a story about Jason. Part of a group of cops, Teresa thought. Charlie was thinking the same thing.

And then Teresa thought that she couldn't possibly divorce him right then. His brother had just died.

Love each other, people. It's the one hundred and twelfth anniversary today of the first Academy Awards. Your host: Douglas Fairbanks, whom many of you will remember for his immortal turn as Che in Carl Marks' late experiment Ernesto in Kinshasa. *A sexy man, Douglas Fairbanks, which I can say because I just got laid. Speaking of which, you could be making love to the partner or anonymous party, real or virtual, of your choice right now. So why are you listening to me? And if you are making love to the partner or anonymous party of your choice while streaming me—you know who you are—I don't want to know about it. Truly I don't. Any and all correspondence on the topic, as assessed by keyword, will be aspaminated. I am reliably informed that my audio listenership, together with feed traffic, indexed according to lucrativity of perclickitude, ranks me in the top five percent of local net, feed, and old-fashioned broadcast traffic. To which I say Amazing! It used to be you had to play music or talk politics to get those kinds of numbers. Or pretend to help people, or try to save their souls. Me, I just talk. And I am interesting.*

THIRTEEN

THREE DAYS after his brother died, Martin returned to the place where it happened, the anonymous vacant lot between a tool-and-die shop and the rail yard that stretched west from the Long Beach Freeway. Meg Twohy was waiting for him in an old unmarked car. She got out of it and said, "Glad you were on time. Only other thing for a girl to do out here is show up in pieces on the tracks."

"Well," Martin said, "let's try to avoid that."

She led him through a gap in the fence into the weedy lot, where dirt footpaths snaked from factory side to rail side along patterns inscrutable to Martin. He stopped when they were near the center of the space and said, "What was he doing here?"

Meg didn't stop right away. When she did, she was holding back curving branches of desert brush determined to return Los Angeles County to its natural state. Traffic from the junction of the Santa Ana and Long Beach freeways thrummed in the middle distance. Some of the traveling cars had old-fashioned dual-pitch horns that always raised the hairs on Martin's neck. The note was rarely heard in these days of smart lanes and automated traffic flow, and something about it made Martin feel at home. This was his Los Angeles. People should be honking their horns on the 5. The new cars, with "horns" that set off warning chirps in other drivers' pods, made it all too personal as far as he was concerned.

"We don't know," Meg said. She looked at him for a long time after she'd said it, as if waiting for him to press her, and just when her scrutiny had made him feel like he should say something else, she looked away and said, "Come on."

How can you not know, Martin thought. He held on to the question, waiting to find out what Meg did know.

At the back of the lot, decades' worth of windblown trash drifted against a chain-link fence to which decades of homeless travelers had applied their trespassing ingenuity. The rail yard beyond the fence stretched interminably away to the east and west, dozens of tracks and sidings winding among thousands of cars bearing the insignias of freight companies that hadn't existed since before Martin was born. "He was on duty, wasn't he?" Martin asked, knowing the answer but belatedly getting around to pressing Meg as he should have done right away. He felt like he had ground to make up, that she had wanted him to say something else at first but now might not respond because he hadn't.

"There's only so much I can tell you." Meg still wouldn't look at him. "I'll give it to you straight, Martin. I shouldn't be here. The only reason I am here is that Charlie and I go way back. Sol is going to give me hell about doing this, first of all because it's not a good use of a detective's time and second of all because he and your father never got along. And no, I am not going to tell you why. So please do not push me."

"So he was on duty," Martin said. He was surprised to hear about tension between his father and Sol Briggs. Cops kept things between them, and presented a united front to everyone else. Even their sons.

Meg sighed. "Yeah," she said. "He was on duty. But he killed his pod right before he came back here."

"So he was meeting someone? He wasn't undercover," Martin said. On-duty cops had GPS transponders in their department-issue pods, and were required to keep them hot unless they had reason to believe that they would be endangered if someone tracked the signal—or unless they were undercover, in which case they didn't carry department pods. Dry wind, scented with creosote and hot asphalt, rustled the trash along the fence. Among the rows of rusting freight cars, Martin saw a human figure moving, too far away to be anything but a shape. Meg wasn't answering him. "He didn't say anything before he killed his pod?"

"It's all in the report, Martin," Meg said. She followed his gaze, and he watched her track the distant figure until it was gone between cars.

"I'm not even going to ask if you went out there and talked to anyone," he said.

"Glad to hear it." Meg shaded her eyes as she turned to face him. "Anytime you want to do our job for us, you can take the exam. Until then, maybe you should stick to writing policies."

So here, Martin thought, was a conundrum. If he backed down, he was never going to get anything out of her that she wouldn't give a random civilian; if he let her goad him, she'd have a different excuse to clam up. The path between meek and obstreperous was narrow. He jumped onto it with both feet. "Meg," he said. "I don't know how to do your job. But I have spent my entire life around other people who do it, so I know what it looks like. What the hell kind of brother would I be if I didn't ask questions?"

Meg dropped her hand away from her eyes and looked out over the rail yard again. A train whistle blew somewhere to the west. "You know," she said, "nobody ever asks a detective if maybe she's done too much legwork on a case." Martin waited. Whatever it was that still hung unspoken between them, he didn't know how to say it. The train whistle blew again, closer, and then a Pacific Coast express blew by on its way to San Diego. When it had passed, Martin felt some of the tension go with it.

"Where was he?" he asked.

She led him to a spot near the southeast corner of the lot. No visible evidence remained that a man named Jason Kindred had died here. If there had been crime-scene tape, evidence flags, any of the physical paraphernalia of investigation—the homeless had invisibly spirited it away. "Right here," Meg said, standing against the eastern perimeter fence.

JASON KINDRED KILLS his pod. This is only one of many things Martin can't figure out, and later Charlie will be equally mystified; but for now, it is the first action, so it comes first in Martin's reconstruction of the events. Jason's squad car sits at the dead end of Noakes, where the street breaks apart into a rutted asphalt lot that was once the yard of a long-dead trucking company. On the other side of the lot is the weedy rectangle where Jason now heads, his hands empty. When his body was discovered, both flashlight and sidearm were where they should have been. Charlie will later decide that the failure of the murderer to take the gun has primary significance, but right now Martin is the one doing the reconstructing, so he is the one deciding what is significant and what isn't. Teresa sleeps next to him. It's a warm night, and Martin is lying on his back, damp with sweat that is slow to evaporate in the closeness of the room. The window is open, but the air is still. Improbably, he and Teresa were having sex twenty minutes before he began his reconstruction of the events immediately preceding his brother's death. Along with sweat, he is damp with her. He inhales the scent and drifts toward sleep. Jason Kindred ducks through a triangular gap in the fence that divides the former truck yard from the vacant lot. He walks directly across the lot, west to east, with the train tracks at his right and the silent aluminum polyhedron of the tool-and-die shop on his left, partially lit by the block's single working streetlight. Dry weeds and desiccated bits of trash crackle and rasp under his feet, but he's not making any effort to be quiet. Someone is waiting there to meet him. A single someone, likely male, wearing worn work boots. Jason and this mystery contact talk for long enough that numerous shiftings of weight and small relocations are visible in the scribbled pattern of their footprints. The mystery contact then walks away toward the tool-and-die shop. Jason stays where he is, waiting. Three bullets rip through him, fired from a distance of approximately thirty feet. The first hits him just behind the left shoulder, burrowing under the scapula before cracking the fourth thoracic vertebra and exiting near the inside of the right scapula. The second shatters his left elbow before splitting his left kidney open and gouging through his duodenum, where it comes to rest. The third hits the left hip bone, deflecting upward at an angle through the already ravaged intestine, perforating the liver, the diaphragm, and the right lung, then exiting at the acromioclavicular joint of the right shoulder. The left brachial, right subclavian, and common hepatic arteries are damaged. With the first impact, Jason takes a heavy step back with his left foot; as the next two bullets hit him, he moves forward again, shuffling and then taking a lunging step with the right foot. Two more steps bring him heavily against the fence. He turns his back to it and slides slowly down to a sitting position, the heels of his shoes digging furrows perpendicular to the line of the fence. At some point he puts his hand on his sidearm. Profound blood loss and the collapse of his right lung compromise his reflexes. Shock, as it sets in, draws blood from the extremities to the torso, where it pours into the peritoneal cavity and out onto the packed earth. Jason has killed his pod. His brother lies feeling the faintest stir of air in the room he will, for some uncertain term in the future, share with his wife. A prickle of evaporative cooling spreads across his stomach and thighs. His testicles creep at the temperature change, then relax again. Martin is sleeping, followed down into sleep by what he does not know, believes he can never know, about the death of his brother in the weeds and the faint wash of streetlight and the fading echo of gunshots out over the iron and cinder arterial jumble of the rail yards, where if anyone hears, they're not talking.

OF COURSE THE first thing he mentioned to Charlie, the following day at Temoc's, was that he'd gotten laid. "This is such a cliché that I genuinely hate to say it," he said, "but I just can't figure her out."

It's not that hard, was what Charlie was thinking. Your wife is in the process of figuring out that she doesn't love you anymore, or if she does, she doesn't love you enough to give up all of the things she has to give up to love you. Which means that she's less interested in the boom-boom than your average healthy woman with Teresa's vim and vigor. "Amigo," Charlie said, and as the words left his mouth he knew he would regret them forever, "never look a mercy fuck in the mouth."

Martin considered this, evaluated the latent offensiveness and cynicism inherent in the idea, and reasoned that although Charlie was an asshole for saying it, he wasn't necessarily wrong. "Wise," he said. "Very wise." And what he was thinking was that maybe his marriage would work out after all.

At which point Charlie made everything worse by adding, "Although why you should need a mercy fuck from your wife is a completely other question."

This time Martin spent a longer time considering. Someone yowled from the interior of Temoc's, the kind of sound that is invariably the product of contact between hot grill and human epidermis. Planes landed and took off from LAX; Temoc's was right on the edge of the satellite parking lots. Martin realized that he had no strength for a confrontation. "So you know what?" he said. "Meg said they think Jason knew the guy, or at least trusted him enough to go in off-pod and empty-handed."

"When you change the subject, my friend, I know you're pissed," Charlie said.

"Sometimes when I change the subject it's just because I want to talk about something else," Martin said. He glanced at his pod, which informed him that he had no messages from known or professionally affiliated senders, and asked if he thought he could ever truly be happy without taking his wife and two lovely daughters to Disneyland. From the interior of Temoc's came an inventive stream of Spanish profanity.

He sat with Charlie watching traffic go by, and the month after Jason's death passed in much the same way. Fruitless speculations, looks askance, and difficult silences. The girls got more attuned to the pressure building between their parents. Hannah talked about moving home to Colorado, needing a clean break from Los Angeles, which seemed like an endless gleaming grave for her murdered and unavenged husband. Her parents were there. Vance planted himself in his corner beyond the pool, counting appearances of honeybees in the flowers and tracking the idiot patterns of the cleaning bot across the bottom of the pool and the lawn bot across the savagely manicured rectangle of grass that was all he allowed himself due to environmental guilt. Every day he had the bot cut the grass shorter and shorter, until by the first of July, he was using it as a putting green. Felicia came out, saw him digging a hole for a cup, and put her foot down. "Goddammit, Vance," she said, in a rare and carefully calibrated indulgence of profanity, "it's bad enough our son is dead. Don't you dare take up golf in this yard."

It was moments like that, Charlie thought, that saw the Kindreds through.

There's a flash demo in front of the Chinese Theatre memorial, I guess having something to do with SAG threatening a strike over avatar rights. Oops, no. I guess it's already over. But watching it made me a little nostalgic for when people made movies, and if their personalities were faked for mass consumption, at least there was a flesh-and-blood person in front of the camera. I'm old! I'm old! Los Angeles, city of hatred for wrinkles and long memories. City of the buff and the buffed, the polished and the peeled, city whose love of glamour is now an industry of virtual necrophilia. And it's the fault of Carl Marks as much as anyone else. I mean, those of us who have a certain number of notches on our belts remember John Wayne in some damn wine-cooler commercial in 1990 or something, but . . . nostalgia. Am I nostalgic for that? Am I nostalgic only for my own long-gone nostalgias? Have my years on this earth prepared me only for recursive nostalgia? I wonder if those are avatars actually striking in front of Mann's. I remember Mann's. I remember thinking, a long time ago, that if terrorists really wanted to fuck us up, they should blow up Yankee Stadium and Radio City Music Hall and—yes, I goddamn well did think this—the Chinese Theatre. I mean, you blow up a bank or a government building, and people wave flags and drop bombs. That works, if that's what you want. But you blow up a dream factory, man, and the dreams go up in smoke with it. And then wouldn't you know it, Mann's burns down after the '29 earthquake and what do I think? It's not the way that place should have gone out. Nature shouldn't destroy dream factories. Only people should do that.

FOURTEEN

MARTIN WAS DISINTEGRATING along with his family in the wake of Jason's murder, unable to do anything about it and unable to address his own grief because his sense of helplessness had arrested him in a kind of mechanistic emotional limbo. He got up, he went to work, he came home. Without knowing it, he'd put the last nail in the coffin of his marriage by devoting so much time to considering his own helplessness that he didn't pick up the fragile marital lifeline Teresa held out. They grew that last critical bit farther apart, each made so self-involved by long-held grievances that they could no longer recognize any gesture of reconciliation. The girls watched it happen, and themselves did nothing because their own efforts to save their parents' marriage inevitably seemed to make things worse. What they didn't know—and perhaps would not have believed had they known—was that their efforts failed because every child secretly and inarticulately understands that if she has to put herself on the line to save her parents' marriage, it is already too late. The child who begs the parents not to divorce is really just getting a head start on recriminations.

Or such was Charlie's view. Martin started haunting Yankee Doodle's, to glean whatever wisps of cop gossip might lead him closer to the truth about his brother's death. Charlie had seen crusaders before, and recognized the kind whose crusade is born from a flailing desire to avenge a loss that no revenge can numb. It was a death spiral, and after scheming for weeks, at last he hit on a way to tell Martin this. "You know," he said one night at Yankee Doodle's. "You keep this up, and you'll be divorced and still not know shit about what happened to your brother."

Martin was cresting on a brief wave of relief at being away from Teresa with a beer in his hand. "Shows what you know," he said. "If she wants a divorce, there's not a thing I can do about it, and I sure as hell couldn't know less about Jason than I do now. So you tell me: What have I got to lose?"

"You think it can't get worse?" Charlie said. "Wait and see." He knew a little about broken marriages, having participated in the breaking of three himself. The rubble was all back east, in Chicago, where his three exes, he was certain, conspired to make him miserable by deciding among themselves which one of them would be civil to him at any given time. And with five children scattered through the wreckage, two of them in college, Charlie still had to deal with the three furies far too often for his own good.

Martin knew Charlie's situation and steadfastly—if predictably—refused to see in it any parallel or relevance to his own. "Charlie," he said, "if you ever think I'm going to get as unlucky as you, here's what I want you to do. Shoot me. And if you can't shoot me, pin a murder on me so I can at least take a buyout and put the girls through college."

When he was at home, he started trying to figure ways to not be at home. The Kindreds started eating out a lot. What the hell, they had the money, and the house wasn't a good place to be. About a month after Jason's death, they had Ethiopian at an old standby with the old standby name of Blue Nile, and Martin digested everything that had happened along with a hedonistic amount of the finest in East African cuisine. By the time he pushed his plate away, he already knew he was in trouble from the injera bread alone. The girls, already disciples of Los Angeles–style body consciousness, barely ate anything, which made Martin feel even more like the stereotypically gluttonous paterfamilias. He'd pinged his parents to see if they wanted to come along, but Felicia apparently wasn't up to a night out—this information conveyed in the tone of voice Vance used to convey simmering disgust—so it was just the four of them.

Allison and Kelly chattered at each other, mostly, and Martin and Teresa didn't have much to say to each other that wouldn't rapidly lead to an argument. Even so, Martin enjoyed himself. He had done well today. He had satisfying work, and excellent children. And he was doing what he could to keep his marriage together, or perhaps a better way of saying it would be he was doing at least as much as he saw his wife doing, and that was where both of them seemed to be setting the bar. The undercurrent of tension made everyone keep things light, and eventually it took; by the time they left the restaurant, they'd genuinely had a good time. On the walk back to the car, they passed an old movie theater, one of Pasadena's dinosaurs, showing a twenty-four-hour retrospective of the films of Carl Marks. Out in front of it, a dozen or so Priceless Lifers and superannuated Maoists were keeping a candlelight vigil.

Martin had a tense moment wondering if they would recognize him, or do anything about it if they did. Next to him, he could feel Teresa tensing as the same possibility occurred to her. They walked by as if nothing was out of the ordinary, and when they'd passed the scene, Martin realized that nothing *was* out of the ordinary. This was the way things were now. People had always kept candlelight vigils, and always lionized charismatic fools. Buyouts wouldn't change that.

LATER, HE COULDN'T sleep, and couldn't find it in himself to care whether he did sleep. So he got in the car and drove, staying out of the smart lanes, south through downtown and then onto the Long Beach Freeway into Downey, where he visited his brother. Martin never went to the cemetery, but this place he did feel a compulsion to visit, this weedy back lot where his brother's life had ended. He parked in the alley at the end of Noakes Street, where the police car had brought him on the day of Jason's murder, and squeezed through a gap in the old chain-link fence. The crackle of dried weeds and distant moan of train whistles would always be part of his memories of his brother now, and he returned to this spot feeling both elegiac and hopeful. "Jason," he said, facing the spot on the fence where his brother had died. "One of these days the guy who killed you is going to take the needle, too. That's a promise."

An avatar sprang into existence at the exact spot. It was Jason, in his dress uniform. Shocked, Martin recognized the academy graduation image used to create it. He had the same photograph in the front hall of his house. "Officer Jason Kindred," the avatar said. "Killed in the line of duty, May thirteenth, 2041. I was the third Los Angeles police officer to die on duty that year. My killer is still at large. If you're here because you know something about the crime, look me in the eye and decide if you want to keep that to yourself any longer." The avatar paused, looking directly at Martin. There was something empty in its eyes that horrified him.

"Someone who will kill a cop won't hesitate to kill others," the avatar said. "Maybe that next person will be a kid, or a pregnant woman, or someone you know and love. If you know something, tell someone. It's the right thing to do."

Martin had heard of this initiative, a product of one of the LAPD's periodic bouts of self-congratulation. Apparently there were avatars like this one all over the city, animated memorials to the thin blue line. He'd always thought it was noble without being maudlin, but now, looking into his brother's face and hearing his brother say things that his brother never would have said, he barely was able to restrain himself from digging up the holocam and stomping it into junk. *Not my brother*, he thought. *You don't piggyback on his death to make everyone fucking sentimental.*

He turned and walked away, forcing himself to calm down, while the avatar behind him said, "You don't want to keep this to yourself."

AFTER THIS, sleep was even farther away. And since it was only eleven o'clock, and he was already halfway there, Martin went to Yankee Doodle's. Charlie was there, scowling at a report on a Buyout Vetting Interview as if someone else had written it. Martin read over his shoulder.

George Bryant, 37. Interviewed at Centinela State Prison, 10/29/39, awaiting transfer to Nautilus-Valley. Bryant is serving 18–30 months for assault and possession with intent. He claims to have planted a bomb under the Macy Street bridge, which collapsed in the '34 earthquake. Per state statute this makes him eligible for a buyout if convicted and sentenced to LWOP. No evidence from post-quake engineering reports (appended) indicates an explosion or sabotage. Bryant himself is unwilling or unable to produce evidence. He hints that he's got "people" working for him who will set off more bombs if he isn't charged. Interview terminated, LA County Homeland Security notified of threat.

Buyout suitability: none

Crazy index: moderate to high

"Why are you working?" Martin asked. "And what's with this crazy index? We've got a new BVI metric every day." Charlie stuck his pod in his pocket and said something unintelligible but certainly profane. Then he said, "I'm working because I am getting obsessive, and I am getting obsessive because your obsessiveness is rubbing off on me, so this is your fault. You son of a bitch."

The usual contingent of cops on the make was there, and several of them came over to shake Martin's hand and crack jokes about the post-Marks demonstration, the brutal details of which had become great fish stories for all the cops who hadn't been there but wished they had. It was maybe not a cop thing, but a human thing, to regret a missed opportunity for violence without consequence. Part of the reason they came up to him now was because of his brother, but part of it was the higher profile of buyouts. Cops were solidifying around the idea; the way Sol Briggs put it was, "What you do is fix some of the shit the courts fuck up."

Martin knew he should feel strange about being congratulated for his role in the death of a human being, but that wasn't the way to think about it. He was a part of what would become a new way of thinking about life and death, transgression and forgiveness. The money wasn't the point. Money was a way of getting people to do things that they knew were right anyway, and the more they did it, the less necessary the money would get. Maybe in a few years, people would be taking buyouts the way disgraced samurai committed seppuku. There was nobility in that, a respectful acknowledgment of an individual human's power over other humans.

"Are you shitting me?" Charlie said when Martin tried to articulate this idea. "If you ever think someone—someone sane, anyway—would walk into that room without a lot of money involved, you're not only naïve but stupid."

"Some friend you are," Martin said. "Did I tell you that the police art people did an avatar of my brother?"

Charlie rolled his eyes. "Never get police and artists together," he said.

Periodically I succumb to a shameful love of statistics and demographic prognostication. So now I will treat you to some. LA County will be eighty percent Latino by 2050. If you're forty years old today, when you were born there were three million white people and four million Latinos in LA County, with a total population of ten million. Now there are two million white people and eight-million Latinos, with a total of nearly thirteen million. So Whitey, you went from a third of LA County to a sixth, and Juan, you went from less than half to nearly two-thirds. I think there's more Asians in LA than Anglos now. Let me say that again: More Angelenos trace their roots to Guangxi than to Glasgow. How about that? And let's not even talk about the decline in the local population of Americans of African descent. There were a million of us in LA County in 2000. Now there's only seven hundred thousand. Put that together with two million of what my great-grandfather would have called ofays, and you only get less than three million out of LA County's thirteen million. So why are all the road signs still in English? Thank God, and I mean this, thank God for the persistence of cultural hegemony. Without it, I'd have to learn Spanish. Fuck, who knows? Maybe I'd have to learn Tagalog. In a hundred years, there's not gonna be a white man or a black man anywhere in Southern California. All we're gonna have is shades of brown.

FIFTEEN

THE NEXT NIGHT, Martin decided to skip Yankee Doodle's. He headed home, looking forward to seeing the girls. Maybe he'd take them out to dinner, since Teresa would almost certainly be working late. She had a startlingly masculine response to their marital problems: She worked all the time and never said a thing. Martin felt displaced by this, and a little uncertain exactly what responses were left to him since she had usurped his gender birthright. He was also a bit preoccupied by the amount of attention his pod and car systems seemed to be drawing, even this long after the Marks finalization. Between them, they'd logged 279 attempted intrusions in the hour he'd spent in Nautilus–LA County sizing up a potential client named Philip de Jonghe. Then he'd come out to find Charlie's backgrounder on de Jonghe:

Philip de Jonghe, 49, initially unavailable for interview, serving LWOP at Yucaipa. Convicted 12/4/39 of premeditated murder. Victim Angelo Suarez, 17, unknown to subject before crime. Shot three times on entrance ramp to smart lane of 710 at Rosecrans. Subject drove to police station and turned himself in. Suarez known to be working with Clanton 14 gang—other members confirm that a hit was out on him for alleged rape of cousin of Cruz Nieves from rival gang MS-13. Further investigation revealed that de Jonghe owed Nieves approximately $27,000 from gambling and drug purchases. Succeeded in interviewing subject 7/17/41, confronted him with this information. He confessed that he killed Suarez because Nieves gave him the choice of that or Nieves having some fun with de Jonghe's daughter. Clear evidence of coercion. De Jonghe's statement referred to LAPD.

Buyout suitability: none

So that had been a wasted hour. By now, Martin was a veteran of both wasted hours and attempted hacks and jacks, since this was one of the favored methods of anti-buyout advocates who wanted to get under his skin. He'd also had his car vandalized maybe a dozen times, and every so often a retro-minded provocateur sent him a threatening letter on actual paper, through the mail. Dissent takes all kinds. The number of attacks was up sharply over the past week or so, which made him wonder if organized buyout opposition was on the rise again, or if the spike in attacks was because the organized groups were falling apart and zealous individuals were taking matters into their own hands. Could be that the buyout guerrillas had come down out of the mountains again, or that everyone was experiencing a wave of intrusions and none of it had anything to do with buyouts; the longest-running (mostly) nonlethal conflict in human history was between those who wanted someone's data and those whose living depended on keeping information where it belonged.

Nautilus paid for top-of-the-line ice, but sooner or later someone was going to get through it if they kept trying two hundred times every hour. That he knew of. It was probably time to see if Charlie had any new toys that were maybe a year or two ahead of the legal stuff, he was thinking, when he got a ping that interrupted his enjoyment of Walt Dangerfield, the only self-styled underground podcaster Martin could tolerate. Dangerfield had interviewed him once, and it was one of the few times Martin left an interview without feeling like part of him had been eaten. Assuming the ping was Charlie, in the automatic way you do when you have someone on your mind and you get a ping, he answered without seeing who it was.

"Mr. Kindred?" The voice was female and business-like, neither of which was like Charlie. You could tell when someone had spent enough time on the phone to be professional in any circumstance, and this voice had that quality. "My name is Janine Shankly, and I'm calling to ask you if we could talk about a possible life-term buyout."

"Are you calling from a Nautilus facility?" Martin slipped into the smart lane on I-10 and turned the car over to John Wayne, only to discover that some prankster had overwritten the Duke with Edward G. Robinson, who informed Martin that they were successfully integrated into the smart lane, see, and would average a projected eighty-two miles per hour over the remaining fifty-three miles to Pasadena, get me? "Sorry, Ms. Shankly," Martin said, trying to reboot the daemon to its factory settings.

He put her up on the windshield, and saw a sharp-featured redhead whose suit and office surroundings said *lawyer*. "Are you often hacked by fans of old gangster movies?" she asked with what he could have sworn was a twinkle in her eye.

"There's a flaw in the car security that leaves the daemon vulnerable," Martin said. "I should tell you right off the bat that protocols dictate I be approached directly by a potential client or family member. Not everybody thinks that lawyers take the right kind of interest in buy-out cases."

"Fear not for your protocols, Mr. Kindred," she said. "I happen to be a lawyer, but I'm calling on behalf of my brother, Everett Shankly."

Martin touched a search key on his steering wheel, repeated the name, and touched the key again. Everett Shankly's arrest, court, and prison records appeared next to his sister's image on the windshield. The family resemblance was immediately apparent. "Okay," he said. "He's at Apple Valley? What did he do?" Nautilus tried to track its prisoners into different facilities based on projections about their likely behavior. Apple Valley was where the company concentrated its population of the indiscriminately violent, those who hadn't killed for a specific reason related to a specific person. Unlike cops, Nautilus risk assessors cared very much about why people did things.

"Everett is in jail for killing five employees of a Chinese restaurant. It happened almost four years ago, but he wasn't suspected for quite some time, and he was only arrested two years ago." Janine Shankly said all of this without a trace of emotion, a sure sign that she had no doubt about her brother's guilt. Looking over the record, Martin at first couldn't figure out why he hadn't already talked to Shankly. He was text-book buyout material . . . ah. There were the notations about various court-ordered competency evaluations. This was a no-fly zone for Nautilus, per the pithy dictum of Scott Krakauer that Nautilus did not do buyouts "on retards or crazy people."

Martin was inclined to put it more delicately. "Ms. Shankly—"

"Janine. Please. If I can call you Martin."

"Of course. Janine. It's very difficult to get a buyout approved in cases where the potential client has a record of psychological treatment or competency issues."

Janine was already nodding. "Right. I think you'll see when you go through Everett's records that those questions were thoroughly investigated and resolved. Everett's never been what you would call normal, but he knows right from wrong. He can feel guilt, and he's had trouble controlling his anger since we were children." Something in her face changed when she said this, spurring Martin to want to change the subject. The factory-installed daemon, defaulting to a feminine coo that always struck Martin as vaguely salacious, informed him that Allison was calling.

He thought the situation over for a minute. "I'll look through the files, Janine, but if I were you I wouldn't be optimistic. Sorry to say that, but I don't want to give you false impressions."

"I appreciate that." Janine's gaze flicked to one side, then back to Martin. "I'm piping you vid of one of Everett's interviews after his arrest. That might give you a better idea of circumstances than anything in his records."

"Okay. I'll take a look at that, too," Martin said. When he broke the connection, the first thing he did was pipe everything she'd sent him straight to Charlie, who could not believe that Martin was cluttering his bandwidth with garbage cases like Everett Shankly. He pinged Martin in a fury for forty-five minutes, then gave up for the night. The next morning, he was back at it, and he caught Martin on his way into the office. "What is this shit?" he demanded. "Have you even read the file? You go from Carl Marks to this?"

Even Charlie was feeling the aftereffects of Marks. The flood of attempted copycats was wearing on them all. Marks' profile had given buyouts a kind of gruesome cachet, to the point where that one deal, almost as much as his brother's murder, hung over everything Martin did. It put him on the periphery of the showbiz spotlight, turned him into a third-rate celebrity, and put life-term buyouts on the radar of the endlessly starving celebrity journalism industry. In less than two years, Martin had gone from an efficient midlevel employee of a risk-management firm to a public lightning rod. Journalists called him for comment on legal issues related to buyouts, and while Nautilus didn't want him answering too many questions, they did send him to seminars on dealing with the feeds. He attended with professional athletes and newly minted actors.

After that, he felt a distance between him and his colleagues—except Scott and Jocelyn. He worked for them, but in some way they saw him as equal because like them, Martin was a face of the company. They also, he assumed, saw him as competition for finite publicity bandwidth, and he stepped very carefully to avoid antagonizing them. Martin believed in saving your bullets for fights that mattered, and the last thing he wanted was to accidentally create lingering bad feeling that might compromise his ability to do his job. As long as he kept doing that, he figured, Scott and Jocelyn would keep on treating him like a prize horse, which was what he wanted. Special but not too special.

It hadn't taken Martin long to figure out that he didn't like celebrity very much. It wasn't just the media attention. He learned to handle the feedheads and underground ambush daemons that popped up trying to catch him doing something scandalous. His pod created new inbox categories for CHARACTER ASSASSINATION and JOB OFFERS, and even those headaches were manageable. But the increased presence of automated regard, the near-constant appearance of daemons trying to sell him something because someone somewhere had decided that their product would benefit from Martin's profile—that galled him. Maddened him, even. It came damn close to making him sympathetic to Carl Marks' pinko rants. He was glad when it began to fade. And all of this, Charlie reflected, collectively made one more reason why Martin should have known not to touch the Shankly deal with the proverbial ten-foot pole. Shankly was made to order for the resurgence of unwelcome celebrity. Didn't do any good to tell Martin that, though. He was pigheaded, plain and simple, especially when he thought his ideals were being challenged. Charlie's pigheadedness, in contrast, was not situational.

ANOTHER CONSEQUENCE of this celebrity, and of Jason's murder, was that Jocelyn called Martin into her office one morning and sent him

downtown for a concealed-carry permit. By the end of the day, Martin
was legally armed with a Sig Sauer SP2047—a gift from Scott, no less.
Its specs rattled around in his head—laser sight, polymer frame,
fifteen-round magazine, old-school Nitron finish, smart grips—along
with the echoes of the test shots he'd fired on the range. He locked it
in the trunk of the car, and after a reasonably civil and sporadically en-
joyable evening with Teresa and the girls, he heeded the call of Charlie and found himself at Jake's Diner. This was another of the ancient
survivors of the turn-of-the-millennium SoCal scene so beloved of
Charlie Rhodes, which usually meant that it was so steeped in nostalgia just walking through the door made you feel a hundred years old.
But Jake's beat Yankee Doodle's by virtue of being close to home and
free of cops.

"A gun," Charlie said. "Seriously? You going to go shoot Priceless
Lifers?" Charlie didn't look happy. He looked, in fact, as if he knew
something that he was going to have to tell Martin but would rather
have spent the evening at the opera with all three of his ex-wives.

"I might," Martin said. "Or I just might shoot you if you don't tell me
whatever it is that's on your mind."

"Two words, what's on my mind: Everett Shankly," Charlie said.

"Give me a break, Charlie. I just asked you to look into it."

"And I did, and I'm telling you, that you're not going to like it. Here,
this is what I have to deal with when you ask me to look into something."
He thrust his pod at Martin, who read:

Sheila del Torre, 27. Interviewed at Bodega Angeleno, where she
works, 7/16/41. Emotional. Interview conducted as a result of
her confession to the killing of LAPD detective Jason Kindred.
She gives her motive as anger over Kindred ending a long-
running affair, said to have continued for five years until shortly
before his murder. Claimed to know the location of the murder
weapon. After her shift, del Torre led interviewer to stated location. No weapon was found. She claimed to know who took it.
Interview suspended to pursue background investigation. Sheila
del Torre found to have an extensive history, under numerous
aliases, of false confessions. Has confessed to at least eleven mur-

ders since 2035, all involving uniformed victims: police officers, firefighters, EMTs. She became extremely hostile when confronted with this information, admitting previous false confessions but insisting that she was guilty of Detective Kindred's murder. Interview terminated when she could not offer any information about the circumstances of his death beyond what was widely reported at the time.

Buyout suitability: none

Crazy index: low to moderate (uniform freak)

"There are a lot of people out there who might want to do buyouts. Tell Shankly he can just serve his time like everyone else. And anyway, you can't shoot me because I bet you didn't even load your fancy new gun."

"Plus it's in the trunk of the car," Martin agreed. "Hope nobody steals the car."

"Don't even joke about that. Do you know what could happen if some larcenous dirtbag got ahold of a Sig registered to you? Martin, Jesus. Have some sense."

"Okay. What should I do with it? Keep it under the pillow to fend off my wife's advances?"

Thunderstruck, Charlie gaped at Martin. When he'd recovered his voice, he said, "You just might be okay after all." Black humor being a quality Charlie admired and Martin typically lacked, at least where his marriage was concerned. Maybe, Charlie thought, he was finally learning.

Martin, under a similar impression and perhaps a bit inordinately proud, arrived home shortly after midnight to find that Teresa had left divorce papers on the kitchen table.

EVERYONE WHO KNEW them had seen it coming. Charlie, owing to a congenital lack of tact, had recently informed Martin that he'd been a divorced guy since the day Charlie had met him. He'd regretted the remark the way he always—later—regretted these upwellings of candor, but Martin had seemed to take it to heart. After that he was marginally less gloomy, by and large, except for certain occasions when the problem of the girls got to him.

Today was such an occasion. "Times like these, Charlie," he said, "I honestly don't give a shit about the job. I'd go to work at a pizza place close to their school if that meant I'd see them more often."

"Amigo," Charlie said. It was what he always said to express support without engaging the specifics of a situation. To Martin, anyway. Charlie considered himself fortunate in his choice of friends because this tactic infallibly worked with Martin, making Charlie feel like a better friend than he in fact knew himself to be.

It was an unspoken basis of their friendship that Charlie would gruffly dismiss any display of emotion on Martin's part. Normally Martin accepted this and understood it, but today he was on the warpath trod by every man who has finally gotten the notice that he has long since known was coming but must nevertheless mortally oppose when it arrives.

So, "Amigo, what?" he said. Belligerently. "What?"

"Amigo by way of saying that I know where you are, and I'm trying to tell you that you ride this out. Like the old Jamaicans say, better mus' come." Charlie fiddled with his glass, centering it on his coaster and then making a pattern of condensation circles on the surface of the picnic table where they were eating burritos and watching the parade of humanity on Sepulveda.

"Shankly," Martin said after a while.

"No," Charlie said. "Bad enough you made me try to make you feel better. I'm not talking about Everett fucking Shankly right now." The parade of humanity continued. It seemed, from the perspectives of Martin's marital bereavement and Charlie's long-term celibacy, to include an uncommonly large percentage of attractive women. Especially for that stretch of Sepulveda. "I might, however, entertain you with a diverting story of a certain party who wished to be considered for a buyout but who was found unworthy," Charlie added.

Martin leaned his head back until his neck cracked. Right, he thought. Distract me from a work problem by telling me about your work problems. Eyes closed, feeling the sun on his face, he said, "Who?"

"You remember Hart Philipakos?"

"I didn't send you that one."

"I know you didn't. But that's where I really learned about Priceless Life. I have to tell you this."

Which was how Martin learned about a seventy-three-year-old double amputee named Hart Philipakos, who had proclaimed himself responsible for the bludgeoning of two Iranian mechanics at a body shop in Simi Valley. Yes, he said, he had killed them. The baseball bat he had used to do it was still in his garage.

And how had he managed to kill two able-bodied men fifty years younger than himself?

He leaned forward in his wheelchair and winked. "Got the drop on 'em," he said. The interviewer's skepticism curdled his temper, and he added, "You don't think I could do it? Go get the bat. I'll show you right goddamn now."

Whereupon the interviewer had thanked him for his time and filed the report from his car. Most of it was already written, courtesy of a quick bit of unauthorized database snooping that disclosed the subject's history. Philipakos had lost his legs in Nasiriyah in 2008, an event that left him with a lingering passion for violence directed against his brothers and sisters of the Islamic faith. He hadn't killed the two Iranians, but at his age and with cancer nibbling at his intestinal tract, he probably wanted to go out with everyone believing he had. The interview itself had been a formality, one paragraph in a report filled out to assuage the rage for order that characterizes law-enforcement bureaucracy. Philipakos was a by-the-book case of someone wanting a buyout because he no longer perceived his life to have any value. The paradox, that a terminal sense of poor self-worth leads people to confess to crimes so their survivors can get rich off the Golden Needle, said something about altruism, maybe, and the confusion of money for value. But at least Philipakos hadn't actually killed in the hope of a getting a buyout. Those were the bad ones, the ones who called the entire enterprise into question by turning its own utilitarian calculus against itself. How was the atonement of a clean buyout to be balanced against the victims of murder as an attempt to game the system?

LAPD, having vested in Charlie the authority to assess the truth of the situation, wouldn't even have to see Philipakos, which would save them the hassle of taking a false confession and charging him for it, and would save the taxpayer from footing the bill for the whole charade. Instead Charlie went out, charged LAPD for his time and mileage, and went on to the next thing.

This was the kind of public–private partnership most people could get behind, but it was an article of faith with Charlie that no solution was so obvious and useful that someone wouldn't complain about it. Sure enough, Priceless Life had gotten wind of Philipakos' confession and sent one of their disposable malcontents to demonstrate. She was about twenty years old, her name was Chloe Kapanen, and she was every inch the well-bred provocateur. Wellesley revolutionaries, Charlie's uncle used to call them. They railed against the injustice of the world with leisure time provided by Daddy's exploitation of Third World labor, and by the age of thirty they became hedge-fund managers. With his uncle's characterization ringing in his head, Charlie decided to learn a little about the opposition from one of its representatives, and she gave him an earful. Priceless Life was a case study in the adaptability of social discontent. In the 1980s it was an anti-abortion group, complete with the occasional clinic bombing or sniper attack on a vilified doctor; then, when Nautilus got their charter to pioneer life-term buyouts, PL was magically reborn as a vocal anti-buyout faction. Listening to Chloe, Charlie developed the theory that the abortion racket had stopped bringing in the donations like it used to, and whoever was running PL saw a chance and took it. Which is another kind of public–private partnership, if you wanted to look at it that way. Mysterious and wise were the ways of the market.

"You never told me about whatsername, Chloe," Martin said.

Charlie had celebrated the end of his story by stuffing his mouth full of burrito, and it took him a while to clear his mouth enough to talk. "I figured you'd done your own homework," he said. He got out his pod. "Here's her picture."

"Hey, I saw her way back at the first Priceless Life demo," Martin said. "At the Ordonez finalization."

Charlie swallowed the rest of his food. "Wonder who else was there," he said. "My point is that the Priceless Lifers, one of these days they're going to remember that they used to shoot doctors and shit."

"And you're telling me that Everett Shankly is going to make that happen?" Martin asked.

"I'm telling you I don't know," Charlie said. "But I tell you what, amigo, when I get pessimistic, I'm usually right."

My son brought me news today that he's planning to get skulljacked. I told him, not until you're eighteen, you don't get skulljacked, unless— and what I almost said was what my old man would have said, which was unless you want to take your skulljacked ass out and sleep on the street. But then I got suspicious, man, I thought what if that's what he's trying to get me to do? Kids are clever, man. Could be my boy doesn't give a shit about getting skulljacked, but he wants me to give him an ultimatum so he has an excuse not to come home at night. All of this, you ask me, is an argument for being childless. Ask the Bangladeshis, there's too damn many people in the world anyway. Speaking of Bangladesh, the Walt Dangerfield Square Mileage Reduction Index for Bangladesh is at twenty-five, that's twenty-five percent of that swampy hellhole now underwater, with the thirty million people who used to live there causing riots and all kinds of unpleasantness in other places. What do we do about it? If we're the Indian army, we seal the border. If we're the Burmese army, we let them come across and then shoot them because it's good practice for our soldiers. Here at home, southern Arizona is security-coded Orange, people, that means you can't go there. People with Orange clearances don't listen to Walt Dangerfield unless it's in super-secret government installations with teams of ninja assassins at the ready. But no one can find Walt Dangerfield! I orbit this culture and look down upon it from afar, beaming my brain into yours, wishing that none of you were listening.

SIXTEEN

THE NEXT MORNING, Martin tried again to get Charlie interested in the Shankly deal. He was in the midst of a lot of maybe deals and didn't have much solid. "Let's just have a look at it, Charlie," Martin said. "We've done prelims on plenty of people who might have looked iffy at the beginning. I'm going to go talk to him tomorrow. I mean, it was his sister who contacted me. You think she's up to something?"

"My sister would be. She'd frame me for Abraham Lincoln's murder if she thought she could get a dollar out of it. Here's what we do. I'll come into the office and we can look it over together."

Charlie hated coming into the office, and Martin was suspicious of his motives. "Actually I'm not planning to be in the office today," he said. "You can meet me at the courthouse if you want, though."

The courthouse was where Martin did his best work, his peerless version of the dance you do when you show up to rain blood money on someone's head. They want the money, and you know they want it, but they also want you to feel nearly suicidal with guilt that you are participating in the execution of their father/brother/lover/husband, and they want you to acknowledge that you are responsible for this event, this two-step of elliptical politeness and averted gazes. Which responsibility, if you are a buyout agent like Martin Kindred, is indeed yours, since you are usually the one who first approached a family member and said, Hey, don't you think Johnny would rather be dead than in jail?

SO THERE CHARLIE was at the courthouse, sidewalk-vendor shawarma like molten lead in his gut and Martin offering a recap of his evening with the girls away from the stony silence of home. They'd gone shopping, they'd taken a walk, stopped by Vance and Felicia's house. The girls had seemed chipper. "I think they're getting used to the idea," Martin said, talking about the divorce. Whenever he got vague, it meant he was talking about the divorce. Charlie thought he understood why, but Martin considered Charlie's understanding of his situation to be fatally deformed by Charlie's own marital past. He let Charlie have his opinions, and Charlie kept on having them because the one thing Charlie had never had during any of his divorces was a real friend to help him make sense of what was happening. He had resolved a long time ago that he wouldn't let Martin go through the same loneliness.

"Yeah, they get used to it," Charlie said. "I'm not going to lie to you, they stay pissed about it for a long time, but they get used to it. And usually they're kind of glad once they understand how bad things were."

Inside, they pounced on a conference room and got down to disagreeing over the merits of a possible buyout of Everett Shankly's sentence. "You want me to go out on this one, I'm happy to bill the hours," Charlie said, "but you should know up front that I don't think it's a live deal. You got a guy who under the laws of a couple of different states would be considered disabled, for one thing. You got how many competency hearings? Five."

"Every one of which came out fine," Martin said. "Nobody ever said Everett wasn't competent. The defense didn't ask for any of those, the DA's office did."

"This is what DAs do, is cover their asses," Charlie said.

"Right, so if they decided the case was good, where are the issues with the buyout?" Martin said.

He knew the answers, but wanted to hear how Charlie would prioritize and phrase them. In Charlie's hierarchy, the problems were: One, buyouts were a paralegal process with different rules from the courts. One-A, because of this, the perceptions about accountability in the public mind were different, and colored by deep cynicism toward privatized corrections. One-B, Everett Shankly presented as different, and was therefore going to be a poster child for all of the self-righteous nutjobs who already thought Martin Kindred was the devil. "You think you're wearing a bull's-eye now, amigo," Charlie said, "just wait until people get word about this one."

"Could be," Martin said. His internal take on the issue of Everett's difference was that all of the disability activists should be cheering. If the disabled were supposed to be treated as normal, why shouldn't Everett Shankly get to do what any other prisoner could? Perceptions aside, however, Martin needed to know if the Shankly deal was solid.

This Charlie couldn't answer. It looked good. Everett was inside for the right kind of crime—murder two—and the initial approach had come through family. The sister was a defense lawyer who had consulted on Everett's case. It was all by the numbers except for Everett himself. "And how is he different?" Martin asked. "I read all this stuff and I can't get a grip on it. He's not autistic, he's got no real mental problems. Is all of this hand-wringing just because he's a little weird?"

"Martin, amigo, what you do is you go see him yourself," Charlie said. "Then you go with your gut. If it was me, I'd never touch this one. It looks like it lines up, but something about it smells bad."

"Good thing you're not the one who has to push it through," Martin said. His pod calendar showed nothing fixed until the next morning, so he could afford the long drive out to Apple Valley. He got there in two hours, or a little more, and was again struck by the uniformity of Nautilus prison construction. Every prison, regardless of its security level, looked like a grocery-store distribution warehouse, only with guard towers and walls. On the inside, however, Apple Valley differed from the lower-security facilities. Because its population was prone to acts of random violence and other anti-social behaviors, contact among inmates was strictly controlled. There were few of the common areas standard in a place like Yucaipa or Oceanside, because it cost Nautilus too much money to perform all the mandated investigations that followed prisoner-on-prisoner violence—known in the industry, with its love of flip acronyms, as POP, pronounced just like dear old Dad. Every Apple Valley inmate wore a transponder and a collar, one to keep track of him and one to light him up with electrical current if he got violent. Martin, as a credentialed visitor, was given a switch that could trigger the collar. The halls between the security check-in and the visitation rooms were lined by tasers, remotely operated by the same security detail that took Martin's gun when he passed from the outside world.

It was all straightforward, with none of the fancy bells and whistles you'd see in a state or federal prison. There, security features had become a playground for defense contractors to deploy their newest toys that the armed forces had declined; Teresa had in fact written documentation on quite a bit of this kind of prison hardware. You had mandatory dosage of aggression inhibitors in prison water supplies, corrections officers in discarded prototype battlefield suits, drones patrolling outdoor areas . . . and still government-run prisons were filthy, violent, and controlled by gangs. Nautilus prisons, by comparison, were exactly what prisons should be: a place to put people who had proved they could not successfully exist in the outside world, and a place where those people were given chances to prove that they should be allowed to return. They were clean, efficient, and boasted crime and recidivism rates much lower than comparable government facilities . . . Apple Valley being the one exception, because here was where Nautilus concentrated its incorrigible population.

One of whom, Everett Shankly, waited for Martin in a consultation room with a live-cam view of the San Bernardino Mountains projected on one wall, and track-mounted tasers in all four ceiling corners. Shankly sat on a plastic chair at a plastic table. He was one of the few people Martin could remember meeting who looked less alive in person than in a mug shot. Although he met Martin's eye and nodded in return to Martin's greeting, a sense of vacancy permeated his gestures. "Mr. Shankly," Martin said, "I'm here because your sister Janine suggested to me that you might be interested in completing a buyout of your sentence." He toggled and time-stamped a recording via his pod. Prison cameras would also be recording the interview, but Martin was cautious enough to want independent copies of everything. The local network genie informed him that it would require access to this recording, and Martin agreed. He had an invisible routine running that would track all of the places the genie visited on his pod, and record any changes left behind. This protected him against not only intrusions from potential rogue elements at the prison but also any outside attack that used the prison network as a conduit.

"Janine said you were coming," Shankly said.

"Good," Martin said. "This is just an interview. We won't be making any decisions today, but before I can go ahead with your buyout, I need to get some information directly from you, and I need to ask you a few questions. Okay?"

It occurred to Martin that he was talking to Shankly the way he used to talk to the girls when they were younger. Something about Shankly's affect made him feel parental, or maybe just patronizing. "Okay," Shankly said. "Call me Everett. I'm not a Mister." His speech was almost without inflection, as if he were giving a bored recital of something he'd been forced to memorize.

"Technically you are," Martin said. "But I can call you Everett if it makes you more comfortable. One of the things I'm going to need from you, Everett, is a set of recorded answers to questions that I'm sure you've already been asked. It's part of the process to make sure that you know all of the consequences of your decisions, and to protect the company, Nautilus, from certain kinds of liability." The comfort of routine helped Martin shake off the impulse to talk down to Everett, but in the back of his mind he was hearing Charlie's reservations all over again.

"Okay," Everett said.

"Do you understand that this interview is happening because you or your designated representative has approached Nautilus Casualty and Property about the possibility of conducting a life-term buyout?"

Everett nodded. "We've got video, Everett, but I'm going to need verbal responses, too, okay?" Martin said.

"Okay. Yes, I understand," Everett said.

"Has anyone put any pressure on you to approach Nautilus about a buyout, or offered to do anything in return for your proposing or accepting a buyout?"

"No," Everett said.

"Do you understand that if a buyout is agreed between you, Everett Shankly, and Nautilus, that the buyout will be finalized within twenty-four hours of signing?"

"Finalized means the needle," Everett said.

"That's right," Martin said. "Can you answer yes or no?"

"Yes."

"Okay," Martin said. "That's the basic stuff. Now I'm going to ask you some more detailed questions. Assuming we finalize your buyout in the next couple of weeks, your disbursement amount will be five million, seven hundred and two thousand, eight hundred eighty-seven dollars. Have you decided on disbursement amounts?"

"That's a Fibonacci number," Everett said.

The difference in Everett's tone caught Martin off guard. All of a sudden, Everett sounded like a regular human being even though Martin had no idea what he'd just said. "A what?"

"You know. Spirals. Galaxies. Flower petals are Fibonacci numbers. The Golden Section. Didn't you take math?"

And now Everett was practically sneering at him. The files had hinted at this aspect of his personality, the deep-seated sense of superiority combined with utter absence of social affect and a possibly related propensity for violence. It was a tricky mix despite the lack of formal diagnosis. Martin felt much less certain of the deal than he had when talking about it with Charlie after lunch. "I was more of an English and history student," he said, "not that it matters."

"Zero, one, one, two, three, five, eight, thirteen, twenty-one," Everett said. "A series each number of which is the sum of the two previous. It describes natural phenomena. The only squares in the whole series, to infinity, are zero, one, and one hundred forty-four."

"Zero is a square?" Martin said. "Oh. Right. Of itself."

"You did take math," Everett said. "Janine has the addresses. I'll give her the amounts."

"We encourage clients to devote some of their disbursements to charitable organizations and valued civic institutions," Martin said. "I'll be more than happy to work with you on making those decisions."

"No," Everett said. His brief spell of animation fell away, a switch flipping inside his head as the conversation turned away from things that held his interest. "Are we done?" His voice was again so flat that only the syntax told Martin he'd asked a question.

Okay, Martin thought. So you're one of those guys whose weird social affect becomes an excuse for being an asshole. Fair enough.

"For now," he said. "After we do some preliminary reports, I'll be back to talk to you again." He pinged security to come and get him, leaving Everett alone with the virtual view and the tasers. On his way out the door, Martin heard Everett saying softly zero, one, one, two, three . . .

"I TOLD YOU," Charlie said. Martin steered into the smart lane on I-15, and John Wayne informed him that they would arrive in Pasadena at twenty after six, pilgrim, unless they were spread-eagled on a wagon wheel. Martin wondered what the drug of choice was among the programmers of aftermarket car daemons.

"I know you did," Martin said. "But ask yourself, are you gun-shy because of Shankly's personality, or because there's something wrong with the deal? How much should his personality have to do with it, anyway?"

The commercial feed scrolling under Charlie's image greeted Martin enthusiastically and asked him whether he could really afford to drive on by the giant annual sale at the Roy Rogers Museum gift shop. "Roy Rogers?" Charlie said. "Is that where Apple Valley is?" Charlie didn't get out of Los Angeles County much, and didn't want to. "Are there deer and antelope playing?" he asked.

"Ha ha," Martin said. "Listen, now I've done the prelim on Shankly, and I think the deal is still good to go ahead. It's not perfect, and we're going to take some heat. What I'll do is talk to Jocelyn about it and see what she says. Meanwhile, you go ahead and start on the vetting. I haven't looked through the court records; how does the arrest look?"

"Arrest looks good," Charlie said. "Cameras in the restaurant returned shit for images, but they at least gave a silhouette that matched Shankly physically once they went back to look. Turns out that the reason they started looking at him was that he said something about the restaurant while he was beating up his sister."

"What? Charlie, Jesus, that—"

"Wait, wait, wait. I know where you're going. But it was in a public place—the chess tables by the Santa Monica Pier. Nobody ever would have done a thing about it, except for a tourist got the whole thing on camera, with audio better than you're getting right now. Janine tried to have it suppressed, but the court ran over her, and so Everett's little domestic problem turned into a lucky break for the cold-case guys over at Robbery-Homicide."

Something about this didn't sit right with Martin. "Janine didn't tell me any of that," he said.

"It's in the file," Charlie said. "She probably figured you'd see it for yourself because she doesn't know you make me do all the grunt work."

Martin turned the situation over in his head as the car slowed on approach to Cajon Pass. After all his worry about Charlie getting cold feet, now Martin himself was having misgivings about the deal, for exactly the same reasons he would have disregarded coming from someone else. "Okay," he said. "I'm going to talk to Jocelyn first thing in the morning. You keep doing what you're doing. If there's anything irregular about the conviction or sentencing, we're not doing this, but if it's just a matter of Everett being extra sympathetic to the bleeding hearts because he comes across as kind of slow, that's not a good enough reason to turn the deal down."

"If you say so," Charlie said, leaving no doubt that he wasn't convinced.

"For now, I say so," Martin said. "But like I said, I also want to get Jocelyn's take on it."

"Okay, hasta," Charlie said, and vanished from the windshield. The car accelerated as the road flattened out over the pass, then slowed to ease down the other side. Martin rubbed his eyes and called Teresa to see if she was going to be home for dinner. She said she would try, and then there came one of those silences. *What is it you want to say?* Martin wanted to say. She was thinking the same thing, he knew it, and he also knew that neither one of them would be the first to ask, just as neither one of them would answer truthfully.

"Well, if you can get there, it would be a big help," Martin said. "I need to stop by the office on the way home and see if I can catch Jocelyn before she takes off."

"You need to talk to her face-to-face?" Teresa asked.

"Need, no," Martin said. "Strongly prefer, yes. There's a tricky case that I'd like to run by her without worrying about who else is listening in."

This was true, but also misleading, since Martin had just gotten through talking about the same case with Charlie out in the open. Part of it was that he trusted Charlie's ice more than Nautilus', and part of it was that plain stubbornness. He wanted Teresa to come home, and he wanted to be the one who worked late for a change, and behind all that he just fucking wanted her to do what he wanted. Also for a change.

"Come on, T," Martin said. "Help me out here."

"Fine. I'll see you later," she said, and then Martin was all by himself, except for Walt Dangerfield, in the traffic that gathered around him as he fell into the Inland Empire.

Today's showbiz news. Britney Spears, with her sixtieth birthday about five months away and her various progeny seeing dollar signs in the new SAG rules about living actors and avatars, has refused to license her avatar rights to her granddaughters' production company. Seems the little Spearses wanted to make a biopic to finance a plan for a line of Britney car and home daemons. Now the kiddies are suing their grammy because she won't go along with it, and millions of seventy-year-old Chinese Britfans—who, I should mention, are weirdo pedophiles, or were when they first became Chinese Britfans—will have to make do with their knockoff versions. I read somewhere that avatar rights to Abraham Lincoln were about to be licensed by the Department of Education, but the NEA's throwing a screaming fit and now Ed's having second thoughts because of all the congressional bitching. Now, what I want to see is an alt-hist, all avatars, that's a story of forbidden love between a committed statesman with a crazy, housebound wife and a music-hall floozy who gets her first lead role at an outdoor performance of La Bohème in Dealey Plaza. Other than That, How Was the Play, Mrs. Kennedy? That's my working title. I'll be reading treatments over the next few weeks, and plan to have the whole thing set up in time for Britney's grandkids to sue me, too. The only thing I'm missing is Carl Marks to put the Britvatar in his remake of Come into the Basement, Anastasia, Dear. Hot! Poor Carl Marks.

SEVENTEEN

HE WAITED until five on the dot before calling Jocelyn, who agreed that she would stick around for another forty-five minutes, but no more. As it turned out, that was just enough time for him to get to the office. She was coming out the front door as he swept into his parking spot.

"Hey, Jocelyn, this won't take long," he said, jumping out of the car and ignoring John Wayne's demand that he put his hat on.

"I sure hope not," she said. "Let's go back inside."

Her office hadn't changed since the first time Martin had seen it. The plants were a little bigger, maybe, and there were different plaques on the walls from different organizations, but Jocelyn had gotten the office how she wanted it the first time. That was how she worked, decisively, with a resolute refusal to second-guess herself. Martin tried to take lessons from this, and one of them was that when he was around Jocelyn, he got straight to the point. "I just came from Apple Valley," he said.

"Oh really?" she said. "Was there happy hunting?"

"Everett Shankly. His sister called me a couple of days ago, and I went out there to do the prelim. I've got Charlie working on it, too, but there were a couple of things in the court record that might be red flags, so I wanted a face-to-face right away. He had competency evaluations, but they all came back clean, and it was the prosecution that asked for them. They came back clean. The problem I see is that Shankly comes across as a little autistic, like he's never quite all there. His sister swears that he's fine, just a little different, but he's also apparently in the habit of punching her around once in a while, so I'm not sure how straight she's being. When I talked to him, he seemed compos, but spacey. No real emotion at all, except when he talked about Fibonacci numbers, whatever those are. Charlie thinks, and I agree, that there's going to be a ton of negative press if we move on this one. On the other hand, if we just look at the facts, it's solid. Weird, but solid. So what I wanted to ask you is this: How much heat are you and Scott willing to take?"

He stopped and replayed what he'd just said. Jocelyn liked to get everything all at once so she could make a decision all at once. Martin was usually more of an incrementalist when it came to arguments or persuasion, but he'd learned that if he stopped in the middle of pitching an idea to Jocelyn, she assumed that he was done and made a decision based on whatever he'd already said. Now she took all of thirty seconds to consider before saying, "It's your case, Martin. Scott and I picked you to be our pioneer in buyouts because we trusted your instincts and trusted that you would do the job. Second-guessing you now would be second-guessing ourselves. If you think it's a bad deal, don't do it. If you think it's a good deal that's going to have a lot of Priceless Lifers screaming their heads off, that's no reason not to do it."

That was it. Jocelyn stood and said, "Time to go home now. Let me know what you've decided."

In the elevator, Martin decided not to do the deal. On his way through the lobby, he cursed his cowardice and decided he'd do it after all. In the car, he decided that he wasn't going to decide until tomorrow morning, and that's what he told Charlie, who thought Martin was being bullied, but then Charlie was always going to think that because he didn't trust either of the Krakauers farther than he could throw a piano. Martin went home. The girls were doing homework, Teresa was in of all places the kitchen, which was good news because she was a marvelous cook. Martin threatened to help the girls with their homework, got the rolling eyes and exasperated sighs he'd been hoping for, and then went into the kitchen. "What's on the menu?" he asked.

Teresa presided over an array of onions, garlic, green peppers, and bunches of fresh herbs. "Nothing fancy. Spaghetti," she said. "Did you see that the Priceless Lifers are planning a demonstration at your office tomorrow?"

"Somebody probably told me and I just didn't look at the message," he said. "Maybe I'll take the day off."

"Allison's got a game tomorrow," Teresa said. The onions went crackling into the pan, and against his will Martin felt himself heating right up with them.

"I know, T," he said. "Also I know that you're telling me because you're planning not to go and you want to make sure I am, because that way you won't have to feel bad about it."

Very deliberately, she set down the knife and turned to face him. "Martin," Teresa said, "whether or not that's true, I don't think it speaks very well of you that your first response to what could have been a simple comment was so confrontational."

"Whether or not that's true," Martin said, "we both know that I'm not wrong. And I'll be at the game. One of us has to."

She turned her back on him and started to chop the peppers. He went into the living room, feeling simultaneously that he should apologize and that she should, and knowing that he wouldn't because she wouldn't. "How's life in algebra?" he asked Allison, who responded that it sucked and she couldn't see how anyone would ever need to know it unless they were going to be a code monkey. Moving on to Kelly, Martin learned that she was conjugating Spanish verbs. His own Spanish lexicon was thematically limited to soccer and musty Calo slang having to do with women and states of intoxication, so he sat with her and enjoyed a few minutes of *Yo creo, tu crees, el cree, nosotros creemos . . .*

"What's Spanish for 'algebra sucks'?" Allison wanted to know.

"Look it up," Martin said. He couldn't believe she didn't know already—or maybe she did, and was just trying to get into the conversation. "Algebra es mal," he said, in an exaggeratedly Anglo accent. "Muy mal!"

"Oh. My. God. Dad, don't ever do that again. Are you coming to my game tomorrow? Probably not."

"I sure am. Four o'clock, look for me pacing the sidelines. I'll be the ref's worst nightmare."

"I will kill you," his daughter promised him. "Kill. If you embarrass me."

"Fear not, hija mia," Martin said. "You know me. Now back to algebra. I'm going to help your mother in the kitchen."

Revitalized, he went into the kitchen, which was now steamy and smelling of tomatoes and oregano. "Let's be nice to each other," he said.

"You first," Teresa said without looking at him.

"Thought I just did." Martin got plates and silverware, set the table, poured beverages according to well-known preferences, looked longingly at a bottle of wine but decided against it out of trepidation that the girls would overreact and worry that he or Teresa or both were descending into alcoholism. "Any time on that demo, the Priceless Life one?"

Teresa sighed. "Martin. Can't you just let me be mad?"

"I could," Martin said, "but why? You're going to be mad until you decide to stop being mad. So why not decide to stop being mad sooner? Besides, you already served me papers. Why get mad about trivial stuff now?"

"Oh, for God's sake," Teresa said. "It's at noon. Now will you leave me alone?"

After dinner, Martin cleared the table. The girls were upstairs, and Teresa was in the bedroom doing something work-related. He brought up Shankly's file on the tabletop and started working through it, looking for something that would settle his opinion one way or another. Later, he noticed Teresa coming into the kitchen, and a moment later he registered that it was after midnight. "When I work late, at least it's at work," she observed.

"T, I have a philosophical question for you." Martin still pored over Shankly's arrest report. "How do you think it comes across if Nautilus argues that Everett Shankly's psychological, what, abnormality is an opportunity for the disabled community? If he's off kilter in one particular way, but compos mentis, then this—I mean, this is what Nautilus might say—this is a chance for an otherwise unproductive member of society to surmount his obstacles and become a fully participatory individual, with control over his own destiny."

While he talked, Teresa had gone to the sink and poured herself a glass of water. She took a long drink, set the glass on the table, and said, "I have a philosophical question for you, Martin. Are you actually serious? Do you really think that anyone with any kind of investment in this issue is going to see that as anything but pandering?"

Martin considered this. "That was two questions," he said.

"Okay, I owe you one," she said. "Now answer me."

"To the first question, yes, insofar as I think that buyouts demand a new way of thinking about agency and control," Martin said. "But no, insofar as I wouldn't actually make the argument because it's too sensitive when the question of disability comes in. Which I guess sort of answers the second question, too. No. They wouldn't. But the idea's worth considering."

"Only if you believe that a buyout is a meaningful action," Teresa said.

Martin nodded. "Yep. That's one of the presuppositions." Surprising, he thought, how here we are having a rational, invested conversation. Exactly what we couldn't do when we thought we might stay married. Or when I thought we might, anyway.

"Well, here's a presupposition," Teresa said. "You are a little clouded right now, and things make sense to you that wouldn't if you had a better grip on anything except your job."

She finished her water and went back upstairs. As he always did, Martin felt a little diminished after one of her exit lines. Pandering, clouded . . . maybe. But it's always easy to point out someone else's faults. "T," he said, knowing she wasn't there anymore, "why don't you just get it over with?"

The tabletop screen when blank white, and then the house daemon— into which Allison had downloaded the persona of some wizard character out of a book—intoned a warning. "The enemy's eye is ever upon us," the daemon said. "We must run diagnostics lest the world of men fall for ever under his shadow."

"Okay," Martin said. The diagnostic ran for ninety seconds, and the daemon came back. "In these dark times," it said, "the enemies of men prey upon the unwary, and crash the systems of those who would oppose them."

"Right," Martin said. "Who crashed us this time?"

"The enemy's forces are legion, and his armies faceless," the daemon said. "This intrusion cannot be traced, nor its origin scryed."

"Scryed?" Martin repeated.

"Discerned, discovered, identified," the daemon said.

So an attack of unknown origin. What with Teresa's mention of the Priceless Life demo tomorrow, Martin figured it didn't take a genius, or a pseudo-medieval wizard, to guess the source of the problem. "Has any data been compromised?"

"This time the threat has been repelled, at great cost," the daemon said. "But darkness looms over the future if network security does not fight to the last of its strength."

"End diagnostic," Martin said. Tomorrow he would download a more comprehensible persona. Maybe it was time for Huckleberry Finn, or at least Anne of Green Gables. He went back to the Shankly file, and by two o'clock he knew a couple of things for sure.

The first was that Everett Shankly was a bomb with a very short fuse that could be lit by just about anything. His counseling records—at least those Martin could access, since he was prohibited from viewing anything from before Everett turned eighteen—characterized him as withdrawn, ferociously intelligent, borderline autistic in his obsession with numbers, and unpredictably violent. From this retrospective view, the bloodbath in Wok to You four years before seemed like an inevitable culmination.

The second thing Martin knew was that he could stand firm on the facts of the Shankly case if he went ahead with the buyout. But with that certainty came the corollary knowledge that Everett's personality quirks, or disability, depending on your predisposition, would make any Shankly buyout such a vortex of opinion that seeing it through might well do the institution of life-term buyouts enough long-term harm in the public mind that finalizing Shankly might become a Pyrrhic victory.

Is it worth it? Martin asked himself. Do you do the right thing every time at the expense of the long-term success to which you've devoted your career? When Kelly came into the kitchen looking for toast and orange juice, Martin realized he'd fallen asleep, and dreamed of this dilemma there on his kitchen table, the center of the one aspiration that he was failing, or that was failing him.

"Morning, kiddo," he said, and made her toast. This he could do.

So what do you think about this Priceless Life group? I want to unpack the word priceless a little. The root price goes all the way back to a Latin root pretium, which means "value" or "worth." Okay so far. But then why isn't priceless the same as worthless? I mean, that's the kind of thing that makes me love language, but when you're naming a group of agitators who are apparently willing to shoot cops (if you believe it was Priceless Life who iced Officer Jason Kindred), that kind of commitment deserves a certain precision of meaning. Technically priceless should mean the same as worthless. Now, whoever named this group can't be held responsible for two thousand years of random deviations of two different words from a misty Latin origin. I'll grant you that. And I will grant you that I am probably the only person in the entire English-speaking world who cares about this. But something about it bothers me. I just can't take these people seriously. I should, yeah, I know I should. And while we're on the topic, or somewhere in the area of the topic, how did Latin somehow come to mean someone who comes from a country that speaks Spanish? Cicero is rolling over in his grave, or would be if he hadn't been metabolized by worms two thousand years ago and then cycled through the food chain maybe a hundred times. I, who probably include in my body a molecule or two that once formed part of that great orator, pronounce myself here and forevermore against the phenomenon of linguistic drift. Elect me to the Académie Française now.

EIGHTEEN

WHEN NOON was looming—really, at about ten in the morning, with no criminals in Greater Los Angeles pinging him in a hurry to take the Golden Needle, Martin allowed himself to use the Priceless Life demonstration as an excuse to vacate the office. He fled to do one of the few things that gave him pure pleasure, rather than the kind of pleasurable satisfaction that comes from meeting an obligation. He went hiking, in a little oasis called Temescal Canyon that had somehow held out against everything the LA basin could throw at it. The trail was shady and cool, climbing over a ridge and then dropping down to a pool at the base of a feathery (though seasonal) waterfall right out of a deodorant commercial. The thing Martin liked best about Temescal was that it was designated Wi-Free, which meant he could get away. Nobody would ping him or stop him on the street for routine vilification, no autorou tines would notice him walking by and insinuate that he probably couldn't live another minute without a particular product or service suggested by his public consumer profile. There was the smell of chaparral, the white noise of the waterfall, the smells of sun-warmed stone and things growing. In Temescal Canyon, everything made sense to Martin, partaking of a logic that needed no justification. When he was here, at the base of the waterfall, Martin could glimpse the possibility of a life free of rationalization. He would never live such a life, had in fact chosen otherwise, but proximity to the ideal made him understand himself a little better. In a natural place, he could conceive of his life as an aspiration toward the natural. If there was to be civilization and therefore laws, laws and therefore punishment, let that punishment be not just humane but human. Let the man who has transgressed take hold of his transgression and turn it into a benefit.

He watched the skips and streaks of stray droplets on the surface of the pool, letting his mind wander. There was someone else near the pool, a young guy standing closer to the waterfall, but Martin neither wanted company nor resented the intrusion. He was capable of being alone even with someone else around. After they'd both been there for a silent ten minutes or so, the guy said, "So. Martin."

No, Martin thought. Not here. Anywhere else I will be the representative, the lightning rod, the guy wearing the bull's-eye. But not here.

He looked up and said, "No."

"Relax," the guy said. "I just wanted to talk for a minute without a whole bunch of other ears listening in."

Martin didn't come any closer to him. "Talk about what?"

"Well, Everett Shankly, of course," the guy said, and Martin felt a cold knot form under his diaphragm. "There's a little more to the whole thing than you know so far."

"Two things," Martin said. "One, I don't talk about ongoing deals. And two, I don't talk about anything out here. Leave me alone."

"Okay," the guy said. "Everybody knows you're a white knight. But when you get back to your car, there's going to be a file on your pod. Don't bother trying to find out where it came from. If you want to know more, stop back here tomorrow, same time." He started back up the trail, stopping a few yards away. "My name's Curt," he said. "We'll talk again."

Martin's car registered no security breaches, and only the expected number of attempts. But just as Curt, whoever he was, had promised, there was a file on Martin's pod—which also said nothing out of the ordinary had happened. He approached the file with extreme caution, probing it with every diagnostic and security routine he had. It appeared to be a simple image-and-text file, with no trace of origin. He isolated it behind a defensive wall that would delete it if it started to run any code, and when he'd satisfied himself that he'd done everything he could to make sure that it wasn't going to damage his pod or the car systems, he decided to go ahead and open it. Then he decided not to. This was the kind of thing Charlie was good at.

As soon as he cleared the Wi-Free zone around Temescal, Martin was besieged by pings. Eleven of them were from Charlie, but then Charlie didn't answer when Martin got back to him, and sitting in traffic on the Pasadena Freeway, the crumbling wreck of Dodger Stadium on his left and hope dwindling that he would get back to Pasadena in time for Allison's game, Martin decided to go ahead and look at whatever the mysterious Curt had left him. His reasoning went something along the lines of: Why would Curt have come to a Wi-Free zone to give him a poisoned file? Running the question back and forth, he decided that his perspective was sound, and he opened it.

It's one thing to be burdened with an awful secret, he would tell Charlie later. Everybody's got awful secrets. But this . . .

The file, in an ancient and arcane format symptomatic of the LAPD's innate aversion to technological progress, was an internal police document, or more properly a collection of documents. The first, a version of which Martin had seen previously, was dated six weeks after the murder of Jason Kindred. It contained a speculative reconstruction of the events leading up to Jason's shooting, a mass of possibly related information, and a final notation that the case was cooling. All of this Martin had seen before. But this version of the report had new material appended. Six weeks after Jason's murder, one of the investigating detectives had added a single page. It consisted of a link to the LAPD's original report on the murder of five people in a Chinese restaurant, and a notation that the suspect in that case—one Everett Shankly—was known to have been in the area of the Delux RentAll near the time Officer Jason Kindred received his fatal wounds.

Flicking past that, Martin came to an embedded video. Porting it to the windshield, he played it while his car crept through the interchange at the Golden State. Construction crews were busy here laying Smar-Trax on all the ramps and merging lanes, which one of these days would improve the traffic but today was congesting it beyond all belief. By the time Martin cleared the interchange, it was three twenty-six. He pegged the odds of making Allison's game on time as a little better than even. The video was amateur quality, with the kind of exaggerated contrasts that betrayed the application of forensic sharpening. A long shot of the ocean backed up and panned the length of the Santa Monica Pier.

Snatches of music and conversation floated from the dashboard speakers, some of the voices growing closer and receding as people walked by the shooter. The thump of a volleyball and the growl of skateboard wheels added to the soundscape. Martin toggled the facial recognition software Kelly had installed in the car to make sure they never drove by one of her friends without her knowing it. The program would tag anyone in the frame whose face had ever been on any screen belonging to the Kindred family. Amazing, Martin thought in passing, how the pressures of middle school socialization create investigative tools. His car eased forward as traffic began to unjam. The video took in the pier for a while longer, then reversed to sweep over the beach, lingering on a bathing suit here and there before continuing the pan. The shot came to rest on the grandiosely named International Chess Park, a cluster of chess tables not far from the base of the pier. Martin counted eleven people sitting at the tables, four of whom were playing chess. The others . . .

The name Janine Shankly appeared over a woman sitting at the far corner of the park. A man leaned over her. "Subject acquired," said a voice that was too loud and too close to be anyone but the shooter. "Talking to female believed to be his sister."

Wait, Martin thought. Charlie said a tourist caught Shankly on camera, and Janine had tried to have it suppressed. But this was surveillance video.

Zooming slowly in on Janine, the camera caught Everett. He was leaning over her, his posture threatening, stabbing a finger at her. "Where's the sound there?" complained the shooter. "Fuck, would you—"

The playback stopped, on a medium two-shot of Everett and Janine Shankly. She looked terrified, and something else. Young. The set of her face was like Kelly's, Martin thought, when she was a little younger, coming out of a nightmare. A terrified child is abject in a way that an adult can't be. A moment of his first conversation with Janine recurred in Martin's mind, and he thought that he'd seen some trace of that child-like terror when she was talking to him. But where was the rest? There must be more, if what Charlie had said about the audio of Shankly mentioning the restaurant was true.

The final frame of the video was tagged with a tiny icon. Martin touched it, and a note appeared: *Meg—this is the guy. See me about gun. SB.*

Sol Briggs. Meg Twohy. The pair of detectives given the lead on Jason's murder.

Martin worked it out. Charlie had told him that a tourist had caught Shankly because in the version of the video that existed in the Shankly file, the audio cues that it was a stakeout had been removed. Martin would have bet his car on it. But Jason . . . if Briggs and Twohy thought Shankly had killed Jason, why were they not pursuing . . .

"Ohh," Martin said softly, as a new understanding cascaded into place. The message wasn't from Curt Whatsisname, whoever he was. It was from someone in the LAPD. Someone who had heard about the Shankly buyout, knew it was going to be a tricky one, and figured that Martin might need a little something to stiffen his spine. Or was it the other way around? Was if from Curt, who had somehow gotten it and was letting Martin know that LAPD wasn't looking into Jason's case the way they usually chased cop shootings? Were they going to be content to let Martin's buyout do their work for them?

Martin pinged Charlie. No answer. "Charlie," he said to Charlie's pod, "meet me at Allison's game. Kickoff four o'clock, same place as last time."

He sat in traffic, feeling determination like a force, a physical expansion in his spine and the bones of his legs. It was all he could do not to get out of the car and start walking, just to be doing something, to be making progress. *This is the guy.* What did they not have? Why hadn't they gone after Shankly for Jason's murder? Work it out, Martin told himself. Break it down. Already he wished he hadn't pinged Charlie because he knew what Charlie would say about the ethical problems of forcing through a buyout based on information that wasn't available to the public. So Martin would not tell him.

HE GOT TO the field at Brookside Park just as the teams were getting their last instructions from coaches, as well as parents who wished they were coaches. As the teams spread out across the field before kickoff, Martin watched his daughter lope to the center circle and hop in place, burning off nervous pregame energy. Allison was rangy, fast for her age, a bit short on ball skills but with a good sense of the game. She scored goals because she got behind defenses and put herself in good positions. Classic goal-poacher, the kind of player that everyone complained about— *doesn't track back on defense, can't beat people one-on-one*—but also wanted on their team because after ninety minutes, there she was on the score sheet. Martin had been trying for years to get her to think about defense, pressure the ball in the opponent's defensive third, but recently he'd come to believe that athletic disposition was just another facet of personality. It was innate, or formed by three years of age, perhaps. Either way, impossible to change at twelve.

The game was still scoreless twenty or so minutes in when Charlie showed up. "I don't know if this is supposed to make me feel youthful or what," he said. "An hour ago I was talking to a guy, you sent him to me, Victor Yeung? I had to bring an interpreter. Jocelyn's going to give me a hard time about the fee. And Victor Yeung, it turns out, did probably kill somebody but he's also got some kind of galloping blood disease that made me scared to death to be in the same time zone with him. No way that one's going to clear."

For a while Martin watched the game. Allison found a seam between two defenders and put a bullet header on goal off a corner kick, but the opposing keeper made a fine save. "Charlie," Martin said. "Remember what you said about Priceless Life and shooting doctors?"

"Yep."

"I don't care," Martin said.

Charlie understood then that Martin was lying to him about something, and that the lie was from that moment forward going to be part of the price of their friendship. He also understood that as long as the Shankly case was open, Martin was going to be unable to care about Victor Yeung or any other potential client. So he waited to see if Martin was going to shed any more light on the situation, and while he waited he considered the last time he had stood along the sideline of a soccer field. It had been this field. Allison was playing, and Teresa was there. For most of the game she cheered apart from Martin and Charlie, but by coincidence she happened to be nearby when Allison scored a goal. For the benefit of all assembled, Martin and Teresa had exchanged a hearty and utterly false high five.

Or maybe not so false. Charlie remembered doing things like that, and knowing he was doing them, and he remembered that it made him feel a little better, the way a white lie comforted a child. Because that's what it was, white lies to comfort a child; even though you know the child sees through it, you pantomime this caring anyway, because it's important to you to do it and in the end it's important to the child that you care enough to lie about precious things. Watching Martin, with a memory at hand of Martin and Teresa, Charlie reconfirmed one of his fundamental beliefs: Anyone who claimed that the truth is always better than a lie . . . those people were zealots, or crazy. People needed to be lied to. They could not get through the day without our necessary lies, Charlie thought. Not because we don't want or need the truth, but because the fact that people are willing to lie to us to spare our feelings means that someone cares. Someone, somewhere, in some way, cares.

High five.

I read today that there have been flare-ups in the water conflict. I mean shooting kind of flare-ups, especially around Phoenix and Las Vegas. You know, if I was a separatist, one of the things that I would make sure of before I separated was that I had enough in the way of resources to support me in the event my separation was successful. Put another way: What the fuck are you thinking, fighting a guerrilla war to stay in the desert? Only in America, man. Only here would we have a sense of entitlement massive enough to make us willing to die for the right to stay in the kind of place that people everywhere else in the world would die to get out of. Wonder if we should call this a civil war. Is it big enough? Is it a threat to the Republic? Is there even a Republic anymore? In my darker moments—and I refer not to my melanin but my serotonin—I believe that the Republic died at the hands of the virtual society. Which of course I have turned to my advantage by becoming Walt Dangerfield, but I'm still grieving. Do I sound sad to you? In another time, I might have been a columnist for the august New York Times, or a respected scholarly journal. But I was born too late, I was born after we'd all been tangled in what we used to call the World Wide Web. As soon as that happened, anyone could say anything and everyone might listen. Nothing was better than anything else. The hierarchies that we depended on to organize our intake of information disintegrated. I'm not sure how I should feel about this. I like doing what I do, and you like me doing what I do, but when there are nutcases fighting an urban insurgency in the remains of a city where I once went to play blackjack, it feels like something ought to be different than it is.

NINETEEN

THE WORD that kept coming to mind when Charlie thought about Martin was *stony*. Something stony had entered into Martin. He didn't spend much time thinking about it, because Charlie Rhodes was defined in large part by his ability not to think about things he didn't want to think about, but when he did, he assumed that the combined stresses of a failing marriage and grieving parents explained the situation. That, and Martin's own lingering grief over his brother's death. Charlie's life had been remarkably free of mourning, so he was unfamiliar with its contours, especially as they were viewed from the outside. Bored on motel stakeouts, he invented and elaborated on various causes that might have provoked the effects he saw in Martin. Any of them could have been true. Martin gave him nothing, so Charlie did what he always did after he'd taken a question as far as the available information would allow. He said the hell with it and went about his own business until such time as new information chose to present itself.

Later he would think that he'd just been missing all of the signals, but at the time he just knew that something was eating Martin, and as a result Martin was being a shithead when it came to their working interactions. Charlie was working five different BVIs for Martin, and three of them he knew to be the rankest bullshit. Normally that didn't bother him, since his rate and expenses didn't depend on the success of an individual deal. He had the feeling that the opposite was true, that his value to Nautilus depended on him turning down a certain number of deals so Scott could go to nervous regulators and congressmen with proof that the company was ethical and self-policing in its generation of market opportunities. Martin, who worked on commission, naturally had a different angle on the question, but he was the straightest arrow Charlie had ever known—which made it all the more surprising when Martin started to give Charlie unmistakable hints that if ever there were corners to be cut, the Shankly deal was the place to cut them.

Item: Martin had previously walked away from potential clients who had undergone competency hearings and evaluations, whatever the result. Not so in Shankly's case.

Item: Martin routinely avoided deals proposed by family members who had been victims of the potential client's propensity for violence. In Shankly's case, the originator was the sister, who on more than one occasion had taken lumps from her brother.

Item: Martin mistrusted cases in which the potential client had pled guilty. His optimal case was the perfunctory not-guilty plea followed by the perfunctory performance by the public defender—à la Christopher Bragdon. Everett Shankly had pled right away, with no effort even to bargain.

This last fact could have been the result of Shankly's worry that if he didn't plead, the state would go for capital murder, and to tie up that last niggling loose end, Charlie sweated his way downtown on the train and hung around the courthouse waiting for the assistant district attorney who had filed all of the reports on Shankly's prosecution. Her name was Consuela Salcido, and she was at the moment engaged in the weekly penance she called Domestic Tuesday. Charlie had long ago decided that if he was ever going to lay his heart on the line for a woman again, she would be the one. Her physique was the feminine version of his, and her sense of humor if anything more masculine. For those two qualities alone he would have married her. The fact that she batted for the other team gave her an aura of irresistible impossibility, which for Charlie sealed the deal, because he was in his own way a knight, and she the object of his courtly passion that would be destroyed if it were ever realized.

"Connie," he said as she escaped from 7B, whence the morning's wifebeaters were being led back to the county bus.

"If it isn't Charlie Rhodes," she said, with a sparkle in her eye. "You testifying in Sixteen?" Which was where certain especially contentious divorce cases tended to land.

"I am here to woo you and make you love me forever," Charlie said, for only by turning his true feelings into self-mockery could he disguise them.

"No shit," Connie said. "Buy me falafel and I'm yours."

Over falafel at Sammy's Halal, they got the catching up out of the way, and Charlie had a chance to renew his admiration for her. She made him quixotic. "Connie," he said after they were both reduced to picking at the remains of their tabbouleh. "Run away with me."

"Only if you promise to keep your dick away from me."

"Then at least tell me something that I'm probably not supposed to know about an old case."

"I knew it," she said. "You smooth talker. What?"

"Everett Shankly."

"What about him?"

"He walked into his first hearing, pled guilty, and never saw the inside of a courtroom after that."

"True," Connie said. "He did do that."

"You threaten to go capital on him?"

Connie scraped baba ghanouj, tabbouleh, and bits of falafel crust into a single heap, which she stuffed into her mouth with the aid of the last slice of pita. "Nope," she said around the mouthful. "We figured a capital case wouldn't go because of his, what is it, some kind of autism. So we were going to go ahead with the standard LWOP, and then he saved us the trouble." She swallowed. "Don't tell me you're vetting him for a buyout."

"Following orders," Charlie said.

"Not Martin's usual type," Connie said, picking parsley from her teeth.

"That's what I thought, too," Charlie said.

Connie glanced at her pod, rolled her eyes, spoke the name of God. "Gotta go. Have you met Everett Shankly?"

"Have not had the privilege," Charlie said.

"You should," Connie said. "Then you should talk some sense into Martin."

Both of those actions seemed good to Charlie, so he carried them out in order. First he went out to Apple Valley, where he was conducted to the same interview room in which Martin had first met Shankly.

Charlie had met more than his share of murderers, and he knew better than to think that they were all menacing, but Shankly was almost comically unsuited to his crime. This guy, Charlie thought, has killed five people. But you look at him, and you'd think he walked with his eyes down to slalom around ants on the sidewalk.

"Everett," he said, and stuck out his hand. "Charlie Rhodes. I'm doing the paperwork on your buyout."

"I thought Martin was doing that," Everett said. He took no notice of Charlie's hand.

"Martin's got me to make sure everything gets done right," Charlie said. He put his hand back in his pocket, and took a minute to get his thoughts in order. The sight of Shankly shook him somehow. A weirdness emanated from the guy, the way Charlie imagined saints or madmen or geniuses had an aura that the lizard hindbrain could detect but the conscious mind never make sense of. "Hey, Everett," he said. "What the hell do you want a buyout for anyway?"

"To take care of the people I hurt," Everett said.

"I say bullshit," Charlie said. "If you were that worried about the people you hurt, you wouldn't have gone as long as you did without confessing. And then you get popped because you're beating up your sister at Chess Park? Jesus. Maybe you did want to get caught, but I can't believe you give a shit about the people you killed or the people they left behind. What I can believe is that you've got something else on your mind. Something that nobody knows about, and that you want to get rid of by taking a buyout. Am I warm?"

Everett was silent for a long time. "Can I call you Charlie?" he asked eventually.

"Call me whatever you want. Just don't lie to me, because I'll know. I was a cop for a long time, kid, and we get so we can smell lies."

A thin smile crept onto Everett's face, then faded away as he spoke. "I don't lie," he said. "I have problems with my temper. I've hurt animals before. I hit my sister sometimes."

"That what you feel guilty about? Your sister?" Bingo, Charlie was thinking. If there's something else there, the buyout goes down the drain. No way it's good if the originator turns out to be on the wrong end of a sex crime.

"Guilty," Shankly said, and his voice emptied out. "As charged. Am I supposed to?"

Three different threads to pick up. Charlie chose one and ran with it. "Depends on what you did," he said. "I never had a sister, but if I had, I'd've wanted to hit her, too, probably. But there's other stuff, you know? Is that what you're feeling guilty about, Everett?"

"No," Shankly whispered. "Guilty but no. Five seven oh two eight eight seven makes me not guilty anymore."

Charlie repeated the numbers in his head, memorizing them. Five seven oh two eight eight seven. Would have been a phone number back in the Stone Age before thirteen-digit dialing.

Then he caught up. That was Shankly's DB amount. For the first time in his life Charlie experienced a feeling of physical nausea brought on by an emotional reaction. Everett Shankly actually believed that he was going to be absolved by taking the Golden Needle. In California, 2041, human civilization had finally come back around to believing you could buy your way into heaven.

Way to go, Martin, he thought. Way to go, champ. You've got them believing your shtick about atonement. Jocelyn was right. You're going to go places, kid.

He got out of Apple Valley before he said something to Shankly that all of them would regret. The drive back cooled him off a little, and by the time Charlie met Martin at Temoc's to compare notes, he thought he was ready for a simple dispassionate effort to talk Martin out of pursuing the deal. Then, the minute Charlie got there, Martin leaned forward—deal-closing posture, he'd called it once—and told him that Nautilus had given the green light for the Shankly buyout. "It's good," Martin added, punching the word. "It's a good deal."

Charlie ate for a while so he would have an excuse not to talk. Martin was looking at him the whole time. When he ran out of food, he still hadn't decided what to say, so he fell back on the Charlie Rhodes method of opening his mouth to see what came out.

"Martin," he said once his mouth was open, "if you do this, you are the dumbest fucking guy I ever met in my life."

"No, if I quit on it I'm the worst coward you ever met. It's a solid deal, Charlie. People are going to think it's ugly, but if you go by the book, it plays." Martin sighed. "And who knows? Maybe this will give the Priceless Lifers the one they can ride to the Supreme Court so we can fucking shut them up once and for all."

"Did I just hear you say that you think this deal ought to go forward because it would be a good test case in court?"

"No. Not because. I think the deal should go forward on its own merits, and I also think it would be a good test case. If we're going to do buyouts, Charlie, we should know why. We should know what it means, and we should be absolutely clear about how it's going to happen."

Once again, Charlie narrated to himself, our hero navigates perilously close to the shores of sanctimony. "I'll tell you about merits," he said. "I think he was fucking her. He's carrying some serious guilt about her, and I'm telling you, I think that's it."

"Who? Janine?" The disbelief on Martin's face would have been charming if it hadn't betrayed the kind of naïveté that Charlie had made it his life's work to stamp out.

"Yeah, Janine. The minute I brought her up, he got all squirrelly. If you'd been there, you'd have seen it, too."

"And you, the human lie detector, did not reach a conclusion?"

"My conclusion was that he wasn't consciously lying, but there was definitely something there that he wasn't going to say unless you forced him into it. I'll pipe you the audio. And you know, what the fuck. I think this deal should have been killed at birth, but if you're not going to listen to me then it doesn't make any difference if he was fucking his sister or not." Charlie counted three planes before another word passed between the two of them. "I'll repeat myself. If you do this. Dumbest fucking guy."

But Charlie knew he was going to, not because he was dumb but because Martin Kindred believed, and could not shy away from a test of his belief. In this he was wrong, but honestly wrong. He had no way to know the truth, and so acted on the truth he had available to him.

WALKING BACK to his office, Charlie was thinking about the character of his friend, and of friendship, and of himself. "I may be dumb," Martin had answered him half an hour before, "but I'm not going to be pusillanimous."

"Pusillanimous?" Charlie had said. "Pusillanimous?" Then they'd both had a laugh and changed the subject because to continue it would have been to run the risk of damaging their friendship, which was dear to them both.

"Hey, guess what," Martin said. "Teresa says she wants me to move out."

"Ah, fuck," Charlie said. "Then you'd better do it. Much as I hate to advise you to give in, amigo, this is one it's better to walk away from."

"Yeah. I know."

"Get a place with bedrooms for the girls, put your own stuff in it. Don't fight the ones you know you're going to lose anyway, Martin. Not unless you have to."

Charlie thumbed the pad next to his office door and stood for a moment before the open doorway considering the fact that at times, he was pusillanimous. Not least during moments such as the one that had just passed, when he should have come right out and said what he was feeling instead of taking the opportunity to say something veiled and obscure. *There's going to be a shitstorm,* he should have said. *You are going to be the most hated guy in Los Angeles. Imagine what the Priceless Lifers will do with Everett fucking Shankly. You think Marks got them worked up? That was just celebrity worship. Everett Shankly is going to come across as a sacrificial lamb. It's going to be like nothing you've ever seen.* Some of it he'd said before, and some of it would have been new, but he should have said all of it.

And he should have said—should have screamed if that's what it took—that Nautilus would throw Martin away like a used rubber if the Shankly buyout went south. Martin knew this, or said he did, but Charlie didn't believe him, because if Martin knew this and was going ahead with the deal anyway, then he was indeed the dumbest fucking guy Charlie had ever met. Inside his office, Charlie considered who else might be in contention for that title.

AROUND THIS SAME TIME, Martin was considering where he was going to sleep that night. He settled on a decent hotel in Pasadena, not far from the house. He'd have to get another place to live, but not until after the Shankly deal was done. The room was done in an American Hotel Moderne so aggressively nondescript that it seemed the designers' singular goal had been to maximize the room's resemblance to some Platonic ideal of the Chain Hotel. It was a non-place for a guy who was suddenly becoming a non-version of what he'd been before, was Charlie's take on it when Martin invited him over for a beer and a look at a little something he'd received via a friendly podjack an hour or so before.

"I have to tell you, Charlie, the timing of this has me thinking," Martin said. "I mean, T suggests I find other accommodations, I do it, and an hour later I get podjacked through hotel security, Nautilus security, and whatever other ice you put on there?"

"Leave me out of it," said Charlie. "I didn't touch your pod."

"Still, the timing."

They drank beer. "So, you here for a while?" Charlie asked.

"Until I find a place. By which I mean until I decide to spend the time on looking for a place. I should do it soon so the girls can get used to it. In fact," Martin went on, brightening a little, "I should bring them along. What do you think?"

"Sure," shrugged Charlie, who could not have cared less whether Martin took his daughters apartment-hunting. But since he had been pusillanimous earlier in the day, his penance was to listen to Martin ruminate about his divorce. "So you got jacked," he said, in the hope of getting things moving, and it worked.

"Yep," Martin said. "Here it is."

The video was decent quality, nothing you'd see on a net feed but better than your average handheld. The man Martin knew as Curt was caught in midsentence as it began, pacing back and forth in front of a group of maybe two dozen people scattered on broken-down couches or sitting on the floor. The room looked like a basement, maybe an abandoned storefront of some kind. Metal shelving lined the walls, cluttered with cardboard boxes, what looked like old signs advertising this or that percentage off retail . . . immediately Martin ran through the closed retail complexes he could think of. There were too many. If it mattered where this was happening, he'd need to narrow things down.

"What happened," Curt was saying as the video began, "was that about thirty years ago, one of your crusader judges appointed by Jerry fucking Brown or someone capped California's prison population at a hundred fifty thousand, when the system had close to two hundred thousand inmates. So the state took a look at what it could do, and decided two things. One, it would let go as many prisoners as it could. So within a year, twenty thousand criminals hit the streets. No training, no job prospects, no nothing. The other thing the state did was decide that if they had too many prisoners, they'd keep the easy ones and get rid of the hard cases. So they signed up every private prison company they could find, and contracted with them to take all of the state's max and supermax population. Presto, another forty thousand inmates disappeared from the state's rolls. Now, the private companies knew that they had the state over a barrel, so they held the state up for a whole lot of money— we've got to build all these new beds, they cost more than a hundred k per max bed, and look at all of the ways we're going to get screwed on land because landowners know we need the space right now, et cetera. Ridiculous sob story, but the state went along with it because it had to.

"Meanwhile, the streets are full of mentally ill ex-cons with drug problems, no skills, and gang affiliations. Guess how many of them end up back in, only for violent crimes this time? So LWOPs tick up, the private prison companies get fatter, but as they get fatter they start to realize that they've got overcrowding problems of their own. That's when they start to go to work in Sacramento, and they get people in Sacramento to go to work in Washington."

Curt stopped to tick off a set of figures on his fingers. "Seventy percent of prison admissions in any given year are recidivists. Sixty percent of those are in for violent crimes. Three percent go back in to serve life without parole. In California, that's six thousand new potential clients for Nautilus and Martin Kindred every year. You want to know why people are looking the other way while prisoners get ground up and turned into money? That right there is why."

He made a gesture with his left hand, some kind of cue, and an image appeared on the wall behind him: Scott Krakauer, in a thicket of reporters. Martin recognized the scene. He'd been standing just off the frame watching Scott massage perceptions of what the buyout charter was all about. "It's a market-driven solution to a problem that has always been artificially and arbitrarily segregated from the market," Scott said.

Martin was mouthing the words along with him, and when the shot froze, Martin could hear the rest of what Scott had said that day. *The courts can punish, but they cannot innovate. They can institutionalize penance, but they cannot compel atonement. And for those of you who say that the life-term buyout does not value human life, I have a question: How does imprisonment value human life? How is a man or woman who sits in a concrete-and-steel box, prevented from any interaction with the outside world except censored letters — how is that life valued? Our program invests those people in their lives again, and does it in the framework of atonement.*

Curt wasn't done yet. "Markets," he repeated sarcastically. "Here's your market. Prison populations have been aging for forty years because of longer sentencing guidelines since the 1990s. Older inmates mean higher per-inmate costs. Those costs amortize back over younger admissions and increase overall costs and the reserve amount companies have to keep against each prisoner. So even if a guy goes in at nineteen and takes a buyout at twenty-two, his projected cost includes all of the costs learned from the company's previous experience with long-term incarceration. In short, Nautilus gets to pretend that they're killing a twenty-two-year-old because he's already eighty-five in some notional actuarial way.

"The older version of a prisoner is used to compel the younger version to die so that older version will never exist," Curt said. "You all know my history, so maybe this is a hobbyhorse of mine, but you tell me: How is that different than having an abortion because you're worried about how you're going to handle a teenager?"

Rustling in the room. "Okay," Curt said. "I'm not going to push that. But whatever rationale you find, you have to see that this is the purest fucking savagery. And get this: Nautilus is trying to get the buyout charter expanded to include Third Strikers serving twenty-five to life."

Which was the first Martin had heard of this. He froze the video with Curt's face centered and clear. "Who is this guy?" he asked. "Can you do your thing?"

Charlie transferred the still to his pod, did a quick capture of Curt's face, and processed it through a couple of marginally legal investigative databases he knew about. "Okay, the name we get is Curtis Laskowski.

Born October 1995." Which made him almost forty-six, a lot older than Martin would have figured. "The crazy makes a guy youthful," Charlie said. "And he's got a lot of crazy. Did a stretch for criminal threatening. No, two, in '22 and '28. Both times, looks like they wanted to get him for planting a bomb at women's health clinics, but couldn't make it stick. Acquitted of terrorism charges." After his last prison term Laskowski had drifted away from right-to-life groups. In 2040 he was recorded at a Priceless Life rally that ended up in tear gas and batons. Martin remembered that one. It was about six months into the program, the first demo that had gotten interesting really. The client's name had been Angel Jaramillo.

"Found a new home," he commented. A sick, watery feeling was spreading through his gut. Curt Laskowski had fed him a doctored file, trying to set him up. I'll kill him, Martin thought. But what do I do about the Shankly case now? I can't tell Charlie about this, I can't just drop it now . . . what's the alternative?

"Yeah, there's no cachet to the abortion stuff anymore." Charlie kept scrolling. "There's an FBI report here that says the Priceless Lifers are having a doctrinal problem, especially since Marks. A lot of new people have come in, from a lot of different other malcontent groups, and some of them think Priceless Life has been passive. They stand up at meetings and give some kind of Trotskyist permanent-revolution line, which always ends up with somebody saying they need to light a fuse and get away."

"So why doesn't DHS break them up?" It seemed obvious to Martin that as soon as anyone started talking about bombs, Homeland Security would be on them like the proverbial white on rice. It was equally obvious to Charlie that Homeland Security, being an entrenched bureaucracy, would steer far clear of the controversy surrounding buyouts. If they came in and broke up anti-buyout groups, the implication would be that the feds were supportive of the buyout charter. No way did DHS want that kind of political entanglement. They'd learned the lessons of their early years.

Priceless Life tended to meet by flash. There were a few identifiable officers, but no scheduled group meetings. No discernible pattern emerged in the schedule or location of their previous meetings. "I need to find Laskowski," Martin said.

"Then you need someone who can tap all of the muni security cams," Charlie said. "And that guy isn't me."

"Is that guy someone you know?"

"You asking me to look?"

Martin sighed. "I was hoping you'd offer without me having to ask."

"So you want to do a buyout that I personally think is real, real borderline. And to make sure that you can bring this deal off without a hitch, you want me to possibly violate some kind of law beyond the kinds of laws I normally violate. And this is in the service of putting you in touch with other people who are or will be against the Shankly deal."

"That's about the size of it," Martin said.

"Then I have two questions, amigo. One is why don't you just call this Chloe whatsername and ask her what you want to ask her, and two is what the fuck is your obsession with Curt Laskowski?"

Oh, Charlie, Martin thought. Because he lied to me, and I believed him, and it turns out that Priceless Life is trying to make me into a stooge and it just might happen because I'm too far into it already to get out. Because if Curt Laskowski was lying to me, then I don't know who killed my brother, and I can't start over again not knowing.

"I met him once before," Martin said. "We had an interesting conversation, but it was a little one-sided. I need to talk to him again."

Again Charlie could tell that he was being asked to permit a lie to pass without question, and again he gave his permission. "Okay," he said. "Have it your way, you dumb fuck. You're lucky you've got friends like me."

The Federal Reserve today . . . I don't give a fuck what the Federal Reserve did. It was important to people whose actions dictate the long-term horizons of my life, but fuck it. I used to believe in infinite horizons. I used to believe that solutions for cancer and global warming were right around the corner, that the bottomless wellspring of human ingenuity would rescue us from the bottomless morass of human venality. That hasn't turned out to be so. When I was a child, I was assured that cancer would be cured by now. Lies. I was assured that there would be suborbital transportation that would move me from New York to Ulan Bator in five or six hours, should I choose Ulan Bator as a destination. Lies. I was assured that vanishing oil supplies would spur innovations in transportation and energy that would mitigate the effects of climate changes. The jury's still out on that one, but I don't think hydrogen cars and more wind farms are going to do the trick when the Chinese are still burning coal like they all live in 1920s Pittsburgh. In short, my auditors, we live in an age of disappointment, and the only reason we don't know this is that we're all too busy fucking Marie Antoinette on the fifty-yard line of Soldier Field while Kurt Cobain and Jimi Hendrix play "Bolero" in an arrangement for two left-handed guitars. In the VR. Someone suckered us, somewhere along the way. The future we bought into was great until we lived long enough to discover that at some point, the future becomes the present, and the fact that it was once the future doesn't mean that it won't be all fucked up once it arrives.

TWENTY

"*I HATE BUYOUTS,*" Janine Shankly told Martin the next day. He had come to double-check Charlie's assessments himself, knowing that his own certainty would be what got him through the blitzkrieg that would come when the full attention of the commentariat focused on Everett Shankly. "And I hate you for doing them," Janine added. She sat back in her chair. "Thought you should know."

"Appreciate the candor," Martin said. He couldn't quite make sense of her demeanor, in particular the way it clashed with the vaguely melancholic but business-like attitude she'd adopted with him the first time they'd talked. Her persona didn't match the office, either, which was liberally vegetated and festooned with all of the typical photographs of sunburned children and indeterminate landscapes. The window was open, and through it Martin could see his car on the street, across a parking lot that was empty save for an Audi convertible, maybe four years old, that he assumed belonged to Janine.

It was one of Martin's signal flaws that he expected a kind of consistency in other people that he never realized was intrinsic to him, and therefore achieved without thinking. His exterior persona was levelheaded to a fault—except with Teresa. It was careful and rational—except where Teresa was concerned. It was resolutely committed to upholding its stated principles—except in the matter of till death do us part. And even there, Martin would have sworn a deposition that he had done all he could to keep the marriage together. Internally, within the stew that was the yang to his external yin, a still small voice put all of this to the lie. The real Martin looking out at you was levelheaded because he was terrified of

his temper; he was rational because he had taught himself intellectual so-
briety as a bulwark against his congenital idealism; he was principled because principle was a way of sublimating his appetites—for recognition,
love, admiration—that he believed had never been and never would be
sated.

Janine Shankly was to confuse him further. "Candor," she repeated.
"I have some more candor, since you're so appreciative. Just because
you can do a buyout on my brother doesn't mean you should. And just
because your brother got killed and you don't know who did it, that
doesn't give you the right to go around turning other people's lives into
money."

"I don't intend to discuss my personal motivations with you, Ms.
Shankly," Martin said. "I think we can both agree that would be less
than professional." His voice took on a bit of extra formality, the one way
he allowed himself to express emotion with people who were neither
friends nor relatives. Janine's mention of his brother was caught in his
mind, spiky and antagonizing. Martin's natural instinct was to fire back,
to use her provocation as fuel for an anger looking for an excuse to manifest itself. Instead he carefully smoothed his initial reaction, substitut-
ing pleasure at his self-control for the more immediate reward of anger.
"Charlie has been through all of the relevant records, but because this
case will draw some attention as it moves forward, I'd like to double-
check everything."

"Shoot," she said. "I've got ten minutes before I need to get going for
a deposition."

And Martin fell into the standard routine. To your knowledge, has
anyone suggested the idea of a buyout to Everett? No. Would you know
if someone had? I believe so, yes. Everett has always been very open with
me. He's a terrible liar. Has anyone approached you to suggest a buyout?
No. Is Everett seeking a buyout because of coercion or pressure? Not
that I am aware of. Is it your belief, having known him all his life, that
he is competent to make the decision to seek and finalize a buyout? Yes.
Has anyone attempted to guide his decision making with respect to the
buyout or its potential disbursements?

Is there any exculpatory evidence that was not presented at his
trial? No.

Ten minutes passed this way, and every time Martin opened his mouth, what nearly came out was the one question he could never ask: Did your brother kill my brother? If he's always been so open to you, how did you not know about that?

Ask him yourself, he imagined Janine replying. I told you he's a terrible liar.

"Did Everett ever rape you?" he asked. It was the first variation from the regular litany.

"I beg your pardon?" she said.

"Were you ever sexually abused by your brother?" Martin asked, rephrasing the question to be less active. He had found that passive voice, the flab and cushion of linking verbs and indirect expression, made people more likely to answer a question that would set them off if phrased directly. It was a mistake, he thought, to be so forthright the first time.

"No, I goddamn well was not," Janine said.

"The reason I'm asking is that any unlawful sexual contact between you and your brother would be grounds to disqualify Everett from the buyout program," Martin said. "And if it were discovered after the buyout was finalized, there could be serious consequences for Nautilus and for you."

Janine stood and leaned over her desk at him. Her voice shook when she started speaking, and rose to a near shout. "I have never been sexually abused or raped by anyone, Mr. Kindred," she said. "And Everett would never do that. He's got a violence problem. He likes to hit things and kill things sometimes. He doesn't like to fuck things, or at least he's never shown any interest that either I or our parents ever noticed. Are you satisfied with that answer? Because I have to go, and you have made me feel filthy."

She walked out. Martin stayed where he was until the sound of her car door opening and closing came through the window. Something vital had just happened, but he couldn't sort out what it was. Charlie was better at this kind of stuff than Martin was. Whenever he touched a nerve, he did it on purpose, and he had preassigned convictions for all possible particular responses. Cops, Martin thought. They know things. I don't know those things because—as my father never stopped reminding me—I never had the temperament or inclination to become a cop.

Vance Kindred had known instinctively whenever Martin or Jason was lying, so they'd learned early on not to do it. Martin to this day was a lousy liar, and he thought he recognized in Janine Shankly some kinship of the dissemblance-challenged. Either Janine Shankly had indeed been molested by her brother, or she was genuinely outraged that Martin would insinuate that she had. He was guessing outrage. The distinction she'd made between *hurt* and *fuck* was one that victims of sexual abuse had long since learned to blur.

To be sure, he pinged Charlie on his way out of Janine's office. "Run down any juvie records you can find, will you?" Charlie had occult pipelines to material, like juvenile convictions, that was purportedly sealed or destroyed after a certain period of time. "On Shankly or his sister," Martin added as an afterthought.

Whatever Charlie thought about Everett's reaction, Martin was going to pursue Janine's. But first he had to head downtown to take a last run through the LAPD file on Shankly—which, because of the cop bureaucracy's hostility toward technology that didn't directly help them apprehend or do violence to possible criminals, was still partially on paper. Whether Shankly was competent or not, if an investigation turned up irregularities at his trial, the possibility that they could be used as the basis for an appeal meant that the buyout couldn't go forward.

Also, Martin needed to see the file because he needed to triangulate what the LAPD records people would hand him with what the mysterious Curt had piped into his car a week ago. The truth, expressed in the plainest possible way, was that if Everett Shankly was guilty of the murder of Jason Kindred, then he would more than likely be going up on a capital charge, which would make him ineligible for a buyout. Balanced against this was Martin's certainty that if the LAPD had enough to charge Shankly, they would have by now, and if they didn't, they never would.

Are you willing to do what is necessary? Martin asked himself. You, Martin Kindred, who make a show of believing in rules. You, the tireless advocate of buyouts as a mechanism of social equilibrium, of atonement and empowerment.

Why not just let Everett Shankly die in prison?

Martin realized an ugly truth about himself. He wanted to be the instrument of Everett Shankly's death. The only way to do this was to exploit his position as a purveyor of life-term buyouts, deforming his role and the process because of his personal thirst for revenge. He could not tell anyone this, not just because he didn't want to implicate anyone but because to admit his intentions would be to compromise his entire identity in the eyes of the people who were important to him. He literally would no longer be himself. Not to anyone who mattered.

So alone it must be. Martin realized that a potential crisis existed for any human being that if encountered would irrevocably divide desire and belief. Everett Shankly was his crisis, the wedge between the reality of Martin and the idealized version of himself he presented to cameras and clients. One of my mistakes, he thought, was that I presented it a little too often to Teresa. It was the kind of lesson that didn't really do you any good because a situation in which you could put the lesson to use was unlikely to arise.

The records clerk said she'd already given Charlie a copy of the file and refused to make Martin another. Having long since learned that police records clerks cannot be reasoned with, Martin pinged Charlie, who confirmed that he did in fact have a copy of the report. "So why didn't you tell me this when you knew I was coming down here?" Martin wanted to know.

"Too busy breaking laws to find your juvie records, amigo. I'm sick of doing you favors and then having you complain about the favors I didn't do you yet, you know what I mean?" Charlie clicked off.

Outside, the sun beat down and the sidewalks shed their excess heat through the soles of Martin's shoes. He daydreamed about snow, weaving his way through the midday crowds between City Hall and the Bradley Metro station, until someone tapped him on the shoulder and said, "Excuse me. Martin Kindred?"

Martin blinked and looked the woman up and down. She was thirtyish, unremarkable. Sunglasses, Dodger cap, pricey sneakers. "That's me," he said. "I'm afraid I don't know you."

"Oh, you don't have to," she said with a smile. "I was just wondering if you're really planning to kill Everett Shankly."

"Am I—" Martin cut himself off and started walking again. The back of his neck prickled, but she didn't say anything else. Then someone else called to him, a ropy black guy in a linen suit, leaning on a fire hydrant. "Hey, Martin," he said. "You still planning to kill Everett Shankly?"

Heads started to turn, and Martin felt the pressure of unwanted attention. "Martin Kindred, hey," came another voice. Martin didn't look. He set his eyes on the sidewalk six feet ahead of him and kept walking. "*¿Está planeando matar a Everett Shankly?*"

Other voices washed over him, in Korean, English again, more Spanish, then languages he didn't recognize, but the name Everett Shankly jumped out over and over. Flash mob, Martin thought. But this one was different. The other time, after he'd finalized Bragdon, they came, delivered a quick message, and left. This time they were after the spectacle. Fuck you, he thought. All of you. I will not be shamed out of doing what is right. He felt the weight of the Sig and wanted to use it. Instead he put his head down and walked faster.

Everett Shankly, Everett Shankly, Everett Shankly, all the way to the Metro stairs. Even the chirp of the fare daemon as it said, "Welcome to the Metro, Mr. Kindred," sounded accusatory. Martin rode back to the office, deciding along the way that the time had come to get a couple of things off his chest. He waited an hour, doing a perfunctory pass through the correspondence sorted out by his desk as professionally relevant, then caught Scott Krakauer coming out of a meeting.

"How about we catch up on the Shankly deal?" Martin said.

Scott glanced at his bare wrist. "I've got a couple of minutes, sure," he said, and clapped Martin on the shoulder. "You look rough around the edges, pal. Problems at work?"

Martin followed him into his office and took a seat on the couch. Scott was a big believer in casual meeting environments. "I got flash-mobbed today," Martin said. "Again."

"About Shankly again?" Seeing Martin's nod, Scott steepled his fingers and put on a great show of considering the situation. Then he said exactly what Martin had known he would say. "We knew this was going to be a tough one. You're not getting cold feet about it, are you?"

If you only knew, Martin thought. "Just keeping you informed," he said. "I don't think it's just going to be flash mobs for long."

"Me neither, but that's okay," Scott said with a shrug. "The Priceless Lifers will get all the net time they can, their donations will spike, a bunch of fatuous college kids will picket out front, and in the end, you know what? We'll do the Shankly deal and come out on the other end looking like we mean business. The rules are the rules, Martin. If this deal is within the rules, we not only should do it, we have to do it." He leaned back, stretched his arms out along the back of the couch, and added, "I know you'll come through."

Martin considered the fact that he felt inarticulately uncomfortable agreeing with Scott. He couldn't formulate exactly why, except to think that he wasn't at all interested in whether the Shankly deal reflected well on the company. Martin knew—or understood from Charlie that he should know—that Scott and Jocelyn considered him a useful naïf who could be counted on to bull ahead through shades of gray because he saw only black and white. He wasn't sure they were wrong about this, when push came to shove, but he also wasn't sure that the Krakauers understood how indifferent he was to the financial fortunes of the company.

Scott's pod muttered something in his coat pocket. "Oops," Scott said. "The wife. Listen, Martin, I know you're out front on this one, but remember, I'm right there with you. Any media comes up, send them to me. This deal's going to be big for Nautilus, and it's bonuses all around at the end of the year if we hit our targets and get the charter expansion moving in Sac."

"Hey, Scott?" Martin said. "Are we trying to expand the charter to Third Strikers? The ones doing twenty-five to life?"

"Where'd you hear that?"

"It's being said."

Scott cocked his head, like a bird trying to get a better angle on something that might be either a twig or a worm. Then he stood and shot out his hand, already moving toward the door as Martin caught up to shake it. "We've got all kinds of plans, Martin, but first things first. No counting chickens. You'll be up to date on whatever we're doing. And listen, flash mobs are scenery," Scott said. "Something to write about in your memoirs. Worse comes to worst, shoot someone. Believe me, if you have any ghost of a reason to be afraid for your personal safety, or the girls', pull the trigger. We'll make it come out all right."

Scott waved and headed down the hall in the direction of Jocelyn's office. "Oh, by the way," he called over his shoulder. "Shankly's been moved to Yucaipa. That's where we'll be doing the finalization. Apple Valley's a little too much for your average person to handle." Martin drifted back toward the top-floor reception desk, wondering if he'd really just heard his boss tell him that he could kill someone and get away with it. *We'll make it come out all right.*

The next afternoon he perjured himself before the Honorable Darshan Singh.

Today is August the second. It's my birthday. The first signers of the Declaration of Independence put pen to parchment on this day. The first subway opened on this day. Adolf Hitler became Führer on this day. Myrna Loy, Shimon Peres, James Baldwin, Peter O'Toole, and some guy who recited pi to forty-two thousand decimal places from memory were born on this day; Wild Bill Hickok, Enrico Caruso, Fritz Lang, and William S. Burroughs died. Wild Bill was killed while playing poker, which is kind of the way I'd like to go. On this day in 1980, I was born, in Emmaus, Pennsylvania. I'm sixty-one. And absolutely nothing of note has happened on that day since, except Burroughs dying. I take this as an omen that it's my day. This morning, in Boston, someone set off a series of bombs triggered by communications from a certain server. If you were getting a ping from that server while you were within sniffing distance of one of those bombs, you set it off. Terrorism-wise, that's good shit. I think it's been a while since we had a good old terrorist attack in LA, hasn't it? I mean, you can't count every random asshole with a racial grudge walking into a McDonald's and only shooting the blacks or the Iranians or the Salvadorans or the Jews. I mean something that makes the rest of us walk around a little scared because it's so random yet so purposeful—by which I mean that it's purposeful but the logic underlying the purpose is inscrutable to rational people—that it makes the entire universe seem a little less stable. We haven't had one of those lately. But I tell you what, if that Boston thing happened here, it might do the trick.

TWENTY-ONE

THE LAST STEP in making a buyout official, and inevitable, was the swearing out of an affidavit to the effect that: (a) the client was making the choice of his own free will; (b) there were no irregularities associated with the client's conviction; and (c) the client was sufficiently in possession of his faculties to make life-altering (or in this case -extinguishing) decisions. Martin stood in the office of Judge Singh on the afternoon of August 2, 2041, and swore to all three of these things despite the fact that he knew one of them to be untrue.

In possession of this secret, he went back out into the city and walked, considering what he should feel and trying to assess what he did feel. If Everett Shankly was going to be removed from the planet, the buyout was the right thing to do. Beyond that, Martin found himself curiously unable to feel. Tomorrow morning he was meeting with a divorce lawyer, even though Teresa's petition hadn't contained anything he wanted to fight about. If anything, she was fairer than he'd anticipated. She would keep the house, get a home-equity loan, and turn the proceeds over to Martin. The girls would spend alternating weeks with each of them, provided Martin lived near enough to their school. Their savings and other assets would be split down the middle. It was all so rational and smooth that Charlie insisted it was a trap. "Someone, somewhere, has an ulterior motive here, amigo," he said. "It may not be Teresa, but you can bet that anytime a divorce looks this easy, someone's getting played for a sucker."

Knowing how much Charlie hated aphorisms, Martin resorted to one. "When all you've got is a hammer, the whole world looks like a nail," he said.

"What the fuck is that supposed to mean? I'm not saying this just because all three of my exes wanted blood. I'm saying divorce brings out the absolute worst in people. There is no such thing as an amicable divorce. Bet on it. You'll find out I'm right."

The worst in people, Martin reflected. And I don't feel anything right now. Maybe that's the worst quality in me, the inability to feel the right thing at the right time.

There was a power in having a secret like Martin had. It made him giddy. He walked, and walked, and walked, navigating the streets of Los Angeles with his secret, knowing that he could stop at any corner, speak his secret out loud, and have it picked up by any one of a dozen devices designed to listen and overhear. In a surveillance society, it's the easiest thing in the world to confess. All you have to do is open your mouth. And so you don't, you walk knowing that you have your life in your own hands because in a surveillance society, you have a secret.

While he was thus ruminating, Curt Laskowski appeared. "Hey hey, Martin," he said out of a cluster of day laborers disembarking in single file from a bus emblazoned WORK TODAY PAID TODAY! "Was thinking I'd have to come to your house or something, but I hear you're getting divorced so it's good we ran across each other."

"How did you know that?"

Curt shrugged. "I know stuff. You know the kind of stuff I know. So listen, we should meet again. Probably at the place, okay?"

Martin wanted to ask if Curt had been on the bus, or were the laborers just cover? There was always something covert about him even when they were standing in the middle of the street. "Why not here?"

"Render unto me a fucking break, man. At the place. Needs to be today or tomorrow for sure."

Interesting, Martin thought. He's been watching Charlie. "I saw your pirate screed the other day," Martin said.

"Yeah?" Curt brightened up. "What did you think?"

"That you're one of those rare people who manages to be naïve, cynical, and paranoid all at the same time. Also that you've lied to me and put me in a situation that could wreck my career."

"Lied to you?" Curt said. "Martin, this is one of those times when being Mr. Black and White isn't going to serve you very well. I would have thought you'd figured that out by now."

There was no good answer for that, under the circumstances. But Martin wasn't inclined to give Laskowski anything. "If people are following you, or following me," he said, "we're not going to be alone anyway. So why not here?"

Curt laughed. "You might never be alone again. But we should meet at the place anyway. Talk about what you did today."

"What I did," Martin repeated. "Weren't you a right-to-life bomb-thrower?"

"People change, Martin. Who knows, maybe even you."

And then he was gone into the welter of the Boardwalk, and Martin realized out of the blue that he hadn't been to see his parents in nearly a month. On the heels of this came the realization that he was avoiding them because he was going to have to tell them that he and Teresa were splitting up. Way to turn over that new leaf, he told himself. Pusillanimous. He would go right then, get that all sorted out. The next few weeks were going to be hard enough without borrowing trouble on the family front.

Even though Vance and Felicia Kindred lived less than half a mile from the Robertson-Venice station, Martin drove, needing the illusion of initiative and a dose of Walt Dangerfield's devil-may-care jolly cynicism. Plus, they'd lived there since before the Expo Line extended that far, so the station seemed like an intrusion on the time when Martin's idea of the house and his neighborhood developed. Where was the closest station when I was a kid? he wondered. Washington and National, he thought. In what, they'd finished it in 2011 or '12. Rancho Park was still a car neighborhood then, and more affluent than the Kindreds could have afforded if Felicia's mother hadn't been living there since the 1960s. Its citizens had watched the Metro come through with the kind of suspicion the Sioux must have felt toward the Union Pacific. In honor of his four-wheeled heritage, Martin stopped to wash his car on Robertson and gave Casa Kindred a ping while he watched the scattering of droplets on his windshield. "What the hell is that noise?" his father wanted to know.

"Car-wash blower," Martin said. "I'm over at the Robertson wash. Mom home?"

"Nope. Why?"

"I'm coming over. Just wanted to see if you were both there."

"See you when you get here." Vance clicked off, and Martin wondered if there was a secret cop bylaw that decreed you could never say good-bye in a voice conversation. He never said hello, either, just acknowledged a new presence by picking up a weeks- or months-old conversation as if it had never stopped. Today he came out to the driveway as Martin got out of the car, and after a full minute gazing intently at the car, he said, "Looks like they did a pretty good job."

"The car wash?"

Vance cracked a smile. "Body shop. Pretty good work. They ever track down who spored the flash signal?"

"I don't know," Martin said. "I'm not sure anyone ever tried, tell you the truth."

"Hell they didn't," Vance said. "Ninety percent of what cops do, they never tell anyone because nobody ever wants to know." He led Martin through the house and out to the pool, where they sat watching the robot wander around underwater. "So what brings you over here?" Vance asked after a while.

"It's been too long. I just noticed that time was getting away, thought I'd see how you were doing."

"Better than you, by the sounds of it. Hear you and Teresa aren't doing so well."

"No," Martin said. "We aren't. She filed papers the other day."

His father considered this for some time. "Sometimes I feel like Felicia and I are the only couple in LA County that's stayed together."

"It's not too late, Dad," Martin said. "You can split up at any age."

"Be strange not to have Teresa around. Especially since we don't see much of Hannah. She drops the kids off once in a while when she needs to take care of something, but . . ." Vance trailed off. There was the Jason-shaped hole again. Martin felt it, and remembered the rustle of trash in the chain-link fence.

"Yeah," he said when Vance didn't pick up the thread. "You hearing anything about the case?"

"Nothing to hear," Vance said. "Nobody knows anything."

Except me, Martin thought. And where do you think I got it?

Someone in the LAPD knew about Shankly but was making sure the word didn't get to Vance. This puzzled Martin. Did his father not want to stay tapped into the police grapevine, or had they decided not to tell him?

"I need to talk to Meg again, see if anything's come up."

"It won't," Vance said. "Meg's a good cop, but her partner's dead-weight. She spends all of her time cleaning up after him. No time for cold cases."

This was new, Martin thought. He couldn't ever remember hearing his father say something negative about a cop around him. Now that Jason was gone, the rules were different.

"You don't close a case right off the bat, you're probably not going to," Vance said, and Martin thought, Not this. He could live with anger and bitterness, but he could not stand resignation. Not when he had an answer that he couldn't share.

"They'll get him," he said, knowing it wasn't true, at least not in any way his dad would ever know about unless Martin told him, and there was no way Martin could do that. Ninety percent of what I'm doing here nobody will ever know about, he thought. Or at least the one most important thing that's 90 percent of the whole.

It was a cop way of doing things. You make sure that the right thing happens, rules be damned. Rules are for lawyers. Cops are for justice. Dad, I'm more of a cop than you'll ever know.

His father was looking at him. "How's Mom?" Martin asked.

"Mad," Vance said. "Mad as hell at everything. Me, the world, every-thing. She's over at Hannah's right now. Best place for her. The grand-kids keep her together a little bit. You should get the girls over here more often."

"You're right. I should. Fact is, I should get home now and see about how things are supposed to work over the next couple of days. Guess I have to look for a place. I'm staying at a hotel now."

Bees buzzed in the flowers. The pool robot finished its war against algae and turned itself off. "Just as long as you don't want to stay here," Vance said.

"No, but thanks for the offer." Martin stood. "I'll figure out what's up with the girls and bring them over here tomorrow, how's that?"

"You know where to find us," his father said, and Martin walked back through the house to his car. As soon as he opened the door, John Wayne said, "Some days the cattle bust through the fence, pardner. Man needs a drink on days like that."

What? Martin thought. Then the Duke went on to inform him that he had no fewer than eight armor-piercing messages from Jocelyn Krakauer, and another three from the little filly, which was what the daemon called Teresa. Advertisements for wine specials and massages sprouted from the dashboard across the windshield. Jesus, Martin thought. What had happened?

He got back to Jocelyn first, and she answered right away. "Martin. I know it's late, but would you mind coming to the office?"

"Any way it can wait until the morning?" Martin asked. "I told Teresa—"

"I've spoken to Teresa," Jocelyn said. "She knows you'll be late. You're at your parents' house, correct? So I'll see you in half an hour." The call ended, and Martin's stomach did the slow roll that came with the mortal certainty that he'd been caught doing something wrong. They couldn't know about Shankly, could they? He dropped the car into gear and drove a hell of a lot faster than he should have, hoping a little that he'd get pulled over so he'd have an excuse not to deal with Jocelyn right then. He had no such luck, however; traffic parted as if Nautilus had worked some spiteful magic, and he was at the office in twenty minutes. Jocelyn was waiting for him in the reception area.

"I've got a little something to show you, Martin," she said, and walked away from him toward her office. He had no choice but to follow.

Her desktop, normally clear of either papers or holo stills, was a collage of both. Jocelyn swept the papers into a stack, set it at one corner, and said, "Play from the beginning."

The holos rearranged themselves into a single flat shot of Martin talking to Curt Laskowski on the street. Behind them, the group of day laborers. "Hm," Jocelyn said. "Interesting chance encounter." The next shot, from a different angle, caught Martin's initial surprise. A sequence followed that swept the viewer around in a 360-degree panorama with

Martin and Curt at the center, time-lapsing through the length of their conversation. "I didn't turn on the sound because I didn't think you'd want to hear it," Jocelyn said, "but all of this was cut with a voiceover pointing out exactly who you are, and exactly who this Curt Laskowski person is. Then they explain that Curt Laskowski is known to be associated with Priceless Life, and that he has a violent past. So far, so good, right? Discredit the Priceless Lifers, make them look like stooges? Well. Then this happens."

The holo jumped to a grainy 3-D vid, obviously shot from three different cameras and then rendered on someone's home setup. In it, Curt Laskowski was talking to Janine Shankly outside Janine's office.

"That son of a bitch," Martin said.

Jocelyn froze the image. Sitting on the corner of her desk next to it, she said, "Oh, I think the situation calls for language a bit more emphatic than that, Martin. How does conflict of interest sound? Corruption? It's a good goddamn thing there's no sound, or who knows what kind of a fucking mess we'd be in."

Martin was getting out his pod to call Janine. "Don't," Jocelyn said. "You've been in court, right? Affidavits sworn out?"

"It's all good to go," Martin said.

"Then you make it go," Jocelyn said. "Tomorrow. First thing, you're out at Yucaipa getting Shankly's thumb. If he's not taking a needle thirty-eight hours from right now, you're out of a job. If he is, then all of this will pass. But it's up to you. Now go."

Martin went. He fingered his pod, itching to call Janine and find out what had passed between her and Laskowski. Had Laskowski told her about the tampering in the LAPD file on her brother? If he had, the deal was off. But if Laskowski was going to do that, why had he shown Martin the file in the first place? Slow down, work it through, Martin told himself. Laskowski's a terrorist. He could have all kinds of reasons for doing what he does. It wouldn't be beyond him to sacrifice Everett Shankly if it meant a political payoff down the road. People willing to kill for a cause, Martin had always thought, were people seeking a cause to kill for. And Curt Laskowski had once without doubt been willing to kill for a cause.

As, the Priceless Lifers would no doubt say, is Martin Kindred.

I'll never be used to it, he thought. In a surveillance society, everyone always sort of assumed that whatever they did was recorded somewhere, but nobody ever figured that what they did was important enough for anyone to care.

And he didn't want anyone to care what he did. Right then, he didn't want to be a public figure, a lightning rod, the face of buyouts and the wrenching questions that came with them.

He also didn't want to be a quitter. Could not be a quitter. Could not walk away from what he knew was right just because it was hard. If Curt Laskowski had lied to him, set him up somehow, that was a separate problem; until he knew one way or another, Martin had to keep going. He had to base his actions on facts and principles. To do anything else was a recipe for becoming like the Krakauers.

Martin let go of his pod. All of it would keep until morning. Right now, Martin Kindred needed to just be Allison and Kelly's dad for a while.

Mars, bitches! Anybody remember that? We haven't been to Mars. I was promised Mars! We haven't been back to the moon. I was promised the moon! I was promised asteroid miners, and harvesting of helium-three from the lunar lithosphere that would make fusion possible and lead to Energy Fucking Nirvana! Instead we get pirate avatars popping up from our pillowcases to sell us Brazilian vaccines while we're busy trying to fuck some woman half our age who swore to us that she'd never been with a man before! Well, that's what happens to me, anyway. There's a bright side to information saturation. But I want Mars! I want rockets and domes on the moon, spacemen! Man, I wanted to be an astronaut. Even after I had to get glasses, I wanted to be an astronaut. That's my excuse for getting fat, disappointment that I couldn't be an astronaut. The future let me down, so I ate a bunch of fucking calzones and fried chicken! The future let me down, so I crawled into the VR rig and pretended I was the Lothario of the spaceways! The future let me down, so I can't get a job! The future let me down by becoming the present! How dare that fucking future. How dare it . . .

TWENTY-TWO

THE FIRST THING Martin did as a divorced dad—for such both he and the girls already considered him—was drop by the house and take them out for dinner. As he pulled up, pinged Allison, and waited for them to come out and get in the car, he realized that he had already begun to train himself not to think of the house as his anymore. Right at that moment, it felt like the training was working, and he gave himself credit for being adaptable.

At first he'd thought they would go to Suzuki-san's, a noodle-counter-slash-retro-diner-slash-adolescent-hangout on the edge of Old Town, but when he announced this plan to the girls, Martin could tell by their reaction that they were trying to figure out how to tell him that they didn't want to go there in his company. "We could," Allison allowed, while Kelly watched her older sister with wide, omigod-you-aren't-going-to-let-this-happen-are-you eyes. "But I thought you hated the music in there."

This was true. Martin hated the shallow, idealized re-creations of the past perpetrated by outfits like Suzuki-san's, and he had in the past grumbled about their cannibalization of his grandfather's culture. Next they'll have segregated seating and extra drinking fountains, he remembered thinking the first time he went there. Now his daughters were forcing him to live up to his curmudgeonliness, and there was nothing he could do about it. Trumped by the social wiles of a twelve-year-old.

"So where do you want to go?" he asked them. "Kelly, you pick."

This earned him a petulant sigh from Allison, but Kelly immediately suggested sushi. O brave new world, Martin thought. He hadn't ever tried sushi until he was in college. That was when you could still get tuna. Now even eel was getting scarce.

So they stuffed themselves with barbecued eel and spider rolls at Yosaku, which was the place where Martin and Teresa had gone out on their first date. The girls were chipper, neither avoiding the topic of the impending divorce nor wallowing in it. "So are you going to get a new place to live?" Allison asked him over edamame.

"Looks like it," Martin said. "It'll be close by here. You guys will stay in the same schools and everything."

"Mom says that people are mad at you because of your job," Kelly said. "Does that mean she is?"

Martin contemplated how to handle this while he worked the third soybean out of a tough pod. "She's worried about you two. And I'm doing some things at work that people don't agree with, so they say things sometimes. I don't think there's anything to worry about, though." Because, he did not add, I have the go-ahead from my boss to kill anyone I think might be a threat.

"How much of our stuff are we going to have to bring to your new place?" Kelly asked.

Amazing, Martin thought. And here I was congratulating myself for adaptability.

"As much as you want," he said. "We'll get you set up. Soon as your mother and I get everything settled, we'll figure out those details. And besides, you don't have to worry about any of that until I get a new place."

He geared everything he said toward Kelly's understanding, knowing that Allison would know what he was doing. She watched him intently, and he wondered what she was really thinking. Part of her duty in these circumstances would be to cushion the blow to Kelly, or so she would think. Allison took her big-sister role seriously. But at some point she was going to come to him on her own and demand the straight story. In this way she was like her mother: Whenever she sensed any attempt at evasion or euphemism, she transformed into a bulldog until she'd gotten at a satisfactory version of the truth.

Or maybe, Martin thought, that's a quality she got from me.

"Dad," she said. "I want you to take me to my game next Wednesday. It's in Oceanside, and Mom said she can't get off work."

The inflection was so adult, so smoothly calibrated to convey the we-need-to-talk subtext, that Martin wondered when Allison had begun to make the transition from girl to woman. He wasn't prepared for her to be so sophisticated and together when she was still walking around in a twelve-year-old body. Girls were different. When Martin was twelve, he had understood that there was a concept called subtlety, but it had never occurred to him that he might be able to figure out how to use it.

After eating, they drove to Silver Lake, where Hannah still lived. She was still talking about selling the house, but Martin didn't think she would. This was good, in his opinion, since he guessed that if she did sell, it would mean she was going back to wherever in Colorado her family was. His mother would have a hard time with that.

He wasn't sure how well Hannah was holding together. She looked hollowed out in a way that Martin suspected was partly drug-induced, and she seemed to float around her home, giving off an aura of liquid ethereality, as if she wasn't entirely present on the same plane of existence. The house reminded him of the bungalow where he'd made his pitch to Leila Ordonez. It was about the same age, with the Craftsman touches still showing through a hundred years of updates both smart and misguided. Hannah's place showed a little less wear, perhaps, and was a bit more given over to the chaos that comes along with two children younger than Kelly. On the edge of his eighth birthday, Bart was the walking image of his father; seeing him, Martin remembered Jason at seven, which meant Martin at nine. Soccer in the park, hikes in the hills on Vance's days off. Scout trips up to Camp Emerald Bay, Lake Arrowhead, and the Circle X Ranch. Nobody had been dead when Martin and Jason were boys.

Bart seemed okay. Pausing just long enough to say *Hey, Uncle Martin*, he charged around the house in a Sensix VR rig, having transformed the house into some kind of military space outpost overrun by aliens in need of slaughter. His younger brother, Zack, carried around the same shrouded aura Martin felt coming from Hannah. When Zack came into a room, things seemed quieter, or seemed like they ought to be quieter.

The idea of death had gotten into him and now everything he saw was colored by it. There had always been a sweetness in Zack's nature, and that was still there, but it had become tied to a contemplative sadness that was heartbreaking in a boy so young. In the throes of guilt over not being committed enough to his nephews' well-being, Martin promised them an outing to a Dodgers game, and then set Allison and Kelly to work on gathering the boys and keeping them out of the adults' hair for a minute so he and Hannah could catch up.

"You look good," she said to him.

Martin laughed. "Compared to what?"

He hadn't been too impressed with what he'd seen in the mirror lately. The stress was beginning to tell; he was losing weight, his eyes seemed to be getting bigger, he didn't like the way his hands had suddenly come to seem all tendon and vein. Martin had never rebelled against the idea of aging, but he did want to age well.

"You don't look so bad yourself," he added in return. It was true if you ignored the sense that a gently impermeable barrier existed between Hannah and the rest of the world. She was a good-looking woman. Charlie, in a fit of tequila-enhanced candor, had once argued that Hannah was a damn sight sexier than Teresa in a raw physical sense, but that T was catapulted into the lead by the erotic intensity of her intelligence. Martin had refused to take part in the discussion.

They talked about the boys for a few minutes, culminating in Martin apologizing for not having been around more. "Never mind, Martin," Hannah said with the weary smile you give someone who is apologizing for something that you both know they will do again. "I heard you're taking them to see the Dodgers. They'll like that."

"Nautilus pays a lot of money for the seats," Martin said. "They might as well be put to good use."

"How do the boys look to you?" she asked. She sounded distracted, a little distanced. As if, Martin thought, she was thinking about something that she couldn't tell him, and was trying to get something across to him without saying it.

Or, equally likely, he was doing a bit of projecting. Wasn't he the one with the secret that he couldn't tell her, not even her who deserved to know it as much as he did? *I know who killed Jason,* he rehearsed. *I've got him. I'm going to make it right.*

"Bart looks great," Martin said. "He was always bulletproof. Zack looks a little quiet. How's he been doing?"

"A little quiet," Hannah repeated to herself. "Yeah. He walks around like the sky has fallen in on him, and he's afraid to look up and see what the sky fell out of, you know what I mean? Like all of a sudden the world isn't how he thought it was, and he doesn't know where anything ends, or begins, or . . ." She was crying, and she leaned into Martin, who shifted his weight and held her, puzzled. He and Hannah had never been par-ticularly close. They'd had fun together at family outings, but this was the first time he'd ever had any kind of emotional interaction with her.

It hit him how distant he had become from his family in the wake of Jason's murder. How alienated he had gotten from the people closest to him, as if the death of one of them had made him mistrustful of the oth-ers. "Yeah," he said quietly into Hannah's hair. "I know what you mean."

Gales of laughter burst from the back bedroom, where Allison had herded her three charges. Martin could hear Hannah listening, and after a moment she said, "It's good to hear the boys laugh. I mean, they laugh, they're little boys. They think farts are funny, and they do stuff with their friends and they laugh. It's not like we live in a tomb." She pushed away from him a little, wiping at her eyes and taking a deep breath. "But you know what? Sometimes it feels like we do live in a tomb. You can't ever get away from the absence."

"My mom's worried you're going to pull up stakes and head back to your family," Martin said.

"I've thought about it. But this is home for the boys, and if I ran back to my home, it would just uproot them. That doesn't get us anywhere. I'm the grown-up; I'm supposed to be the one who can handle this stuff." Hannah reached out and gripped Martin's arm just below the shoulder, squeezing briefly before letting her hand slide down to rest at his elbow. "Please come around more, Martin. It's a cliché, and I know I'm not supposed to say it, but the boys need a man around. Your father is great, but he's almost seventy. Bart and Zack need someone who can give them some of what their father would have."

"Okay," Martin promised. "I will."

"Shit," Hannah said. "I hate myself when I get all needy. How are you? Things still rocky with you and Teresa?"

"About as rocky as they can get," Martin said. He gave her the capsule summary of the divorce as it stood. "The girls seem to be doing really well with it," he said, unable to keep all of the surprise out of his voice. "Almost makes me wonder if we should have done it sooner."

He'd been looking off to the side while he talked, and when he looked back at Hannah, he caught a sudden mischievous twinkle in her eye. "You're not seeing someone, are you?" she asked with a lopsided smile.

Oh, Martin thought. Bart and Zack aren't the only ones who need some of what their father used to give them. "No," he said. "It isn't like that."

"I'm not, either." Hannah held his gaze. Her smile was gone.

"No, Hannah," he said.

"It's not because you're Jason's brother," she said. "It's because I can trust you."

If you knew what I wasn't telling you, Martin thought, what would you do? He shook his head. "Really, Hannah. No."

"I know," she said. "I know. I don't even really want to. I just want to want to."

From the back bedroom, more gales of laughter. "Things sure get happier when you're around," Hannah said.

HE DROPPED THE GIRLS off at about nine, and was watching them go toward the house — Kelly still young enough to want to run everywhere, and Allison walking with the twelve-year-old's exaggerated sense of world-weariness — when it occurred to him that since he was there, he should grab a couple of things. He hopped out of the car and caught up to the girls as they were going inside.

Teresa came out of the dining room and said, "Hello." The girls vanished.

"Figured I'd pick up a couple of things," Martin said.

She nodded. "Okay. But I'd like to have some rules about how we go into and out of each other's places."

"Soon as we both have a place, we can talk about those kinds of rules." Martin left her there and went into the bedroom. He was packing a week's worth of clothes, and throwing in some of his personal tchotchkes, when he sensed her in the doorway. He stopped what he was doing and turned to await whatever she was going to say.

"I'm not divorcing you because I don't love you, Martin," she said. "And I'm not divorcing you because you devote more love to your work than to your family. And it's not even because you refuse to see the consequences for us of how Jocelyn and Scott are putting a bull's-eye on you so they can sit back and count their money. I've been thinking about this, and in the end, the reason I'm divorcing you is that you have put the girls—also me, and also yourself—possibly in harm's way, not because you had to but because it was the only way you could think of to prove something to your father. I've seen the flash demonstrations and the Priceless Life feeds where your name comes up. How long do you think it's going to be before one of those people is on our front lawn? We should have been more important."

Martin said nothing. He turned away from her and finished putting random things from the bureau top into his bag. Cuff links, an old analog wristwatch. When he had everything he wanted right then, he turned back to Teresa and said, "Excuse me."

"Talk to me, Martin."

"What do you want me to say, T? You want me to fight so you can feel better about something you've already decided to do? No. I don't want this. You do, and you can get what you want, and there's nothing I can do about it. So where's the point?"

She stepped out of his way. "Okay, Martin. At least tell the girls good night before you go."

As if I wouldn't, Martin thought. *And she knows it.* He didn't take the bait, though, not because it wouldn't have been cathartic to fight but because he had enough windmills to tilt at already. Even a white knight knows when he's got enough hopeless battles to fight.

Ladies and gentlemen, kids of all ages, there is rain and rumors of rain. If you're counting, it's been forty-four days since our last measurable precipitation here in El Pueblo de Nuestra Señora la Reina de los Ángeles de Porciúncula, the previous nomenclature inserted at the suggestion of the marketing guys who dare to suggest that my show is a little too Anglo. Ay caramba! Coming up tomorrow, an entire show done in a pidgin patois of Arabic, Tagalog, Lao, Amharic, and Hindi. A ratings bonanza, twenty-four hours from right now. Don't. Miss. It. I might even get a brown person to do it for me. Oh, wait. I'm a brown person. Aaaaahhhh, I need to get in touch with my inner sacred lost brown language that united my people in the face of their oppression and suffering. Nobody speaks nigger anymore, by which I mean everyone does. Damn you, Whitey! Thirty years ago you got Obamafied and now what's an honest American of African extraction to do? I was all behind the multicultural society, but look what it got me. I have to tell you that my ancestors come from a Land Over the Sea, and were brought here in the Bonds of Slavery. You wouldn't know otherwise. Bandwidth is color-blind, but at some point I have to come out into the light of day. Then I am seen.

TWENTY-THREE

THE SKY to the west and south, out over the Pacific, was a jumble of thunderheads. In the other direction, Los Angeles and the Valley huddled against the advancing storm under a blanket of smog the color of a dirty cigarette filter. Martin couldn't remember the last time it had rained. May, maybe? And here it was August. He left his pod in the car, feeling as he walked away toward the trailhead that he was going naked toward a battle that would be fought with weapons he didn't understand. He went up the trail, thinking that if Jocelyn and Scott knew he was out meeting Curt Laskowski, they might just fire him. They rarely asked what he did with his time out of the office, assuming that he was chasing deals— which generally was true. But Martin also knew that they tracked employee pods, and would note that his was offline. The Los Angeles basin contained a number of Wi-Free zones, but few of them were in places where a buyout agent might reasonably go to conduct business. DBs were another story, but after closing out Marks, Martin hadn't been doing too many DBs. All of the post-Marks weirdos were clogging up his work hours, and he just hadn't been as efficient because of Jason. Throw in the Shankly deal and all of its peripheral complications, and what you got was lousy productivity. He would probably hear about it.

And it all might be for nothing, at least today. He and Laskowski hadn't made any kind of specific arrangement, and it was a day later than Laskowski had wanted to meet. Plus, after the swirl the video feed had caused, Laskowski might not want to meet anymore. There were enough hidden agendas on all sides that nobody could have any clear idea of what anybody wanted.

Except me, Martin thought. Always except me. Everyone always knows what I want, or thinks they do. The difference isn't that I don't have a hidden agenda, it's that I know everyone else does, and they don't know that about me. Curt Laskowski being the sole exception.

Martin wasn't entirely correct in this diagnosis, as Charlie would have told him had either of them been prepared to have the conversation. Charlie knew that something about the Shankly deal had gotten under Martin's skin, and also knew that Martin wasn't going to tell him what it was. At the exact moment of Martin's contemplation of Pacific thunderheads, Charlie Rhodes was sifting through Everett Shankly's juvenile records, which turned out to be extensive and maybe illuminating. Shankly had done three stretches in juvie, and had acquired there all the skills that juvenile detention so readily taught: the proper use of force and intimidation, of course, and the manipulation of authority through the judicious use of snitching. Charlie immediately piped this over to Martin, and the information waited patiently on a server until Martin's pod came back online. The truth was, Charlie himself was the only person involved with Everett Shankly who had no duplicity in him. What he wanted, he said he wanted, which was for Martin to do the right thing and lose neither his life nor his self-respect. It was unclear to Charlie how meeting with Curt Laskowski furthered anyone's goals, except maybe Curt Laskowski's.

On the trail up to the waterfall, Martin wasn't thinking about any of that. Unusually for an Angeleno of his age and background, he enjoyed being disconnected from the supersaturated information environment. He liked the woods, and was disappointed in himself for not passing that feeling along to his girls. Teresa had never felt it, really. She was a city creature, and preferred her nature at a distance, a thing to be admired rather than touched. Martin was no mountain man, but he found a peace in remote areas and Wi-Free zones. He also felt a sense of imminence—which he wished he could experience as immanence—in the lack of daemons and pings, as if the brain trained from birth to filter and sort a storm of information couldn't quite believe in silence, and could only understand it as a gap bounded by noise on all sides.

"You didn't show up last time we were supposed to meet," Laskowski said, snapping Martin out of his hike Zen. Martin looked around, realizing that he'd only come as far as the first juncture on the trail from the parking lot. From here you could go to the waterfall where he'd first met Laskowski, or up to Skull Rock and along a ridge with a fine view of the city and ocean.

He didn't have much patience for Laskowski's complaint. "Tell me about Janine," he said.

"Hmmm," Laskowski said. "Janine. You want to go up to Skull Rock?"

Martin shook his head. "Prefer to stay somewhere a bit less camera-friendly."

"Martin, man, you've got to learn to keep an even keel here. You think you're out there, doing your thing, the lone knight, and you get all fucking discombobulated when you all of a sudden find out that your decisions are important to other people. And that their decisions turn out to be important to you. You're fucking dense sometimes, man."

This was not the first time Martin had heard this criticism, but he sure didn't want to hear it from Curt. "Easy for you to be calling me dense when you've been playing me for a patsy, Curt. Maybe you ought to explain to me why I shouldn't go talk to Meg Twohy about how you tried to suborn me into doing a bad buyout."

Laskowski shrugged. "Do it. Then Everett Shankly will rot away in prison, and still nobody will ever admit what happened to your brother, and you'll hate yourself for the rest of your life because you didn't do anything about it. What the fuck, you think Meg Twohy doesn't know about this? You think that she isn't hoping that you'll do Shankly so she and every other cop over there who knows about it can go home at night knowing that they got a cop-killer?" Laskowski glanced up at the sky. A few raindrops were falling. "If you're looking to the LAPD to make trouble for me, you really don't know what's going on here."

"Then tell me. Because what it looks like is that you fed me bad information so you could turn around and scream to everyone who would listen that I'm not following the rules."

"I did do that," Laskowski said. "And now it's time for the next part of the plan. You want to know what it is, since you're too far in to say no anyway?"

Martin took a slow, deep breath, let it out, and said, "I don't think

I've ever threatened anyone physically in my life, but when this is over, you better look out."

"Seems to me I better look out *until* this is over," Laskowski said. "I mean, I hacked the cops, I got you in trouble, and depending on how it all comes out, Nautilus is going to be in the shitter, too. Which makes you in more trouble. And given that Nautilus is run by ex-cops, I would guess that however much trouble they get in, they're going to make sure that I get it worse. So. Want to hear how we avoid all that?"

"I'm all ears," Martin said.

Laskowski nodded. "Good man. Hey, how much do you think I could get for a buyout?"

"You're what, forty-six?"

"Yep."

"I don't know," Martin said. "Maybe two million. Depends on your health screenings, that kind of thing."

"Healthy as a horse," Laskowski said. "Two million, huh?"

"Stop wasting my time."

"You misunderstand me," Laskowski said. "That's what this is all about."

Laskowski fell silent then, and Martin couldn't find anything to say. It's not possible, he thought, that all of this has happened because a disaffected aging abortion radical needed some way to go out in a blaze of glory. There's too much to it. Too many easier ways for him to get headlines. The wind picked up, and even within the shelter of the canyon walls it set up a creaking in the dry trees and lifted the waterfall's spray across the pool. Martin felt it on his face.

"I guess you could say I've been a seeker," Laskowski said. His typical sardonic tone was gone. "Looking for something easy to believe that would give me a reason to be angry enough to justify things that I wanted to do anyway."

"Don't confess to me," Martin said. "I don't want to hear it."

"We're not that different."

"We couldn't be more different," Martin said. "You're willing to take me down, take anyone down, to get what you want. Not what you believe in, what you want. Don't you fucking dare compare that to what I do."

Laskowski was nodding. "Right. Belief. That's my point. It's time for a different kind of belief now. Nobody believes that human life is sacred anymore, or even priceless. We're all just arguing over where we're going to start the bidding, and that includes you."

This is not what I meant at all, Martin thought, and on the heels of that: This is what happens when you break the rules that define what's right so you can do what's right. I'm sitting here in Temescal Canyon being made into an object lesson in the difference between commitment and dogmatism. He said, "I can't believe I'm sitting here getting a lecture on belief from a guy who used to blow up abortion clinics."

"Once," Laskowski said. "Once I did that. And it was only a pipe bomb."

"So when one of your crazy friends blows the hands off my daughter with a pipe bomb, I'm supposed to say, Well, what the hell, it was only once?"

"This isn't about you, Martin. You don't get that. That's why your white knight pose is such bullshit. A real white knight knows that it's never really about him, it's about what he represents."

Martin got up and started to walk away, but Laskowski stood, too, holding up a hand to stop him. "I lied about being healthy," Laskowski said. "I mean, I'm healthy now, but I have good reason to believe I won't be. I've got three close relatives who died of Lou Gehrig's. Every time I get up in the morning and my fingers are numb because I slept funny, I'm convinced my body's started ringing the funeral bells already."

"That's going to make it hard for you to get a buyout," Martin said, with what he considered a minimum of sarcasm.

"You know what? Fuck you," Laskowski said. He held out his left arm, with the inside of the forearm turned up. A snake smartattoo, obviously flash and badly done, slithered from elbow to wrist along the path of a prominent vein. "I've got the gene. Right there on chromosome twenty-one. Scrape and see."

"Forgot my sequencer at the office," Martin said.

"Martin, goddammit. I don't want to live through that," Laskowski said. "In confidence, I'm telling you this. I gave you your brother's killer, motherfucker. That's our little secret. And my gene is our other little secret. You owe me this."

"Save the self-pity. The gene doesn't mean you're going to get it," Martin said.

"That's not the point, either. At least I'm in good company. Mingus, Leadbelly, Hawking . . . a guy could do worse." It started to rain, and Laskowski turned his face up to accept it. Again Martin started to walk away. "Here's the thing, Martin," Laskowski said. His eyes were still closed, his face still upturned. He smiled. "If anyone ever deserved a buyout, it's Everett Shankly. He's a murderer, but he's also fucked up in a way that meant the world was never going to give him a square deal. So you and I don't disagree on that. But when you start using Shankly as the thin end of the wedge, so all of a sudden we turn around and every prisoner serving a long sentence can just take the needle instead, payout prorated to the length of incarceration? No. You can't get behind that, but that's what Nautilus wants. So what I'm trying to do here, I won't lie to you. I'm trying to let you get what you want, and what Shankly deserves, so that everyone will see how wrongheaded buyouts are. Think about it. It's a square deal."

Martin believed him. The same way that he'd heard Janine and believed her when it would have been easier to think she was lying, he listened to Curt Laskowski and found that Laskowski's strange truth had a more compelling logic than all of Martin's preexisting theories about why he might lie.

But because Martin believed Laskowski, he also felt that his secret had been diminished, that it no longer had power. Curt knew. Two people knowing a secret is one too many.

"No," he said. "I can't promise you that."

"It's a better deal than you're going to get from anyone else," Laskowski said.

Ladies and gentlemen—I grow fond of this mode of address—I'm gonna guess that the Priceless Lifers are going to earn their malcontent protestor stripes today. Word on the wire, by which I mean the wireless, is that a big thing is going to come down, and I can't help but be excited. Who wouldn't be? Someone other than a desert separatist lunatic might just show a little backbone today. If it happens, and I don't even know what it is, I'm going to lose my shit. I'm going to dance a jig, I'm going to drink whiskey and chase girls who would think my sons are too old, I'm going to believe again that there is immortality in the passage of human spirit down through the generations. That's not too much to ask, is it? From the Priceless Lifers? Maybe today they're going to find out which lives are priceless. Mine I sold a long time ago, and I didn't get as much for it as I thought I was going to. So I sit here in my spiderweb and watch it all go by, and I tug at strands, and the things that nourish me, the things whose blood I can suck and grow fat on, are the courageous doomed actions of people who have the misfortune to preserve a shred of idealism in the face of the world in which we all do this thing we call living.

TWENTY-FOUR

EVERETT SHANKLY'S last words were, "Do them in order, Martin." They echoed in Charlie's head for a long time after Shankly had been finalized and Martin ran himself into the emotional oblivion of imploded ideals.

The storm had passed overnight, and Charlie was up early looking at the scrubbed sky over LAX. Far out over the Pacific, there was still a hint of receding darkness. Charlie yawned, sipped coffee, pronounced aloud several Anglo-Saxon words as the arthritis in his neck reminded him that he was on the back side of his threescore and ten. Then he spun up the terminal in his bedroom that was dedicated to crawling secure servers known to harbor chatter from various radical groups including Priceless Life. The terminal daemon sorted through all of the filters he'd set up to track various threads into various folders of varying priority, and came up with all kinds of noise from Priceless Life sources. One of them was talking to someone at LAPD, which didn't surprise Charlie because he'd seen it before. Probably a community liaison working through a permit for one of PL's planned demonstrations. The rest of the Priceless Life traffic was internal, old-fashioned SMS with auto-scrubbed content upon receipt. That meant a flash demo was in the works.

Charlie switched over to a tap he had running on feeds from some of the newsdrones that circled over Southern California. Each of them spawned raw video on a wallscreen hanging across from Charlie's bed. He'd had nine taps the day before; two of them had been found and killed overnight. Watching the remaining seven, he saw flashing lights and uniforms surrounding three sheeted bodies in Little Ethiopia, a live

movie shoot at Doheny State Beach, traffic snarls on the Long Beach
Freeway and at the Orange Crush, another murder scene in Santa Ana,
a gossip stakeout on an actor's place in Beverly Hills, something going
on at the East Hollywood train station . . . all of it typical. He wondered
what was on the two feeds he'd lost overnight.

He pinged Martin to let him know about the Priceless Life chatter.
"Why are you calling me at six in the morning?" Martin wanted to know.

"Because you're doing Shankly today and I knew you'd be up,
amigo," Charlie said. "Plus I wanted to give you a heads-up that the
Priceless Lifers are on the march."

"Tell me more."

Martin had left the hotel early, before dawn, when the smell of rain
still hung in the quiet streets of North Pasadena. There was a murmur of
traffic from the Foothill Freeway, and the chirping of birds. Everything
smelled clean. Even the flowers smelled better as they opened themselves to the day. And today was the day that Martin Kindred was going to
avenge his brother. He drove out to Yucaipa staying out of the smart lane,
skipping from lane to lane, moving a little too fast in the grip of a super-
stitious belief that no cop would pull him over on the way to finalize
Everett Shankly's buyout. When he got off the freeway, he pulled into a
diner to have breakfast, knowing it was going to be a long day. After
Shankly was finalized, there would be media. There might be protests.

His meeting with Laskowski was heavy in his mind. You've been
warned, Martin told himself. Laskowski's in it for a reason. He's playing
both sides, but the only side he's really on is his. A useful lesson, maybe.

Finalization was scheduled for nine o'clock. It was seven thirty when
the waitress brought Martin's eggs, and seven forty-five when he got back
in the car, jangly with coffee but paradoxically serene of mind, even with
Walt Dangerfield spouting his own inimitable take on the Shankly deal.
"Buy *me* out!" he screamed. "That's when all of this will be different,
when some random motherfucker can fill out a buyout form like you're
applying for a no-fee *credit card*! We finance anybody! *That's* the brave
new world! That, people, is when there's no turning back!"

No turning back. Dangerfield was right. Laskowski had been right
about that, too. Martin was committed to this course of action, come
what may.

Which was exactly what Charlie was afraid of. Had been afraid of night and day since Martin had brought up the Shankly deal a month before. It stank in every way a buyout could stink without running directly afoul of charter prohibitions.

He called in a favor from Klaatu, his go-to source for nuggets of prohibited information. Like, say, the specific terminal within LAPD headquarters that someone in Priceless Life had contacted. *Hola K'tu,* he pinged, *run this down for me?* He attached the record.

Waiting for Klaatu, he ran a couple of BVIs.

Vincenzo Alvarado, 61. Pled to sixteen counts of aggravated sexual abuse of a minor. Interviewed at Lancaster State, where he is in protective solitary. At the time of the interview, Alvarado was recovering from multiple assaults in Pelican Bay resulting in serious internal injuries as well as facial disfigurement. Contacted Nautilus to consult about a buyout after these assaults; primary purpose of interview was to ascertain whether coercion was a factor. Alvarado denied this. He stated that several of his attackers joked that they were going to drive him to want a buyout, but that none of them said anything about profiting from it should he choose one. His given reason for wanting a buyout is to spare himself years of similar abuse, as well as leave something for his victims. Difficult to assess how genuine this sentiment might be. Alvarado is aware that his advanced age means a less profitable disbursement, but wishes to go ahead despite this. No irregularities surfaced during a search of his arrest and trial records, and his testimony reflects the substance of his initial contact with Nautilus.

Buyout suitability: poor for reasons of age

"Klaatu, you son of a bitch," Charlie said. "Where are you?" He dove into another BVI.

Esteban Hinojosa, 29. Confessed to murder of Sheila Hollimon, 23, found dead 3/5/41. Hinojosa arraigned, charged with murder, rape. Held in LA County Jail pending trial. Contacted Nau-

tilus before beginning of his trial. Prior to initial interview, background research indicated that Hinojosa was bipolar and that his
adherence to medication regimen was sporadic. Further interviewing of family members indicated Hinojosa was recently
upset about losing his job and not being able to support his family; allegations of serious drug habit unsubstantiated until com-
pletion of prison-intake laboratory screening. Strong suspicion
on this investigator's part that Hinojosa committed the murder of
Sheila Hollimon—if he committed it—out of concern for his
family. If this proves incorrect, his history of psychological illness
makes his eligibility for a buyout highly questionable.

Charlie was ready to kill himself. It had been ten minutes since he'd
pinged Klaatu, whose median response time was something less than
ninety seconds. No way could Charlie face another BVI, not in his
frame of mind. And then came the sweet signal, Klaatu's own pingtone:
"Gort! Klaatu barada nikto!"
     Charlie popped the message and read:
     Briggs, Solomon E., Det. Sgt.
     "Ah, shit, amigo," Charlie said. An hour later, when he was talking
to Martin, he said, "Sol Briggs is talking to someone in Priceless Life."
     Silence from Martin. Charlie watched him thinking this over. All
around the image of Martin, raw feeds from the newsdrones. Won't be
long, Charlie thought, before I'll be seeing him through those feeds. Just
getting a head start now.
     "What should I think about that, Charlie?"
     "You should think that there's some kind of game, and that you don't
know who's on which team, and you don't know the rules, and you don't
know what's at stake. And if I was in that situation, I would get the fuck
out of it. Promptly."
     Driving the last stretch on Oak Glen Road, Martin was hearing
these words in his head, over and over, and against them he was hearing
Meg Twohy's narrative of his brother's last moments on earth, and he
was hearing Curt Laskowski saying that the argument wasn't whether
life was priceless, but where to start the bidding.

My bid is in, he thought. Not to be retracted. I would not be who I am if I backed out now. All of the other players are about to find out that they don't know my rules, either.

A daemon popped up on his windshield, looking a lot like Jerry Torres, the gate guard. Martin wondered if Jerry got likeness residuals. "You are entering a temporary zone of heightened security," it said. "Please allow a scan to determine your admissibility."

"Allowed," Martin said.

"Good morning, Martin Kindred," the daemon said. "Please proceed directly to the staff parking area and wait for escort." It vanished without waiting for a response.

Martin was wondering why the change in procedure when another daemon bloomed from the dashboard, this time a forgettable turn-of-the-century sex symbol. "Hey there, killer," it said. "We know you've got a lot on your plate today, what with your blood sacrifice to shareholder value, but we hope you'll spare us a little time." It blew him a kiss. "See you soon."

Then it, too, vanished, leaving Martin with a sharpened sense that the day was going to bring as much uncertainty as resolution. He shifted in his seat, feeling the press of the Sig against his rib cage. A mile or so down the road, just before the turnoff, his pod security blew wide open and the names of every buyout client he'd ever finalized started to scroll across the windshield, looking as if they'd been written in the sky over Yucaipa. In sixteen months, he'd done forty-nine. His windshield started to look like a holo version of the Vietnam Memorial, which he'd visited once as a child because his mother's uncle was among the names. The effect had to be deliberate, he thought. One more example of Priceless Life being conscious of how they framed their position. Fifty thousand wasted lives in Vietnam equals forty-nine convicted murderers and pedophiles. Sickening.

He pinged Charlie. "You getting this?"

Charlie's face on the windshield had names running across it. "Yeah," he said. "Priceless Lifers have some pretty good worm doctors, amigo. I can't even find the routine they're running."

"Comforting," Martin said. Then he passed a small stand of trees be-

fore Yucaipa's perimeter fence and saw what the day was really going to
bring.

After the trees, a large roadside sign announced the turnoff from
Oak Glen to the prison access road. Beyond it was a quarter-mile stretch
of asphalt laid in a sweeping curve around the perimeter fence to the
prison gate, which faced the foothills. And lining the road on both sides
along the entire quarter of a mile, chanting and waving banners, were
hundreds of protesters. More lined the naked slopes above the northern
end of the prison property. The sky was thick with drones, and two small
planes trailed banners reading BUYOUT = MURDER FOR PROFIT. "Looks
pretty exciting on the feeds," Charlie commented. "By the way, Floyd
Ingram is a dud."

He had gotten himself together enough to put together another in
his life's endless string of negative BVI reports:

Floyd Ingram, 41. Contacted Nautilus 4/14/40, following guilty
plea of murder 4/11/40, and sentencing to LWOP 4/12. Victim
Julio Brown, 59, Ingram's brother-in-law, found dead of stab
wounds 10/18/39. Ingram turned himself in and confessed
1/3/40. Prior to interview with Ingram, a background search un-
covered medical diagnosis of HIV-3 on 11/17/39. Evidence con-
necting Ingram to murder of Brown heavily circumstantial, case
dependent almost entirely on Ingram's self-incrimination and his
admission that he was in Brown's company the night of Brown's
death. Results of investigation forwarded to Los Angeles district
attorney's office, as well as Ingram's family and public defender.
No interview with Ingram conducted due to questions regarding
Ingram's ulterior motive and rigor of LAPD investigation.

"Who cares about Floyd Ingram, Charlie? Look at this." The mass of
bodies closed onto the road, leaving only a gap wide enough for Martin's
car. None of them touched him. He drove slowly through the curving
gauntlet of protesters, keeping an even speed and staying in the middle
of the road as individuals and small groups danced out to shout or wave
a sign before melting into the mass of people that converged behind
Martin and followed the car toward the prison's gate. He began to feel

like the crowd was pushing him along, propelling him toward the same act they claimed to protest. Vultures, he thought. How many of you are here because you're ghouls who want in on the death of Everett Shankly and the media lynching of Martin Kindred? And how few of you really know how you feel about life-term buyouts? Or how you should feel?

They drove him on, and Martin got a sparkle of panic at the base of his skull. He had come here of his own free will, because he was doing something difficult and unpopular but that he believed in, and as soon as he'd turned onto this final stretch of road a mob of anonymous protesters had robbed him of the chance to take the final steps on his own. The sparkle of panic radiated down into his hands, and as it hit his fingertips it transformed into anger.

He stopped the car. Instantly they converged on him, and his horizons contracted to the faces and palms beating flat against the windows. Moving slowly and with purpose, Martin opened the door. He did not push anyone with it. He worked the latch and eased it open as the protesters on that side of the car faded back far enough that he could get out and stand in a tight semicircle of open pavement.

A young woman spat at his feet. "Take the needle yourself, monster."

"If I ever do something like Everett Shankly did," Martin said, "I will." He was looking her in the eye as he said it, but his eyes wanted to jump away because as the words left his mouth he heard them for the lie they were. He had done something that you could take a buyout for, or in about an hour he would have. Perjury leading to capital punishment was a crime carrying a sentence of life without parole. If you wanted to get technical about it, a buyout wasn't capital punishment, but Martin despised those kinds of semantic split hairs. That was a distinction Scott Krakauer would make in the interest of a sharp sound bite. Martin knew that he had perjured himself, and that as a result of that perjury Everett Shankly was going to die.

But Everett Shankly deserved to die, and Martin was at peace with what he was about to do. Ninety percent of justice takes place off the books. Maybe Charlie was right that someone other than Curt Laskowski was trying to game the buyout system. Maybe he was even right that Martin was vulnerable because he didn't know what the game was or who was playing. What Charlie didn't understand, because Charlie had never met an ideal he was interested in subscribing to, was that belief demanded risk.

He walked, as the thunder of the crowd gradually overwhelmed his hearing and became a cocoon of white noise. He walked slowly and with purpose, straight down the double yellow stripe at the center of the road. The chants and slogans imprinted themselves in the part of his brain he'd carved out to store invective, but they didn't reach him emotionally. These people screaming at him were vultures and ghouls. Not one in a hundred of them knew the first thing about how buyouts worked.

As Martin approached the guard booth, Jerry Torres rolled the gate back just far enough for Martin to walk through without having to turn sideways. The protesters formed a wall across the chain-link gate as it rolled back into place. They did not touch it—for a protest mob, they were preternaturally disciplined or afraid of the police—but they formed ranks against it and boomed their slogans through the parking lot inside Yucaipa's walls. Jerry came down from his gatehouse perch long enough to say, "You sure brought 'em out today."

"I sure did," Martin said, and he was a little startled to hear a note of pride in his voice that he wasn't sure was ironic. What Charlie would have said was, *Fuck self-examination, do your job if you've decided to do your job.*

Charlie was in fact thinking something along those lines as he monitored the feeds and watched Martin go through the gates, the road beyond the fence swallowed by the mob. Martin walked to the prison's front door and inside as the gate guard—whose name Charlie could never remember—returned to his post. He had taps running on Martin's pod and Martin's car, and both were under siege. He could track some of the incursions, but others were coming from nowhere. Uneasy, Charlie thought again that Martin had stirred something up and didn't know how deep or far it went. He'd tracked the origin of the signal that brought the flash mob together at Yucaipa, and it occurred to him that if every self-respecting Priceless Lifer was out at the prison, now might be a good time to have a look at the actual physical location where the anti-buyout wackos made their plans.

That meant tearing himself away from Martin's crowning achievement-*cum*-fatal error, though, which Charlie was loath to do. But Charlie hated dithering worse than he hated an honest dumb mistake, so he forced himself to go with the impulse. He got up, threw on jeans and a shirt from the back of his chair, and headed out to see what the lair of a bunch of social malcontents might actually look like.

Did anyone catch Ingrid Bergman and Mos Def in the new Othello? "By heaven, I rather would have been his hangman!" But that's Roderigo, and who gives a fuck about him? Even though the recently departed Michael Douglas makes for a fine conniving lieutenant, especially since they spawned the avatar from old footage of him in The Streets of San Francisco. Enough to make you think that SAG is on to something when they strike over live-actor quotas in movie production. And who would have thought Haley Joel Osment would have made such a badass Iago? This I have to read:

> Others there are
> Who, trimm'd in forms and visages of duty,
> Keep yet their hearts attending on themselves,
> And, throwing but shows of service on their lords,
> Do well thrive by them and when they have lined their coats
> Do themselves homage: these fellows have some soul;
> And such a one do I profess myself. For, sir,
> It is as sure as you are Roderigo,
> Were I the Moor, I would not be Iago:
> In following him, I follow but myself;
> Heaven is my judge, not I for love and duty,
> But seeming so, for my peculiar end:
> For when my outward action doth demonstrate
> The native act and figure of my heart
> In compliment extern, 'tis not long after
> But I will wear my heart upon my sleeve
> For daws to peck at: I am not what I am.

You remember Popeye? He yam what he yam? He's the anti-Iago, the one character any of us ever knew who was fully and completely himself. The rest of us, we're Iago, man. We aren't what we are. I'm not Walt Dangerfield, but what the fuck am I?

TWENTY-FIVE

INSIDE YUCAIPA, Martin could feel eyes on him. The prison staff professed to be agnostic on the topic of buyouts, but they knew controversy when they smelled it, and they didn't like it. So today they didn't like Martin, because he'd brought a sea of yelling people to their front gate. The internal booth officer who usually shot him a wink while she checked in his sidearm wouldn't look him in the eye today, and the screws who escorted him down the hall to the viewing chamber maintained a chilly silence. It wasn't necessarily a hostile atmosphere, but it sure wasn't welcoming, either.

Janine Shankly was there, and Scott Krakauer, and the same priest who always came whenever the client didn't specifically request a cleric of a particular stripe. One half of the room's seating was filled with the extended family of Shankly's restaurant victims. Martin had a fleeting impression that he could tell how many generations each of them had been in the country by how emotional they appeared; those born in China, or first-generation, sat more impassively than those whose families had crossed the Pacific about the time the first Kindreds had made the trip from Derbyshire in 1880 or so. You're a hate criminal, Teresa would have said to him with a gleam in her eye, the way she always did when he made a harmless and probably correct assumption about ethnicity and behavioral tendencies. At least she might have before they'd stopped talking to each other with any kind of gleam at all.

The other side of the room, on Martin's right, was empty save for Janine, Scott, and Sol Briggs. Scott and Sol were sitting together in the back row while Garret Lau fidgeted around near the doorway, wanting to be somewhere else but stuck there because he'd attended every other buyout during his tenure at Yucaipa and stopping now would call even more attention to the specific circumstances of Everett Shankly. Add Martin to the right side of the room, and the pairs of guards at the door and just on the other side of the glass, and there were thirty-seven people whose field of vision included Everett Shankly. No cameras, no attendees without a family or professional interest. Buyout finalizations were not public events, although Scott wanted them to be. He had visions of ancillary revenue streams.

Martin had visions of being ignored. Anonymity was fast becoming his fondest wish. He'd been dumb enough to think, once upon a time, that a little celebrity wasn't a bad thing. Carl Marks had disabused him of that notion, and Everett Shankly was making it look like a bout of derangement. So what was this, apotheosis? Once, Martin had gone to a shrink, who had told him that he was the kind of person who was always striving to do higher and better things. Martin thought this was okay, but then the shrink went on to tell him that his underlying reasons were destructive. You're never good enough for yourself, the shrink said, and you shoot higher and higher because you know sooner or later you won't be able to go any higher—and it's that failure that you really want, because it will confirm what you've suspected all along.

He sat next to Scott because to do otherwise would have brought the controversy into his work environment, and as soon as he'd come to rest on the plastic chair Scott leaned in close and started talking, his mouth close to Martin's ear and one hand on Martin's shoulder. "This one's bold, Martin," Scott said. "I love it. Admire it. This is the kind of thing I can live with even if it fucks up, because it sends a message about the kind of company we are."

"No fuckup here, Scott," Martin said. "You know that."

"Right," Scott said. "Remember Carl Marks. You've seen the shitstorm before, right?"

Martin felt a brief squeeze on his shoulder, and Scott leaned back into his chair. Martin kept his eyes front, on the figure of Everett Shankly on the gurney. It occurred to him that he had become something of a connoisseur of human behavior in the face of death. He'd still never had a client make a break for it at the last second, or require restraints, but he'd seen wailing rage and whispered psalms and everything in between. Character was never more evident than under the shadow of death that must be met willingly.

Jocelyn sat on his other side, surprising and unsettling him. A sighting of both Krakauers in the same place never occurred without careful planning, and usually meant media relevance. Martin began to understand that he might just have gotten himself into something bigger than the Carl Marks deal. He nodded at Jocelyn, who shot him a wink that shocked him into returning his attention to Everett Shankly.

Carl Marks had died with all his personality quirks intact. The inflated sense of self-worth, the messianic charisma, the auteur's hauteur. Many actors and performers make a great show of not understanding where their public and private personae end and begin, but Carl Marks genuinely didn't. He died as if the needles were fake and the doctors and guards working for SAG scale. As if someone might bring him back from the dead to get the next take that much closer to perfect.

There was an air of the impossible about Everett Shankly. He looked like a child in the dentist's chair, as if everything about him had been calculated for maximum pathos. He seemed to radiate the sense that he could not possibly have killed anyone. Martin had seen quite a few murderers who were normal people, without any unusual malice toward humanity in general. And he had seen a few who inhabited the oddly gentle child-like space of certain kinds of insanity. Everett Shankly felt different. You looked at him and were certain he could not have killed anyone, so certain that it seemed he must emit some kind of pheromonal innocence.

It was a good thing, Martin thought as he watched the tech slide the shunts into Everett's elbows, that human beings are rational enough to overcome our instincts. He wasn't feeling rational at the moment. He was feeling angry, and anxious, and most of all cheated because he wasn't able to bring his parents and Hannah here and let them see that Jason's murderer was meeting a just end. He didn't want the secret, rebelled against the idea that it had to be a secret, could barely restrain himself from a foolish promise to stand up and denounce Everett

Shankly as the murderer of Jason Kindred at the moment the injections began to roll into Shankly's veins. He wanted Shankly to die knowing he hadn't gotten away with it, and for a moment, as the doctor stepped back and prepared to give the signal, Martin was willing to destroy his career and his life for that one moment of acknowledgment.

Then, as the doctor said, "Everything checks out," that willingness drained out of Martin, and he was a spectator at the death of a man whose death he had helped to broker. The sodium thiopental flowed into Everett Shankly, and Shankly's eyes began to close.

"Do them in order, Martin," he said.

Thirty seconds of silence passed, and no one else in the room looked in Martin's direction or gave any other sign that they had heard Shankly speak. The doctor gave a signal, and the pancuronium bromide shut down Shankly's muscles. Thirty seconds after that, potassium chloride stopped Shankly's heart. Two minutes after that, Everett Shankly was declared dead. *For you, Jason,* Martin thought. *That's not the only reason he deserved it, but as far as I'm concerned, this was for you.* The techs draped a sheet over Shankly and the doctor started in on the paperwork releasing his body to Janine, who was going to have him cremated. Simultaneously, Jocelyn and Scott tapped Martin's shoulders. Jocelyn shot him a wink and spoke under her breath. "Big day for us, Martin," she said. "A lot of the storm is going to blow around you."

He nodded. The Krakauers got up, shook hands with Garret Lau, and left. Martin sat until the relatives of Shankly's victims had filed out, their faces stony with grief, some of the younger women crying. The only other person in the room was Sol Briggs. Martin wondered briefly if Briggs was feeling reflective, as most people did in the aftermath of a death. Reflection led Martin back to Curt Laskowski. *A real white knight knows that it's not about him, it's about what he represents,* Laskowski had said, but he was wrong. The real white knight acknowledges no difference between him and what he represents.

"What was that he was saying at the end?" Sol asked. Martin shrugged and said he didn't know. But he did, and Sol would know soon if he bothered to run back the vid of the finalization that regulations mandated. The audio in those was always flawless, so much so that Martin hadn't watched one since the first. Without the audio in this case, all he had was the remembered echo of Everett Shankly's voice, saying *Do them in order, Martin,* before he died.

THE LITTLE SLICES and slivers of concrete and rusty barbed wire trapped along interstate rights-of-way and in the crotches of interchanges, or re-sected from neighborhoods by railroad planners—those used to be ei-ther gathering places for the city's homeless, or secret hideouts for criminals and smugglers. Nobody wanted to go there, because there was nothing there to go to; so the people who didn't want anyone around went there precisely because the nothing that repelled other people looked like opportunity to them. Then along came municipal broad-band, and all of a sudden you could run a business from any of these places, where before the cable guy wouldn't go. Now you didn't need him. You needed a pod, maybe a server if you had a lot to keep track of and you were too paranoid to entrust your data to public storage. But the crannies of Los Angeles that used to be the sole preserve of homeless hermits and gangs who needed a good place to process drugs or torture snitches . . . now they were full of underground podjackers, pirate nar-rowcasting malcontents of every political persuasion. This was the breeding ground for the furtive discourse of paranoia and would-be rev-olution. Walt Dangerfield would no doubt be found here.

The signal that had spawned the Priceless Life flash mob came from such a place, a rambling interconnected warren of corrugated tin shacks that might once have been a railroad office or a contractor's temporary headquarters. Charlie got there at about the same time Martin was walk-ing through Yucaipa's front gate. He did a sweep and found the local se-curity daemon a cut above average, which meant that it took a full minute for his pod to convince the daemon that he didn't exist and hadn't actually picked the lock and let himself in.

Right away the olfactory smorgasbord of old marijuana smoke, dry-ing fast-food grease, and the sweat of the intensely committed told him he was in the right place. Every hideout of every knot of dilettante revo-lutionaries had smelled like this for the past hundred years. The hide-outs of other cohorts that smoked a lot of pot and ate fast food were similar, but Charlie could always detect the lingering tang of self-righteousness in a place where post-college idealists went to bicker and congratulate themselves. He could see a sprinkling of status lights near the back of the room. A terminal cluster, probably, powered down because anyone who might have wanted to use it was out at Yucaipa giving Martin hell. A bar of light glowed dimly from the bottom of a doorway behind the cluster.

"Hey there," he called out. "Anybody home?"

Mostly this was Charlie's standard tactic to avoid getting shot, but he was also curious to find out which of the Priceless Lifers would have been the one selected to staff the fort while the rest of the gang had all the fun. They didn't seem like the type to leave lights on.

The door opened and Chloe Kapanen walked out, framed by a spill of flat white light from what could only be a news feed. "Huh," Charlie said. "I wouldn't have figured it was you."

"The door was locked, Mr. Rhodes," she said.

Charlie nodded. "Sure was."

"I'm going to assume that you gave a yoo-hoo as a way of saying that your intentions are aboveboard."

Charlie nodded again. "Sure are."

Leaning against the door frame, Chloe said, "So you're here to have some kind of conversation about Martin Kindred."

"Actually I want to know why you're not out with the rest of the kids at Yucaipa," Charlie said.

"Because I hate demonstrations," Chloe said. "Next question."

"What's Laskowski's deal?"

"I don't know. Next question."

"You don't know meaning you don't know why I'm asking, or you don't know meaning you don't know why he did whatever he did that set Martin off?"

"What makes you think Curt did something to set Martin off?"

"People who answer questions with questions are liars," Charlie said.

Chloe rolled her eyes. "No," she said. "Often they are just people who are being asked questions that they don't have enough information to answer. And now you can stop trying to bully me."

"You don't want that," said Charlie. "The only other tactic I know is charm."

She sat at one of the chairs in the terminal cluster. "Okay, there's your icebreaker. Now you've got me warmed up. My defenses are down. Go in for the kill."

Charlie sat two chairs away, noting that there were seven. The number of Priceless Life bigwigs, or the number of chairs that happened to be there? So easy to force patterns, react to them, and then find out they were never there. "So listen," he said. "Why is Sol Briggs talking to someone in your organization?"

There was a long silence. Charlie thought she was about to answer, but just then he got a ping from Martin's pod. He listened, said, "Fuck," listened some more, and said, "No way. You want a name, it's Curt Laskowski." After another moment, he broke the connection.

"What?" Chloe asked. "Why did you tell them Curt?"

"Your demo just went south. Way south." Charlie was already headed for the door. "There's cops down, and a whole lot of other people, too."

"It was peaceful," she protested, and Charlie wouldn't have known it beforehand but that was exactly the one thing she could have said that was guaranteed to set him off.

"Kid," he said, "nothing like this ever happens unless both sides are ready for it to happen. You want to bitch and moan about police brutality, you go right ahead, but you goddamn well better look in the mirror, too. Somebody walked up to Sol Briggs and blew him away in his car. Which lives are fucking priceless?"

He stalked out into the heat, with way too much to do and not nearly enough time to do it.

You have how many years on this planet? First twenty, you don't know what the fuck is going on. Last ten, you're thinking about the next time you have to take a piss. So there's maybe fifty in between, sixty more recently. Unless you're in Bangladesh, or Florida. How many hurricanes is that in the last six years, on top of an extra foot or so of ocean? Florida's gonna be a chain of islands before I shuffle off this mortal coil. Unless I take a buyout, which even though I have met Martin Kindred and know him to be a stand-up guy will never happen because I'm too goddamn old. Yes, LA, I'm old! I was born in the twentieth century! I was alive when Neil Armstrong walked on the moon! I have conscious memories of Ronald Reagan! And yet you listen to me. Listen to me! In another ten years, you'll be able to swim from Miami to Tampa, and along the way you're going to see a lot of bewildered and misanthropic fucking alligators, man, because they had it good down there for a while. So long, Everglades. So long, everything. I think the end is coming. I have a feeling of impending impendingness today, and it impends. The sky is falling, the British are coming, the bases are loaded with two out in the ninth.

TWENTY-SIX

WHEN MARTIN walked out of Yucaipa, his car was exactly where he'd left it in the middle of the road. From this distance, it looked untouched. Sol Briggs was with him, and during the hour they'd spent inside Yucaipa, San Bernardino County sheriffs had formed a cordon around the demonstration. Half of them seemed to be panning video cameras across the crowd. Martin was no good at estimating crowd size, but there had to be thousands of people there, thick on both sides of the road as far as he could see. The sides of the nearest hills looked like the lawn at a music festival, and the air buzzed with drones and helicopters. Two of the copters bore the seven-point star of the county sheriff's department. Something bigger than a demonstration about Everett Shankly was happening, Martin thought. One buyout all by itself isn't worth this.

"Your car?" Briggs said. Martin nodded.

Briggs popped the locks on his unmarked. "I'll give you a ride."

They were in no hurry to get to Martin's GTO, and Briggs barely touched the accelerator once they'd cleared the prison gate. "Fuckin' do-gooders," he muttered.

"They can't all be here because of Everett Shankly," Martin said.

Briggs was fiddling with his pod. "Nah. I guarantee you ninety percent of 'em are here because this is the cause of the day, and now they can say they went to a demonstration. They've got Everett figured for a martyr, and you for Pontius Pilate. I'd watch out if I were you. A whole lot of the old Priceless Lifers used to be in the anti-abortion racket. Not your true believers, but the spooky freaks who all they want to talk about is pipe bombs and sniper rifles."

This was by far the longest speech Martin had ever heard Briggs deliver. He considered it, and remembered again what Scott had told him. *Pull the trigger. We'll make it come out all right.*

"Maybe I should be afraid," he said. "I don't think I am, though."

"Don't be afraid. Be careful," Briggs said.

They were almost to Martin's car. "Sol," Martin said. "How come you've been talking to people inside Priceless Life?"

Briggs didn't answer. He parked next to Martin's car, passenger-side-to-passenger-side. Martin became aware of an intensifying roar outside. The crowd had figured out he was in Briggs' car. *Give me something, Sol,* Martin thought. *You know what I just did. Now you owe me.*

"Okay," Briggs said. "We can talk about this later." He opened the door, and the sounds of the mob poured in. Martin opened his own door, and was struck by the way that seemed to make things a little quieter, as if more sound was escaping than coming in his door. *Later,* he was thinking, *later we'll talk about it and I'll know,* and that was when the mob surged forward, over the sheriff's cordon toward Briggs' car, and somewhere out of the mass of bodies Curt Laskowski appeared. The inside of the car boomed with gunshots, Martin lost track of how many. Briggs' blood spattered across Martin's face and shirtfront. His eyes flinched shut, and the gunshots kept coming, punctuating the swelling madness of screams and the thump of bodies against the car. Martin rolled out the door and fell into the space between the two cars. Other gunshots were cracking over the crowd noise, and fragments of window glass rained down on his back. He stayed right there, listening to the sounds of riot suppression until a tear gas canister went off near the car and drove him out into the open.

He was in a suddenly vacated space, eyes streaming, hands held out away from his sides. He didn't want to be there, but didn't want to run. Around him, distorted by gas and tears, he could see bodies on the pavement. Chopper blades thumped low in the sky, and he could hear heavy engines approaching. Panic gnawed at him. The police were going to show up and kill him. They would think it was a setup. Or they would take him for one of the rioters, and with a cop down—maybe more than one—the responding uniforms were going to be out to put some hash marks on their side of the scoresheet. "I'm Martin Kindred!" he shouted. "Martin Kindred!" He blinked, tried to wipe his eyes clear on his shoulders, and realized he'd smeared more of Sol Briggs' blood on his face. There would be records of what happened in Briggs' car, Martin thought. They'll prove I didn't do anything. But I might not live that long.

I was set up, he thought. Set up so it would look like I set Briggs up. All of the elements of the Shankly buyout reshuffled themselves, settling into a new pattern. Laskowski had driven everything from the beginning. Martin began shouting his name again, adding that he couldn't see. An amplified voice boomed from a riot wagon coming down the last stretch of the prison access road. "You in the middle of the road! We have detected a firearm! Lie facedown on the pavement right now and keep your hands where we can see them!"

Martin sank to his knees. "I'm Martin Kindred," he called out. "I was in the prison on business." He put both hands flat on the burning pavement and let himself down in a reversed push-up until he was prone.

Boot soles hit the road not far from him. "Do not fucking move!" a cop shouted. "We will shoot!"

"Read my pod," Martin called. "I'm Martin Kindred. I work for Nautilus Casualty. I do buyouts."

"Do not fucking move!" the cop repeated. Running footsteps approached, and a knee punched into Martin's back, crushing the air from his lungs. The muzzle of a gun ground into the base of his skull. The cop holding him down tore the gun from his belt and zip-tied his hands together. Martin tried to speak, but he couldn't get any air. The cop searched him and came up with his pod. Weight shifted on Martin's back as the cop handed the pod off. His blood thundered in his ears, and he felt himself starting to black out.

Then somebody said something to someone else, and the knee disappeared. Martin hauled in a huge breath, too fast; his compressed lungs couldn't handle it all at once, and he started to cough until he thought he was going to pass out again. He rolled onto his side and tried to get up; someone helped him, and then his hands were free. Gradually he got his breathing under control, and his vision was clearing. He looked around and saw a circle of cops in riot gear, no longer pointing their guns at him but not pointing them anywhere else, either.

Into the circle came another cop, not in uniform. "You know a guy named Curt Laskowski?" he asked.

"I've met him," Martin said.

"Any reason why he would have been here today?"

"He's in Priceless Life," Martin said. "They were all here today."

The look on the detective's face said that he wanted to stomp the shit out of somebody, and Martin would do. "Did you see him?"

"I—I don't know," Martin said. "Sol was getting out of his car, and then somebody . . ." He realized he was talking with his hands, making a gun out of one of them and crooking the thumb over and over. "I just tried to get away."

"Didn't return fire with your fancy civilian weapon?" The detective had Martin's Sig in his hand. He sniffed the barrel, ejected the clip, and pressed down on the top cartridge. "Guess not," he said. "Got to love an armed citizenry. Stay here."

The detective walked away, leaving Martin to take in the aftermath of the riot. There were nine bodies that he could see: eight anonymous demonstrators and Sol Briggs. He thought of Sol's last moments, the contemplation and indecision on his face, the nebulous promise. What were you going to tell me, Sol? Martin wondered. And why couldn't you say it in the car? Such a strange moment. Thinking back over the fifteen years he'd had interactions with Sol, Martin couldn't remember ever seeing anything like introspection. Sol Briggs made decisions and executed them. He did what he did, right or wrong, and moved on, leaving the cleanup for someone else.

Which he had now done permanently. Briggs lay on his back, shirt torn open, the apparatus of lifesaving stuck to the pavement around his body by drying blood. Bullets had torn part of his face open, exposing broken teeth and his jawbone. Powder burns on his skin looked like fresh tattoos. Martin wondered if anyone had told Meg Twohy yet.

The detective returned. "Should have introduced myself," he said. "Javier Beltran, Robbery-Homicide. And you're Martin Kindred. You knew Briggs, and you knew the guy who's our first impression for the shooter, and something fucked up is going on here. So you're going to come with me and we're going to talk about it."

"I didn't do anything," Martin said.

"Maybe not," Beltran said. "But we're going to make sure of that before you not doing anything gets any more cops killed. I'm going to treat you like a human exactly until you give me a reason not to. Deal?"

Martin started to stand up. "Sounds like an offer I can't refuse," he said.

"Now you're getting the idea," Beltran said, and led Martin to a car.

DETECTIVE JAVIER BELTRAN turned out to be a decent guy. The first thing he did was hand Martin his pod and say, "Call your wife."

Martin shot Teresa a message that he was fine and would call her when he got done talking to the police, and that if the girls wanted to call they should, but there was no reason for anyone to be worried. *Nobody was after me,* he wrote, which might have been true. *Make sure they know that.*

Then it was back to the situation at hand, which was how to play interrogation rope-a-dope with Beltran without appearing to be anything but confused and forthcoming. Beltran starting things off by unburdening himself of some personal opinions. He thought buyouts were more trouble than they were worth, which meant he viewed Martin as an agent of social unrest, and this opinion was confirmed in his eyes by the day's events. Once they got that out of the way, though, things smoothed out. "You had a brother on the job, right?" Beltran asked Martin when they were coming down into the city. "I hear he was the real deal."

"Yeah," Martin said. "He was."

"Well, then, we sure could have used him." Beltran paused as if weighing his options. "We've got maybe six thousand demonstrators who got the fuck out of the area at high speed once the shooting started. And we've got ten of them still on the ground, but my guess is none of them is our shooter. Another three or four hundred ended up in wagons headed to San Bernardino for processing, but my guess is our shooter isn't there, either. You know why I'm guessing that?"

Martin shook his head. "No," he said.

"Because the math isn't in our favor, and because I'm a cynic. Just by the odds, we've got a five to seven percent chance of having lucked on to the shooter. Once we get the raw news feeds and can run his face, we get a leg up, but until then he's a free agent. That's a bitch of a head start. Reason I'm telling you all this is that I have a feeling you know something about the situation that might help us make our process more efficient. Am I wrong?"

"I've met Curt Laskowski twice," Martin said. "He's a member of Priceless Life, and he has a history of terrorist activity for anti-abortion groups. I think he's one of these guys who just likes to be around when violence happens, and if that means he has to start it himself, that's what he does."

Beltran was nodding. "Okay. Appreciate the character analysis. But what's the connection with Sol Briggs?"

"I don't know," Martin said.

Now there was a terrible kernel of selfishness in Martin's responses. He didn't want anyone to know what he had done, not just because he would end up in jail but because then the act would no longer be his. Once the cops had hunted Laskowski down, the Shankly deal would be just between Martin and Jason, and Martin wanted it that way.

So why hadn't he given Laskowski up?

Because I still might get away with it, he thought. Maybe I should be willing to take the punishment for breaking a law even if the law is unjust, but I'm not. It's a cop game now, and I'm playing by cop rules. Ninety percent of what happens, nobody ever knows about.

Martin wasn't a cop, though, as his family and Charlie had endlessly reminded him, and rarely do civilians get to play by cop rules—as Beltran reminded him. "Why do you want to play this coy, Martin? Family guy like you, wife, daughters?"

Martin was silent.

"Look," Beltran said. "Slack you want, slack I can give you. I'm not looking to bust your balls, and your family's earned a favor."

Martin was silent. Then, just as Beltran was about to speak again, he said, "Thanks. But the best favor you can do me is to let this play out. I haven't hurt anyone."

"Have it your way," Beltran said. "But I'm just going to warn you that the next time we talk to each other, things might be different."

"How's the investigation into my brother's murder?" Martin asked.

He was looking out the window, not wanting to challenge Beltran by looking him in the eye. The ice was thin.

Now it was Beltran's turn to be silent. Neither of them spoke until Beltran turned north on the 605 instead of keeping straight on I-10 into downtown. "I'll drop you somewhere where you can change your shirt," he said.

Is there any two words in the English language . . . let me start that over. Are there. Are there any two words in the English language that provoke the same kind of response as cop down? No, there are not. Cop down means there's someone out there who values his own life so little that he's willing to do the one thing guaranteed to make that life absolutely worthless. He's willing to kill a cop. If you're willing to kill a cop, either you've convinced yourself that you're bulletproof, or you don't care what's going to happen when the bullets start hitting you. Well, there's someone like that out there right now, because today at the Shankly soirée somebody shot a cop. Whereupon the rest of the cops waded in and pounded the living shit out of everybody but the guy who fired the shots. So, as the great Vonnegut would have said, it goes. Riots and rumors of riots. People, man. I mean, if you're not going to kill a cop because you're in a mad fury about the injustice of commercialized state murder, when are you going to kill a cop? It makes absolute, incorrigible sense. If you're a certain kind of crazy person.

TWENTY-SEVEN

THE FIRST THING Martin did when he got back to the hotel room was pour himself a drink from the minibar. Then he ran the ice upgrade from the stick Charlie had given him. Then he called the girls to say good night.

Kelly didn't have her own pod, but Martin figured that she was more likely to be with Allison than with Teresa, so it was Allison he called. Then, like a memo from the universe confirming that he never knew quite as much as he thought he did, Kelly answered. "Dad," she said. "You were in a *riot*. It was on the *feeds*. People got killed."

"I'm okay, kiddo," he said. "I would have called sooner, but I had to talk to the police about what happened."

"Why were you there? Was it work?"

"Yep. Work. I had an appointment out there." Martin started to formulate a Kelly-level explanation of the Shankly PR problem, but she was already on to other topics. Her dad was okay, that was all there was to it. So they chatted about school, about whether the remake of *The Princess Bride* should use live actors who resembled the original cast or avatars, and about the difficulties of carrying on a summer-camp romance when everyone else thought Tony Blanco was the cutest boy in the room, too. Then she wanted to know what was the definition of an animal, and whether gnats and plankton counted, and then, with no change in tone, she said, *ByeDaddyloveyouAllison!* And was gone.

I'm going to hear her grow up as a voice on the phone, Martin thought. See her as phosphors rearranging themselves on the screen of my pod.

Allison was furious at him, which she demonstrated by bursting into tears as soon as she got on the line. Martin calmed her down as well as he could given the fact that they were five miles apart and she was a twelve-year-old girl. The truth was, she was tough in the way that Teresa was tough, but because Allison was still growing into it, sometimes knowing that she was tough was enough to make her dissolve into tears. "Dad," she said when she'd pulled herself together, "can you get another job?"

"I don't know, Alli," he said. "Maybe I could, but my job is important, and it's important that someone does it well."

"Find something else important!" she said. "Something important and not dangerous!" After a moment's thought, she added, "You could be a veterinarian. They're important."

"That's not a bad idea," Martin said. If, he added to himself, I was fifteen years younger and any good at anatomy.

"So when are you going to come and get your stuff? Mom says you're moving out."

Martin took a breath to bite down on his initial response. "Sometimes," he said, "your mother puts things a certain way when I would put them differently. We'll talk about this all together. But in the meantime, my stuff is going to stay right where it is. Why, you in a hurry to take over the extra bedroom?"

A laugh from Allison was just what he needed, and he got it. Then she was gone, and Teresa was on. "I'm going to go right ahead and apologize for phrasing that that way," she said.

"Well, thanks," Martin said. "How about we get our story straight between us grown-ups before we tell the kids anything else?"

"We should. If you live that long."

"Come on, T."

"Come on, hell," she said. "You were in a car that had thirteen gunshots fired into it. And you're going to put yourself in the same situation again. First it was Carl Marks, and now it's Everett Shankly, and next time it'll be someone else. Maybe you don't care what I want anymore, Martin, but the girls don't want you in the spotlight."

"I don't want to be in the spotlight, either," Martin said. "But the job is important."

"Bullshit. It's important for you to think your job is important." There was a pause. Teresa looked offscreen, said, "Yes, honey, I know," then returned her attention to Martin. "Let's have lunch tomorrow or the next day. Get some things settled. Okay?"

"Sure," he said. "Good."

Teresa clicked off.

Then he stripped and got into the shower, staying there for a long time. He imagined each particle of Sol Briggs' blood sluicing down his body and into the drain, platelet by corpuscle. It did not purify him, but he wasn't guilty of Briggs' death. He was a bystander, a knight on other errands, slowly being stripped of anything except belief in the rightness of his actions. *She asked me to move out,* Martin thought, *and here I am. I call my daughters, I consider looking for a place to live, I waste money on a hotel room because it's a form of self-destruction I can afford.*

He got out of the shower, dried off, and threw away all of his clothes. Then he shaved, dressed, and sat down with his pod, knowing that Charlie would ping at some point but unwilling to start a conversation he knew neither of them really wanted to have.

Do them in order, Martin. He cracked the file containing the Shankly DBs. There were twenty-one of them, in eight different amounts.

Morgan Macallister, 100 Main Street, Newport Beach. $196,418.

Jaime Hernandez, 4637 Kimberwick Circle, Irvine. $832,040.

Lawrence Apire, 8881 East Foxhollow Drive, Anaheim. $75,025.

Lillian Huerta, 2260 Angela Street, Pomona. $121,393.

Antonio Ocampo, 132 East Oberg Street, San Dimas. $121,393.

Luther Henry-Scontras, 2841 Sanborn Avenue, La Crescenta. $196,418.

Angela van Bronckhorst, 1047 East Spazier Avenue #313, Burbank. $75,025.

Ibrahim Suleyman, 3285 Tareco Drive, Los Angeles. $514,229.

Emma Clinton, 7100 West Sunset Boulevard, Los Angeles. $196,418.

Janine Shankly, corner of La Brea and West 20th, Los Angeles.
$1,346,269.

Dorothy Esterhazy, 3419 West 43rd Place, Los Angeles.
$75,025.

Nigel Washington, 8731 Baring Cross Street, Los Angeles.
$317,811.

Miguel Tavarez, 1727 East 107th Street, Los Angeles. $46,368.

Andrea Finn, 11479 Linden Street, Lynwood. $196,418.

Fu-Ping Yan, 7455 Firestone Boulevard, Downey. $121,393.

Alejandro Zuniga, 8023 Slauson Avenue, Montebello.
$317,811.

Israel Loring, 2100 South Garfield Avenue, Monterey Park.
$75,025.

Mahmoud Hassan, 2719 Michigan Avenue, Boyle Heights.
$196,418.

Bruce Nguyen, 3357 Opal Street, Los Angeles. $121,393.

Victoria Evanson, 1382 La Puerta Street, Los Angeles. $46,368.

Armando Galarraga, 4450 Dunham, Los Angeles. $514,229.

The total was right, and as DB lists went it wasn't too onerous. The longest one Martin had ever done ran to thirty-six entries, and took him four days to finish. Leave it to a number freak like Shankly to get strange with the amounts, Martin thought. He'd seen a lot of clients take out frustrations or perpetuate grudges with disbursement amounts. Christopher Bragdon had left each of the three mothers of his four children a single dollar, and the vast majority of his disbursement had gone to a Wilmington charity well known (at least according to Charlie) to be a front for the Aryan Brotherhood. In the end Bragdon's prison gang buddies had been more important to him than his children. One more check mark on the pro-buyout balance sheet, as far as Martin was concerned. A guy like that didn't deserve to be on the earth.

Since he'd be doing the disbursements himself, Martin automatically started plotting out the most efficient way to get through them. Then he caught himself, hearing Everett Shankly's last words again. What do I owe him? Martin thought. He'll never know how I do them. What difference does it make?

But he was confronting the strange power of a dying man's last request, and Martin found that he couldn't rationalize it away. Was it so much to ask, that the DBs be done in a certain order? Everett Shankly was gone, Jason was avenged. It seemed somehow . . . *churlish* was the word that boiled up out of Martin's college vocabulary, to ignore Everett's last request out of spite. I am not a churlish person, Martin thought. Ergo (another college word) I should not do churlish things. Human civilization is the conflict between principle and instinct. I am being ridiculous.

It was a problem for tomorrow, he decided, and drained his glass.

CHARLIE HAD SPENT the morning talking to crazy people, the day committing property crimes and trying to shepherd Martin through messes of Martin's creation, and the evening wondering how it was that life continually punished him for being loyal to his friends. Now he was, with the aid of several beers, putting himself in a reflective frame of mind. Against his better judgment he was at Yankee Doodle's, oppressed by its macho bonhomie and sickly fascinated by the predatory mating rituals of the middle-aged cop. Normally Sol Briggs would be at the center of the whorls and spirals of bar-stool courtship, saturnine and feral, grinning at a brutal joke while his eyes roved over the curves of women no older than his children. Charlie found himself a little sad that Sol would no longer be around. He'd been a disgusting human being, but good for a laugh; in candid moments, Charlie saw some of himself in Briggs, used Briggs as a touchstone to make sure he wasn't giving in to his own baser impulses. His death seemed like a memento mori personally addressed to Charlie Rhodes.

He went outside, wishing he had a cigar. It had been nearly three years since he'd smoked one, but if you couldn't use the death of a disliked casual acquaintance as an excuse to indulge a fatal habit, what use was life?

Martin was maintaining radio silence. Charlie thought about going to look for him, but Pasadena was a long fucking way from Long Beach at this time of night, and if Martin wanted to stew, Charlie wasn't in the mood to interfere. The coming days were going to get a whole lot shittier, and maybe it was best just to let everything sit for a few hours. While thinking, he fiddled with his pod, wanting to do something but uncharacteristically confused about what it should be. One possibility was to shake Chloe Kapanen harder until he knew for sure what she'd known about Laskowski. The downside to that was that she might go to the LAPD, and Charlie had no way of knowing whether it would be one of his friends or enemies who would take the call. A second possibility was find Laskowski himself and hogtie him for the uniforms. Or just kill him.

Contemplating this option, Charlie stepped into uncomfortable territory. In his life he'd killed three people, all of whom were in some way trying to do him serious bodily harm. He'd never been particularly traumatized by this, but he wasn't looking forward to the possibility of doing it again, and the act he was considering was utterly different. It was one thing to hear a bullet go by your head and return fire. Nobody could blame you for that. If he just smoked Curt Laskowski, no matter how good he made it look, he would always know what he had done. Any one of his ex-wives would have said that Charlie Rhodes left a trail of human wreckage in his wake, but he didn't see it that way. He'd spent his life trying to make the best of bad situations, and he was too old to make the jump into vigilante murder now.

Which didn't mean he couldn't join a manhunt now and then. Aha. Thus presented with the decision, Charlie grew so resolute that he walked away from a half-full beer, straight to his car and into the Los Angeles night, plotting out an itinerary that would lead him to Curt Laskowski.

We have a name for the shooter of the cop yesterday, one Curtis Diogenes Laskowski. Now, there's a name that says Stone Killer. Am I wrong? Of course not! Because even if I was, none of you could tell me! Ha! O o o o that barbaric yawp. The drugs are getting to me. So Curtis Diogenes Laskowski blew away a cop named Solomon Briggs. Detective Briggs, this cop-hating narrowcast buccaneer wishes you nothing but the best in the afterlife of your choosing. And Curt Laskowski, you are one lucky crazy gringo. Have fun in prison. If you ever get there. Apparently buyout deal maker Martin Kindred was in the car, right? First his brother, now this. I bet right now, nothing would clear a room of cops quicker than Martin fucking Kindred walking through the door. But I forgot this Diogenes thing. The famous Cynic, who believed that independence and happiness came from freedom from social mores, who believed that all civilization destroyed the individual . . . we could use another Diogenes. And as a bonus etymological lesson, I am happy to inform you that the word cynic comes from a Greek root meaning "dog." The dog is cynical but idealistic, too, isn't he? He'll take a shit wherever he pleases, but you can hit him and he'll always come back for more. And dogs don't lie. They might want to, but when you come home and someone has torn up the trash all over the kitchen, I guarantee you the dog is going to look guilty and cop to the crime as soon as you look in his direction. Honest, cynical, idealistic, all at the same time. I wonder if Curtis Diogenes Laskowski is that kind of guy.

TWENTY-EIGHT

IN THE MORNING, Martin decided to comply with Shankly's last wish. Not so much out of a feeling that he was obliged to Shankly, but that he was obliged to a standard that he had failed by breaking the rules to get the Shankly buyout done. So his penance would be adhering to Shankly's rules. He felt good about the decision for the length of time it took him to get ready for work.

A message from Scott and Jocelyn had arrived at five forty-seven that morning suggesting that Martin ought to drop by the office before heading out into public spaces again, and further suggesting that earlier was much better given the previous day's turn of events. Martin trolled the feeds and saw that Curt Laskowski was the subject of an impressive manhunt, and that most of the demonstrators arrested at Yucaipa had been processed and sprung with summonses for disturbing the peace. No surprises there, nor was it a big shock to see the mainstream feeds ignoring or downplaying the civilian casualties. It was all by the book: People who got killed in riots either had it coming or should have known better than to put themselves in that situation.

Flipping over to MSNBCNN, Martin blinked at the sight of his house besieged by real human reporters. He pinged Teresa. No answer. Then he pinged Allison and Kelly's school, and was reassured to find that both of them were in class. "We're getting a lot of interview requests, though," the secretary complained. "We've only got one officer, and she's having a hard time keeping all of the reporters away. This isn't good for the students, Mr. Kindred."

Since when did secretaries issue judgments to parents? Martin wondered. "You can let your administrators know that I'm doing what I can to keep a lid on it," he said. "I'll pick up the girls today. Please don't let them get on a bus."

His next call was to Charlie, but he got a signal-unavailable ping-back. Either Charlie was in a Wi-Free or he'd shut down for some other reason. Uneasy, Martin left his room and took the stairs down to the hotel lobby. The GTO was in the shop getting windows put in and wouldn't be ready until after lunch, so the plan was to start the DBs then after talking things over with Scott and Jocelyn.

Camera lights hit him the second he came out of the stairwell, and the lobby erupted in shouted queries. *Martin! Mr. Kindred, what do you know about Curt Laskowski? Why hasn't Nautilus made a statement? Are you divorcing your wife? How do you feel about Detective Briggs' murder? What was it like in the car? Why were you in his car? Did you say anything to the demonstrators?*

Was Everett Shankly innocent?

Martin stopped. He was almost to the door, but he turned to face the ring of lenses and microphones, taking off his hat and raising it over his head for quiet. "I have one thing and one thing only to say," he said. "I did the Shankly buyout exactly as I would have done any other, following the same procedures and adhering to the same set of rules. Apparently Everett Shankly became some kind of cause célèbre for people who are against buyouts. Fair enough. But what happened yesterday had nothing to do with Everett Shankly's guilt or innocence. It had to do with a mob mentality. I think instead of turning this into a media circus, we ought to be thinking about the family and colleagues of Detective Solomon Briggs and the others who lost their lives yesterday. Now please leave me and my family alone."

He turned again, feeling the waves of questions breaking over his back, and walked out the door.

"This has turned into a problem, Martin," Jocelyn said when the three of them were settled in Scott's office. "How are we going to manage it?"

"Which part of the problem?" Martin asked.

He was asking Jocelyn, but Scott answered. "Our primary concern at this point is that you were in the car with Sol Briggs when Laskowski killed him. It's going to be very easy for people to think that you were acting as some kind of spotter for Laskowski, and I'm afraid some people are already thinking that. Put together with the initial controversy over Shankly's buyout, and we've got a situation."

"I can't prove a negative," Martin said. "People are going to believe what they believe about that. The evidence will show different once it's all examined."

"That might be," Jocelyn said. "Assuming all of the evidence is examined."

There was a pause. Martin wondered if Jocelyn could know about the LAPD's interest in Shankly for Jason's murder, and if she was trying to give him an opening. Then Scott stepped in again. "Also assuming that the public narrative of this isn't set in stone before the police have a chance to look at all of the relevant information."

"I'm not following," Martin said. "Didn't we decide that this deal was worth pushing through even if people screamed and yelled about it?"

Scott adopted a pained expression. "I do remember that conversation. The problem is that the situation has gotten more serious. We've got to take the long view here. At first it appeared that the return on the Shankly deal, in terms of pushing the envelope of what the public was willing to accept, would be worth the trouble. Now . . ." He shrugged. "No plan survives events. Things have changed."

"We're taking a lot of calls from Sacramento and Washington," Jocelyn said. "People who were supportive of expanding our charter are having second thoughts."

"It's hard to overestimate the impact of a cop getting killed," Scott said. "Apart from the fact that we knew Sol Briggs personally."

How careful they were to alternate, Martin thought. Setting up a rhythm. When people set up a rhythm, it's to prepare for some kind of punctuation.

"We took a lot of punches during the Carl Marks deal, but it was worth it then," Jocelyn said. "The combination of celebrity, controversy . . . we needed it then, and you were terrific."

Scott picked up the thread. "Now we don't need it so much, though. Truth is, we don't need it at all. It's not helpful, it doesn't move things forward. Things might stall. As executives of this company, we have a responsibility to prevent that."

"And on a personal level," Jocelyn continued, "we have a responsibility to pursue the agenda. We believe, Martin. This isn't just about the money. Although," she added with a smile, "I'm sure you remember that money was a part of the conversation from the beginning."

I do indeed, Martin thought. You said something about actuaries and bow ties, and a goddamn lot of money.

"It's very important that we appear to be taking this situation seriously. I mean, we are, but we have to demonstrate that in a particular way. Which usually doesn't have anything to do with the relevant steps we're actually taking." Scott was getting serious, leaning forward and then back as if he couldn't get settled. With Scott, posture was everything. Martin could tell he was building up to the point of the whole conversation.

Just as he figured out what it was going to be, Jocelyn put it into words for him. "We'd like you to resign, Martin," she said. "It may not seem fair, but it's the best way to move the company forward in view of what's happened."

Of course, he thought. They rode me while the business grew, and now that it's got its own momentum, I'm the logical sacrifice when perception problems get serious. From the outside, it looks like Nautilus is shedding someone who's too tied to the early days of the program. They can make a show of recognizing that the next step in expanding buyouts means changes, and they can express simultaneous regret and optimism. And there I go back onto the market, branded by both what I've done and how it came to an end.

"I assume you're going to fire me if I don't agree?" Martin said.

"Afraid so," Scott said. "In fact, we probably should just fire you, but it didn't seem fair, after all you've given to the company. Best that the public narrative has you leaving on your own terms."

"Okay, then, I want to do the Shankly DBs before I go," Martin said.

The Krakauers looked at each other and reached an unspoken agreement. "Sure," Scott said. "No problem. We can do that."

HE FLOATED OUT the door, in possession of one more secret. Not for long, though. Martin had a distinct sensation of imminence. As soon as the announcement of his resignation went out, it would be widely assumed that he was pushed out the door. How long would it be before other secrets came out? If Curt Laskowski survived his capture, what incentive did he have to protect Martin?

Things were going to get a lot worse, Martin thought. He pinged Charlie, text only: *Allowed to resign.* Then he started walking to the Metro station. The car wouldn't be ready for another couple of hours, but since he couldn't do DBs without it, Martin had some time to sit in train cars and consider his situation. In a couple of days he would be jobless, tagged as the guy who started the Yucaipa riot and got an LAPD detective killed. It was going to be a rough couple of years. At least forty-nine buyouts meant quite a bit of money in the bank, even if Teresa was going to end up with some of it.

Maybe the thing to do was take the bull by the horns. Martin cataloged what he knew that might be able to help him. One: LAPD was looking at Everett Shankly for the murder of one of their own, but hadn't made the move. Two: Curt Laskowski had access to LAPD documents, via either intrusion or inside friends. Three: Sol Briggs had been in touch with Priceless Life.

A possible version of events presented itself, which fit the known facts but was so counterintuitive that Martin thought he'd also have to believe in the Tooth Fairy if he took it seriously. Briggs was pipelining information to Priceless Life, and had willingly given Laskowski the file on Shankly. If it was true, the cynicism of it was breathtaking: Laskowski deliberately allowed a bad buyout to take place, and allowed the organization to be manipulated by the cops, so Priceless Life got its rallying point and the LAPD got their cop-killer.

It didn't fit, though. If the LAPD liked Shankly for Jason's murder— if they knew he'd done it but also knew that they didn't have enough for the DA's office to prosecute—there were other ways of solving the problem. Everett Shankly would not have been the first suspected cop-killer to suffer a random street shooting.

Occam's razor, Martin told himself. It's too elaborate. What's the simplest solution that fits the facts?

He took a deep breath and pinged Meg Twohy. She didn't answer. "Meg," Martin said. "I'm sorry about Sol. And I need to talk to you. Urgently." He paused, wondering what else he could say, and then broke the connection. Now, he thought. This needs to happen right now. He headed downtown, pinging Meg constantly and when he wasn't pinging her pinging Charlie to ping her. When he got off the subway, he strolled into the plaza in front of the library, found himself a bench that was a bit out of the way from the main pedestrian flow, and kept pinging. About forty-five minutes later, Meg appeared. "What, Martin?" she said. "What do you want?"

"I just wanted to tell you," he began, and then stopped. "I'm sorry about Sol, Meg. I think Laskowski set me up, I think he was pulling strings—"

She cut him off. "Didn't you just get through telling Javy Beltran that you didn't have any idea what Laskowski was planning?" she said.

"Of course I didn't," Martin said. "But I've been trying to figure it out. Meg, I've got kids. You think I'd put myself next to a guy when I knew he was about to get killed? I'd have to be awfully trusting that Curt could shoot straight."

"I thought of that."

"And?"

"It makes me feel better. A little," she said. "I don't have any way of knowing that you didn't have some other plan, though. Try this one on: Sol was supposed to let you out before Laskowski opened up. You like that? The department does. Maybe Laskowski decided to take you out since you knew about the plan."

"So he managed to hit Sol six or seven times and completely miss me? Come on, Meg," Martin said.

"The average shooter with a pistol misses much more often than he hits. If you run the probabilities, it's unlikely but not impossible. For the record, I don't think that's what happened, but I'm telling you as a favor that I'm in a minority right now." Meg looked up and down the street. "Now what did you want to tell me so urgently?"

"I got fired this morning."

She squinted and looked up at the sky. "Hmmm, wonder if I won the pool. I think I had ten o'clock."

"It was actually closer to eight thirty," Martin said. "They're going to let me resign once I finish the Shankly DBs."

"Which is when?"

"A couple of days from whenever I get my car back," Martin said. "Which should be whenever I get to the shop."

"And I need to know this why?"

"Because someone's pulling me around, Meg, and I don't know who it is, and I was hoping you might be able to shed some light."

"And I would do this why?"

Crossroads, Martin thought. He paused long enough to get what he wanted to say exactly right. "Because I took Jason's killer off the street."

She stood up. "Don't call me again," she said, and walked away.

I am frenetic. I am the screaming id that wants to kill anything it can't fuck and fuck anything it can't kill. I am the monkey let out of the Skinner box. I am the college kid who was homeschooled and finds himself at UCLA. The universe is too big, the pleasures too many and various, the time I lost too much ever to make up and my hunger to make it up therefore too great ever to sate. I am the wendigo, cast out for crimes against the tribe and transformed into a monster with a heart of ice who must eat and eat and never be full. I am appetite. I am wishing, in short, that I had been in the heart of the maelstrom out at Yucaipa. Everett Shankly I could not give a shit about. You kill five people, you get what's coming to you. But to be in the mob, to be free . . . I've got a VR rig in my head, and there I'm seeing the muzzle flashes. There I'm hearing the thwop of the helicopter rotors, there I'm weeping with tear gas and ducking my head when the batons come down, and you know what? Because it didn't really happen, I love it. I'm proud of myself for imagining it. I wasn't there, but I wanted to have been there, and this fake courage feels to me like the real thing. Man, I didn't know until just now what an asshole I was.

TWENTY-NINE

CHARLIE SAT BACK on his bench in Chess Park, listening to a bell some-where tolling noon. To give himself a new perspective on things, he'd taken the exact spot where Janine Shankly had taken a couple of punches from her brother just before his arrest. This part of the beach and the Santa Monica Pier were occasionally swallowed up in a pirate Wi-Free zone that existed between suppressions of its suppressor. Today the suppressor was up and running. Charlie figured it would be a cou-ple of hours before Santa Monica IT found it and baffled it again.

He'd gone on the hunt for Laskowski figuring that the permanent Wi-Frees would be the place to begin, but pretty quickly he'd seen that LAPD had those under close surveillance. Laskowski would have gone to Plan B right away, and the problem was that Charlie didn't know what Plan B was. Your average killer either went to ground among people he knew or headed for the nearest border. Laskowski had murdered out of some ideological conviction, which was a wild card. Was he in some Priceless Lifer's basement right now? In their headquarters listening to Chloe lecture him about how he'd set the movement back?

He could also be facedown in the water under a pier somewhere, Charlie thought. But that wasn't likely. Laskowski knew his way around the Wi-Free pirate underground, which largely existed to create spaces for pocket networks to run without the content taps that came with mu-nicipal Wi-Fi. It stood to reason that he could move with the pirate Wi-Frees, hiding out from the security infrastructure until he made some long-term plans.

That was Charlie's working hypothesis, and it had led him here. He didn't like the symmetry of it—too easy for Laskowski to come back to the place where the whole thing had started—but the pier Wi-Free was one of the more durable pirate pockets. Laskowski would feel safe lost in the physical crowds, and in the warren of restaurants, bars, and illegal squats that hunkered on and around the pier.

A couple of other known Priceless Lifers hung around in a place called Sneaky Pete's, carved out of what had once been a video arcade and was now one of the seamier VR barracks Charlie knew of in Greater LA. You had to know Pete's was there to find it, and to get there you had to go through the barracks, which Charlie did with great reluctance. Martin owed him for that, if for nothing else. Stacked six high along the walls were bunks modified to hold complete sets of deadman VR gear, the kind that took you on your trip without you moving your body. In the middle of the room were booths, partially closed off, for that portion of the clientele who wanted physical motion along with their cortical stimulation. Charlie hated VR, or at least the people who tripped. They were disappointed Singularity zealots, getting what they could from the faded promise of the post-human future. Worse, they were by and large exactly what you would expect them to be: poor specimens of humanity using their trips to gratify desires that real life never offered. Once, Charlie thought as he navigated through the booths trying not to look at the simulated depravity within, I'd like to see someone using VR to explore an art museum or something. It would go a long way toward restoring my faith.

Instead he breathed air thick with hormones and the scent of bodily fluids, and tried to stop his ears against the more vocal trippers as they found their crescendos. Inside Sneaky Pete's, the atmospheric bouquet ran more toward marijuana and whiskey fumes, with a hint of sour puke. Not a sea breeze, but an improvement from the barracks. Charlie scanned the faces in the room, planning his approach to the bar so he got at least a profile look at everyone in the place. He didn't see Curt Laskowski.

He did see Meg Twohy.

Charlie double-checked for Sol Briggs, felt like an idiot for doing so, then felt like an idiot for feeling a stab of sentiment that Briggs wasn't around anymore. Two nights in a row, to be feeling bad because a walking bag of shit like Sol Briggs got smoked; age was turning Charlie into his mother. Next thing he knew, he'd be glued to daytime soap feeds and lining up for revivals of *Arsenic and Old Lace.*

Although, he considered, that wouldn't be all bad, especially if the alternative was walking up to a cop who would know why he was there. But he did it anyway. "Meg," he said, sitting next to her at the bar. "Buy you a drink?"

"You fucking well better, after the last day," she said. "I lit a match to my career first thing this morning, to keep your friend out of jail."

"What the fuck," Charlie said. "Why'd you do that? He won't work that hard for himself."

"The problem with guys like Martin is that they have this weird influence." Drinks arrived. Meg downed much of hers, and didn't refuse when the bartender asked if she wanted another. "He's so committed to what he believes that even when he's a fool, you want to cut him a break because he believes."

"Not enough people believe," Charlie agreed, and killed his own drink. The bartender wasn't in such a hurry to get him another. Nice to be in your thirties and fiercely, competently sexy the way Meg Twohy was. "So, lit a match," he added.

"Tcchhh," she said, striking a fingertip against a palm.

"Tried to call off the dogs?"

"Suggested we should approach the investigation logically."

"Ah," Charlie said.

Meg started in on her next drink. "Although the truth is, I'm not going to be brokenhearted if emotion trumps logic when we find Laskowski."

Charlie waited to see if she would keep going. When she didn't, he said, "Speaking of whom."

"No idea," she said. "We're trolling the Wi-Frees, as you can see, but they come and go too fast to keep track of, and he's more tapped into that scene than we are."

Charlie decided not to mention Meg's unconventional stakeout tactic of sitting at the bar with a row of drinks. She'd just lost her partner, even if he was a professional liability and lousy human being. "Mind talking about Everett Shankly for a minute?" he asked. She shrugged. "Okay," Charlie said. "You picked him up for a domestic that a passerby just happened to catch on video, and then he ended up going down for multiple murder. How'd you get there?"

"When we pulled him in for the thing with his sister, he confessed practically the minute we put him in the interview room," she said. "Before we even told him what we wanted. So we skipped the domestic charges and went right with the multiple murder. Does that offend your sensibilities?"

"Not if Janine was okay with it," Charlie said.

"Oh, she was," Meg said.

I just bet she was, Charlie thought. "And she defended him, right?"

"As much as she could," Meg said. "She got the hearings put off as long as she could, did every evaluation known to man, the whole works. But he pled guilty as soon as we stood him up in front of a judge. She may have told him that he was going down on a capital charge if he didn't, but I don't think the DA would have done it given all the competency questions."

"He was cleared for trial, though, right?"

"Oh, yeah. He was weird, but he wasn't disabled. Still, once all those evaluations go into the trial records, juries get real skittish about the needle. DAs don't want the hassle of a capital proceeding if the sentence is going to be life anyway." She killed off another drink and banged the glass on the bar a little harder than she had to. Ding ding, Charlie thought. Detective Twohy, going off duty.

"But then it didn't make any difference because he pled," he prompted.

"Nope."

"He say why he was confessing?"

"Who cares?" Meg said. "He did it, he confessed to it. The reasons don't matter."

That right there might be the reason I'm not a cop anymore, Charlie thought. He and Martin shared a belief that reasons mattered. Martin had even quoted a poem at him once: *The last temptation is the greatest treason / To do the right deed for the wrong reason.* It was one of the wellsprings of Kindred family conflict. Martin was all about reasons, the cops in the family were about results. The two worldviews coexisted poorly, was one way to put it.

He caught the bartender's attention with a twenty, pointed it at Meg, and laid it on the table. "Sorry about Sol," he said.

"Yeah," she said. "Watch out for Martin."

That's what I do, Charlie thought.

Halfway back through the infernal scene in the barracks, his pod made just about every sound it was capable of. The city had gotten to the pier Wi-Free again. He stroked the screen to life and saw that Martin had pinged maybe a dozen times. Then he saw that he had another dozen or so messages from Chloe Kapanen, which was weird.

Who first? Where was Laskowski? Okay, Charlie thought. Chloe first.

MARTIN PICKED UP his car at twelve thirty, reopened the Shankly DB file at twelve thirty-three, and was on his way to the first address at twelve thirty-four. Fired, he thought. Allowed to resign. My last couple of days, and I'm going to do it right. "Pilgrim, I gotta tell ya, yer goin' awful fast," John Wayne said.

He slowed down, easing into the smart lane on the Long Beach Freeway and rolling with the automated flow all the way down to Newport Beach. The address turned out to be in Balboa Pavilion, near where the ferries left for Catalina. Private clubs with mirrored windows alternated with the kind of odd business that could only exist at the intersection of Ocean and Narcissism. One such enterprise was Davy Jones Sportfishing and Burial at Sea, which was the registered occupant of the first address. Martin walked in and approached a leathery Hawaiian-shirt-clad guy wearing a captain's hat embroidered with the business logo. "I'm looking for Morgan Macallister," he said.

The guy looked him up and down before deciding he wasn't a customer. He pointed back in the direction of the door. "Morgan's out in the marina. Look for a catamaran named *Betsy*."

Wandering through the marina, Martin realized how much he didn't know about boats. He thought he'd know a catamaran when he saw one, but it took him a while to track down *Betsy*. She was about forty feet long, gleaming dark blue in the sun. Martin stood at the bottom of the gangplank leading up to her foredeck and wondered if he was supposed to ask permission to come aboard. "Hello?" he called.

"Hey, hang on a second," came an answer from somewhere inside the boat. Footsteps pounded up a flight of stairs and a twentysomething Adonis wearing canvas cutoffs and nothing else appeared at the top of the gangplank. "What's up?" he said.

"Are you Morgan Macallister?"

The kid's face got crafty. "You a process server?"

"No. So I take it you are Morgan? My name is Martin Kindred, from Nautilus Casualty and Property. I'm here to deliver a disbursement from the buyout of Everett Shankly."

"A what from the what of who?"

"If you have a bank account," Martin said, "I'm about to make it a lot fatter."

That got young Morgan Macallister moving, but it was clear right away that he'd never heard of Everett Shankly and didn't know why he should be receiving nearly two hundred thousand dollars from a recently deceased total stranger. "What the fuck?" he said, succinctly.

"There's no stipulation in the rules that you have to leave the money to people you know," Martin explained. He'd done quite a few DBs in which individual payouts had gone to movie stars, charities, favorite bartenders, even pets. The rules precluded neither mischief nor malice. The only prohibitions were that clients couldn't give to Nautilus employees or employees of any law-enforcement organization, unless the recipient was a family member.

"A hundred and ninety-six thousand bucks?" Macallister repeated, for the fourth or fifth time.

"All you have to do is tell me where to send it," Martin said.

Macallister whipped a battered pod out of his pocket, tapped it to life, and said, "Ready when you are, man."

Every time Martin did a DB that had some weirdness to it—seemingly random or unknown recipients—he started looking for the logic. Today was no different. The next address was in Irvine, and as he crawled along the streets of Orange County, he concocted and discarded all kinds of scenarios. Shankly loved boats. Shankly knew Macallister, but neither of them wanted anyone to know. Shankly wanted to be buried at sea.

Hm. Martin pinged Janine. She answered right away, looking bright and sharp, with only a shadow around her eyes to tell that she'd just lost her brother. "Janine," Martin said. "I'm doing the disbursements on your brother's case. He asked that I do them in a particular order, and I'm respecting that wish. The first one was at a place that does burials at sea. Was that something he wanted?"

"No," she said. "He never said anything about it. Why is my brother's psychology so interesting to you?"

Because your brother's psychology means that I don't have a brother anymore, Martin wanted to say. Instead he signed off with, "Just making sure I'm covering all the bases. Thanks."

The temperature rose maybe ten degrees between Newport and Irvine. The address was in a regular Orange County neighborhood, the house a modified ranch occupied by one Jaime Hernandez. It occurred to Martin, not for the first time, that he never would get anywhere in Greater LA without the GPS in his car leading him right to it. He had a general idea of where things were on a map, but individual addresses—often individual names of towns and cities—were meaningless. Anyone knew where Newport Beach or Anaheim was. But all the smaller communities—where were they, and how did they all fit together into the asphalt patchwork of the Los Angeles basin? The map was not the territory, and Martin didn't even have a clear idea of what the map looked like. He was twice removed from the territory, his experience of the city where he lived so completely mediated that he had come to experience the medium rather than the city.

Jaime Hernandez was not at home. No neighbors were out on the street. Martin ran through a database or two and found that Hernandez worked at a bank in Santa Ana. Half an hour later he walked into the branch and waited for Hernandez to finish opening a new account. Then he introduced himself. "I know who you are," Hernandez said. "I haven't killed anyone."

Martin wasn't sure whether to smile or not. "Well, let's keep it that way," he said. "I'm here because you were designated as a recipient of some of the proceeds of Everett Shankly's buyout."

"Shankly? The one from yesterday?" Hernandez looked confused. "I didn't know that guy from Adam."

"Doesn't matter," Martin began, and he explained the rules. He had a feeling he was going to be doing a lot of that. Echoes of Carl Marks again; the director's DBs had all been to communist organizations and random purveyors of Marxist theory.

"How much is it?" Hernandez asked.

Martin glanced at his pod. "Eight hundred thirty-two thousand and forty dollars."

Heads turned in the lobby. Jaime Hernandez looked like he might faint.

"Are you shitting me?" he said.

Martin shook his head. Slowly Hernandez took out his pod and brushed a sequence across its screen. He held it out, his hand not entirely steady. Martin touched his own pod screen, and several sets of numbers in several computers changed, adding maybe fifteen years' worth of salary to Jaime Hernandez's account.

"We recommend that you consult with a financial adviser," Martin said. "I've taken the liberty of sending you a couple of names that have worked with buyout disbursements before."

Hernandez was staring at his pod screen. "Thanks," he said.

"Have a nice day," Martin said, and left the bank, eyes on his back.

The rhythm of it was easy. You walk up, shock someone with a financial windfall, on to the next. It was easier when there was no close relationship between the client and the recipients, because family members often wanted to make a big show of vilifying Martin and despising buyouts before they allowed him to make them rich. The next address was near the intersection of 241 and the Riverside Freeway in a distant part of Anaheim sandwiched between Orange and Yorba Linda. Once this had been a land of shiny McMansions; now the shine was off them and they were home to immigrants just getting a foothold in America. The recipient was named Lawrence Apire. He was from the Sudan, spoke minimal English, and possessed neither a pod nor a bank account, which meant Martin had to print him out a physical check for $75,025. Apire looked fearful, as if he thought he might have agreed to something when he accepted the check. As much as was possible, Martin reassured

him that the money was his free and clear. "I'd suggest you get it into a
bank as soon as possible, Mr. Apire," he said. Apire nodded. Like Macallister and Hernandez, he did not know Everett Shankly.

Fine, Shankly, Martin thought as he headed for the next stop in
Pomona. You give your money to a bunch of strangers. That makes you
look cold-blooded, like your last gesture from beyond the grave is one
more Fuck You to the families of the people you killed. I may not be in
the buyout game anymore after this deal, Martin thought, but if this is
the real Everett Shankly, I'm gladder than ever that I did it. Even if no
one will ever know.

He trolled the feeds to see what news there might be about Curt
Laskowski. Manhunt, arrests of Priceless Life ringleaders on suspicion of
obstructing an investigation. That caught Martin's attention. He wondered what the cops had found.

A jack-in-the-pod appeared on his windshield. "Hello, Martin Kindred! We notice that you've had your car worked on a couple of times in
the last few months, and thought you should know about Foothills
Mazda's new model-year—" Car ice froze the jack, and Martin remembered the word he'd heard Walt Dangerfield use. Aspaminated. He'd
missed part of a report about the Priceless Lifer arrests, and he ran it
back. No names were given. He pinged Charlie, whose pod was live
again. No answer.

Neither Lillian Huerta of Pomona nor Antonio Ocampo of San
Dimas had any personal relationship to Everett Shankly. Nor did Luther
Henry-Scontras of La Crescenta. Martin had now driven in a rough
semicircle, from swankiest seashore Orange County to a plebeian office
building in the shadow of Burbank. He had been recognized a few times
and heard a few stray comments come his way. He was doing his job for
probably the second to last day, and he was coming to the end of a marriage as well. Everything was ending. Which meant, as his mother
would no doubt point out to him the next time he saw her, that Martin
Kindred was ripe for a new beginning.

He looked down the list and saw that Janine Shankly was number
ten. She lived in Mid-Wilshire. Between Martin and her stood Angela
van Bronckhorst of the Spazier Grand Apartments, Ibrahim Suleyman

who lived up in the Hollywood Hills, and Emma Clinton of 7100 West Sunset Boulevard.

Ten was a nice round number. Martin headed for the Spazier Grand Apartments and bestowed upon Angela van Bronckhorst approximately seventy-five thousand dollars that she tried to refuse and then agreed to accept only if she could immediately donate it to Priceless Life. "I find you verminous," she said to Martin, this seventy-year-old matron in careful reproductions of expensive clothing.

"It's a free country, Ms. van Bronckhorst," Martin said.

"Not if you and your people get your way," she said. "Soon you'll have us optioning pieces of our bodies for the right to breathe air and drink water."

Martin tipped his hat and left. He had a similar conversation with Ibrahim Suleyman, who lived in an expansive used-to-be-Moderne villa overlooking the Hollywood Reservoir. "What do I need with half a million dollars?" he said. "And blood money. No thank you."

"You're free to pass it right along to anyone you want, Mr. Suleyman," Martin said. "All I'm required to do is be present at the initial transfer into your account."

"What if I give it back to you?" Suleyman said. "Hm? What then?"

Martin thought about it. He genuinely wasn't sure, and told Suleyman so. "Probably it would look bad, and I'd refuse it anyway. Give it to your pool boy, the IRS, a charitable organization or political party. Whoever. I'm not asking you to make use of the money or believe in it. All I need to do is hand it to you."

"The placing of value on human life is an affront," Suleyman said.

"I'm not here to argue with you, Mr. Suleyman," Martin said.

"No," Suleyman said. "You are following orders, I'm sure. And I'm sure you have convinced yourself of your reasons." He held out his pod. "Give me this blood money so I can get rid of it and get rid of you."

Ten minutes after Martin had left Suleyman's house, Suleyman pinged him. "Why is this Everett Shankly giving me money anyway?"

"You've already asked me that, Mr. Suleyman. I don't know. A number of Shankly's recipients have been unfamiliar with him personally." All of them, was the truth.

"I sent the money to the sister of the policeman killed yesterday because of this," Suleyman said.

"Glad to hear it," Martin said.

"And you're sure you know nothing about why I was on this list? This Shankly person, he never mentioned me by name?"

Ah, Martin thought. Here was familiar territory. It was impossible for the rich and powerful to believe that things happened to them randomly, because that meant they weren't in total control of their environments. To the rich and powerful, this was an intolerable message from a universe they had spent their lives trying to get the upper hand on. "I'm afraid not," Martin said.

Suleyman broke the connection. Martin imagined him stewing as he gazed out over his million-dollar view. For some reason the image satisfied him in a way that made him feel a little sullied.

Emma Clinton worked as a mechanic at the corner of Sunset and La Brea. The building had been a gas station once, probably around the turn of the millennium. It still retained the imprint of what must have been a mandatory layout for big gas stations at the time: double banks of pumps on two sides of a glass-walled convenience store, with a car wash off to one side and flat awnings covering the pumps. Now the convenience store had been built out into a garage specializing in water separators and fuel-cell service, and all that remained of the pumps were the curbed platforms they'd stood on. Martin stood on the corner, envisioning what the intersection had looked like in, say, 2003. He wondered where he was on a map. Seemed like he was circling back, but a full circle back to Newport Beach would have taken him through quite a bit of the ocean. What was Shankly's point?

And more to the point, why was Martin bothering to do this? That's what Charlie asked him when he finally pinged back, jolting Martin out of his reverie. "Everett Shankly's a dead murderer, amigo," he said. "Even you can't think you owe him anything."

Except I do, a little, Martin thought. Or I owe it to myself, and Shankly's the way that I can see that. "What's it going to hurt?" he said.

"What, you don't spend enough hours of your life sitting in traffic?"

Charlie had a point there. It was almost six o'clock, and the streets were jammed. That much hadn't changed in LA since the 1960s. They could build subway tracks under every street in the city, and there would still be traffic jams overhead. It was some kind of congenital disorder that afflicted all Angelenos. Once Martin finished with Emma Clinton, who had her head stuck under the hood of a gold-flake '27 Lexus, it was probably going to take him twenty minutes to crawl the couple of miles down La Brea to Janine Shankly's address. Then he'd be turning around and hacking his way northeast to Pasadena. Annoyed, Martin said, "So I'm sitting in traffic. I said I'd do it, now I'm going to do it. Where have you been?"

"Trolling the Wi-Frees for Curt Laskowski," Charlie said. "Guess your itinerary doesn't much matter anyway if you're only on the job until you finish the DBs."

"Guess not," Martin said.

"You okay with it?"

"No," Martin said. "I'm getting thrown to the wolves, and I probably should have seen it coming, or at least that's what everyone's going to tell me."

"You've been fucking set up, is what you've been," Charlie said.

Martin took a minute to measure his response. "Charlie, let's do this. How about we grab a beer. You tell me how I'm being set up, and we'll look at the help-wanted ads together. Sound good? Say nine?"

"Nine," Charlie said. "Fix your attitude between now and then. Or maybe you'll get arrested and it won't matter." He clicked off.

Martin stared at his pod as if it would explain Charlie's mood. I'm the one who saw a guy killed yesterday, and lost my job this morning, he thought. When do I get to be the one who takes out his frustrations on someone else?

He looked up to find Emma Clinton standing next to him. "Closing up here," she said. "Now what was it you wanted to . . . hey. You're the guy from the riot thing. The buyout guy."

"Martin Kindred," he said. They shook hands.

"Let me guess," she said. "You're here to give me a bunch of money because you've discovered that Everett Shankly and I were secret lovers."

Distracted by the conversation with Charlie, Martin didn't catch on to the joke right away. "Oh," he said. "Well, sort of. Actually I am here to give you some money."

"What?" She backed up a step.

"Really. You were on Everett Shankly's disbursement list."

"Oh my God. How much?"

Martin told her, and she repeated the figure. "A hundred and ninety-six thousand dollars. Oh my God." Unconsciously her hands came together in a prayerful gesture. "Oh my God."

That right there is why I do this, Martin thought. "All I need is your pod," he said.

She fished it out of her coverall and watched the screen as Martin made the transfer. "Why?" she asked. "I mean, why me?"

"I don't know." Martin could have sworn there were tears in her eyes.

"Out of all the people in Los Angeles," she said. "I've got two kids in college, I thought they were going to have to leave . . ." Now she was crying, and making no attempt to hide it. "And the garage, I had to put so much into it and I thought I was going to lose it anyway." Emma Clinton hid her face in her hands, then wiped tears away, leaving war-paint streaks of grease under both eyes. "You know, he was a murderer, but he did a wonderful thing for me. Do you understand how that feels, Mr. Kindred? Can you understand that?"

"I think so," Martin said.

Then his pod lit up. Incoming from Caitlin Frost. He didn't take it, but he left the screen live so he could see her message. "Hi, Martin," she beamed at him. "I understand you're leaving Nautilus? Sure would love to get a comment from you. You're on Sunset and La Brea, right? I'll be there in ten minutes."

Shit, Martin thought. Leaving a beatific Emma Clinton standing in front of her closed garage, he made tracks for his car and headed not south toward Janine Shankly but east toward home. By the time he'd covered the mile and a half to the Hollywood Freeway, he had 116 messages chirping and cajoling on his pod. By the time he got to the Pasadena Freeway, there was at least one drone overhead.

By the time he got home, he had to shove his way through a phalanx of reporters. Like a flash mob, he thought. The signal goes out, they manifest. Then another signal, another manifestation. He ducked the barrage of questions and lights, escaping through the front door into the house that was almost no longer his.

The first thing Teresa said to him was, "Thought we were having lunch today."

"Sorry about that," he said. "I got fired. Threw a wrench into the day's plans."

"Martin," she said, the way you say somebody's name when you mean it to stand in for a long lecture about innocence transforming into gullibility.

He let it pass. "Yeah," he said. "Where are the girls?"

"Upstairs. I told them they weren't leaving the house until this blows over. So when is this going to blow over?"

Martin was watching the play of lights across the living room curtains. The house network was shut down, he assumed because the less scrupulous members of the Fourth Estate would be worming avatars in to get clandestine vid. Now he was conscious of how different this was from the Carl Marks deal. Then, he'd faced the media attention because, as his grandmother would have said, he'd known it was a snake when he picked it up. Carl Marks was a celebrity, a lightning rod. To be associated with him was to get a secondary jolt. Now Martin was the source of the uproar. He was the one who shocked by association.

"T," he said. "Do you think I've done something wrong?"

She knew what he meant. Not have I made mistakes, but have I done something wrong. It took a long time for her to answer. Then she said, "I don't think you could have done anything differently."

Which wasn't what he needed to hear, but wasn't wrong, either.

Manhunt. Who doesn't love a good manhunt? I'm thinking all the way back to John Wilkes Booth, Pretty Boy Floyd . . . now the hunt is on for Curt Laskowski, and the rest of the world stops. It's an excuse to talk about something that isn't happening but will be interesting when it does, except that when it does the story will be over. Ain't that a bitch? And it's an excuse to devote bandwidth to something other than all that depressing shit coming out of the Dust Bowl Two, and the water sloshing over the Gulf Coast, and the crushing of the movements in the desert Southwest. I mean, who wants to talk about real intractable problems like the insufficiency of currency in a truly globalized and truly virtual market when you can talk about whether the LAPD had flushed Curt Laskowski out of the Wi-Free in Koreatown? Hell, I don't. Believe me, I love the trivial, the exploitative, the voyeuristic, and the reprehensible. Every once in a while I lose track of myself and talk about something rel-evant, but that isn't me. I don't give a shit about the Issues of the Day, or the Problems of Civilization and Humankind. I can't. Because I can't fix it, I don't know the people who can, and all I can do is take care of the people near and dear to me. If I am kind to people I meet on the corner, if I love and am loved, if I teach my children and minister to my elders, the rest of the world can burn.

THIRTY

THE WAY the day had gone, Charlie was sort of hoping Martin wouldn't show up for their beer. The last thing he wanted was to have to be civil to a pack of feedheads out of respect for Martin, when what both Martin and the feedheads needed was a straight right to the chin. He was into his third beer when Martin came in the alley door of Jake's Diner at five to ten. "You're late, you're stupid, and you're probably trailing reporters like the smell of a fart, amigo," Charlie said. "Why should I be happy to see you?"

Martin took a seat, contemplated this question, and said, "I'm about to be single and unemployed. You're going to be seeing a lot more of me."

"Terrific." Charlie eyeballed the remaining volume in his glass, decided it wasn't worth preserving, and drained it. "I have a theory," he said.

"Maybe I do, too," Martin said. "But let's hear yours first."

"Mine goes like this. Laskowski killed Briggs because he's a shit-for-brains wacko who can't stand being involved in something nonviolent. But why Briggs, then? Seems to me that if he's in the movement, and the movement doesn't like buyouts, then the people to go after are the people who do buyouts. That makes the Krakauers and you persons of interest. So I'm thinking about this, and I recall that you, amigo, were behaving in an unusual way at the beginning of this whole Shankly deal. Which in turn led me to remember a certain conversation, maybe a couple of weeks ago, when you and I both knew you were lying about something but I let it go. I'm turning all this over in my head, and putting it together with whatever I can scrounge up about Sol Briggs, and you know where it leads me? It leads me to your brother, Martin. Briggs and Twohy caught the call when Jason went down. You get all squirrelly when Shankly's sister comes calling, and then yesterday when the deal is done a certain Priceless Lifer, whom you've met before and about whom you are also squirrelly whenever he comes up in conversation, smokes Briggs. This tells me some kind of communication was happening between you and Briggs and Laskowski that I so far don't know about. Now you fucking level with me."

Charlie kept his voice down, but the heat came through. Martin could feel people turning to look at them. "Okay," he said. "You probably remember telling me that if I did the Shankly deal, I was the dumbest guy you'd ever met."

"Dumbest fucking guy, I believe is what I said."

"Right. I stand corrected. Well, I'm starting to believe you."

With a mocking heavenward gaze, Charlie said, "At last."

Martin leaned in closer to Charlie and kept his voice barely above a whisper, but even so, he was taking a terrible risk when he said, "Everett Shankly killed my brother."

Charlie didn't move, didn't look at him, didn't say anything, until after nearly a full minute he scooted his stool back from the bar and said, "This conversation needs to happen somewhere else."

Fifteen minutes later they were standing in a corner of the parking lot just inside Gate 8 of the Santa Anita Race Track, not too far away in Arcadia. "There's a Wi-Free in the Arb over there," Charlie said, pointing across Baldwin Avenue to the LA County Arboretum. "It laps over to this part of the track lot."

Martin looked around, then felt foolish. It wasn't like he'd be able to see a difference. "How do you know about these?"

"Part of the job," Charlie said. "You make a living finding people, you need to know where they can hide from the things you use to find them."

"Are there lots of philandering tax cheats hiding out in the Arb?"

Charlie ignored this. "You're in the shit, you know," he said.

"Yeah," Martin said.

"I saw Meg Twohy today. She said she's been trying to protect you."

"Tell her I appreciated it next time you run into her."

"You may see her before I do," Charlie said. "Way she tells it, most of Robbery-Homicide wants to haul you in and beat some kind of conspiracy confession out of you."

"Charlie, I know someone set me up. What I can't figure out is who. You know the thing that Batman always says, the question that always eventually solves the crime?"

"What are you talking about?"

"Batman, you know, the World's Greatest Detective. The one question he always asks is, *Who benefits?*"

"Batman?" Charlie said. "That's not Batman, asshole. Or if it is, he's quoting."

"Quoting who?" Martin said. He couldn't believe it wasn't Batman. All the comics he'd read, nobody had ever said anything about quoting.

"You're gonna love this," Charlie said. "It's Karl Marx."

"No shit," Martin said. He considered this. "Fucking irony." Then he snapped out of it and went on. "But that's the question. Who benefits here? Priceless Life has got a martyr, but they can't make use of him because one of their guys killed Briggs, and now they look like loose cannons. Briggs is dead. I'm about to lose my job. You're going to keep on doing BVIs either way. Jocelyn and Scott are scared to death of what the fallout is going to be. Who benefits?"

"How much money is Janine getting?"

"A million three something."

"So she sure as hell benefits."

Martin didn't see it. "No. She defended him, she tried to get him not to plead, she made it very clear to me that she was going to be keeping a close eye on me and that if I screwed up she was going to nail me. And she loved her brother, Charlie. In a brokenhearted, sad kind of way, but she loved him. You didn't get that impression when you talked to her?"

"Who benefits, amigo? Janine benefits."

"No," Martin said again. "She still doesn't know how much she's getting. What if he'd left her a dollar? Or nothing? How does she benefit then?"

"You tell me," Charlie said. "After you tell me whatever your bullshit story is about how Everett Shankly killed your brother."

Martin didn't just tell him. He played the vid Laskowski had given him before they'd met in Temescal Canyon for the first time. Charlie watched it, then played it again. When it was over, he leaned against the fence around the parking lot and thought hard. The wind shifted, and Martin could both smell lake water from the Arb and hear the whicker of insomniac racehorses from the stables to their south.

"Shankly asked me to do the DBs in order," Martin said. Charlie kept quiet. "And I spent all day today making a big circle from Newport Beach around through San Dimas and then over through the Hollywood Hills and back down toward Mid-Wilshire. Everett did this on purpose, Charlie. He wanted to get one last little dig in, tell me he had me running around in circles. He didn't know I had seen that file."

"Or he was just nuts," Charlie said.

Martin shook his head. "The last address on the DB list is four-four-five-oh Dunham, city of Los Angeles. Know it?"

"No," Charlie said.

"What if I told you that Dunham Street runs along the side of a big railyard not too far from the Santa Ana–Long Beach interchange? And that earlier this summer a cop named Jason Kindred turned up dead there? Everett wanted to taunt me, Charlie. But he was building a puzzle I'd already solved."

The light at Gate 8 and Baldwin turned yellow, red, then green again. "Christ," Charlie said. "I use more than ten sheets of toilet paper when I take a dump, I feel like a war criminal. How do people do stuff like this?"

He thought for a while, piecing it together. "So Laskowski takes out Briggs because Briggs got him the file, which he gave to you, which made you do a buyout on a bad guy who was even badder than we knew when we did the deal? In other words, Laskowski takes out Briggs for giving him a file that Laskowski used to bait you into creating a situation Laskowski wanted? Are we talking about shutting him up?"

"You're the one who noticed that Briggs was talking to Priceless Life," Martin pointed out.

"Okay," Charlie said. "So Laskowski's cleaning up after himself, plus he's crazy. Ask yourself the *Who benefits* question again, though. What's he got to gain?"

"He told me he's afraid he's going to get sick," Martin said. "ALS or something. You want to know what I think, it's that Curt Laskowski wants a buyout."

"So he kills a cop? How does he know he'll live to get to trial? Or that he won't go down on capital murder? There's more to it," Charlie said. "Has to be. I still think it comes back to Janine."

"No, it doesn't. You answered your own question about her."

"Still, you should talk to her."

Martin told him about his brief conversation with Janine that morning after the first DB at Davy Jones. "She say anything weird?" Charlie asked.

"No, and she didn't seem agitated that I'd called. It's a dead end, Charlie."

"Will you stop and think for one fucking minute?" Charlie shouted. "You have been set up from day one on this, and the one person who had to be involved was Janine Shankly. Now why aren't you talking to her?"

Martin didn't answer. The stoplight changed. Red. Green. Stop. Go.

"I can't fucking talk to you right now," Charlie said. "You did this, you lied to me, you dragged me into it, and the whole time I was trying to help. Leave me alone for a while, Martin. You got what you wanted."

He walked away. Martin watched him cross against the light and vanish into the shadowed perimeter of the Arboretum. You got what you wanted. The same thing Laskowski had said, or close enough. But Martin sure didn't feel like he had what he wanted. Not at all.

ON A LATE-NIGHT Colorado Boulevard bus headed back to Pasadena, Martin tried to reassess the situation. Everett Shankly kills Jason Kindred. LAPD knows this but cannot pursue it, so they leak the knowledge. But why use Priceless Life as the vector? How did they know that Curt Laskowski wouldn't take the file to the feeds and wreck the Shankly buyout for good? That kind of publicity would also have meant that Shankly would never go on trial for killing a cop.

Priceless Life needed a martyr, and they got one. If they could ever prove that Martin had deliberately done a bad buyout, then the buyout charter itself would be threatened. Were there Priceless Lifers in LAPD? Didn't seem likely. So what did Priceless Life have that made it necessary for them to be part of the setup?

Back at the hotel, Martin took the elevator. The feedheads were gone. They'd be back in the morning. In his room, he read over a package of severance documents Scott had sent. It was generous. In the morning he would set out early, finish the Shankly DBs, and move on. He'd get a place near the girls' school and try to get used to the way the world felt when you woke up by yourself in the morning. He'd stay clear of politically charged work, and politically charged conversations. He would admit that Charlie was right about things sometimes.

Ambitious, Martin thought. Best to get a good night's sleep before beginning.

HE CAUGHT JANINE at home, before she'd left for work. It was seven fifty-five, too early for the wakening city to have driven the smells of ocean and eucalyptus out of the air. Early in the morning Los Angeles is a beautiful place to be. Janine's condo was in a newish building built on the bones of something that had itself been newish when it was redeveloped. Martin would have bet the lot had been through three designs in the time he'd been alive. Mid-Wilshire in Martin's childhood had been one of the clean, upscale places—not Rodeo-style flash and glitz, or Brentwood-style opulence, but a self-consciously muted display of wealth. Mid-Wilshire made you feel good about yourself and your prospects. Now it wasn't quite so upscale, but still nice. The neighborhood had aged nicely— certainly had aged better than the subdivision in Anaheim that had been destined for ruin the minute its foundations were poured.

She greeted him without emotion, and they got right down to the transfer. While the servers were talking to each other, Martin asked, "Did you ever wonder if Everett had killed anyone else?"

"I beg your pardon?"

"Sorry," Martin said.

"Why are you giving me such a hard time?" Janine asked. "You insinuate sexual abuse, you ask about burial at sea, now you want to know if Everett's some kind of serial killer. He's dead, Martin. Let him be

BUYOUT   279

dead. And leave me alone." Tears stood in her eyes, and broke down her
face when she saw the number on her screen. "A Fibonacci number,"
she said. "It figures."

"You recognize Fibonacci numbers just by looking at them?"

Janine dabbed at her face in a non-makeup-disturbing way. "If you
had a client—not to mention a brother—who was as obsessed as Everett
was with Fibonacci numbers, you'd be able to recognize a bunch of
them, too. I bet I could give you the first forty or fifty in a row, just because he used to whisper the sequence to himself all the time."

"I think he was doing that while I was interviewing him, too."

"That was Everett," Janine said. "A little strange, a lot violent, but
only sometimes. The world is a hard place for someone like Everett. But
he made it a lot harder on a lot of other people."

Martin touched the brim of his hat and started to walk back to the
car. Janine called after him. "Are people happy when they get the
money?"

"Some of them are," he said. That seemed to satisfy her. Martin got
into the GTO, and in the rearview mirror he saw her get into her own
car and drive away.

AND ON AROUND into the maelstrom, swooping in toward 4450 Dunham,
where secrets Martin already knew had been promised by a man he'd
killed under false pretenses. Okay, Everett, Martin thought. Even now, I'll
give you this one. Think of it as a penance for me bending the rules,
which I shouldn't have done even to rid the world of the guy who killed
my brother. He gave $75,025 to a stylist in a beauty salon on West 43rd
Place, who took it and then told him he needed to get right with God on
his way out the door; $317,811 to a weeping seventy-year-old paraplegic
on Baring Cross Street in South Central; $46,368 to the night watchman
at the Watts Towers on East 107th Street; and so on. On Linden Street,
near the intersection of MLK and Atlantic, Martin thought he'd have to
call an ambulance when an octogenarian lesbian couple both clutched
their chests upon finding out that they were a little less than two hundred
thousand dollars richer. Linden Street, Firestone Boulevard, Slauson Avenue, South Garfield, Michigan, Opal, La Puerta . . .

And then 4450 Dunham. Martin stood in the street. From the front, 4450 Dunham was an old, ordinary light-industrial building. Metal siding and roof on a concrete foundation, a faded sign at the roofline saying PREFAB METAL. Facing the street was a glass office door, and to its right a ramp down to an open loading dock. Inside, he could see men working at lathes, the sounds of the machines not quite drowning out shouted instructions in Spanish. Running along the western wall of the building, to Martin's right, a driveway led to the vacant lot where Jason had been murdered.

He opened the office door, announced by the jingle of a bell. The reception area was empty. The sound of machine tools came through the wall to his right, and salsa floated from a hallway that extended in front of him toward the back of the building. A lean Mexican in work clothes came down the hall toward him. "What can I do for you?"

Martin glanced at his pod and said, "I'm looking for Armando Galarraga."

"You got him," the guy said, pointing at a patch on his shirt embroidered with his first name.

"Mr. Galarraga, my name is Martin Kindred. I'm doing disbursements on the buyout of Everett Shankly, and you are a named recipient."

"Everett Shankly? From the riot a couple of days ago? I saw that on the feeds. You got the wrong guy. I didn't know him."

"Yeah," Martin said, "I've been hearing a lot of that. But it doesn't matter. He wanted you to have some of his buyout money, and I'm here to oversee the transfer."

Galarraga looked uneasy. He scratched his head, stroked his mustache, ran through an entire repertoire of gestures designed to convey uncertainty. "There's no downside for you," Martin said. "It's tax-free, and you can do whatever you want with it."

"Yeah, but I didn't do anything to get it," Galarraga said. "Can't you just give it away or something?"

"No, but you can. All that has to happen now is we let our pods talk to each other for a minute, and you're . . ." Martin confirmed the figure. "Five hundred fourteen thousand two hundred and twenty-nine dollars richer. From there, it's up to you what you do with the money."

Galarraga froze when he heard the figure. "Five hundred thousand?" he repeated.

"Plus a little more."

"And I don't have to do anything?"

"Not a thing. I'll pipe you a package of documents along with the transfer, suggesting financial advisers and things like that. But the truth is, you've just had a bag of money fall out of the sky." Martin gave Galarraga an encouraging smile. "So shall we?"

"I guess so," Galarraga said. He got out his pod, but still looked doubtful. Then he saw Martin's sig on the transfer message. "Your name's Kindred?"

Martin nodded.

"That was the name of the cop who got killed out back."

"Yeah," Martin said. "He was my brother."

"Oh man, I'm sorry. And now you're back here working. Some coincidence, huh?" Galarraga stowed his pod and patted the pocket as if he'd just put a bunch of real money in it. He was old enough for cash to have been much more common than it was now; the gesture looked old-fashioned, emptied of meaning.

"It sure is," Martin said. "Life is funny that way. Mind if I take a walk around the back?"

"No, no sweat," Galarraga said. "You go on. I'll leave you alone."

You pour yourself into something. Doesn't matter what it is. You pour yourself into it because at one point you think it's important. Then maybe you figure out that it isn't important, but by then you've invested too much, and the investment is important even if the thing you've invested in isn't anymore. Is that too general? I will specify. Once I believed that I had something to say about life and politics and art and culture and all of this other shit that somehow is critically important even though you can go days without thinking about it. So I started talking to anyone who would listen, because I needed people to listen. Then I realized that I was doing it for myself, to be listened to, instead for other people because I thought I was saying something they needed to hear. That's a tough pill to swallow, and a hard trip to take. Out on the other side of it, I said to myself, you know what? Keep talking. That's all you have, the talking. The listening doesn't matter. You talk into the void, because it's all a void, and instead of knowing someone is listening, you trust your sanity and your worth and your life to the possibility that someone might listen. And you know what? That's enough. The possibility is enough. Once there might have been certainty, but now the possibility has to be enough.

THIRTY-ONE

CURT LASKOWSKI sat on the other side of the fence, feet braced against the slope of the track embankment, looking out over the expanse of rust and smoking a hand-rolled cigarette. He looked over his shoulder when he heard Martin's feet crunching through the dry weeds. "You a wanted man yet?" he asked.

"Why should I be?"

"Well, right now you're associating with someone known to you to be the murderer of one of LA's finest, and I don't see you calling the cavalry."

"I still could," Martin said.

"Sure," Laskowski said.

Martin sat and leaned against the fence, at an angle that kept both Laskowski and the spot where Jason had died in his field of vision. "Was it worth it?" he asked. "Do you think you did the right thing?"

"Which thing?" Laskowski asked. "What do you think I did?"

"At the very least you sold out your organization for a personal goal."

Laskowski laughed. "What, by killing Briggs? Martin, you're two steps behind. I killed Briggs because he was going to come after me. You had this conversation with Charlie last night."

"How do you know about that?"

"I like Charlie," Laskowski said, ignoring Martin's question. "You should listen to him more. But you guys kept talking about who benefits, and you don't see the obvious answer."

"It's you," Martin said. "That's the obvious answer."

"No, you fucking idiot." Laskowski threw his arms up in the air. "Pay attention! Who benefits? Nautilus benefits."

Martin saw it then. By teasing Martin with the Shankly file, Jocelyn and Scott had tricked him into doing a bad buyout, created a controversy that they stage-managed by firing him, and at the same time cemented a public perception of the primary opposition to buyouts as a violent mob of cop-killers.

And they had done all of it by manipulating Martin's grief at the murder of his brother. Carl Marks had whetted the public appetite, and when attention was at its most intense, they turned Martin into a symbol of the excesses his job was designed to prevent.

"They gamed you from the beginning," Laskowski said. "And along the way, they got me, too."

It all fit. It fit so well, in fact, that Martin couldn't believe it was true, except there he was. Reality trumped belief in the end. But there was just one loose end, he thought. "How did they know you'd come through, Curt? Why use Priceless Life to get the file to me?"

"This is the best part," Laskowski said. "Jocelyn and Scott promised me Briggs. It's an awesome deal. I get to off a cop, and then—here's the kicker—I'm supposed to be the next buyout Nautilus does, once the dust settles from all this shit. And you know what I'm going to do? Every fucking cent of my buyout is going to go to Priceless Life."

The audacity and the cynicism of this setup were so staggering that for a moment all Martin could do was admire it. "Chloe's going to have a problem," he said.

"Chloe's going to go crazy, is what she's going to do," Laskowski said gleefully. "I hate her, I hate life, I hate you. I'm going out, and I'm taking it all down with me."

This was a balloon stretched so tight that Martin couldn't resist sticking a pin in it. "What if she just takes the money?" he asked. "Argues that she's going to make something good out of something bad, et cetera and so on?"

"No, she can't do that." Laskowski stabbed a finger through the fence. "That's *your* line, remember? Even if she wanted to take the money—which that greedy bitch, I'm sure she does—she couldn't, because the only rationale she could have is exactly the same line of bullshit you guys at Nautilus have been peddling. If she takes the money, she's a hypocrite; if she doesn't, she's denying the gift of me, Priceless Life's first martyr."

"You're crazier than I thought," Martin observed.

"You are not the first person to tell me that," Laskowski said.

"What makes you think the cops won't just punch your ticket?"

"Ah," Laskowski said. "That would suck. But then Chloe gets her martyr with no complications, and at least I go out in an interesting way. Not a bad alternative scenario."

"So, you planning to turn yourself in now?"

"Already did," Laskowski said, holding up his pod. "I'm surprised they're not here already."

Which was when Martin heard the drones, and knew that Curt Laskowski had neglected to mention one other part of his plan. "Taking me down with you, Curt?" he said.

"Everyone, man," Laskowski said. "Everyone."

THEY BROUGHT MARTIN in, were about to book him, didn't book him, stuck him in an interview room to stew for three or four hours, then finally decided to get things moving by having Javier Beltran come in and give him a hard time for a while.

"I told you the deal wasn't going to be as good next time," he said.

Martin nodded. "You did say that. Am I being charged with a crime?"

"Maybe," Beltran said. "You commit a crime?"

"Nope," Martin said.

"Okay, then, let's talk." Beltran sat down. "Laskowski says that you're dirty as sin, that you were in on some kind of plot to use the Shankly buyout to get at Sol Briggs because you had some kind of grudge against him that had to do with your brother. Right?"

"That's wrong in so many ways that I don't even think I can list them all before I start to forget some," Martin said.

"Which ways is it right?"

"None," Martin said. "I was doing my job finishing up the disbursements on the Shankly buyout, and at the last address I ran into Laskowski."

"The address that just happens to be where your brother got killed."

"You'd have to ask Everett Shankly about that," Martin said.

"Funny," Beltran said. "Did you kill your brother?"

Martin was so blindsided by this question that he couldn't speak. "What?" he finally managed to say.

"Did you kill your brother? Simple yes-or-no question."

"No. And fuck you for asking."

"Settle down," Beltran said. "Why was the last disbursement address where your brother was killed?"

"You want me to guess? I think it's because Shankly killed him. And I think someone in here knew it, and I think you know all this already."

Beltran stood. "Hey, Martin?" he said at the door. "We could have taken you and Laskowski down this afternoon, and nobody would ever have said a word. You might want to think for a while about why we didn't."

He shut the door behind him. Half an hour later Meg Twohy came in. "Let's go," she said without looking him in the eye.

Martin stood up and stretched. "Okay. But can I ask you a question?"

"You can ask."

"What about the file where you guys had someone talking about Shankly and Jason?"

She looked stricken. "Martin, I swear to God I didn't know anything about that. That was Sol."

"Who else?"

She shook her head and walked him out to the front steps, where she handed him back his pod and his gun. It was dark. "In there, just Sol," Meg said, and walked back into the building. Martin nodded. She didn't have to say any more.

He took a cab back to his car, and caught up on the feeds along the way once the cab daemon had finished its spiel about how Mr. Dileep Premachandran was guaranteed by the city of Los Angeles to be a superb, careful, and efficient driver. The city was in a froth over the capture of Laskowski—and the fact that Martin was there when it happened. Analyses of this fact ranged from the straightforward, using interviews with Armando Galarraga to point out that Martin had a good reason to be there, to the wildly conspiratorial. These varied from hints that Martin was an LAPD mole in Priceless Life to accusations that he was under threat of indictment for conspiracy in Sol Briggs' murder, and so had agreed to sucker Laskowski into appearing where the LAPD could get him. There were 1,496 messages in his inbox. The pod daemon had created three new categories: INTERVIEW REQUESTS, PERSONAL COMMENTS, and CRACKPOT THEORIES. All but sixteen of his messages had been tracked into one of those categories. Thirteen of those sixteen were related to the end of his tenure at Nautilus. The other three were from Teresa. Text only, the same thing repeated each time: *Don't come here. Call when you're ready to follow through on what you say.*

"Sucks being a scapegoat, doesn't it, sir?" the cabbie said.

Martin looked up at the rearview mirror and saw dark eyes, prominent nose, bushy mustache. He couldn't place the cabbie's accent. "Pardon me?"

"I've been seeing you on the feeds. No way this is your fault. Whenever someone gets caught up in something like this and resigns, hey, that's like a guarantee from God that people higher up the food chain are involved. Am I wrong?" The cabbie kept a bare minimum of attention on the road. His eyes, cheerful and wise, bored into Martin.

"No," Martin said. "I don't think you're wrong."

"I knew it," the cabbie said. "You're not perfect, but you try to do the right thing for the right reason."

"Yeah, I do," Martin said.

"Well, that," the cabbie said, "is the road to madness. But you should still try to do it."

"We're kindred souls . . . Dileep," Martin said, glancing at his pod to get the cabbie's name again.

"You say that as a joke and a pun, but it might be true," Dileep said.

"This is a shtick, right?" Martin said. "The funny wise Indian cabbie? You auditioning for something?"

"Auditioning for life, man," Dileep said. "And even if it is a shtick, who can say it isn't real?"

Out of the cab and onto the street in front of Prefab Metals again, Martin leaned against the door of his car and called the girls. Allison answered. "Dad," she said. "You have to stop getting arrested. It's really embarrassing."

Martin didn't know whether she was serious or not. The ability to inspire that confusion, he knew, was one of the secret weapons of the girl on the cusp of adolescence.

"I'll keep that in mind, kiddo," he said. "But I wasn't actually arrested. The police and I just needed to talk some things over."

Kelly had a different set of concerns. "Are you really like an undercover policeman?" she asked. "That's what Caitlin Frost said."

"Caitlin Frost needs clicks, sweetheart," Martin said. "She's not always right about everything, but she says what she thinks will make people pay attention to her."

"You say that about me," Kelly said.

"Only when it's true," Martin said. "And it's different with Caitlin Frost, because a lot of people believe what she says. You, on the other hand, are such a goofball that everyone knows not to believe you."

In mock fury, Kelly said, "I am not a goofball and everyone should believe me."

"Well, you tell everyone that I'm not an undercover policeman. I'm about to get a new job, but that won't be it." Martin said good night and clicked off, strengthened and saddened at the same time by the sound of the girls' voices. Seeing them didn't affect him in quite the same way. Their voices were what he carried with him, and the remembered sensation of their hands in his, or the weight of their bodies when they were younger, sleeping over his shoulder. Absences. Absent voices, absent children who have grown into semi-present older children.

Absent brothers.

Martin started to cry. The street was empty, nobody here but us scapegoats, and he let it go, looking up at the muted stars. The whole thing had been a death spiral, from the minute Santos had called him. Everything had collapsed since then. Now here I am, he thought, at the center, and maybe I can start all over again. I have to be a better son. I have to be a better father. I have to be a better friend. Time for that new leaf to be turned over for real. What better time? My marriage is gone, my job is gone, my reputation is gone, my brother is gone. What else to do but start over?

It was nine o'clock. Martin decided to go see his parents. He would confess what he had done. All of it. Pushing the buyout, letting his hunger for both revenge and acceptance drive him away from what he believed, neglecting the people he loved because he didn't know how to let them help him heal. All of that. It would be more sentiment than his father had ever had to survive from Martin in a single sitting. If it didn't kill the old man, a better relationship might come out of it.

Driving through Los Angeles in the afterglow of revelation, he felt purged. Not clean, but purged. Learning to be at peace with having done things he regretted. Everett Shankly could have his little message from beyond the grave; he was still dead, and it was time for Martin Kindred to start living again.

The last thing he needed to do was fill out the closure report on Shankly's finalization. Martin decided to do it at the office, and then take what he wanted from his desk and walk out the door for the last time. No sense waiting until tomorrow.

He got to the office at about ten and left the Sig in the car so he wouldn't get flak from the security guard catching the last few innings of the Dodgers game, and went up to the office. Sat in his chair and allowed himself to breathe in the fact that he would never be in this office again after the next hour or so. It wasn't a bad office. He'd had worse. But he'd never worked for worse people, and although Martin wasn't a big believer in recriminations, he was also learning that it was as much of a problem to put yourself in a situation where you wanted to be recriminating as it was to actually be recriminating when the situation seemed to warrant it. A perspective shift, he thought. That's what I need.

A buyout finalization form had three parts. The first reproduced the original agreement, attested by agent and client. The second contained the forms from the finalization, including the death certificate and doctor's attestation that the finalization was carried out in a humane and efficient manner. The third concerned the disbursements. Using an interactive map of Los Angeles, Martin linked pictures of each of the disbursement addresses and files containing each individual recipient's acceptance of the transfer. Working through them in order, Martin replayed the sweep around from Newport up into the foothills and then back down into the city, the tightening spiral that led to . . .

He saw it then, all of it. Twenty-one glowing points of data on his desktop, and between them stretching an imagined gentle curve that took a shape built from Fibonacci numbers.

A Nautilus curve.

And it ended on the precise spot where Martin's brother was murdered.

He tried to read it a hundred different ways, tried to force it into a pattern other than the one he knew it already formed, but when he put it all together with everything else . . .

Who benefits?

Nautilus had killed Jason Kindred. That's what Everett Shankly was saying.

So what do you think about the Dodgers? Looks like one of those ninety-win, almost-make-the-playoffs kind of seasons to me. I would almost prefer incompetence, since then I wouldn't have to spend all of this time believing, and agonizing over the possibility of being disappointed. My grandfather once told me that sports could teach you something about being a man. I believed it. In some ways, I still do, but I don't know what it is to be a man when I can opt the other way if I'm willing to undergo a minor surgery and take some pills. I don't know what it is to be a man when I never played sports. I don't know what it is to be a man when I can go in the VR and be a woman if I want, or a dog, or Diogenes the Cynic. I almost wish that the cops weren't going to kill Curt Laskowski, because I'd like to go into the VR and be him, just to see what it is that made him do what he did. How can you rationally analyze the circumstances of your life and conclude that randomly killing a cop at a demonstration is okay, is the thing that you must do? You can't. Not rationally. So the answer is that rationality isn't the answer, which brings me right back to the Dodgers. Rationally I know they will crush my hopes. But every April, and even every August when things are still marginally possible, those hopes spring up again. Hope is a fucking dandelion. A cynical, Diogenes dandelion. It challenges us to live up to ourselves.

THIRTY-TWO

THEY GOT ME, Martin thought. They didn't just sucker me into betraying my principles, they made me party to the execution of a man for a crime he didn't commit. If Shankly hadn't killed Jason, how could Martin know that he was guilty of the restaurant shooting? Had Jocelyn and Scott done that, too, or hired someone to do it? Adrenaline surged through him, the lizard part of his brain was screaming *run!*

He mastered it, forcing himself to think. He was in the office. Jocelyn and Scott did not know he knew what he knew. As far as they were concerned, he was still buying the simple explanation, which was that Curt Laskowski's madness had driven everything to this point. They would know he had seen Laskowski, would assume that Laskowski had told him his version of the truth, and they would react accordingly. So he had a single advantage, which was the message from Everett Shankly.

Janine, he thought. She must have been in on it, too.

John Wayne appeared on his desktop. "Ya can't be too careful round these parts," he said. "Looks like we got rustlers in the chaparral."

Someone was trying to break into the car? Now? Martin killed his desktop screen and headed for the door. John Wayne's voice spoke from his pod. "They got me, pilgrim."

"Shit," Martin said. By the time he'd gotten down the nine floors on the elevator and out to the parking lot, he'd convinced himself that someone had stolen the car, but it was there. Nothing looked disturbed. Got me? Ah, he thought. Stupid Western-movie idiom. The daemon meant they'd broken in. He calmed down a little. His insurance company—a subsidiary of Nautilus—had been getting a workout from him lately. After this, he'd have to go somewhere else, since the company's auto coverage wasn't worth it without the employee discount.

All of this ran through his mind parallel with a flash inventory of what someone might steal. He'd have to file a report. The car had pretty good intelligence, but it was embedded and hard to get to. There were some fixtures, a couple of custom displays, nothing really out of the ordinary . . .

The Sig.

Ever so carefully, Martin walked a perimeter around the car, looking for anything a thief might have left behind. He saw nothing. Then he went to the driver's-side door, popped it with his pod, and opened it without touching anything except the bottom corner of the door panel, with the toe of his shoe. The interior light came on. Martin leaned in, braced a hand on the cloth of the driver's seat, and used a pen to pop the glove compartment. The Sig was gone.

He backed out of the car, leaving the door open, and pinged Javier Beltran. The detective answered voice-only. "Javier," Martin said. "My car's been broken into, someone stole my gun, and we need to talk about Everett Shankly right now."

"Where are you?" Beltran came on visual.

"Parking lot of the office. Nautilus."

"Don't move. I'll be there in ten."

Waiting, Martin felt a clock ticking down, but he didn't know toward what. Who would know he had a gun and break into his car to steal it, without making it look like an actual random street break-in? Without John Wayne, as augmented by Charlie's anonymous hacker friends, Martin probably never would have known the Sig was gone until he went looking for it. Laskowski was in prison; was some other Priceless Lifer looking to frame him for something? Or were Jocelyn and Scott looking to take care of loose ends?

He pinged Charlie. "Fuck you," Charlie said when he answered.

"No time, Charlie. I'll apologize later, but you need to get to Janine Shankly's now, pronto. La Brea and Twentieth, piping you the address right now. May be a wild goose chase, but if it's not, you might save her life. Go. Please."

"I'm going," Charlie said. "Fuck you." He clicked off.

Martin piped him not just the address, but the entire disbursement report. He drew a connect-the-dots curve on the map, and added a note. *Watch for Krakauers.* As soon as he'd sent it, Beltran was pinging him. "I've got an aerial on you right now," he said. "I'll be there in three minutes. Don't go anywhere, and don't use your pod again. Who'd you ping?"

"Charlie Rhodes," Martin said.

"You call the cops, you call a PI. Who's next?" Beltran clicked off. In almost exactly three minutes, Martin saw headlights turn off Figueroa into the far end of the parking lot. He waved and the headlights moved toward him. The car stopped twenty yards away, and Javier Beltran got out.

"You touch anything?" he asked.

"I got a message from the car daemon," Martin said. "I came down and everything looked okay, so I opened the door to make sure. That's when I noticed the gun was gone."

Beltran had a flashlight out and was playing it over the open door and the interior of the GTO. The beam lingered over the glove box. "What kind of gun?"

"Sig P2047."

"The one you had the other day. Nice piece," Beltran said. "Work issue?"

"Yeah. Well, issued through a work license. The gun was—"

Three shots from directly behind him cut off what he'd been about to say. Martin flinched and spun to his knees, ducking his head and covering his ears. He saw Beltran jerk to one side and drop, falling against the rear tire of the GTO. When Martin looked back to the source of the shots, he was looking at Scott Krakauer.

"He's right," Scott said, considering the gun in his hand. "It is a nice piece." He tossed it at Martin's feet. "You can have it back now. But if you pick it up, I'm going to shoot you with mine." Another Sig appeared in Scott's hand. "And just in case you're thinking about something heroic like jumping me and choking the life from me with your bare hands, I should tell you that there are people keeping an eye on your girls who will know if your gun goes off again."

"Smart," Martin said.

Scott inclined his head. "We try to cover our bases. They're good people, very loyal. Maybe a little too inclined to mix business and pleasure. Two in the house, one very frustrated lookout, and then there's my wife to oversee things."

Charlie would have said that you could always tell when someone is lying because liars elaborate needlessly. Martin hoped he was right, but whether Scott was lying or not, Martin wanted him to keep talking. The longer he could keep him talking and not shooting, the more time he was giving the universe to introduce some confusion.

"Even cops don't just get to kill cops," he said. "This is all pretty far gone, Scott."

"You've got it all wrong, Martin. You're supposed to be asking me how I knew you'd figured things out. And you're supposed to be railing at me for killing your brother—which I did with that gun there, by the way." Scott pointed at the Sig near Martin's feet. Seeing Martin's expression, he parodied it, shooting up his eyebrows and making a comically exaggerated O of his mouth. "But how did the chip not register that it had been fired? Pirate Wi-Free, baby. It's a great thing to be able to carry around a pocket-size widget that can poke the surveillance state in the eye. Anyway, that's why I wanted you to have that gun. Keep it in the family."

"So you could steal it back?" Martin said.

Scott tapped his temple with the barrel of his own gun. Add recklessness to egomania, Martin thought. "I figured this was a good way to figure out who you trusted on the force," Scott said. "Which meant who we shouldn't trust and should seize any opportunity to get rid of. Anyway, thanks, Martin. For your work, for everything, really. And for this." Holding up his right hand, Scott peeled what looked like a latex glove off his right hand. He held it up so Martin could see the whorls and patterns in the latex. "Straight from your employee file. Surprised you haven't asked me how I got the gun to fire. I could have just overridden it, but traces of that kind of violence linger, you know? And hey, good move not going for your piece just now. It might have worked."

Scott stuck the latex glove mold in his pocket. "If you want to run for it when the uniforms respond, you'd save us a lot of trouble. But if you play it right, you might be able to avoid a capital beef. Hey, maybe you can sign yourself up for a buyout? How's that sound?"

"I was wondering when you were going to get to buyouts," Martin said. "You killed my brother, you killed some cops, you killed I don't know who else. For buyouts?"

"No," Scott said. "Fuck buyouts. Funny how you, of the indomitable principles and invincible idealism, don't recognize a fellow idealist when you're staring at one. Buyouts aren't the point, Martin. They're the embryonic stage of the real thing. We're capitalizing human life, is what we're doing. You've been able to sell your organs for twenty, thirty years. Old hat. You've been able to get your insurance company to pay off early on your life policy for maybe fifty years, ever since AIDS got bad. Older hat. But the thing about human life is that it occurs across time. It's not the body that's worth something, it's the time. So what if you can capitalize the time that a human being hasn't lived yet? God! Imagine the market! We started with felons because they're always the thin end of the wedge on stuff like this. There were art exhibits made from Chinese prisoners around the turn of the millennium. But let's say you're a dirt farmer in India, wherever. You've got too many kids, the wife has one more. You can sell the time your kid is going to be alive, expressed as the amount of resources that kid will consume and converted into the projected cash value of those resources, currency of your choice. Blam! Then you find someone who is willing to pay for that kid not to consume those resources. This is the brave new world, man. Now it's prisoners, but in twenty years there are going to be booths all over the world where you can walk in, wave your pod or your ID card or just let the machine fucking sniff your DNA, and on the screen inside will appear a figure. There will be two buttons, Yes and No. You press No, you walk out. You press Yes, lights out—but the cash flow to your survivors can mean they live a life you never could have given them. That's the pure market. Labor isn't the strength of the market anymore, it's time. Specifically unlived time, because unlived time means anticipated expenses, and anticipated expenses are uncertain. The more uncertainty you eliminate from the market, the more stable you make what's left behind. And along the way you cull the herd, keep it healthy. Good management. And good environmentally, too.

"When you can press that Yes or No, and realize the cash value of the potential inherent in your life, that's when the dream of Karl Marx—pardon the pun, or homophone, or whatever—that's when it dies. Finally. Once and for all. That's when we reach the end of history. And Jocelyn and I are going to make it happen."

All through this, Martin tried to surreptitiously scan the skies for drones, or the roads for slowing headlights. Anything that might mean help was on the way. But he was alone, and he'd made it that way, hadn't he? Family in danger, best friend alienated and probably shitfaced at Yankee Doodle's. He had two chances. One was that the chip on his gun would provoke a visit rather than a call from LAPD. The other was that he would get a chance to go after Scott, and then figure out what to do about Teresa and the girls. Thin, thin odds.

But then he understood. Scott had fallen into the same trap as Carl Marks. He was living his role, no longer able to separate vision from reality. None of what he was talking about would ever happen, and buyouts were lethal performance art to him, nothing more. He's performing, Martin thought. Like all of us perform when there are cameras everywhere we go. It's a pantomime of what might have been real, all of it. From the beginning.

Scott was looking at him. "What, no opinion?" he asked. "You were a part of it, Martin. An unwilling part, maybe, but I don't think so. Not entirely. You believe. You believe in buyouts, and if you don't believe the rest of what I've said, it's because you—like everyone else—haven't thought the issues raised through to their logical conclusion."

Martin got a ping. He looked at Scott. "Probably the cops, isn't it? Asking why my gun's been fired?"

"Answer it," Scott said. "Careful what you say."

Martin did. "Janine Shankly's dead," said Charlie. "I'm outside your house. Say something non sequitur if you think the girls are in danger."

"Yes, Officer," Martin said. "Yes, I did." He paused.

"Okay, amigo," Charlie said. "Don't do anything for a couple of minutes."

"I'll wait right here," Martin said. Charlie clicked off.

"Well done, Martin," Scott said. "It's not impossible that we could keep you on, you know. I said I could make a shoot go away. This one would be tough, but I might be able to do it. What do you think?"

Martin didn't have to fake surprise, or a surge of desperate gratitude, although he hated himself for the gratitude. "Is that really possible?"

"Might be," Scott said. "You've been good for the team, Martin. Think you can handle moving forward with this? You're eyeball-deep now. No getting out. From every angle, you're dirty as hell, but there might be a way out. Consider this a personal invitation. In a couple of years buyouts are going to be about as controversial as brushing your teeth. You ready for the big time?"

Mindful of what Charlie had said, Martin took as much time as he thought he could to think about it. "Scott," he said. "How do I know you're not just setting me up for something else?"

"You don't," Scott said. "But from here, it doesn't look like you have much to lose."

"What do you want me to do?" Martin asked. Then he shook his head. "Never mind. You're right, I've got nothing to lose. I'm in," he said. He looked around, at Javier Beltran lying dead next to his car, and at the Sig lying between his feet. "This looks bad, though. Shouldn't I have the gun on me when they show up? I mean, if we're going to try to make it go away, I shouldn't seem like I'm trying to get rid of it, and it shouldn't look like you're covering me."

"Good thinking," Scott said. "You're getting the hang of this."

"Thanks," Martin said.

"Go slow, though," Scott said. "We're still developing a trusting relationship, right?"

"Right." Martin bent down and picked up the Sig, keeping his eyes on Scott the whole time. Scott was relaxing, but not all the way. He watched Martin carefully, and then his eyes flicked away at the sound of sirens just as Martin was returning the Sig to his belt holster. Before Scott could look back at him, Martin raised the gun again and shot Scott twice, carefully, aiming for the center of mass. Scott went down with a look of child-like surprise on his face, dropping his gun as his knees hit the pavement. His hands flailed weakly toward the wounds in his chest.

"That's culling the herd, chief," Martin said. Scott looked puzzled for a moment, as if he couldn't quite piece together what Martin meant. Then he died.

The sirens were closer. There was no way Martin would survive an encounter with the police. He started the car, backed around away from the bodies of Javier Beltran and Scott Krakauer, and pulled out onto Figueroa, counting three sets of lights a couple of blocks back. As he made the left onto Fifth, the first two cars squealed into the Nautilus lot; the third blocked the driveway. Then they were out of sight.

He figured he had maybe a sixty-second head start. Traffic cams and LAPD drones would pick him out soon enough by homing in on his pod signal. Martin threw his pod out the window; he'd already sent Charlie everything he needed to make his case, if he ever got a chance to make it. But already a new idea was forming in his head, of making a different kind of case altogether.

Martin floored the GTO, feeling it leap ahead as he came up to the freeway ramp. He was beyond principle, beyond ideal. He no longer had work and family. He had found vengeance empty and belief suicidal, and what remained for him was the caveman's urge to kill whatever threatened that which was dear to him. Screaming around the ramp onto the Pasadena Freeway, Martin wound the GTO up and sped for home.

Hey, you know, it's a relief to be talking about something other than this whole Laskowski cop-killer fake drama. Here's the other thing I think is interesting. I remember, a while back although I haven't pulled the file because listening to my own voice is like being dead, talking about Othello. The thing about Othello is that you have an idealist and a cynic, plus racial tension and frustrated love, or lust anyway. I said something about Iago, and you know who Iago is? Right now I'm thinking Curt Laskowski is Iago. Once he had beliefs, then he lived, and then he found that the beliefs didn't survive the living. So he had either belief or life, and what kind of choice is that? But there's a middle ground. It involves a little self-deception, but we all know how to do that. You convince yourself that satisfying your basest impulses, to fuck and kill and avenge, is actually a way of expressing your belief. I think Curt Laskowski knew this a long time ago, but didn't let himself know that he knew it until his back was against the wall. But here's what I'd want to tell him: Your back was always against the wall. You're born with your back against the wall, and you live with your back against the wall, and if you ever get your back away from the wall it's because you drop your principles and fight. I can't blame him for that. I can blame him for what he did, but no. I'm not going to judge him for why. Fuck, I said I wasn't going to be talking about Laskowski, and then there I go talking about Laskowski. I can't wait to talk about the Dodgers again. Who lost last night, six to four.

THIRTY-THREE

"PILGRIM, ya got the law on yer tail," John Wayne said.

Martin looked behind him. No lights. He looked up at the sky. No lights. "You mean contact or pursuit?"

"They sure would like to talk to ya," John Wayne said. "But they ain't found you just yet."

"Automated response," Martin said. "Request immediate response to home address, emergency priority. And request ambulance to Janine Shankly's home address, on file."

Probably Janine had been killed with his gun. Martin's only prayer of surviving the next hour was to have the cops second-guessing the situation enough that they wouldn't just put him down to make sure. He had to make them more interested in getting the story than ending the story so they could spin it without him around. That meant two things: first, make sure his family was safe, and second, find Jocelyn Krakauer.

"Ping Charlie, and ice it up," Martin said. "Route it through Mars, make it armor-piercing. Need him to tell me right now what's going on at home."

Ten seconds later, Charlie's face appeared on the windshield. "You kill a cop?" he asked.

"Nope," Martin said. "But I did kill Scott."

"Jesus, amigo. There's nobody home at your house."

"What?" Martin was coming up on the end of the Pasadena, where it spilled into the South Arroyo Parkway. He downshifted through the last curve, the GTO's engine rising to a redlined howl, and torched the first red light. That'll tell them where I'm going for sure, he thought. "Nobody? You sure?" He couldn't bring himself to say, *No bodies?*

"They're not there," Charlie said. "If that's what Scott told you, he was blowing smoke up your ass. I did punch the tickets of a couple of anonymous goons who were hanging around in a car by your driveway."

Martin put it together. Scott had wanted to let him go from the parking lot so he could run home—straight into a bullet. So where were Teresa and the girls?

"Be there in five," he told Charlie. "We're going for a ride up to Casa Krakauer."

THE KRAKAUERS LIVED on a mountain road off the Angeles Forest Highway, with no official designation beyond the Forest Service designation NF-2N74. Climbing out of La Canada Flintridge, Martin asked Charlie if he had a portable Wi-Free bomb. "Now why would I have one of those?" Charlie said, producing one from his pants pocket.

Martin held out his hand. "Can I have it?"

"What do you want it for?"

"Better you don't know," Martin said.

Charlie put it back in his pocket. "Amigo, you have more than enough trouble. If you're going to get into more, maybe you shouldn't be in a big hurry to do it alone."

"Okay," Martin said. "Fair enough. Plan A is to call Jocelyn and tell her that I'll get out of her hair and forget about the whole thing if T and the kids are waiting outside her house when I get there."

"Has the virtue of being direct," Charlie said.

"Plan B is that I go in there and kill her."

"Amigo," Charlie said.

"I'm not kidding, Charlie. They killed my brother, threatened my family, destroyed my reputation and my career, and Scott had it all planned out that I would die tonight." Martin looked over at his friend. "You think he came up with that on his own?"

"Watch the road," Charlie said. This seemed prophetic about a minute later when they came around an ascending curve to find a state police roadblock, two cars and five rifles with their barrels in steady hands, aimed at Martin's side of the windshield.

IT WAS AN INTERVENTION, was how Charlie would characterize it later. What you did when your friend stopped listening, stopped caring, was so far gone into himself that he couldn't see the way out into the world again. Or if he could, had despaired of the world so completely that he wanted out, if only he could find someone to do it for him.

Item: Shankly wasn't Priceless Life's martyr. Curt Laskowski was. He was the one who sacrificed himself to bring down Martin Kindred, and Nautilus, and maybe the buyout program itself. And all he had to do was what came naturally to him anyway.

Item: Martin Kindred would not have survived the night unless Charlie had taken some kind of action.

Item: The guy who had killed Jason Kindred was dead, and his co-conspirator already under arrest, by the time Charlie had climbed into the car with Martin in Pasadena.

Conclusion: It was over. Time to move on.

But that didn't make Charlie feel any better about the look of betrayal on Martin's face when he'd figured out what Charlie had done. No one gets hurt feelings like the potential suicide who's finally got the guts to do it and then is thwarted.

Laskowski pled guilty on the day that the buyout charter of Nautilus Casualty and Property was suspended. Jocelyn Krakauer hunkered down behind a wall of lawyers and eventually survived because there was no proof that she'd known anything about anything. That wasn't enough to satisfy anyone, so the rest of the system's weight came down on Martin.

He'd been willing to go to prison, if only long enough to get in touch with his successor at Nautilus. But there would be no successor, and no buyout, so when a Los Angeles County grand jury returned murder charges against Martin in the deaths of Scott Krakauer, Javier Beltran, and Janine Shankly, Martin became the thing he feared the most: one more life destined to be spent looking at the world through bars. He refused to plead at his hearing, demanded to represent himself, behaved in every way as if he needed to hear the state pronounce its evidence against him. As if he needed his sins read into the record, even the ones he hadn't committed. As if, in short, he needed to be seen as a sinner.

Which people were only too happy to do. Martin's gun had killed all three of the people he was charged with killing—and had killed his brother. The district attorney's office was holding off on charges in the Jason Kindred murder until they saw if they could get Martin for something else. Martin's real crime—the perjury that had sent Everett Shankly to receive the Golden Needle—went unnoticed. The DA refused to charge him, on the grounds that Shankly was buyout-eligible anyway since he had never been charged with Jason Kindred's murder and turned out not to have been guilty of it, so Martin's perjury didn't materially affect anything, and anyway the DA had better things to do, like try him for multiple murders. The trial promised to be a sensation. The victims were the femme-fatale sister of a man many people considered innocent, a decorated homicide detective, and the visionary leader of one of Southern California's most controversial businesses. In the public mind, Martin was already a loose cannon because of the Shankly buyout and his subsequent firing-in-all-but-name; it made perfect sense for him to be the sacrificial lamb that would tie off the story of Everett Shankly with a neat, life-term bow. Symmetry and irony, all at once. Even if the DA hadn't wanted to prosecute, he would have had to.

He'd been placed in a county-level facility run by the Texas holding company whose cornerstone property was the former Corcoran State Prison. The company was known as CoCo, and from his cell Martin watched it all happen. He had been assigned a public defender by the name of Lester Aworuwa, whose opinion was that he should plead and hope for a life sentence. Martin would have done this if he'd thought there was any chance of a buyout, and he tried to explain his reasoning to Charlie, who stopped by the prison about once a week. Charlie wasn't having it.

"I told you when you took the Shankly deal that you were the dumbest fucking guy on the planet," Charlie said. "Now you're just proving me right. You've got it in your head that you need to do something honorable here, but you're confusing honor with obsession, amigo. You keep thinking that if you just insist on the way you want things to be, things will be that way."

"They might," Martin said. "But okay. If I've got this all wrong, what should I do?"

"Fight," Charlie said. "You're going down for shit that you either didn't do or that anyone else would have done. That's when people fight. You want honor? What's fucking honorable about letting the system steamroll you because you feel guilty that they won't nail you for the stuff you did do? That's fucking narcissism, is what it is."

Martin took this in. Exhaustion had dulled his responses to everything since his arrest. He was sleepwalking, letting the final acts of the Shankly drama happen without his active participation. The only thing he could feel was a need to see the girls, and a guilty terror about what might happen when he did. "Charlie," he said, "I don't know what to do. Maybe I deserve this."

"Where do you get off pitying yourself?" Charlie said. "Your ideals went and kicked you in the nuts. Now maybe you need to figure out some other way."

"Some other way," Martin echoed. "To what?"

To live, Martin, Charlie thought. But if he had to say it out loud, it wasn't going to do any good. He went off to stew in his highly individual broth of misanthropy and love. When he was done doing that, he walked around the neighborhood ignoring work, feeling autumnal, elegiac, even maudlin. Everything was ending—but things ended. He'd long since given up expecting anything to go on forever. The difference was that everything was ending hurtfully, disastrously, in exactly the way that maximized harm and grief to everyone. Leaving no one better off, no one even in a position to think that with time, the events of these past two years would be something they could learn from. All of the scars would remain. None of them would instruct.

He reeled himself back in, savagely cursed his introverted and therefore unknown tenderness—or perhaps it was the introversion he cursed, or the invisibility. In any case he cursed the qualities of his personality that he always chose to hate at times like this, when to be emotionless would have been to ride away unscathed. Perhaps emotion was not, in the end, weakness. But it sure wasn't strength, either.

Charlie decided to act.

CONNIE SALCIDO wasn't happy to see him, especially because he was happy to see her. But Charlie couldn't help it. She was the forever-inaccessible woman of his dreams. "Let me take you to lunch," he said, falling into stride next to her in the downstairs lobby of the Los Angeles County courthouse.

"It's three o'clock, Charlie." She didn't slow down.

"Afternoon espresso, then. Or a weekend in Tijuana."

"Oh, now you've got me." Connie stopped. "Seriously, Charlie. You're radioactive around here right now. I talk to you, someone's going to yell about Martin Kindred. You're fun, but you're not worth that kind of flak."

"Connie," Charlie said, "I have been in love with you for ten years. If you have a single ounce of respect for my devotion, you will hear me out just for a second. Then I swear I'll never say anything about it again. No jokes, no nothing. It'll be strictly business from then on."

"Asshole," Connie said. "Your dumb jokes are the only thing that make you bearable."

Which hurt his feelings, but she walked with him. And when he started telling her what he wanted, ten minutes later in the plaza in front of the main branch of the library with a Wi-Free bomb going off in his pocket, she didn't walk away.

MEG TWOHY was harder to crack. At first she terminated his proposal with extreme prejudice, which he'd known she would do. He let it go. The next morning, after a visit to Klaatu, he came back loaded for bear. He hit her with everything, not caring whether he burned every professional bridge he'd ever built, not caring whether she was disgusted by him as a human being. Charlie was infected, however briefly, by the kind of insidious idealism he'd often savaged in Martin. He had a worthy goal, and was willing to go to great lengths to reach it. It felt good, this releasing yourself into something larger, more abstract. As long as you didn't let it go on for too long.

They went back and forth, Charlie asking Meg to break the law because Martin had not broken the law and then Meg telling Charlie that Martin had broken the law, just not the one that was going to put him behind bars. Charlie came back with his last, desperate play, the one that was either going to work or put a stake through the heart of Charlie's career. Not to mention possibly landing him in jail himself.

"Meg," he said. "All those years you stood by while Sol did shit that should have had him eligible for a buyout, and it ate you up. I could tell it ate you up. It was killing you. Now Sol's dead, Meg. You don't have to do things that way anymore."

She didn't say no.

"Meg," Charlie said. "Please. Enough sacrificial lambs. I'm begging you."

People were walking around them, in and out of the library or cutting through it on their lunch breaks or sitting on the concrete steps because they had nowhere else to go. Charlie watched Meg watching them, and thought of Martin sitting in his cell because he couldn't go anywhere, either. He'd never believed he could go any way other than the way he'd gone. That was his problem.

"This thing you have," Meg said. "You're sure it will work?"

"It's Klaatu, Meg," Charlie said.

And then he bit his lip and didn't look at her, almost didn't breathe because the calculus she was performing was so delicate that anything he did might upset it. Charlie had sweat in his mustache. His nose itched. He stayed still.

"If it doesn't work," Meg said, "I promise you that I will kill you, Charlie. I mean that literally. I do not exaggerate."

Charlie held out the thing from Klaatu. "It'll work," he said.

Carl Marks is having the last laugh from his dialectical hereafter. He kicks the buyout program into the public-awareness stratosphere after a career lionizing the people who tried to engineer a better world by killing off a whole bunch of the disagreeable people cluttering it up, and then the buyout program goes down in flames because the people running it turned out to be a bunch of the most conscienceless motherfuckers you ever did see. Ideals, man. Fuck 'em. I never had any. If I, Walt Danger-field, ever espoused ideals, I was kidding. K-I-D-D-I-N-G. The whole thing goes up in smoke, and up in smoke is where it should be. I mean, we live in a world where species that might have cured cancer by virtue of their dermal secretions are driven to extinction because somebody thought it might be a good idea to build houses in a swamp at the base of a mountain range. If the houses get buried in a mudslide, you know what? This is what you get for not wanting to cure cancer. This is what you get for thinking on a human scale. As human beings, it's our respon-sibility to think beyond the human scale. When we don't, you get guys like Carl Marks. I was watching the movie that made him again last night, The Assassination of Leon Trotsky, *and the thing that got me was not De Niro's performance as Stalin—which is better than Goulet's but never would have worked in Koba!—and it wasn't the fucking deranged pathos of Trotsky dying by the ice pick after a life devoted to the idea of a vanguard revolution. It was the idea of a vanguard revolution, a group that sees farther and knows better than everyone else. There's your ker-nel of why no human system ever works. Communism looked for equal-ity, but people aren't the same. Capitalism rewards success, but not everyone has the tools to be successful. So what do we do? Theorize? Fuck that. We make movies, we get away with what we can. We are kind to the people around us. Any more than that you can't expect from a human being. I believe, without reason or justification, that when he had the ax in his head Trotsky knew this. Carl Marks didn't. I won't watch his movies anymore.*

THIRTY-FOUR

MARTIN FOLLOWED the feeds from his cell. Priceless Life was demonstrating daily outside the jail, calling for a permanent end to buyouts and a swift life sentence for Martin. Curt Laskowski killed himself in Yucaipa when he could no longer escape the fact that he wouldn't be able to take a buyout. Three days after his suicide, Martin got an actual paper letter from him: *Martin. Jim Jones, Iscariot, Brutus. Good company.*

This gave him something to think about other than his impending martyrdom/comeuppance. A cult leader, a traitor who might also have been a revolutionary, and a conspiratorial assassin who might have done the right thing. For Curt Laskowski, that was indeed good company. What company would Martin Kindred place himself in? The category of idealists was too big to handle, even if pared down to include only those idealists who endangered lives for their ideals. Jim Jones, Judas Iscariot, and Brutus would all fit that category, too. Comparisons, as the Knight of the Doleful Countenance knew, are odious.

And Curt Laskowski, in the end, was one more idealistic egomaniac who by the end of his life had only the ego. A useful counterexample for a guy in Martin Kindred's situation, or so it seemed to Martin, insofar as it mattered. If he was going to be spending the rest of his life in Corcoran, neither his ideals nor his ego would matter to anyone but himself.

Which was maybe the way it had always been, and in the buyout work he'd found the perfect way to create the illusion of relevance. When you've been a stooge, and you knew all along that someone was trying to play you for a stooge, you discover the truth about your ability to rationalize. Martin rationalized heroically, coming up with every excuse under the sun about why he'd had to do what he did the way he did it. Anyone else in my spot would have done the same, he thought, including pulling the trigger on Scott Krakauer.

If he ever got a chance, he was going to tell Charlie that, and Charlie was going to tell him that sure, divorce sucks and murdered brothers should be avenged, but when you sublimate your grief and heartbreak into the systematic liquidation of people who never did anything to you, it's time to admit that you have a problem. Martin actually caught himself performing both sides of that imagined conversation, sotto voce, in his cell. He spent most of his time alone, as was to be expected. CoCo had no desire for his controversy to rub off on them, so he was placed in a segregated population consisting, it seemed, of all of the people who would excite irrational grudges or predatory instincts in the general population. As an affiliate of the criminal justice system and a white-collar Anglo who had never been in a serious fight, Martin fit on both counts—although the COs (known as CoCoCos) never let him forget that they'd just as soon lock him in a room with a dozen hard cases and leave for a long weekend.

Teresa came less often than Charlie, and Martin's parents hadn't visited once. His father had recorded a message, and watching it Martin realized that he was never going to inhabit the same universe as the old man. He'd tried to do what was right, and then he'd tried to take the cop's attitude toward means and ends, and it hadn't worked. To his father, he was a murderer, and the sideshow about Jason was an unforgivable trespass on the dead son's memory. Something felt right about this final rejection, and eventually Martin puzzled it out: It meant he never had to try to live up to the old man again. He'd done things his way as a reaction against the old man, and been belittled; he'd tried to do things the old man's way, and been vilified. What remained was to do things his way, for his reasons.

If he ever got the chance in the world again, which according to Lester was unlikely.

Teresa refused to bring the girls. Martin hadn't seen them in a month, but he couldn't blame her. He couldn't get angry about anything. At first she brought him clothes to wear to court appearances, and papers to sign as their divorce moved along. Then something unexpected happened. She started to ask how he was. She brought him books, and things the girls had done at school. She asked him if there was anything she could do.

"Send me back in time a couple of years," Martin said, and smiled. It was a weak and rueful smile, but it was the first one he'd felt on his face in quite a while.

A little quirk of a smile around Teresa's mouth lifted Martin's heart for reasons he couldn't articulate. "What would you do differently?" she asked.

"Have different reasons," Martin said.

"What a chickenshit answer," Teresa said. "What good do different reasons do if you wouldn't have done anything different?"

"That's the point. I would have. If I'd had different reasons, I would have done different things." The smile vanished from Teresa's face, replaced by a certain set of the muscles that Martin had long since learned to recognize as a signal that he'd said something wrong. "I'm not talking about us, T," he added. "I meant my dad, Jason . . ." He trailed off. "What did you think I meant?" he asked finally, even though he was pretty sure he already knew.

She came back, at least part of the way. "For a minute there I thought you were going to tell me this all happened because I didn't love you enough," she said.

"No, T," Martin said. "I wasn't going to say that."

For a while there was nothing to say. Then Teresa stood up. "I should get back to work," she said.

"Yeah. I'd like to see the girls."

"It's complicated, Martin," Teresa said. She left, and the waiting CO took Martin back to his cell. The control I have, he thought, is not over what happens but over how it happens. You grant certain people in your life power to wound you, and then there are others who have that power without you knowing it. Those are the people who say things that remove a little of the happiness from your life. Permanently.

It's all so tenuous, Martin thought, it all hangs by a thread. Everywhere people are forced to do wrong and can only console themselves with the knowledge that someone else would have done it worse. But even the reasons are in themselves wrong. Is it better to be a competent

buyout agent, arranging the deaths of prisoners according to strict ethical standards that mean lots of people who might benefit from them
cannot receive them—or to be corrupt, railroading the innocent while
welcoming the guilty, and spreading the buyout benefit as widely as possible? Different individuals win and lose, but take a step back and you
can see that the pattern is the same.

But nobody can see a pattern while they're inside it. A rat doesn't
know he's in a maze. He just knows that the world smells like cheese he
can't find.

Pusillanimous? he heard Charlie saying, incredulously. Another smile
of regret prompted a comment from the CO. "Something funny, cop-
killer?"

If he denied it, he was asking for a baton to the kidneys. If he tried to
explain it, same thing. Martin erased the smile. "No," he said. Back in
his cell, he thought about the girls and about being pusillanimous.
Then he went to the bars and demanded a call to Lester Aworuwa.

"Lester," he said when the public defender showed up in the visiting
room two hours later, visibly burdened by poor diet and failed ambition,
"I have been pusillanimous. My brother and I will never go fishing. It's
time to fight."

Three hours later, after arguing over the language of court filings,
drafting letters, and drawing up subpoena lists, Lester staggered back to
his office and Martin returned to his cell. His own actions, his own
terms. Jason, he thought. You're dead. I loved you, and now you're dead.
I thought I could make that all right. He stayed up late looking at Allison's algebra homework and Kelly's Spanish exercises, and then he read
the hate mail that got through the CoCo censors. It was gratifying to
know that so many obvious lunatics hated him with such annihilating
passion.

First thing in the morning, he got some terminal time and key-
boarded a long text-only message, feeling like he was a child again learning e-mail on his mother's PowerBook. *Amigo. I have been pusillanimous,
and the dumbest fucking guy on the face of the earth.* The terminal daemon informed him that *fucking* would not be permitted. He deleted it
and went on. *So you're right. I was wrong. Twenty-four hours ago I would
have taken a buyout and been glad of it. That's how far gone I was. Now—*

and maybe this is just because a buyout is no longer a possibility, maybe I'm already suffering early symptoms of Inmate Litigiousness Disorder—now I want to fight. I know I don't have to ask you to stand with me.

He thought there might be more, but already he was so far into the territory of sentimentality that he dared not go any deeper. Martin looked at the message for a long time, until someone in line behind him said, "Oye, cabron, send your fucking message, all right?" Then he deleted it and walked away. Having thought it was enough. Having believed it, even if only for as long as it took to keyboard it in, was enough.

Feedback informs me that I'm getting a little bit dreary lately. To combat this impulse, I am at this very moment doing a complicated and joyous dance of West African origin, which in days gone by might have brought forth a god. Since We the People are without gods despite devoting an inordinate amount of our time trying to carve our Republic, which may or may not be alive, into the Procrustean form desired by those who want gods in the Congress, no gods are forthcoming as a result of my dance. But something else might arrive, equally mysterious and irrelevant to your daily lives and loves. I am going to tell you who I am. My name is Travis Kellerman. I grew up in Pennsylvania, and I came to LA to go to grad school in 2007. Look where it got me. I watched things come apart, and other things come together, and you know what? I decided to do this. I have a master's degree. What kind of master? Doesn't matter. And fuck this, it's all a lie. I couldn't tell you who I am anymore, I don't know, I've been Walt Dangerfield and Walt Dangerfield is all I want to be. I never even heard of anyone named Travis Kellerman. I've never been to Pennsylvania. Although I would go if I got the chance. I hear it's nice, a little warmer than it used to be so it's kind of like Georgia now sometimes, only you can still see snow. I'd love to see snow. Is there . . . oh. News! News saves me from my own self-involvement! Oh. My. God. Are you shitting me? Ladies and gentlemen, Martin Kindred—

THIRTY-FIVE

EVEN IF MARTIN had sent the message, Charlie never would have gotten it. As Martin was keyboarding in the concrete depths of CoCo–Los Angeles County, Charlie was standing on the lip of a bluff that fell perhaps two hundred feet to the churn and spume of the Pacific Ocean, southwest of Lompoc. The nearest road was a quarter of a mile away, if you didn't count a two-lane dirt track that ran along the line of the bluff for as far as he could see in either direction. The morning air had a little nip to it here at the edge of the sea. In the right and left pockets of Charlie's canvas coat were the pieces of a disassembled Sig Sauer SP2047.

It was a good gun. In the last year it had been used to kill four people that he knew of. The most recent was Scott Krakauer. Before that, Javier Beltran, Janine Shankly . . . and before that, Jason Kindred.

Charlie felt sullied by the virginal glow of sunrise, spilling out across the expanse of the Pacific to fade into the predawn darkness still visible on the horizon. Because he, too, would have killed Scott Krakauer if he had done to Charlie what he had done to Charlie's friend, Charlie was about to become an accessory after the fact by throwing the pieces of this gun into the ocean. If by some chance he was observed doing what he was about to do, and if by some further chance divers were able to recover parts of the gun, Charlie was cutting straight to the front of the line for a Golden Needle, in the unlikely event that buyouts were ever reinstated. And that he decided to take one, which was even less likely. He inhaled until his lungs were on the edge of embolism, and still wanted more of this seacoast air. Nothing could make him willingly leave a life that included dawn on the Pacific coast.

His being discovered was unlikely. Drones were few and far between, and nobody lived or worked within a mile of where he was. He could barely hear the occasional tires on the pavement of the Coast Road. The subroutine he'd given Meg, courtesy of Klaatu, was guaranteed bulletproof by the only hacker whose guarantee Charlie trusted. Still and all, *unlikely* was a good word to describe the chain of circumstances that had led him there. Charlie had long since learned to stop trusting long odds to save him from his own errors. Yet here he was, because Martin was his friend.

The trigger between the index finger and thumb of his right hand felt warmer than the morning air. He took it out of his pocket and scanned the sky for drones, listened for traffic on the Coast Road, glanced back along the line of bluffs for signs of motion. Camera lenses, startled birds. Any sign that someone might be watching.

He was alone.

Strange feeling, being alone. Free of the nets, out of the city, standing on the lip of a lichen-covered rock in one of the last places in coastal California where human presence looked like it might not be fatal, Charlie felt a watery uncertainty in the part of his brain that needed routine, habit. He'd read somewhere that people saw in the ocean what already existed in their unconscious minds, and two hundred feet below his boot soles was chaos. How long since he had allowed himself an unmediated experience? And how fucking ridiculous that this is what it took.

Fucking Carl Marks, thought Charlie. If there's no crackpot celebrity there to spike the interest of the idiot hoi polloi, maybe none of this ever happens. But you could blame Jackson Ordonez, too, for being first, or either of the Krakauers for offering the job, or Martin for taking it. It was about that time, it seemed to Charlie—much too late for the knowledge to do anyone any good—that the Kindred marriage began its final decline. It wasn't just that hindsight was 20/20; sometimes the human tendency restrospectively to create patterns out of random events became a way to convince ourselves that we have something to feel guilty about. It all came too late, and it came down to Charlie to make sure it all meant something. The only act that ever had meaning was the breaking of pattern. The monkey wrench in the plan was the meaning of life.

He flicked the trigger out over the water. As it fell, he thought of the procession of fingers that must have squeezed it over its years of service. He knew who two of those fingers belonged to. Martin was the last, and this had all been about Martin, because Martin was Charlie's friend and because it was important that there were still people in the world who thought human life was valuable and the right thing worth doing because it was right. If you were Martin Kindred, Charlie thought again, you'd have killed Scott Krakauer just like he did.

And you probably would have killed Everett Shankly, too. Channeling his ten-year-old self, who had dreamed of being Mariano Rivera, Charlie wound up and fired the magazine out over the breakers. He followed it with the barrel.

Charlie's line of work once had meant getting to be friends with secretaries and desk sergeants; now it meant that he had quasi-professional acquaintances who spent all of their time writing podjack scripts when they weren't getting him illicit access to raw newsdrone feeds or interrogation records. The business had changed, along with everything else, and he was old enough to remember when it was different. So he knew people, and he knew everything anyone else did about what had happened over the previous eighteen months involving Martin Kindred, except what Martin never told anyone, and because Charlie considered himself a student of human nature, he thought he could make a pretty good guess at that. Put the facts together with a little trained guesswork, and you get a picture. That's what he did. He didn't think he was wrong.

He'd had a month to think about it, to test events against what he knew and remembered about Martin Kindred, and Teresa, and the Krakauers, and the way that years of friendship left you able to predict exactly what someone is going to feel, to reconstruct how they got from one place to another even if you weren't there while it was happening. Out over the ocean went the slide and a couple of loose springs and levers.

Face it, he told himself. When you came up on that roadblock, you knew what he was going to want, and you knew what you would be willing to do to prevent it. Now you're doing it. It was true. He'd known. He'd known that he would have to destroy their friendship because to do otherwise would mean that they had never been friends at all.

He had no doubt that he was destroying his friendship with Martin, who might have forgiven him the roadblock intervention. But never this. With this act, Charlie had joined the ranks of those who in Martin's eyes had trespassed against ideals because of flawed, emotional, contingent human relationships. The irony did not escape him that he was doing this because Martin himself had, however briefly, joined those same ranks, and now wanted back out. He threw the hammer off to the left, sidearm, as if he could skip it across the coastal updraft all the way to Mexico. It ricocheted off a rock and vanished in the spray.

But that's what friends did. A good friend saved his friends from themselves routinely, without asking thanks or praise. Charlie Rhodes was many things—a lousy husband, a problematic father, indifferently committed to the ethics of his profession—but nobody could ever say that he wasn't a good friend.

Sometime in the next couple of hours, if Connie lived up to her end of the bargain, Martin would get a visit to his cell. He would be processed out by early afternoon, back into the world, freed by the failure of the chain of custody to keep track of the weapon used in the murders of Janine Shankly, Javier Beltran, and Scott Krakauer. There would be no principled stand, no martyrdom, no acquiescing to despair, and Martin would never forgive him. Charlie could see that, and he hated the way he felt misused yet again. Martin had to live with himself. Everyone had to do that. But it was so much harder when you allowed yourself, even for a moment, to believe that you had the answers. Then, when you were cast out to take your place among the multitudes with everyone else, there was a sense of having fallen that no good deed would ever be able to shake.

In other circles, the message would be going out, propagating from its origin somewhere within Priceless Life or Nautilus or somewhere else, Charlie would never know and in the end it didn't matter, through the inner rings of the dedicated and disaffected, from there to the Kuiper Belt of activist dilettantes who didn't have an audition that day so might show up and told all of their friends because what the fuck it might be cool, and did you hear who might be there? Somehow through the selective willful blindness that has always allowed Los Angeles to present itself as the land of dreams rather than the grinder of souls it has always been, the message would reach a critical mass of dissemination before its recipients had a chance for any response but to join the herd.

Martin Kindred is getting off.

It would all begin again. Flash mobs, drones piping their images to inexhaustible feeds, canned outrage. Or maybe it would all stop. All the cynicism about showy wealth and clandestine power, it would feed on itself, and lie dormant until the next outrage appeared.

And people like Charlie would watch, and act when it looked like it might do some good to act, and continue to believe that it was worth being a little better than the world seemed to want you to be. The last piece of the Sig, its slide, went out in a long arc, its matte black absorbing the sunlight until it vanished into the surf. Charlie's rotator cuff ached. He scanned the sky again and decided to stay there for a while, where the sea beat itself against the rocks. Some day it'll win, Charlie thought. But none of us will be around to see it.

ABOUT THE AUTHOR

ALEXANDER C. IRVINE has written fourteen books, among which are *The Narrows*, *A Scattering of Jades*, and *The Vertigo Encyclopedia*. He has also written comics (*Hellstorm: Equinox* and *Daredevil Noir*) and media-related fiction and nonfiction (*John Winchester's Journal*, *Batman: Inferno*, *The Supernatural Book of Monsters, Demons, Spirits, and Ghouls*). His short fiction is collected in *Pictures from an Expedition* and *Unintended Consequences*. He has won the Locus, Crawford, and International Horror Guild awards and been nominated for the World Fantasy Award and a Pushcart Prize. He spends most of his time in Maine and teaches at the University of Maine in Orono.